Pride, Prejudice & Permutations

A COLLECTION OF PRIDE & PREJUDICE VARIATIONS

TIFFANY THOMAS

ISBN: 978-1-956548-09-9

For my parents, without whom I would never have been able to finish this story before my fourth child was born.

Table of Contents

An Attempted Compromise

What happens when Caroline Bingley and George Wickham team up to force Darcy into a compromise? Laced tea, an accidental death, and an elopement!

Chapter 1

Caroline Bingley looked down at her arm in disgust. There, on the sleeve of her favorite dress—the burnt orange one—was a black ink stain marring the delicate French lace that had cost a fortune in London.

She had been attempting to write a letter—something she never did—to impress Darcy whilst in the library with him. Instead, all she managed to do was ruin her sleeve.

She had sent her maid into Meryton to fetch some lace to make repairs, but the stupid girl didn't seem to know the difference between tangerine and apricot. Sighing deeply, Miss Bingley resigned herself to having to go into the savage little backwater town herself.

The carriage ride into the hamlet itself was uneventful, albeit a bit boring. The scenery was nothing to the grand landscape that surrounded Pemberley, and she yearned for Darcy to finally make an offer so she could enjoy the riches that would come from being his wife.

The carriage began to slow, so she looked out the window to verify that they had arrived. To her dismay, she saw her brother and Darcy on horseback, approaching the Bennet sisters.

"Am I to never escape those women?" she muttered to herself angrily.

Miss Bingley had only just rid Netherfield of the presence of the two eldest girls and not a moment too soon. Darcy paid that Miss Eliza a dangerous amount of attention, and now all of Miss Bingley's well-laid plans to become Mistress of Pemberley were in jeopardy.

She watched helplessly as she saw Darcy's eyes fix on Miss Elizabeth, who was standing with her sisters amongst a small group of soldiers. When one stepped slightly closer to the chit, Darcy's flickered to the man. To Miss Bingley's astonishment, Darcy turned bright red with anger.

As Bingley looked at his friend riding towards Netherfield, he failed to hide his bewilderment. Her brother bowed his head in farewell, gave one last longing look at the elder Miss Bennet, and then followed his friend.

"Interesting," Miss Bingley mused aloud as the scene played out before her.

She waited until the party had disbanded; then she descended from her coach. After purchasing the necessary lace—*although this was a far cry from the high standards of London*—she left the shop to discover the soldier who had so upset Darcy directly in front of her.

"Oh!" she exclaimed as she stepped back to avoid a near collision, causing her to drop her purchase.

"My apologies!"

The handsome soldier in regimentals dipped a low bow with a flourish, his eyes raking down her body as his head descended. He spied the dropped parcel, smoothly picked it up, and handed it to her.

"Thank you, Mr. ...." Miss Bingley's voice trailed off.

"Wickham. Lieutenant George Wickham, at your service."

"Thank you, Mr. Wickham."

"And you are?" he asked.

"Miss Caroline Bingley," she said, performing a short curtsy.

"Ah, the mistress of Netherfield," he said with a charming grin.

"Why, yes. Do you know the estate?"

"I am familiar with your brother's name. He is the good friend of Mr. Darcy, I believe."

"Yes, our families are very close to one another," she said proudly, lifting her nose in the air. "Are you acquainted with Mr. Darcy?"

"You will never meet anyone more acquainted with him than I, having been acquainted with him since my infancy. How do you find him?"

"He is the perfect houseguest," she gushed. "Ever so polite and attentive at all times."

"I am glad to hear it," he replied. "Mr. Darcy can please where he chooses. He does not want abilities. He can be an amiable companion if he thinks it worth his while. Among those who are at all his equals in consequence, he is a very different man from what he is to the less prosperous. His pride never deserts him, but with the rich, he is liberal-minded, just, sincere, rational, honorable, and perhaps agreeable—allowing something for fortune and figure."

"This does not describe yourself?" she asked, preening at this evidence of Darcy's regard for herself, as he had never treated her rudely.

"We were born in the same parish, within the same park; the greatest part of our youth was passed together; inmates of the same house, sharing the same amusements, objects of the same parental care. My father began life in the law—but he gave up everything to be of use to the late Mr. Darcy and devoted all his time to the care of the Pemberley property."

It was here that Wickham paused and seemed to blush. "Forgive me, Miss Bingley, but I fear I have overshared with you. I have a warm, unguarded temper, which led me to be the favorite of the late Mr. Darcy and caused his son no small amount of jealousy. He had not a temper to bear the sort of competition in which we stood— the sort of preference which was often given me. The fact is that we are very different sorts of men, and he hates me."

Here tears filled Wickham's eyes. "But until I can forget his father, I cannot wish for anything but the best for my oldest friend."

Miss Bingley, whose heart was not easily touched, was moved to some compassion. "I am very sorry to hear it. To me, Mr. Darcy has always been the best of men. In fact," she hesitated before continuing, "I daresay I am one of the few who can claim his good opinion.

The longer we spend together in the same residence, the more certain I am of it. Perhaps I can do something for you once I am Mrs. Darcy."

"Do you mean to say"—Wickham stepped closer and lowered his voice—"that Mr. Darcy may be making you an offer of marriage?"

"I have no reason to suspect otherwise," she said with a satisfied smile.

"Then I am very happy to hear that my old friend is able to win someone as worthy and beautiful as yourself."

Miss Bingley lifted her chin smugly for a moment, then remembered the scenes from the last few days with that horrid Miss Eliza. "There is one thing that causes me concern however," she whispered.

"What is that?"

"I think he may be in danger of a fortune hunter. One of the local ladies, a Miss Eliza Bennet, has been using her arts and allurements—along with her sister—to entrap my brother and Mr. Darcy."

Wickham gasped. "But surely he would not be able to tear himself away from a creature as wonderful as you!"

"I would normally agree with you, but this girl seems to have ensnared my poor Mr. Darcy."

The conversation was interrupted by the shriek of a horse in the road, and the sudden noise jolted Miss Bingley to a recollection of herself and their surroundings.

"Upon my word!" she exclaimed, taking a step back from Wickham, alarmed at how closely she was standing next to him. "I should not have been sharing such things with you."

She hastily turned to go around him and board her carriage. He stepped to the side to allow her to pass, but as she moved in front of him, he gently grasped her arm. "I would like to help you, if I may, Miss Bingley," he said, sincerity evident in his eyes. "I want nothing more than to help my old friend get what he deserves."

A tremor of excitement raced through her. This was just what she needed! "Of course, Mr. Wickham. Your generous nature does you credit," she murmured, attempting to remain calm.

"When can I see you again?" he asked with a grin. "There is much we should discuss about the best way to bring you and Darcy together."

One of the carriage's horses gave a snort, and Miss Bingley thought quickly. "I usually take a small walk in the gardens each morning when my brother and Mr. Darcy have gone to the study after breakfast. Perhaps you might join me around ten in the morning tomorrow?"

Wickham bent at the waist. "Your servant, Miss Bingley."

She hastily climbed into the carriage, aware of just how much time she had spent in Meryton, but gave him one last long look through the window. It was all she could do to suppress a squeal of excitement. Darcy may be hers before long!

Chapter 2

Elizabeth Bennet frowned as she watched the handsome Mr. Wickham attend to Lydia at their Aunt Phillips's card party. The story he had related to Elizabeth only solidified her disdain for the arrogant gentleman Mr. Darcy. She knew he was prideful—his refusal to dance with her or acknowledge her looks was only her first piece of evidence—but she had no idea how resentful he could be!

Poor Wickham. She couldn't help but remember the fury on Darcy's face when they had encountered one another in Meryton the other day.

Elizabeth's thoughts remained focused on the soldier's story throughout the evening and into the next day. Only a note from Netherfield had succeeded in pulling her from her musings.

"Miss Bingley invites you and myself for tea this afternoon?" she asked Jane in surprise. "I wonder what on earth for."

"Clearly she wishes to further a friendship with us," Jane said, her eyes shining. "I believe she is more amiable than you give her credit for."

Elizabeth thought back to the harsh looks and snide remarks she had received from Miss Bingley during their time spent at Netherfield while Jane was recovering her health.

"Perhaps," was all she replied.

The time arrived to go to Netherfield. As the carriage bundled along the road, Elizabeth mentally prepared herself for the onslaught of impertinent questions and sly smiles she expected from Miss Bingley and her sister, Mrs. Hurst.

To the Bennet sisters' surprise, they were greeted not only by the

Netherfield ladies but also by the gentlemen. Bingley practically bounced to Jane's side, his face beaming with delight as the two settled on a sofa. Elizabeth took her seat on a comfortable settee while Hurst stretched himself out on a small sofa, clearly already in his cups despite the early hour. Darcy crossed the room and looked out the window to the right of where Elizabeth sat.

Miss Bingley and her sister sat together on chairs near Hurst's sofa, a small table in front of them. The hostess rang the bell, then turned to the group and said, "I am so delighted you could all join us! I have a wonderful new tea from town that I wish for everyone to try."

"I say, I didn't know you were much of a tea drinker," said Bingley with some surprise. "I thought you always said you preferred the same blend and that experimentation was for those who were too unrefined to know their own tastes."

Miss Bingley flushed scarlet and darted a glance at Darcy. "Nonsense, Charles! I declare I like nothing better than to try the latest fashions, whether in clothing or tea. And I'm determined to share this tea with all of you."

Turning to the Bennet sisters, she said condescendingly, "I daresay it will be unlike anything you have ever experienced here in the country."

Thankfully, any further snide remarks were interrupted by the housekeeper's entrance with a tea tray. After laying it on the table in front of Miss Bingley and Mrs. Hurst, the housekeeper offered a curtsy and left the room.

Miss Bingley made herself busy, filling each cup with water and tea. Elizabeth thought it was somewhat odd that throughout the process, the hostess moved to the front and back of the table instead of remaining in her seat, but Elizabeth imagined it was something in fashion in London.

Beaming widely, Miss Bingley delicately carried the teacups, along with small biscuits, to each of her guests. She batted her eyes when she served hers to Darcy, who gave a curt thanks but remained facing the window.

"Now, I shall be quite offended if you do not drink the entire thing!" she cried gaily.

Mrs. Hurst nudged her husband with her foot, startling him awake. The man looked around blankly, then after a discreet motion from his wife, rolled his eyes and sat up, taking the last cup from his sister-in-law.

Elizabeth obediently raised the cup to her lips, inwardly rolling her eyes at the dramatics and machinations of the elegantly dressed lady. As soon as the liquid reached her taste buds, she choked. The tea was bitter, even with the copious amounts of sugar and honey that had clearly been added to disguise the acerbity.

At first, Elizabeth thought it was a cruel prank Miss Bingley had played on her to show her superiority. One glance around the room, however, showed that the other guests were doing their best to hide their expressions. It was clear that it was the tea in general that was at fault, not just her own cup.

Noting the hesitancy with which her guests were taking another sip, Miss Bingley urged in a shrill tone, "Come, come, drink up! I went through quite a lot of trouble and expense to give my visitors the very best!" She herself grimaced as she took a large swallow, then forced a pained smile as if to provide evidence of her enjoyment.

In an effort to get the experience over with as quickly as possible, Elizabeth and the rest of the crowd gulped their tea as quickly as politeness would allow. Once finished, she stuffed her biscuit in her mouth to remove the foul taste from her mouth.

After everyone finished their tea, hushed conversation began around the room. Bingley and Jane spoke quietly to one another from their spots, and Miss Bingley conferred with Mrs. Hurst. Darcy's determined gaze remained fixed on something outside, leaving Elizabeth to her own thoughts. As no one appeared to be paying her any attention, she absentmindedly tapped her fingers on the armrest, playing a simple melody she knew by heart.

"Für Elise?"

Elizabeth's shocked gaze turned to Darcy, who was still looking out the window. "Why, yes," she replied. "I must confess to some surprise at you knowing it. Do you play?"

He shook his head. "No, but my sister does. It is one of her favorites, and I hear her play it almost daily."

Elizabeth opened her mouth to ask another question, but before she could make a sound, she was interrupted by a small shout from across the room. "Miss Bennet!"

Bingley was looking at Jane in surprise. To Elizabeth's surprise, her sister lay unmoving across Bingley's lap. His arms were around the elder Bennet girl, whose head lolled to one side.

Letting out a cry of horror, Elizabeth stood quickly in alarm. She swayed as a bout of dizziness assailed her, but a hand grasped her arm.

Darcy had spun from the window. "Are you well?" he asked her in a slurred voice.

"Are *you*?"

His face turned white, then green.

He shook his head, the motion causing him to lurch to the side. Fortunately, he released her arm before collapsing to the ground.

Elizabeth looked frantically around the room, searching for aid. Bingley had slumped forward, his arms cradling Jane's head with his face in her bosom. Neither of them made any sound. The same was true of Miss Bingley and Mrs. Hurst, who were collapsed in a heap on each other. Hurst remained in his prone position, his empty teacup having fallen to the floor beside him, shattered into pieces.

"What on earth?" Elizabeth whispered to herself. "Are they all dead?"

This horrifying thought caused her to rush across the room and shake Jane. She was relieved to see her sister's chest rising and fall-

11

ing as though she were asleep. Bingley's head rose along with her. Elizabeth desperately tried to move the man's face away from her sister's décolletage, but his neck refused to support itself and kept flopping down.

Frantic with worry, Elizabeth ran towards the bell, hoping a servant could summon Mr. Jones, the local apothecary. Before she reached it, however, the door opened behind her. She spun around and saw an officer standing in the doorway.

She sighed with relief. "Mr. Wickham!"

Chapter 3

Elizabeth looked into the handsome visage of Wickham, made even more so by the red uniform he wore.

"I have never been so relieved to see anyone in my life!" she cried. "Something dreadful has happened."

Wickham stared at her in confusion, then looked around the room before returning his gaze. His normally carefree face had tightened, and he gave her a harsh look. "Did you not drink the tea?"

She gasped and stepped back from the fierce intensity on his face, then shook her head. The faint dizziness she had felt earlier returned, causing her brain to feel foggy. "Th-th-the tea?" she stammered.

"Yes, the tea. Miss Bingley added quite a bit of laudanum to it. Did you not drink it?"

"I-I-I... Well, yes, I did, but why would she do that?"

"Because she wanted everyone to be unaware of the compromise she was about to put into motion. How on earth are you still awake if you drank it?"

Understanding finally dawned on Elizabeth. "Laudanum has never worked for me. Most tinctures and teas don't. Even when I had a broken leg as a child, it took four times the regular dose of an adult's for me to get any relief from the pain."

Wickham's eyes widened in surprise, then narrowed. "Well, that does present quite a problem."

"How do you mean?" she asked, fear trickling into her mind through the fog.

13

Letting out a great sigh, Wickham shook his head and said, "You see, Miss Elizabeth, Miss Bingley greatly desires to marry my old friend. She will resort to any means necessary, including compromise. Of course, Darcy is of such a resentful nature that any blame cannot be allowed to be placed back on the lady. She is willing to share half her pin money with me once she is married. All we needed to do was put everyone to sleep, then allow servants to discover Darcy and Miss Bingley in her bedroom, unclothed. Of course, seeing how everyone else was asleep, an accident with the tea will be to blame."

Elizabeth gaped at Wickham's matter-of-fact explanation. "You would ruin Mr. Darcy's life all for monetary gain? Did you not tell me that you felt so much love for your godfather you could never betray the son?"

Wickham gave a burst of laughter. "Oh, you poor, foolish girl," he said in a mocking tone. "I had thought you cleverer than that."

His face changed into one of hatred as he bared his teeth. "I have long since wished to have my revenge on Darcy, and now I shall have it. Nothing can stop me!"

Looking over at her, he gave her a wolfish grin. "Of course we'll have to do something about the fact that you are still awake. I cannot have you ruining everything."

Elizabeth's heart clenched with fear, and she looked around desperately as Wickham stalked towards her. "Come now, Miss Elizabeth," he cajoled. "If you don't fight me, I promise to make this quick and painless."

The gleam in his eyes told her otherwise. When he reached out to grasp her arms, she kicked him. Years of roaming Hertfordshire as a child with the Lucas and Goulding boys had taught her much about the more sensitive parts of a male's anatomy.

Wickham let out a curse as he collapsed to his knees, cupping himself between the legs. "You little—"

Elizabeth did not wait to hear the foul word he was about to say.

14

She ran for the open door, flew down the hallway, and made a bee-line for the front entrance. She looked around desperately for a servant as she ran, but the house was strangely silent.

Making a quick decision, she bolted out of Netherfield's main door and flew down the steps. She could hear frantic footsteps behind her, accompanied by oaths mingled with grunts of pain. "I swear, you stupid chit, you will pay for this!"

Elizabeth looked around frantically. The paths to the sides of the house were lined with hedgerows whereas the road to the stables was completely open. Not knowing what had happened to any servants, Elizabeth determined her best chance would be to hide before Wickham could get outside and see the direction she had taken. She took a bracing gulp of air, then pushed herself into the bushes.

The hedges pulled at her dress, but she tugged until she was all the way hidden amongst the branches. Forcing herself to take deep, quiet breaths, she turned around to ensure she was far enough back to be hidden. She arranged a few of the thicker bundles of leaves to wrap in front of her, further concealing herself.

Elizabeth could hear boots coming along the gravel walk, and she held her breath, only daring to allow the faintest of wisps to come in and out of her mouth. Her lungs burned, but she refused to give them what they so desperately craved.

Wickham shouted her name several times, yelling in vexation. Finally, he stomped away and took the path towards the stables. Grateful she had chosen to avoid that route, she sat silently for several long minutes.

Just as she had determined to leave the shrubbery, she heard a carriage. With trembling hands, she brushed aside a branch to see out. She held her breath, half-expecting Wickham's wild eyes peering back at her.

To her tremendous relief, Wickham was not directly in front of her. In fact, he was in front of Netherfield, inexpertly driving her father's carriage! He pulled to a stop at the door, then descended from his perch and ran inside. Minutes later, he returned, carrying a limp Miss Bingley in his arms.

Elizabeth pressed her hands tightly against her mouth, fighting back a cry of alarm at seeing the unconscious woman being roughly shoved into the carriage. Wickham then ran back inside. Elizabeth debated whether to risk going to Miss Bingley's aid, but Wickham's loud footsteps moments later made her grateful she'd remained hidden.

The soldier exited the manor, although he was no longer dressed in the red coat of the militia. Instead, he wore a black coat that Elizabeth recognized as Darcy's. In his arms, Wickham carried several pieces of fine silver, jewels, and a coin purse. These were dumped unceremoniously on top of Miss Bingley's prone body on the floor of the carriage. He took a moment to use a white cloth to bind the limp woman's hands together before shutting the door.

Watching helplessly, Elizabeth couldn't help but bite back a cry as Wickham leaped back into the driver's seat of the Longbourn carriage. Blood from her lip mingled with tears flowing down her face as she watched her father's carriage disappear from view.

Elizabeth stared at the empty drive, completely lost to time, unaware of the drizzle that came from the clouds. It wasn't until a freezing rain fell in earnest and she began shivering that she came to herself. She ran into the building, barely aware of her dripping gown and soaked shoes. A glance into the drawing room showed everyone to be in their same positions, with the exception of Darcy, who had been rolled over, his coat and cravat removed.

That must be what Mr. Wickham used to tie Miss Bingley's hands, she thought absentmindedly.

Elizabeth had little desire to enter the room, so she ran towards the hall leading to the servants' staircase. "Hello? Hello? Is anyone here? Please, help me!" she cried as she ran.

She reached a narrow set of stairs and quickly made her way down them, continuing her calls. Just as she was about to despair, a door flew open, and the Netherfield housekeeper exited her office.

"Who on earth is causing such a fuss?" the elderly woman demanded harshly before realizing who was in front of her. "Miss Elizabeth," she gasped in horror. "What on earth?"

"Please, you must help me! He's drugged them all and kidnapped Miss Bingley!"

Chapter 4

Mrs. Weston, the Netherfield housekeeper, had been a resident of Meryton since before Elizabeth was born. She had served at Netherfield since her twelfth year, when she began work as a housemaid. Rising through the ranks, Mrs. Weston had seen more than her fair share of unique tenants to come through the estate that hadn't been visited by its master in half a century.

When the spoiled Miss Bingley had declared a holiday for all the servants except for Mrs. Weston, the butler, and a maid and footman, Mrs. Weston decided to not look a gift horse in the mouth. After all, the poor workers deserved a break from the inconsistent whims of a capricious mistress.

The complete and utter shock she felt upon viewing the poor girl's state moved the elderly woman to a volume of shouts she hadn't used in more than two decades. She immediately shouted for the footman by name. Within a few moments, the young man, alarmed by shouts, skidded to a halt in the doorway to the hall from the kitchen and gawked.

"Fetch Mr. Jones, at once!" Mrs. Weston bellowed before yelling at the maid to heat water immediately.

Elizabeth watched all of this with a vacant expression and blank mind. Now that she had contacted someone who could take matters in hand, the shock of all that had occurred finally caught up with her. She trembled violently, but when Mrs. Weston made to lead her towards the kitchen, Elizabeth shook her head frantically and pulled away. "No, I must go to Jane!"

Dashing back up the stairs, Elizabeth ignored Mrs. Weston's

calls to slow down and be careful. Instead, the girl ran faster, desperate to return to her beloved sister. She flew into the drawing room and stopped only when she reached Jane's side.

Behind Elizabeth, Mrs. Weston gasped. She had hurried after Elizabeth at a speed she didn't know the older woman could possess. Ignoring the housekeeper, Elizabeth sank beside Jane on the sofa and tried to rouse her, but she remained limp. Tears filled Elizabeth's eyes as she cried, "Jane, Jane!"

Hands grasped her shoulders, trying to pull her away. "No, let me go!" cried Elizabeth as she fought to free herself.

"Miss Elizabeth, Miss Elizabeth, come away or you might injure her," Mrs. Weston said firmly.

Elizabeth was no match for the strength of a woman who had known decades of hard labor in service. When she realized her efforts were futile, Elizabeth turned and wept into Mrs. Weston's shoulder. The two remained in that position until a knock on the open door announced the arrival of Mr. Jones.

"Good God in heaven!" the apothecary cried as he looked around the room. Spying the only two conscious people, he continued. "Miss Elizabeth, what on earth happened here?"

Several servants crowded in behind him, gasping and pointing as they murmured amongst themselves. Suddenly conscious of the situation, Elizabeth followed the gesturing fingers towards her sister and Bingley, who were in a scandalous position on the sofa.

"Oh Lord," Elizabeth groaned. "The gossip!"

She stood and attempted to pull the couple apart, but her arms had no more strength. Mrs. Weston barked at two manservants by the door, ordering them to come help set everyone to rights, but they were too terrified to move.

Mr. Jones let out a startled cry of alarm when Elizabeth turned to face him. Her dress was torn in numerous places, in addition to being soaked and filthy. Her arms and face were covered in long, deep scratches that were bleeding, and leaves were caught in her half-unbound hair. "Miss Lizzy, I insist you sit down immediately," he said in a firm voice.

Unable to find the strength to argue, Elizabeth sat and mutely stared around the room as Mr. Jones came to her and felt her forehead. Frowning with concern, he looked at Mrs. Weston. "She is feverish. She needs dry clothes, fire, willow tree bark tea, and a bed immediately."

She nodded, took Elizabeth's arm, and guided her away. Before they made it a few steps, however, a groan came from behind them. Everyone turned to stare at Darcy, who was rising to his feet. "What the devil?" he asked hoarsely, looking around blearily.

Upon seeing Elizabeth and seeing her disheveled, wounded state, his eyes widened, then sharpened into a focused gaze. "Elizabeth! What happened? You are injured!" He took a step towards her but swayed on his feet.

Mr. Jones hastily leaped forward to steady the tall gentleman. "It appears you have all been drugged with laudanum."

Darcy looked around the room again, this time seeing clearly. When he spied Bingley and Jane entangled on the sofa, he let out a strangled cry. He tried to cross the room to them, but Mr. Jones kept a firm grip on Darcy's arm.

"Mrs. Weston, please take Miss Elizabeth out before her fever worsens," Mr. Jones stated firmly.

The housekeeper nodded and tugged on Elizabeth's arm, pulling her out the door and up the stairs.

Turning his attention back towards his patient, Mr. Jones said in a strong voice, "Mr. Darcy, clearly everything is in chaos at the moment. We must do the most pressing things first. Now that Miss Bennet has been taken care of, I need to examine you. Once complete, I will tend to the others."

Still groggy from the drugged tea, Darcy merely nodded at the command, which reminded him much of his cousin, Colonel Fitzwilliam.

Mr. Jones quickly checked Darcy's eyes and listened to his heart. As he did so, both Bingley and Jane stirred. Bingley was the first to awaken, and he smiled dreamily at Miss Bennet, which caused the peering maids at the doorway to titter. Alarmed at the sound, Bingley startled in his seat and looked around wildly. Upon realizing the public and scandalous nature of the situation, he immediately straightened, startling Jane out of her own haze.

"Oh my goodness!" she cried, sitting up and turning a furious shade of red.

She and Bingley both stammered their apologies to one another. Jane was near tears, and she buried her face in her hands. Darcy was struck by the similarities between Jane and his sister, Georgiana, and his heart was touched by the young woman's obvious mortification.

"It is all right, Miss Bennet," Mr. Jones said softly as he reached her side. Placing a hand on her shoulder, he added, "The tea you all drank was drugged. None of you are responsible for acting improperly on purpose."

The apothecary examined the embarrassed couple, then crossed the room to where Mrs. Hurst was asleep near the tea things. He felt her pulse and announced that her heart sounded strong, which produced a sigh of relief from the entire party.

Going lastly to Hurst, who was prone on the smaller sofa, Mr. Jones knelt and spent a long time placing his fingers on the man's neck and wrists. Finally, he sat back and ran a hand through his hair. "I am afraid that the laudanum was too strong for this man. Mr. Hurst is dead."

Chapter 5

Two hours later, the inhabitants of Netherfield once again found themselves congregated in a sitting room. This time, however, there was no tea to be found. Instead, the servants poured coffee, chocolate, and lemonade for the guests.

Included in their company were Mr. Bennet, Mr. Jones, and Sir William Lucas, who was acting as magistrate. Elizabeth, who had been bathed, warmed, and tended to, was the last to join the group. Upon her arrival, the awkward silence that had descended was interrupted.

"Now, Miss Elizabeth, can you please explain to us what happened?" Sir William asked in a gentle voice. "Mr. Jones informs us that Mr. Wickham was here and that Miss Bingley has gone missing?"

Elizabeth nodded shakily and began to recount the events of the afternoon. When she reached the point where an unconscious Miss Bingley was transported to the carriage and bound at the wrists, Jane let out a horrified gasp.

"We must recover her at once!" Bingley cried, leaping to his feet from Jane's side.

"Must we? I say she's made her bed, and she can be left to lie in it." Mrs. Hurst's voice was laced with venom.

All heads turned towards the newly widowed woman in the corner. Mrs. Hurst, upon awakening, had been unable to speak since the moment she was informed of her husband's death. Her hand rested on the small swell of her belly, heretofore unnoticed, as she continued. "My sister has already caused my child to lose its father before its birth. I'll not have her poison the only family I have left."

"But surely, there must have been some kind of misunderstanding," Jane said faintly.

Elizabeth pressed her lips together and shook her head. "No, Jane, there has not. I'm not entirely certain as to the cause of Mr. Hurst's death, but Miss Bingley and Mr. Wickham knew exactly what they were doing when they entered into this kind of illicit relationship."

"I can answer that," Mr. Jones interjected. "It is my understanding that Mr. Hurst was already in his cups by the time the tea was served. Any medical person could tell you that it is extremely dangerous to mix laudanum and alcohol. The two combined can easily be fatal."

"He wasn't always this way," Mrs. Hurst spat out. "He only began drinking when Caroline moved in with us. She drove him mad, he'd say, and it was the only way he could handle being around her. Not only did she turn my husband into a stranger, but she has ended his life entirely."

Mr. Jones nodded in agreement. "I can safely say that Mr. Wickham and Miss Bingley are both directly responsible for the death of Mr. Hurst."

Bingley went pale. "Does this mean they will be arrested for murder should they return?"

Everyone looked at Sir William, who cleared his throat. "Naturally, it is difficult to determine at this stage. Their intent plays a large role in determining an arrest, and they will need to be thoroughly questioned before any further steps can be taken."

"Well, surely Wickham should be arrested for kidnapping," Darcy burst out, speaking for the first time. "Whether or not he intended to kill Hurst doesn't negate the fact that he took an unconscious woman against her will. They're probably halfway to Gretna Green by now."

"You think he'd marry her?" Bingley's eyes widened in disbelief.

"Yes," Darcy said firmly. "This isn't the first time he's attempted to run off with a young woman in possession of a large dowry. When his plans went awry, he probably panicked."

The room fell silent. Bingley looked from Jane to Mrs. Hurst, then said uneasily, "Well, I don't suppose much would be gained by going after them now. They have hours ahead of us, and we would never reach them before my sister was totally ruined. Too many servants have seen things as it is."

Mr. Bennet cleared his throat. "And that very matter is the reason I insisted on being here."

All eyes turned towards the elder gentleman. He cleared his throat again and shifted in his seat. "I'm afraid the rumors are already spreading through town. My wife's sister came to Longbourn with tales of a sordid tea party only minutes after I received your note, Mr. Bingley."

Elizabeth let out a groan. "Dare I ask, Papa?"

Mr. Bennet's lips tightened. "The story I heard was that Mr. Bingley had seduced Jane on the sofa. When you attempted to intervene, Mr. Darcy forced himself on you, causing your injuries and the loss of his jacket." Mr. Bennet hesitated, then said, "I'm afraid the two of you are quite ruined."

"And we are the scoundrels," Bingley said sorrowfully.

Jane burst into tears, and Elizabeth wrapped her arms around herself. "What happens now?" she whispered.

"That entirely depends," Mr. Bennet said, looking intently at Darcy and Bingley.

Darcy's stone face grew even more fearsome, but Bingley appeared elated. He looked towards Jane. "Miss Bennet, while this isn't the way I would have had things turn out, I have to admit that I find you the most angelic and incredible woman of my acquaintance. Will you marry me?"

Jane bit her lip and glanced towards Elizabeth, who gave her sister a reluctant nod, for she knew just how deeply Jane's affections ran for Charles. "Yes, Mr. Bingley, I will marry you."

With that resolved, Elizabeth turned towards her father. "Papa, could we not say that I tried to stop Mr. Wickham from hurting Mr. Darcy and that is how I became injured? Certainly we could put out a story that doesn't involve forcing me to marry a man I barely know."

Darcy's eyebrows rose at this. "Miss Elizabeth, I am more than prepared to do my duty as a gentleman, regardless of the unpleasantness of the situation."

Elizabeth's eyes flashed dangerously. "I would prefer to marry for love—or not at all—than to spend the rest of my life with someone who finds me merely 'tolerable' and considers marriage to me to be 'unpleasant.'"

Turning her back on the gentleman, whose face moved from confusion to understanding, Elizabeth pleaded with her father. "Papa, please. I am sure we can find another way."

Mr. Bennet let out a tremendous sigh. "I'm afraid, my dear girl, that there is no other choice. The gossip has spread, and you know our little village well enough to understand that any other story won't have nearly as much power against the excitement of scandal."

Elizabeth's eyes filled with tears, and she hugged herself even more tightly. Darcy stepped forward and said, "Mr. Bennet, might I speak with your daughter in private?"

Mr. Bennet scowled at the tall young man. "You may speak with her just outside the door, but it will remain open and you will stand where I can see you at all times."

Darcy nodded in solemn agreement, then extended his arm to Elizabeth. She stared at it for a long while. Just as Darcy thought she would refuse, she stood and silently took it.

Once in the hallway, Darcy ran a hand through his hair. "Miss Elizabeth, I don't even know where to begin. I can't apologize enough for the circumstances we are in right now, but please allow me to assure you that I do not find the idea of marriage to you to be unpleasant."

Elizabeth looked up at him in surprise. "I don't understand."

He sighed. "I know I was a beast at the assembly when we met. I truly did not know that my words to Bingley had been overheard, but I vow that I had not even looked at you for more than a moment before responding to my friend. That night, I would have said the same thing about any woman. I simply wanted to be left alone."

She nodded slowly, and he continued speaking with hope lightening his heart somewhat. "As for marriage being unpleasant, I meant the circumstances of being forced into the situation and for the trauma you must have endured in facing Wickham alone. I regret that my words were so poorly misinterpreted."

He hesitated, then pressed on. "I have not the talent of explaining my feelings well. Oftentimes, what I meant in my head has a very different meaning than what comes out of my mouth. It is part of why I choose to simply remain silent rather than speak."

At this point, Darcy stopped speaking and moved his gaze to the floor, awaiting her response.

Elizabeth paused, then said, "Thank you, Mr. Darcy, for your gracious apologies. I must admit, my opinion of you has been quite poor up until now. However, seeing the perfidy a man like Wickham can conceal, I am forced to concede to the uncomfortable notion that I am not nearly as proficient at making out a person's character as I had thought."

"Wickham has charmed many a person, including my own father," Darcy hastened to assure her. "You are not the only one whom he has fooled."

She nodded in acceptance. "My concern now, Mr. Darcy, is that I simply do not know you. How can I agree to spend the rest of my life in the power of someone who is a stranger to me?"

"I can see why that would be an alarming notion," Darcy said. "I don't see that we have much choice, however. So what can I do to make the process as tranquil as possible for you?"

She sighed. "I just wish we could become more acquainted with one another and make the choice for ourselves."

Darcy took her hands in his own. "I know I may not be your choice, but you were already mine. Your wit, your charm, and your beauty have captivated me beyond any woman I've ever met. I swear, Elizabeth, I will do everything in my power to make you happy. Whatever you wish, I will give it to you. I cannot give you the time for a formal courtship before a wedding, but I will court you every day afterwards until you choose me for yourself."

Elizabeth blinked back sudden tears. "Then, yes, Mr. Darcy, I will marry you."

Epilogue

One year later…

Elizabeth glowered at her enlarged belly and rubbed her hand over the top. "Stop that, you," she scolded with a smile. "I know you're as eager to be born as your papa is to see you, but you mustn't continue trying to leave by kicking your way out."

"Talking to our son again, my love?" Darcy stood in the doorway, arms folded as he watched his wife with a hint of amusement on his lips.

"Our daughter seems to be a very active sort," she informed him.

Darcy laughed and crossed the room. "She takes after her dear mother, then."

Elizabeth wrinkled her nose. "So long as I do not turn into my *own* mother, I shall be content with whatever child God decides to give us."

He finally let out the grin he'd kept at bay and leaned down to kiss her. She let out a low moan and returned his embrace with equal fervor.

True to his word, Darcy had spent the first two months of their married life courting Elizabeth. Spending time together, holding hands, and stealing a kiss or two finally led to a true marriage of mutual happiness and love for the both of them. The evidence of that love scandalized the servants on a daily basis.

Elizabeth sighed gently as Darcy moved behind her and kneaded her shoulders to work out the tense knots that had formed. "How goes your letter?" he asked.

She frowned, looking down at the paper that held only two lines of writing. Several crumpled attempts lay scattered around her feet, and a few were across the room, having been thrown there in a pique of frustration.

"If I have to tell Mama one more time that we will not be hosting a season for Lydia until she finishes school, I swear I shall never read her letters again."

Mrs. Bennet had been ecstatic when she heard the news that her two eldest daughters were to be married to the wealthy gentlemen of Netherfield. It was only when she was heard to lament that Mr. Hurst had died instead of his wife, else she'd have another daughter married, that Mr. Bennet finally responded.

The appalling behavior of both Mr. Wickham and Miss Bingley had caused Mr. Bennet to finally consider the very real dangers that existed in the world, especially to women who chose to act outside of propriety. Hearing his two youngest and silliest daughters giggle at the comments of their equally silly mother about a poor widow whose husband was murdered by her sister was the last straw.

Kitty and Lydia were immediately sent away to separate schools—partially funded, of course, by Darcy and Bingley—and special masters were hired for Mary. A companion was hired for Mrs. Bennet, as well, in an attempt to curb most of her excessive manner. While considerable improvements had been made in all four women over the last year, the latest letter from Mrs. Bennet showed there was quite a long way to go. A year of lessons could not overcome a lifetime of absurdity and inanity.

Fortunately for Mrs. Hurst, none of the comments made by the senseless Mrs. Bennet reached her ears. To her great relief, she gave birth to a healthy baby boy, who could inherit the Hurst estate. Finally free of her pernicious sister, Mrs. Hurst mellowed into a loving mother who was content to live with her in-laws and raise her son outside of the immoral ways of the ton.

As for Miss Bingley, she returned to Hertfordshire as Mrs. Wickham, along with her new husband. The time on the journey to and from Gretna Green allowed Mr. Wickham to work his charms, and the vain woman became convinced that the elopement was the intent all along, due to her darling George's instant love for her from the day they met.

Tragically for the gullible young wife, her husband was immediately arrested upon their arrival at Netherfield. He was charged with the murder of Mr. Hurst, and Mrs. Wickham was named his accomplice. Their attempts to justify their actions held no sway over the judge, and it was only by Darcy's influence that they were transported to Van Diemen's Land instead of being sentenced to death by hanging.

As everything had happened in Hertfordshire, the scandal was minimal. Instead, word was put out that the couple eloped and chose to leave for either the Continent or the Americas—no one knew which—and soon the gossip moved on to another scandal.

In the end, Miss Bingley's actions resulted in unhappiness to no one but herself and Mr. Wickham. Whether that happiness was due to "that Eliza chit" gaining Pemberley, or actual feelings of remorse for her actions, no one will ever know for sure.

But one thing that was known by everyone was that the Darcys were the happiest couple in the world, all because of an attempted compromise.

No Less Brittle Than Beautiful

What happens when Lydia Bennet bumps into Mary, sending her crashing into the arms of… George Wickham? The resulting compromise at Aunt Phillips's card party leads to a ruined reputation and a marriage neither of them wished for. Will Mary and Wickham be able to sort out their differences and find a happily ever after?

Chapter 1

Mary Bennet scowled as she watched her younger sisters flirt with the officers and their new friend on the streets of Meryton. It was clear from the smug look on his face that the handsome new gentleman was accustomed to and appreciated the fawning of women and girls. Mr. Collins was entirely ignored by all of the Bennet daughters in favor of this new acquaintance.

He was, Mary had to admit, very handsome indeed. She could almost see why her sisters were so enraptured. Even Elizabeth eyed the man with a bit more enthusiasm than she typically did other newcomers.

Just then, two horses approached the group. Mr. Bingley dismounted and immediately went to greet Jane. Mary looked on with faint approval as she watched the two interact. They would be a good match, if their mother didn't run the man off like she did the last one.

Unfortunately, our younger sisters may aid her in that endeavor.

Lydia and Kitty were still full young the last time a gentleman had expressed interest in Jane, so it was their mother's conduct alone that sent the suitor running to London. That, and Jane's paltry dowry.

Mary's attention turned towards Bingley's riding companion, Mr. Darcy.

Well, now this is unexpected.

Mary watched out of the corner of her eye with interest as Mr. Darcy turned red upon seeing the newcomer, who had turned a ghostly shade of white. The man on the ground gave a slight tip of his hat, but the man on the horse turned his back without acknowledging the gesture and rode off.

Mr. Bingley, upon seeing his friend's departure, hastily bid farewell to Jane before remounting his horse and following after Mr. Darcy.

The gentleman was eventually introduced to Mary as Mr. Wickham. He had recently come from town with Captain Denny and was on his way to join the regiment at Meryton. Upon closer inspection, Mary could see he was several years older than the other young officers.

He is a bit old to just now be taking a commission, Mary thought with consternation. *I wonder what his story is.*

One thing that Mary secretly enjoyed was learning the stories of individuals. It wasn't so much wishing to hear gossip about them but rather to understand their motivations and why they made the choices they did. Elizabeth fancied herself a studier of character, but Mary knew that Elizabeth's conclusions were superficial at best.

It was only when a person's experiences and past history were exposed that their true character could be revealed. Each person was born a blank slate, and their character was shaped and formed by the events in their lives. Once uncovered, their motivations were plain to see and their actions could be anticipated.

Of course, Mary did not get much character study from other members of her social class. The vanities and shallowness of the upper classes did not provide much of a challenge. It was the tenants and the servants who were of the most interest to Mary, and she regularly visited with those who farmed on the Longbourn estate, not only to care for their needs, but to understand them as people.

None of her family was interested in her insights, however, so she had taken to writing them down. Using the excuse of copying Fordyce's Sermons as a cover, she tried to make connections and anticipate behaviors. Already this year she had predicted two marriages and a move to another county.

Part of Mary's studies included her family. She knew that her mother's nerves and silliness were a direct result of her husband's dismissal of her concerns over the years. Furthermore, she knew her father's disinclination to improve his wife stemmed from a laziness that came from overindulgent parents.

Mary's innate skill at understanding people and getting them to confide their stories in her was the motivation behind her study of scripture. She had always felt a strong desire to do that which was right, and seeing how people reacted to the events in their lives—whether for good or ill—caused Mary to search for advice in the scriptures that would prevent her from making the same mistakes as others.

It was with some concern, therefore, that Mary watched her younger two sisters interact with Mr. Wickham. While the girls had flirted with the officers, there was something different about the way they spoke with the dashing new lieutenant.

Mary did not like it. She knew from seeing the maids with the footmen and the farmers' sons that many a girl lost her way to a handsome face. As Lydia and Kitty had less resolve than even a scullery maid, Mary felt nothing but dread over this newcomer.

As the soldiers escorted the Bennet daughters—and Mr. Collins—to Longbourn, Mary resolved to do everything in her power to keep Mr. Wickham as far away from her younger sisters as she could.

Unfortunately, that resolve kept getting interrupted by Mr. Collins. Mary felt quite sorry for the bumbling fool of a parson. He was not vicious, and it was apparent to her that he suffered from a severe lack of self-esteem. Mr. Bennet had once mentioned that the senior Mr. Collins was a mean, miserly sort of man, and Mary understood immediately how Mr. Collins would be.

While Elizabeth felt nothing but amusement and vexation at the man of God, Mary felt nothing but pity and helplessness. She tried to do what she could to keep him from provoking her elder sister, as she knew it would lead to nothing but heartache for Mr. Collins.

Unfortunately, her efforts to request his help on items of great doctrinal importance couldn't prevent his attachment to Elizabeth's beauty at the urging of Mrs. Bennet, the one mother figure in his life—other than Lady Catherine, of course.

Mrs. Bennet was elated to see her daughters return to Longbourn with such handsome gentlemen, and they were immediately invited in for tea. Mary watched the interactions, a sense of foreboding welling up within her. She couldn't put her finger on it, but there was something wrong about Mr. Wickham. It was almost as if his eyes didn't match the words he said or the expressions on his face.

It was with great relief that Mary watched the men take their leave. Following convention, they bowed over each lady's hand. When Mr. Wickham took her fingers in his, a small jolt of energy shot up her arm. She lifted startled eyes to his handsome face.

His blue eyes, which had appeared cold throughout the entire visit in spite of his smiles, were clouded with confusion. It was clear he had felt the same connection she had, and he hastily released her hand. A smooth mask fell over his face, and he turned to join the other officers on their way out the door.

Mary surreptitiously moved near the window and watched out of the corner of her eye the redcoats make their way down the drive and towards Meryton. The last thing she wanted was for Lydia to notice and tease her about falling for one of them.

That night, as Mary crawled into her bed, unaccompanied by any of her sisters—as they each shared with the one closest to them in age, leaving her alone—she thought back to her interactions she'd had that day with Mr. Wickham.

The spark between them had been unlike anything she had ever experienced herself, but she'd heard enough from Kitty and Lydia to know that it was common in romance novels that featured "love at first sight."

Don't be silly, she scolded herself. *Even if there were an attraction—and I must admit that he is probably the most handsome man I have ever seen—there is a very big difference between lust and love. And as the Good Book says in Galatians chapter five, if I walk in the Spirit, then I will not fulfill the lusts of the flesh.*

That can't be so difficult, can it? I will increase my devotions, and I will not allow anything untoward to occur. I am mistress of my own destiny.

Chapter 2

Mary awoke the next morning, feeling confident about her decisions of the night before. She took an extra half hour in her morning scripture study and prayer; then she went downstairs for a light breakfast.

To her relief, there was no one else in the room. Elizabeth and their father had already eaten, and the remainder of the family were still abed. Mary took a few biscuits to eat on the way before putting on her boots to walk towards the Smith's tenant farm with a basket of goods.

The Smiths were a large family of seven children, the eldest of whom was a young woman named Harriet, who was about the same age as Mary. Mr. and Mrs. Smith were kind and welcoming, and Mary felt more at home in their small tenant home than she did at Longbourn.

She watched as Harriet began kneading out dough on the counter. Mrs. Smith was once again with child, and her age was causing severe complications. The midwife had ordered the hardworking mother to begin her confinement, even though there were still three months left until she was due to give birth. Harriet, who had been working as a seamstress for the dressmaker, was now at home to take her mother's place.

The two girls chatted as Harriet worked—Mary was never allowed to help, though she had offered many times over the years— and Mary found herself confiding in Harriet about the reaction she had to Mr. Wickham.

Harriet frowned as she looked at her landlord's daughter. "You be careful, Miss Mary," she warned. "The militia is better at harming the communities in which they reside than protecting them. They leave debts at shops and debts of honor, and more than one girl finds herself with a sprained ankle. For all this Mr. Wickham being handsome, don't ignore your first impressions of the man."

"I certainly won't forget them," Mary assured her friend. "His eyes were empty and blank, and his smile never once reached them. It was almost as if he didn't have a soul. It makes me wonder what could have happened to him in his life to reach that level of apathy. The only time he changed was when he took my hand."

Harriet's frown deepened. "I've known many a girl who convinces herself that she will be the one to change the scoundrel, but it always ends in heartache. You're too smart and too kind for that, Miss Mary. Don't let yourself be swallowed up."

Mary repeated her assurances that she would not fall under the spell of a man such as Mr. Wickham, but Harriet continued to worry. "I will ask around town about him," she said, "and see what I hear of him."

"You know I don't like to gossip," Mary warned.

"Oh, I know," Harriet said, giving Mary a sly smile. "But it would be helpful in your study of him, would it not?"

Mary agreed that this was so, and the conversation turned to other topics. Harriet was especially useful to Mary in helping to care for the tenants because she knew of needs that the tenants themselves felt too uncomfortable to share with the landowner—especially one as indolent as Mr. Bennet.

Her heart lightened somewhat by her conversation with her friend, Mary walked back to Longbourn with her empty basket, which had been filled to the brim with meats, breads, and cheeses. As she walked, she felt an inexplicable pull towards Meryton. With a gasp, she realized it was because she was hoping to interact once again with Mr. Wickham.

Stop it with this foolishness, you silly girl, she scolded herself.

Resolving to read her scriptures upon her return, she was dismayed to discover upon arriving home that the entire family had been invited to a card party at their aunt's home that evening. Lydia and Kitty were crowing about the officers having been invited.

Mary did her best to excuse herself from the event, but Mrs. Bennet refused to acknowledge the request. "How will you ever find a husband if you do nothing but stay at home and read sermons?" she declared shrilly.

Sighing, Mary went upstairs and put on her plainest gown, ignoring the temptation to dress her best and do her hair in a becoming manner. She knew she could look nearly as pretty as Kitty if she tried, but she had little desire to be pursued by a man who was more interested in the outside than the inside.

Mary winced as she pushed the final hairpin into the severe bun that would cause a headache by the end of the night. Lastly, she added the spectacles that were made with a clear glass and didn't actually make a difference to her eyesight, which was just as normal as her sisters.

Mrs. Bennet frowned at her middle child when she saw what she was wearing, but as Mary had delayed in coming down the stairs, there was no time for the matron to insist on a wardrobe change. Instead, she ushered her daughters into the carriage—Mr. Bennet had chosen to remain at home, as was his wont—and they headed towards Meryton.

Most of the guests were already present when the Bennets finally arrived at the home of Mr. and Mrs. Phillips. As promised, many of the officers were present, including Mr. Wickham. Mary studiously avoided looking in his direction and instead contented herself to sit in a corner, where she pulled a small copy of the Old Testament from her reticule. Turning to Proverbs chapter thirty-one, she began to read in earnest.

Unfortunately for Mary, her sister Elizabeth had chosen a seat nearby. Within minutes, Mr. Wickham had engaged Mary's elder sister in conversation, which was loud enough for Mary to get an earful, even though she had little desire to do so. She scowled at the pair and tried to focus on her scriptures, but she simply could not prevent herself from overhearing what he had to say.

Mr. Wickham began by casually inquiring about Netherfield and how long Mr. Darcy had been staying there. Mary could not help but roll her eyes as Elizabeth eagerly listened to every syllable coming from the smooth officer's lips.

When Mr. Wickham said, "Till I can forget his father, I can never defy or expose him," Mary betrayed herself with a snort. Elizabeth did not seem to notice, having been caught up in the story, but Mr. Wickham's eyes flickered over to Mary in surprise.

Mary gave him a sharp look that clearly communicated her disbelief in what had been said. This caused a look of disquiet to come over Mr. Wickham, and he faltered somewhat in his conversation. Elizabeth had to repeat her question in order to once again command his attention.

A short time later, Lydia interrupted the conversation, begging Mr. Wickham to join her table. When he tried to demur, Lydia petulantly changed her request into an invitation to dance. Mary was prevailed upon to play the pianoforte, which displeased her greatly, and she exacted her revenge by playing as ill as possible.

Once the dancing was complete, Mr. Wickham came to stand by the piano. "You play delightfully, Miss Mary," he said with a winning smile.

Mary's traitorous heart fluttered in her chest, but she fixed him with a cool look of disdain, one eyebrow raised. "Thank you," she said flatly.

He paused, disconcerted. "Might I have the pleasure of your company for a few minutes, perhaps for a turn about the room?"

She searched for an excuse to avoid doing so but was unable to think of one. Heaving a sigh, Mary rose from the bench. Mr. Wickham extended his arm to her in a gallant fashion, and she hesitated for a long moment before taking it. Just as before, a small shiver of energy shot through her as they made contact.

Her eyes darted towards him to see if he had experienced the same sensation. Other than a widening of his eyes and a small sheen of perspiration across his brow, he gave no sign of having been similarly affected. Her years of observations, however, told her that he was not unaffected.

"I must tell you how delighted I am with Meryton," he said lightly as they walked. "I've never received a warmer welcome anywhere."

She raised an eyebrow. "I find I am quite surprised to hear that. You seem to have the happy manners of someone who makes friends easily. Although, I daresay, I wonder at your ability to keep them."

His smile dimmed as his steps faltered, but he quickly regained control of himself. "I hope to always—"

"I don't know what you want from me, Mr. Wickham, but I must be frank. I have little desire to further any acquaintance with you. I do not trust you; you are hiding something at best or are intending to be harmful at worst."

A look of utter shock crossed his face, but before he could respond, Lydia cried, "Look out!"

Mary felt something—or someone—shove into the back of her. She was thrown into Mr. Wickham's arms, and the two of them tumbled to the floor, limbs becoming intertwined.

As they struggled to free themselves, a tearing sound alerted Mary to the horror she would find when she looked down. The bodice of her dress had been torn, revealing her stays and shift—and Mr. Wickham's hand had the unfortunate convenience of resting on her bosom.

She frantically shoved his hand away and pulled the torn part of her gown up to cover herself. Mary looked around in dismay to see the entire party staring at them, their looks ranging from horror to concern to amusement.

Mary didn't think the situation could be any worse - with a gig-gling and drunk Lydia standing over them, hanging on the arms of Denny - until her mother wailed, "Oh, Mary, you foolish child! What have you done? We are now all ruined!"

Chapter 3

Wickham stood glumly at the front of the chapel, wondering how his life had come to this. He was about to marry a plain, shrewish woman, with no dowry to even make it worth his while.

Next to him stood Captain Denny, and in the pews sat Colonel Forster, Fitzwilliam Darcy, and Colonel Fitzwilliam, all three wearing stern looks on their faces.

The day after the debacle at the card party the week prior, Wickham was unceremoniously hauled in to face Mr. Bennet. Colonel Forster insisted on attending the meeting, during which the commanding officer assured the enraged patriarch that Wickham would act the gentleman and marry the lady whom he had ruined.

Never mind the fact that it was the girl's stupid, youngest sister that caused the problem by drinking too much and stumbling into Mary.

Never mind the fact that Wickham had no money, and his newly betrothed had no dowry.

Never mind the fact that the girl had begged her parents to not force her into the marriage.

What was done was done. Wickham had toyed with the idea of absconding in the middle of the night, but Colonel Forster had reminded his ignominious lieutenant that the penalty for desertion during wartime was death. Wickham valued his life too much to risk it.

Fortunately—or perhaps unfortunately—Darcy had heard about the situation and came to offer a solution. Wickham had no idea why his former friend chose to get involved, especially after what had occurred in Ramsgate that summer, but he wouldn't look a gift horse in the mouth.

In exchange for selling his commission, Wickham would take on an apprenticeship with Mr. Phillips. The law had, after all, once been his choice of profession until he realized how little it paid. Darcy settled a small amount on Mary Bennet for her own particular use, and the couple would live in the small apartment above Mr. Phillips's offices.

In exchange, Wickham would be closely monitored for good behavior. He would have a small wage from Mr. Phillips—which was rare for an apprenticeship—but it would be conditional upon the quality of his work *and* his wife's happiness. If she were mistreated in any way, or if Wickham chose to stray not only from his marital vows but also from his promise to avoid gambling and drink, then he would be sent to debtor's prison.

Mr. Phillips would send weekly reports to Darcy, who would keep Wickham's vowels in a safe at Pemberley. Colonel Fitzwilliam, whom Darcy had summoned via express when the scandal erupted, would remain for several weeks to ensure Wickham was "settling in" to his new life correctly.

Wickham let out a sigh as he shifted his weight on his feet. The Bennet girl—*Mary*, he reminded himself—was late, and he just wanted the entire debacle over.

He knew he was extremely fortunate that Darcy had been present, and he grudgingly admitted that the situation would have been much worse had he been left to his own devices. An internship with the law was preferable to taking an unhappy wife back to the barracks to live on a meager income.

The word *wife* made Wickham cringe somewhat. The idea of being tied down to one woman for the remainder of his life—especially when his income depended on his faithfulness to said woman—sounded like a lifetime of hell. Especially when that woman seemed entirely impervious to his charms.

The reminder of Mary's words the night of the card party caused him to frown. Wickham had no idea why she could see straight through him. A plain spinster was typically the perfect target for him, but this one seemed to not react to him at all.

Except when we touch.

His frown deepened at the memory of the first time he touched her hand at Longbourn. Never in his life had he reacted in such a way to a woman—and he'd had plenty of experience. The air seemed to crackle when his fingers met hers, but he'd contributed it to a random occurrence.

The fact that the energy was so much more intense the second time when she took his arm was even more troublesome. What was it about the plain, mousy girl that inspired such a reaction in him?

There was no time to continue pondering, however, as the doors to the church finally opened to admit the Bennet family. A beaming Mrs. Bennet ushered her four other daughters up the aisle and into the pews. Once they were settled, Mary and her father came through the doors.

Wickham was disappointed to see that she was dressed in her same style of a plain gown and severe coiffure. A small part of him had hoped she would magically transform into a beauty as her other sisters were. Oh, why couldn't it have been the second or youngest daughters who had fallen into his arms instead of the severe middle girl?

He watched her approach the front of the church, then turned to face the pastor, an older gentleman who had known the Bennets since Mrs. Bennet was Miss Gardiner. The clergyman gave Mary a tender smile, then turned a stern gaze to Wickham, who swallowed. The elderly man's light blue eyes seemed to bore into Wickham's very soul, leaving all of his sins exposed.

Wickham barely heard any of the ceremony; it was as if it were all a dream. He vaguely remembered saying "I do" and giving her a peck on the cheek, but other than that, everything was a blur. He signed the registry, then handed the pen to Mary—his new wife. She took it stiffly, then turned to walk down the aisle. Out of habit, he offered his arm to her. She took it, and the same jolt shot up his arm.

Well, perhaps this is an indication that tonight won't be as terrible as I thought it would be.

The newly married couple made their way down the aisle and out into the fresh air. Mrs. Bennet followed behind, urging everyone to Longbourn where the wedding breakfast was to be held. Wickham helped his new bride into the waiting carriage, then followed in behind her.

The silence was deafening on the way to Longbourn. Mary stared out the window, her stiff back looking as though it might snap in two if she straightened any further. Wickham tried to think of something to say, but it was one of the very rare occasions where he was at a loss for words.

The broken look on her face, however, reminded him eerily of his mother's expression whenever his father failed to come home from the night. It was not a look he wanted to see on anyone ever again, and it caused the wall he'd placed around his heart to crack just the tiniest bit.

Upon arriving at Longbourn, the pair descended from the coach and entered the house. They were greeted by many well-wishers who congratulated them on their marriage. With each word of felicitation, Wickham could see Mary shrink into herself more and more.

In an effort to boost his spirits, he put on a winning smile and accepted the best wishes with charm and grace. There was absolutely nothing he could do about the situation, and he was stuck in this backwater hamlet, so he might as well go ahead and make the most of it. For her part, Mary sat silently at the table and nodded stiffly at each person who approached her with congratulations.

Eventually the breakfast—which lasted late into the evening—

came to an end. Wickham escorted Mary to the carriage, being followed by Lydia and Kitty, who giggled incessantly about the night's upcoming events. He gave them all an elaborate bow, then followed his wife into the carriage.

Mary was just as silent on the journey to their new home as she had been after the wedding. Wickham felt himself growing nervous about the wedding night. It wasn't something he had put a lot of thought into—after all, bedding one woman was just the same as another, at least to him. It dawned on him, however, that taking an unwilling wife to bed—especially when she was supposed to be the *only* woman he could bed—would be very different.

While he had seduced many a woman before, there was something different about the idea of forcing his attentions on an unwilling participant. Just the idea of it made his blood run cold. Had it been any other woman, he would have been confident that his charms would eventually sway her.

His wife—Mary Wickham, as she was to now be called—was a different story. For the first time since he'd been a teenager, he felt insecure about his ability to woo a member of the opposite sex.

He still had not decided what to do when the carriage arrived at their new residence in Meryton. Wickham had not yet been to the set of rooms where they would live, but as they entered the apartment, it was clear that Mary had been busy getting everything situated.

Wickham scarcely had time to look around when the door closed behind them; he and Mary were finally alone, and it was their wedding night.

Chapter 4

Mary winced as the sound of the door closing behind her husband echoed loudly in their room. While she had been alone with Mr. Wickham in the carriage, it was very different from being in their apartments with a bedroom just a few feet away.

Trembling slightly, she removed her bonnet and gloves, placing them gently on the small table near the door. She then walked past her husband and into the bedroom, where she sat stiffly on the bed, waiting for what was to come. She closed her eyes and braced herself for the unknown.

Over the prior week, she had worked hard with her sisters to make the small rooms as comfortable as possible. Her new home opened into a hallway with a sitting area to one side and a small kitchen to the other. A third room, the bedroom, was positioned at the end of the hall. Everything was decorated and furnished with the help of Jane and Elizabeth, who had taken Mary under their wing after the appalling debacle at the card party.

Mary had finally begun to feel comfortable with her new situation until the night before her wedding, when Mrs. Bennet had come into Mary's small room to speak with her privately about her wifely duties. According to her mother, Mary would need to lie very still. There would be pain and blood, but if she closed her eyes and imagined herself somewhere else, it would all be over quickly.

Unfortunately, the apartment only had one bedroom and one bed, so there would be no way to retreat afterwards. Mrs. Bennet—who was used to having separate chambers from her husband and therefore did not consider this—told Mary that once she was with child, she could then sleep apart from her husband.

All of this information put Mary into a state of distress she had never before known. It was one thing to imagine having to be with Mr. Wickham during the evenings, but it was quite another to imagine sharing a bed and having him touch her in her most private places.

She jumped slightly when she felt the weight of him settling on the bed beside her. Squeezing her eyes shut even more, Mary clenched her fists so tightly that her fingernails dug into the palms of her hands. A light brush of fingertips on the top of her closed hand caused her to flinch away.

"Mary, please look at me."

She forced herself to open her eyes and turn towards her new husband. Completely unsure of what to expect, Mary was surprised to see a soft look on his face.

"I have never taken an unwilling woman to my bed, and I do not intend to start now," he said.

Mary blushed fiercely at this. "I know my duty, Mr. Wickham," she said stiffly.

"Please, call me George. We are married, after all, and will be spending a lifetime together."

She hesitated. "Perhaps just Wickham," she suggested as a compromise.

He smiled. "I think that it would be best if we gave ourselves time to become accustomed to our new situation. I know that this marriage is the last thing either of us wanted. I do not intend to make it worse by forcing a consummation. I can wait until you are ready."

Mary's startled eyes met his. "I... I had not expected... that is, I would be very grateful for that."

"It has been a long day for both of us, I imagine. Perhaps it would be best if we retired for the night and spoke tomorrow. I noticed a settee in the sitting area. I will sleep there tonight in order to give you some privacy."

Her eyes widened at this unexpected display of courtesy coming from a man she had deemed cold and a fraud. "That is very good of you."

Mr. Wickham—*Wickham*, she reminded herself—gave a small nod, then stood from the bed and left the room, leaving her to herself.

***

The next morning, Mary awoke with the sun, as she was wont to do. It took her several moments of blinking and looking around to remember where she was. As the memories of her wedding the day before came flooding back to her, she groaned and buried her face in her pillow, which was damp from the tears she had shed the night before.

Mary prided herself on being a student of character, but Mr. Wickham—*Wickham*—was an enigma that she had still been unable to figure out.

Well, nothing will be discovered unless I leave this bedroom.

She got dressed—which she was used to doing on her own, as her sisters often monopolized the maid's attentions—and made her way to the small kitchen that contained a small table. To her very great surprise, Wickham was standing at the small stove, stirring a pot of what appeared to be porridge.

"Ah, good morning, Mary," he said with a smile. "I was unsure of your morning habits, so I took it upon myself to make a simple breakfast. I'm afraid we haven't quite figured things out about hiring a maid or anything. Fortunately, I have developed a few skills as a poor military man. Please, help yourself to the tea."

Mary raised an eyebrow at this characterization of himself, but she chose to not respond. "Thank you," she said instead, taking a seat at the table and pouring herself a cup. "I have to admit some surprise as to your own early appearance."

He shrugged a shoulder. "I admit to preferring to be a lie-abed, but my few short weeks in the militia had me waking up at the crack of dawn for drills, and this morning, I still felt the urge to get my pistol for target practice."

"So long as you don't intend to make me your target," she said with a smirk.

Wickham looked back over his shoulder from the stove, eyes wide with surprise. Then he gave a small chortle and said, "I do believe, Mary, that many people underestimate your wit."

"Well, with Elizabeth constantly using hers..." Mary's voice trailed off, a bit embarrassed that she had confided so much of herself.

She clamped her lips tightly together, then raised her teacup to her mouth and took a small sip. The room, which had felt comfortable only moments before, grew confining with the increased tension in the air.

After several long minutes with only the sound of a stirring spoon in the pot, Wickham filled two bowls with porridge and brought them to the table. He immediately began to eat, but Mary took a few moments to bow her head in prayer before she began as well.

It was only after a few bites that she saw him staring at her. "You really mean it," he said, his voice tinged with surprise.

"Mean what?"

"Your beliefs. Those proverbs you quote. The devotion you present. You actually mean all of it; it isn't just for show."

"I beg your pardon?" Mary felt a bit affronted at this remark.

"Well, it's just... you see, I've never met anyone who actually lived in private what they spoke about at church unless someone else was watching them. Even Darcy, the insufferable prig that he is, doesn't take the time to pray before a meal when it's just himself and maybe a friend."

She raised an eyebrow. "I can assure you, Mr. Wickham, that I take my beliefs very seriously."

"Wickham, remember? And yes, I can see that you do. It just surprised me, that's all."

Mary had no response to this, so they both fell back into eating quietly until Wickham interrupted the silence again. "Why?"

She had to swallow a mouthful of porridge before responding. "What do you mean *why*?"

"Why do you take it all so seriously? I mean, I know society requires us to profess beliefs to the world, but what makes you actually do it?"

She gave him a long, measuring look before finally saying, "Wickham, I believe in the word of God. I believe there is more to our existence than just this life, and I believe that when I reach my dying day, I will stand before God and report to Him everything that I have done. So I guess the better question is why *don't* you take this life more seriously?"

Chapter 5

Mary's words rang in Wickham's ears over the next several weeks. *I believe I will stand before God and report to Him everything I have done.*

His first inclination was to blow it off, but he simply could not get her words out of his head. Even as he fell into a routine of working with Mr. Phillips all day and then spending his evenings with Mary at some card party or other social function, the idea that there was more to this life stayed with him.

Wickham had never really considered what would happen after death before. He was sure that his father and his godfather were probably in Heaven—they were, after all, both the very best of men—but the idea of reporting to God everything he would do had never once occurred to him.

As he watched Mary also become accustomed to their new arrangement, he was amazed by her quiet diligence and devotion. She studied her scriptures, said her prayers, and frequently wrote in her notebook. When he asked her what she did all day, she usually said she was visiting her father's tenants or working on sewing projects for the needy in the parish.

She was incredible.

Even when he had toyed around with the idea of taking orders, Wickham never contemplated what it meant to be responsible for the well-being of those in the parish. He figured all he would have to do would be to say a few sermons and pass the collection plate. Mary's interactions with her local rector, however, began to change his entire viewpoint.

Wickham had little doubt that if it were Judgment Day, Mary

would be admitted to Heaven within two seconds of explaining to God what she had done on earth.

But what would I say?

The question resonated in his head over and over again. Each time he went to do something, like use some coin at the bar or even feel a temptation to head to the barracks for an off-the-books game of chance, he imagined himself before an all-powerful being, trying to justify it.

Along with affecting his current judgments, it seemed as though every action in his life, every mistake, every sin, was brought to his mind over the prior month. His wild actions at university, his jealousy towards and betrayal of Darcy, and his callous treatment of gentle Georgiana, Darcy's sister.

As Wickham became more acquainted with Mary, the more he saw bits of her that resembled Miss Darcy. Her love of music, her quiet demeanor in company, and her eagerness to do the right thing.

One day, Wickham realized with a start that if anyone dared try to treat Mary in the way that he had treated Georgiana, he would not hesitate to end that fool's life. It was this new understanding that caused him to go to Netherfield as soon as he'd received word that it was once again occupied by Bingley, Darcy, and Colonel Fitzwilliam in expectation of Darcy's and Bingley's upcoming nuptials with two of the Bennet sisters.

The two men entered the drawing room where Wickham sat, their faces grim. "What is it you want, George?" the colonel demanded angrily.

For the first time in his life, Wickham looked at Darcy with remorse. It was as though the scales had fallen away from his eyes and he was seeing the truth for the first time.

"Only forgiveness," he replied.

Darcy's eyebrows flew up his forehead. "Excuse me?"

"Darcy—Mr. Darcy—I have come to apologize for the complete and utter monster I have turned into. I have been a selfish being all my life, and I took everything I had for granted. No, worse—I just discarded it in a manner that I will always regret. And with us about to become brothers with your marriage to Elizabeth, I could not waste a single day in speaking with you."

The two cousins exchanged glances. Darcy's face was imperturbable, but Fitzwilliam's was furious. "You dare to apologize now?" he seethed. "After everything that you have done? What's the *real* reason for doing this?"

Wickham's heart sank at this doubt, but he knew it was well deserved. He swallowed hard. "It is because, one day, I will have to stand before God and justify every one of my actions. I cannot look upon my past behavior without abhorrence. I do not blame you for not trusting me; indeed, I wouldn't believe me if I were you. I don't expect you to, but I do swear that I will do everything in my power to atone for my past misdeeds."

With that, Wickham gave his former friends a deep bow, then left the room.

***

Mary looked anxiously at the clock, wondering where her husband was. It was an hour past when he usually came home, and her heart ached at the idea that he had fallen back into his sinful ways.

Over the months, so many changes had occurred in her family. Jane and Elizabeth had become engaged to Mr. Bingley and Mr. Darcy, and their father had taken a firmer hand with Kitty and Lydia. His anger over Lydia's behavior causing Mary to wed a man so completely her opposite had finally moved him to action.

The last several months together with Wickham had been more pleasant than she had ever expected. There was nothing that particularly stood out, but Mary couldn't help but feel as though there were a softening in Wickham that had never been there before. He frequently asked her questions about why she did the things that she did.

At first, she expected him to mock her. After all, Lydia was so attracted to him, and he seemed to be just a male version of her younger sister. Instead, however, he became pensive after each discussion. Their conversations became something for her to enjoy rather than fear.

He felt like a friend.

The clock struck seven, and Mary could bear it no longer. She left the kitchen, having barely touched her food, and went to her bedroom. She opened her scriptures and her notebook, and read over everything she had observed about her husband in the prior months. Had she missed something that would have caused him to revert to his former habits?

She lost track of how long she sat on her bed, tears smearing the ink on her pages as she read through the book of Psalms. At last, she heard the front door open.

"Mary?" Wickham called.

Unable to answer, she closed her eyes. She didn't want to see the evidence of his debauchery. Would his clothes be rumpled? Would he smell of alcohol? Would his eyes be bloodshot?

"Mary?"

She jumped at the sound of his voice just a few feet away. The shock forced her eyes open. Wickham was looking down at her with concern.

"Good God, Mary! Are you all right?"

She burst into sobs, unable to hold her emotions in check. "Where were you?" she choked out.

Understanding crossed his face. "Oh, Mary, I am so sorry," he said, sitting next to her on the bed.

He put his arm around her shoulders, causing her to tense up. Other than the occasional hug from her father, she had never had a man touch her in such a way, but the familiar jolt that coursed through her each time Wickham and she touched caused her anxiety to ease.

"I went to Netherfield to speak with Darcy and Fitzwilliam," he told her. "I owed them an apology. It took much longer than I expected to return; the horse lost a shoe along the way."

She sighed in relief, and he pulled her closer to him. "I'm so sorry I doubted you," she whispered. "That was very wrong of me to assume the worse of you."

Wickham shook his head vehemently. "No, Mary, you actually had every right to do so." He hesitated, then said, "I think it's time I told you about my past."

For the next several hours, he related everything to her: his abuses towards Darcy, his affairs with women, and his attempted elopement with Georgiana.

After he finished speaking, she sat quietly for several minutes. Just when he could bear the silence no longer, she asked softly, "Why are you telling me all of this?"

"Because I don't want to be that person anymore. The very first day of our marriage, I asked you why you do the things you do. Do you remember what you said?"

Mary shook her head, and he continued. "You told me that you expected one day to give an accounting to God of all your dealings on earth. That stayed with me, repeating over and over in my head until I realized that I had much to be ashamed of."

"That was never my intent—"

"I know it wasn't, but I am so grateful for what you said. It gave me a perspective on life that I never before considered. Without you, I would have remained the selfish beast that I was. You have saved me, Mary, and I love you for it."

With that, he leaned down and kissed her gently, and the two opposite individuals who had married one another at last became united.

Epilogue

Mary laughed as she watched her husband and Darcy run across the front lawn of Pemberley, racing each other towards a ball. The Wickhams were visiting the Darcy estate as they did every year, and watching the two adult men compete with one another was always the highlight of the trip.

"Who's winning this time?" Elizabeth asked as she sat next to Mary.

Mary looked at her sister's extended belly. "Should you be out here in this heat?"

Fanning herself with one hand and holding a glass of cool lemonade in the other, Elizabeth pulled a face. "I will not be forced into confinement one second more than is necessary, thank you very much. Spending the last month of pregnancy in bed just about killed me the last three times."

Mary smiled in agreement, although she had very little knowledge of the matter. It had been eight years since she and Wickham were married, and a little over seven years since they began sharing a bed. There had been several times she had thought she was with child, but there was always significant bleeding after a few months and before the quickening.

Wickham frequently reassured her that he was happy with their little family as it was, just the two of them, but she caught the occasional look on his face when he saw the Darcy and Bingley children—it was the same wistful look she had as well.

She rested her hand gently on her flat stomach. It had been four months since her last courses, but she didn't dare say anything to anyone other than the midwife for fear of yet another disappointment. Wickham had mentioned it, but she informed him that courses could frequently be irregular after a miscarriage—which was the truth, at least according to the midwife.

Mary knew that if she had shared her suspicions with her husband, he would have insisted they not travel to Pemberley that year. She knew how much he treasured these visits, however, and would not allow him to make that sacrifice, especially if it turned out to be for nothing.

Darcy beat Wickham to the ball by just a few steps, causing Wickham to jokingly accuse his friend of cheating by having longer legs. Darcy retorted that it wasn't his fault Wickham refused to eat his vegetables when they were children, causing the eldest Darcy boy—a young lad of the age of six—to frantically ask if he was eating well enough to grow as tall as his father.

This caused Elizabeth and Mary to laugh, and Elizabeth assured her son that as long as he ate as much as his nurse instructed, he would grow as tall as God wished him to be.

Mary's smile widened when she heard a familiar shout, and she turned to wave hello at General and Kitty Fitzwilliam, who were coming down the path with their two-year-old twin girls. His regular visits to Netherfield to check on Wickham had caused Fitzwilliam to develop a close relationship with Kitty, whose character had improved greatly with her father's increased attentions.

The Fitzwilliams eventually relocated to Derbyshire upon their marriage, where Kitty lived at Pemberley when the newly appointed general had to travel. Eventually, he retired, and his father the earl gifted them a small estate halfway between Matlock and Pemberley.

Thankfully for Mary, Jane and Bingley decided to purchase Netherfield, which prompted—for the Bingleys' sanity—Mr. Bennet to severely curtail his wife's ability to pay calls on her eldest daughter. Under his strict command, the woman was only allowed one visit per week to last just thirty minutes. Anything more resulted in the lowering of her pin money for the next quarter.

The arrival of the Fitzwilliams caused Darcy and Wickham to call for an end to the game. A cheerful—but sweaty—Wickham came and sat on the ground near his wife's chair. "How are you, dearest?" he asked, resting his head on her knees.

Mary caught the surprised expression on Darcy's face at this evidence of intimacy and familiarity. It had taken three full years for Darcy to accept that Wickham's transformation was legitimate, but now the two were as good of friends as they had been when they were boys. Even so, Mary could tell that Darcy could not truly understand how someone as charismatic as Wickham had fallen for someone as pious and plain as Mary.

Wickham told Mary he thought she was beautiful long before he saw her away from her plain gown and false glasses. It had taken several weeks from their first kiss to actually come together as man and wife, and the look on his face when he saw her in a flattering nightgown and hairstyle was something she would never forget.

He had fallen in love with who she was on the inside, which gave her the courage to let him truly see who she was on the outside as well.

Her ruminations were interrupted when she felt a fluttering in her stomach. "Oh!" she cried out, dread filling her at the sensation.

No, I can't bear this again. She began to pant, the anxiety causing her to lose her breath.

Wickham immediately shot to his feet. "Mary, are you unwell?"

"Doctor," she gasped out.

Wickham swept her into his arms and practically ran towards the house, followed closely by Elizabeth, who kept up with his pace in spite of her pregnancy.

He laid her gently on the bed, then sat next to her, holding her hand tightly. He refused to leave her side as she panted heavily and Elizabeth mopped her sister's sweaty brow with cool cloths.

Finally the doctor arrived, and Wickham was forced to leave the room, partially dragged out by Darcy, who offered his friend a glass of brandy in the study.

Mary explained everything to the doctor, who carefully felt around her stomach. Elizabeth opened her mouth to ask a question, but then closed it when the doctor said, "Based on everything you have told me, Mrs. Wickham, I believe you are with child."

"I thought as much," she admitted, to Elizabeth's surprise. "Am I losing this one as well?"

"I actually think you must have felt the quickening," Elizabeth burst out, then blushed and said, "I apologize, Doctor."

The elderly gentleman laughed. "Mrs. Darcy, you know you need never apologize to me. But, yes, I do agree with you. The movement you described—and the fact that it was without pain—leads me to believe your baby has reached the size where you can feel its movements inside of you."

Mary looked between her sister and the doctor, eyes filling with tears. "I never thought... that is, I didn't think I could... Oh, I must tell George!"

"I will fetch him after I see the doctor out," Elizabeth assured her.

Within a few painfully long minutes, Wickham entered the room. "Are you well? What has happened? What did the doctor say? Neither he nor Elizabeth would tell me anything."

The tears in Mary's eyes dripped down her face. Wickham dropped to his knees beside the bed and grasped her hand with his. "Please, God," he begged, "don't let her be dying."

She squeezed his hand, touched by his fervent prayer, and said, "No, my love, it is quite the opposite. I am with child, and I felt the quickening! It so startled me, I thought perhaps I was losing another babe."

The despair on her husband's face changed from misery to relief, then from relief to joy. "A baby?" he whispered. "The quickening?"

Mary explained about her suspicions and being unwilling to ruin their trip. He rolled his eyes and placed a hand on her cheek. "You silly girl," he said fondly. "You are of infinite more value to me than a trip to Pemberley."

She turned her head and leaned into his palm. "Who would have thought eight years ago that we would be where we are now?"

He smiled. "I thank God every day that Lydia tripped and forced us into a compromise."

A broad smile crossed her face. "I once lectured Lydia that a woman's reputation is no less brittle than beautiful. At the time, I hated that society's norms forced us together for no reason. But now I can't imagine anything I would wish for more."

Wickham leaned over and tenderly kissed her on the forehead. "Nor can I, my love. Nor can I."

Keep Your Breath to Swell Your Song

The famed Bonnet Family Singers are known throughout the ton for their beautiful voices. Though their performance for the prince regent threw them into the spotlight, they have chosen to keep their identities a secret. The rumors say they are daughters of a gentleman, but no one knows for sure. All Mr. Darcy knows is that there is something familiar about the way Miss Elizabeth Bennet sings at Lucas Lodge.

Chapter 1

"Oh, Brother, I am so glad you brought me tonight!"

Mr. Darcy smiled fondly down at his younger sister, Georgiana, trying to mask the pounding that had begun in his head. They were sitting in their box at the Theatre Royale in Covent Garden, waiting for the performance to begin.

There was nothing he despised more than being out in public amongst the members of the *ton*, but this was the most animated he had ever seen his sister about anything.

"Remind me again why we're here," he said.

Georgiana sighed and rolled her eyes. "Because this is the only time the Bonnet Family Singers are performing in public! Everyone has been absolutely dying to hear them sing ever since the prince regent spoke so highly after hearing them at the Duke of Waverly's gala."

He raised an eyebrow at this information. "I thought the Duke of Waverly only invited close friends to that event. Charles mentioned his sister was infuriated to not be able to attend, and not even our uncle received an invitation."

She nodded furtively, her head bobbing up and down in her enthusiasm. "And the prince regent *never* compliments *anyone* for their singing—this was the first time! Since then, they've been in high demand, but they rarely ever accept invitations to perform anywhere."

"Why are they called the Bonnet Family Singers? Is that their name?"

Georgiana shook her head fiercely. "That's part of their popularity—no one knows who they are! Rumor has it that they are of the gentry and are a family of five daughters, but no one knows anything more than that."

"How is it no one recognizes them when—?"

Darcy's words were interrupted by his sister's hiss at him to be silent. The principal manager of the theater had come onto the stage to introduce the act. Darcy leaned back in his seat, wondering how long he would have to remain before being allowed to retire to his home and the quiet and peace of his room.

Light applause sounded as the gentleman left the stage, and all waited with breathless anticipation. Darcy tried once again to ask his sister about the singers, but she gave him a glare that was so ferocious he decided he could ask at another time.

His questions were answered, however, when five women came out of the wings from behind a curtain. They were each wearing enormous bonnets that shadowed their heads. Beneath their bonnets, an intricate mask covered their faces, except their mouths and chins.

Four of the ladies moved into a line at the center of the stage while the fifth went to the piano on the left.

Darcy had never heard the theater so silent before, especially not when so filled with people. He wagered there was not a single seat or box that was empty in the entire building, which boasted of being able to hold over three thousand people.

The women were silent for a long moment, then the one at the piano played a simple scale. The women began to sing "Robin Adair."

What's this dull town to me
Robin's not near
What was't I wish'd to see
What wish'd to hear
Where all the joy and mirth
Made this town heaven on earth

Oh, they're all fled with thee
Robin Adair
What made th' assembly shine
Robin Adair
What made the ball sae fine
Robin was there
What when the play was o'er
What made my heart so sore
Oh, it was parting with
Robin Adair
But now thou'rt cold to me
Robin Adair
But now thou'rt cold to me
Robin Adair
Yet he I loved so well
Still in my heart shall dwell
Oh, I can ne'er forget
Robin Adair

Darcy's eyes widened at the gentle harmony that came from the performers' lips. He had never heard anything so pure or melodious in his life, and he had attended dozens of operas from world-famous singers.

When the song ended, the entire arena burst into applause and cheers. The women waited unmoving, as the audience voiced their approval for the beautiful music. After several minutes, the shortest girl stepped forward and raised a hand, and the large auditorium went instantly quiet.

Darcy's eyes immediately focused on her form, which was light and pleasing. In a strong French accent, she said, "Thank you very much. Now, we would like to perform a song in honor of all of those serving against Napoleon. Our prayers are with the brave men who keep our land safe."

She stepped backwards, and the tallest girl took her place in the front. She opened her mouth and sang "The Soldier's Widow."

Sad was the plaint of the wand'ring stranger,
Hungry and pale was the infant she bore;
Return'd from the land of misfortune & danger,
She hop'd to find peace on her dear native shore.

O neat was her cottage, and great was her treasure,
A treasure to her more than diamonds or pearl
In the smiles of her William consisted her pleasure,
And the fond caresses of her little girl.

Duty commanded, her William attended,
And she could not bear with her soldier to part
She roam'd oe'r the field when the battle was ended,
She kiss'd his pale lip, & she pressed his cold heart.

They bore her away, of all comfort bereft her,
Affliction her dart at her bosom did hurl;
Oh no, little darling, one comfort is left her,
The sweet smiling kiss of her dear little girl.

After the first verse, the other sisters joined in with a soft harmony for the remainder of the song. As the words flowed through the room, Darcy closed his eyes and pictured his cousin Colonel Fitzwilliam, who had recently returned injured from a campaign. While Darcy had heard this song before, it had never resonated with him as fiercely as it did now.

The song came to a close, and the audience sat in awed silence before erupting into applause. This time, Darcy joined the rest of the room in clapping. When it began to die down, Georgiana leaned over and, with tears in her eyes, whispered, "I wish Richard could have been here for this."

Darcy nodded, but there was no time to respond, as the shortest girl once again raised her hand for silence. Stepping forward once again, she said, "We appreciate being able to perform for you tonight. Our final song is for all those who have felt or still feel love."

She then began to sing, "Voi Che Sapete Che Cosa E Amor."

Voi che sapete che cosa e amor,
Donne, vedete, s'io l'ho nel cor,
Donne, vedete, s'io l'ho nel cor.
Quello ch'io provo, vi ridiro,
E per me nuovo capir nol so.
Sento un affetto pien di desir,
Ch'ora e diletto, ch'ora e martir.
Gelo e poi sento l'alma avvampar,
E in un momento torno a gelar.
Ricerco un bene fuori di me,
Non so chi il tiene, non so cos' e.
Sospiro e gemo senza voler,
Palpito e tremo senza saper,
Non trovo pace notte ne di,
Ma pur mi piace languir cosi.
Voi, che sapete che cosa e amor
Donne, vedete, s'io l'ho nel cor,
Donne, vedete, s'io l'ho nel cor,
Donne, vedete, s'io l'ho nel cor.

Questioningly, Georgiana turned to her brother, who replied, "It's Italian. Here is what it means: You who know what love is, ladies, see if I have it in my heart..."

The other three women joined in for the majority of the song, but then stopped, for the last three lines were sung as a solo by the shortest singer in the front.

She ended by holding the last word as a strong, clear, pure note for longer than Darcy thought possible. As the echo of her voice died away, the chamber's occupants leaped to their feet and applauded.

Darcy remained in his seat, stunned. He had never heard anything more exquisite in his entire life. The woman's voice was pure and passionate, and he yearned to hear more.

The women onstage waited until the applause began to die down, giving curtsies of acknowledgment. Then they turned and filed off the stage, disappearing completely.

Chapter 2

"Wasn't that just incredible?" Georgiana asked Darcy excitedly as he escorted her out of the private Fitzwilliam box.

There were many calls for an encore, but the ladies never returned to the stage. Eventually, the uproar died down, and everyone chattered amongst themselves. Darcy was eager to get his sister out of the noise and back to Darcy House before he was forced to mingle amongst acquaintances.

They were unaccompanied that night, as the remainder of the family was in Matlock to spend time with Richard, who was recuperating. This lack of companionship meant there was no one to rescue him or his sister when the matchmaking mothers of the *ton* realized his presence.

"Can we please go backstage and meet them?" she asked once they had reached the stairs.

Darcy's eyebrows flew up on his forehead. "Georgiana," he said, hesitating, "I do not mean to be indelicate, but the things that occur behind stage at a theater are not something that a well-bred young woman should be exposed to."

"Oh."

Her face fell, and her look of disappointment wrenched his heart. "But," he added, "if you promise me to remain in the carriage, I will go back and see what I can do."

Georgiana's face lit up with joy. "Oh, you are the best brother ever!"

He chuckled, then lifted her up into the carriage. Motioning for the two footmen who usually accompanied them to stand guard near the door, he swiftly went back inside and headed towards the rear of the theater.

The men who were guarding the doors to the backstage area were preventing many people from entering. Darcy pushed his way to the front of the crowd, but his progress was halted by a hand on his shoulder. He spun around to see the face of a grinning Charles Bingley.

"Darcy!" the younger man cried. "Wasn't that the most incredible thing you have ever heard? I daresay, the song about the soldier almost moved me to tears. I've never seen or heard a more angelic woman. I think I may be in love—I must meet her!"

Darcy rolled his eyes at his friend's boyish eagerness over yet another infatuation with a woman he barely knew. "How do you know she isn't old and ugly?"

Bingley's eyes widened; then he laughed. "With a voice and curves like hers? There's not a chance!" He paused, then added, "But why are *you* back here? I know meeting up with an actress or an opera singer isn't really your thing."

Stiffening, Darcy coolly responded, "Not in the slightest. Georgiana expressed an eagerness to meet the singers in person, and I told her I would arrange it."

With that, the two gentlemen made their way through the crowd, which had grown larger in the few minutes they were speaking. Darcy's great height made it easier for him to push his way to the front, with Bingley trailing after him.

Once he reached the door, Darcy said, "I would like to meet the singers who performed tonight."

One of the guards snorted. "You and everyone else, but we're under strict orders—no one enters tonight to disturb the ladies."

"Certainly an arrangement of some kind can be made?"

Darcy began to reach into his pocket, but the man shook his head, looking offended. "No, sir, there's not enough fortune in the world that would tempt us to open this door for anyone."

Darcy started to give up, but the thought of Georgiana's disheartened face caused him to give it one more try.

"Now see here!" he said in a commanding voice. "Do you know who I am, who my uncle is? I demand you let me back there this minute!"

The man raised his eyebrows. "And my orders come directly from the prince regent himself, who promised the ladies they would remain undisturbed if they agreed to perform tonight. So unless your uncle is the king, I will not be opening this door."

There were a few snickers, and Bingley put his hand on his friend's shoulder. "C'mon, old boy. We should go."

Darcy's cheeks flushed in embarrassment, and he allowed Bingley to pull him away.

***

Elizabeth Bennet was standing near the door that connected the backstage with the front area of the theater. She had just spied Lydia and Kitty with their ears pressed against it, giggling.

"What are you two doing?"

The youngest of the Bonnet Family Singers giggled again. "Listening to all the gentlemen trying to get back here and see us. It sounds like quite a crowd! If only we could meet them; I'm certain I would make them all fall madly in love with me."

"Get away from there," Elizabeth seethed, grabbing their arms and pulling them away. "The only reason Papa allowed us to perform in public tonight was because the prince regent himself assured us our identities would remain private. If our names or faces got out, we would all be ruined."

"I wouldn't mind if they all knew who I was," Lydia argued. "I'd be married quicker than any of you."

"No, you wouldn't," her elder sister responded fiercely. "You would be used and discarded. The only reason we even do this is because Aunt Gardiner serves on the board of trustees for an orphanage along with Her Grace, and we were volunteered to sing for their charity event. Had we known how out of control this would become, Papa would have never allowed it. Now, get back to the room with Jane and Mary."

Exasperated, Elizabeth watched Lydia and Kitty grumble their way back in the direction of their other sisters. As Elizabeth made to follow them, she heard shouting coming from through the door.

"Now see here! Do you know who I am, who my uncle is? I demand you let me back there this minute!"

Her eyes widened with fright, and she dashed after her youngest sisters to return to their room where their parents and the Gardiners waited.

"We must leave immediately," she gasped, closing the door behind her. "There is a large crowd out front, and they are shouting and demanding entry. I'm not sure the guards will be sufficient."

Mrs. Bennet began to wail and flutter her handkerchief. "Oh, my poor nerves! I knew we never should have agreed to allow the girls to perform in public. Their identities will be discovered and their reputations completely ruined. We will be cast out of Longbourn to the hedgerows when your father is dead."

Her husband raised his eyebrow and said in a dry tone, "My dear, I believe you were the one who insisted upon this concert when the prince regent offered to contribute five thousand pounds apiece to the girls' dowries from the proceeds. With such an income, even if you are all ruined, I'm certain you could live quite well on such an amount."

"Nevertheless," interjected Mr. Gardiner, "I agree with Lizzy that we leave immediately. There can be more danger from men of London who are in their cups than just a ruined reputation due to identity."

"Excellent point," Mr. Bennet said, slamming his book closed with alacrity and standing. "We will go out the back entrance and head to the carriage ourselves instead of waiting for it at the usual place."

Elizabeth gave a sigh of relief. They were finally going back home to Longbourn.

Chapter 3

Two months later...

"Oh, Mr. Bennet! Have you heard the news? Netherfield Park is let at last!"

Mrs. Bennet came bustling into Longbourn, fluttering about with excitement at the news she had just heard from Lady Lucas. Lydia and Kitty followed closely behind her. Hertfordshire so rarely obtained new neighbors that this was a novelty indeed.

"Has it?" he asked in an uninterested tone, turning the page of his newspaper.

She ignored his indifference and sat herself on the sofa. "Yes, and he is a single man of large fortune! Can you believe it? He has five thousand a year! What a good thing for our girls."

He smirked from behind his paper. "How so? How can it affect them?"

Elizabeth, who had been sitting with Jane and Mary near the window, hid a smile.

"Oh, Mr. Bennet!" she cried again. "How can you be so tiresome? You must know I am thinking of his marrying one of them! He will probably like Jane the best, as she is so beautiful."

"What a good joke if he were to fall in love with me!" Lydia interjected, giggling. "I should be the first married of all my sisters."

"Well, we shall see tomorrow night at the assembly," Mrs. Bennet replied. "Lady Lucas heard it from Sir William that he promised to attend and bring a party of guests."

"Am I required at this event?" Mr. Bennet asked, a look of alarm on his face.

"You do not wish to be present when one of your daughters sets eyes on her future husband for the very first time?" Elizabeth asked with a hint of sarcasm.

Mr. Bennet glared at his second daughter when Mrs. Bennet squealed. "Oh, I had not thought of that! Yes, Mr. Bennet, you most definitely *must* attend."

The battle of attendance at the assembly was waged between Mr. and Mrs. Bennet for the following twenty-four hours until at last he conceded, if she promised to leave him in peace until it was time to go. She eagerly acquiesced and spent the remaining time overseeing her daughters' preparations.

As they left, Mr. Bennet gave his wife and youngest daughters a stern look. "Now remember, there is to be absolutely *no* mention of singing or increased dowries. Anyone who so much as breathes a word of our secret will have their pin money taken away for a year, in addition to spending said year locked in her room."

"I don't see why the gentlemen can't know about the girls' new fortunes," whined Mrs. Bennet. "It would greatly improve their chances of making a good match."

"It would also increase their chances of discovery," Mr. Bennet replied sharply. "The entire town would want to know where the money came from, and their conjectures might end up leading to gossip more damaging than the truth."

Mrs. Bennet murmured under her breath, but grudgingly acquiesced. The ride into Meryton to the public rooms that hosted the assembly was long and tense.

Upon arrival at the assembly, Mrs. Bennet was disappointed to see that the Netherfield party had not yet arrived. As they waited for the dancing to begin, Elizabeth ensconced herself in the corner with her good friend, Charlotte Lucas. It took several minutes to find her, as Elizabeth was by far the shortest of her sisters—and the majority of the people in attendance.

They chatted about the latest gossip in the neighborhood while watching everyone line up for the first set. It was halfway completed when the door opened to admit a large party of strangers.

Mr. Bingley was announced, along with his sisters Miss Bingley and Mrs. Hurst, and two other gentlemen by the names of Mr. Hurst and Mr. Darcy.

Charlotte was able to identify each of the new arrivals, and Elizabeth was struck by the grim—yet handsome—mein of the tall Mr. Darcy.

"They say he owns half of Derbyshire," Charlotte whispered.

"Must be the miserable half," Elizabeth replied in jest, looking at the man's aloof expression.

The girls giggled, but then Elizabeth caught her mother waving her over from across the room. She sighed and excused herself to her friend, then made her way over to where her sisters and Mrs. Bennet stood. The matriarch pinched the girls' cheeks and brushed at their gowns. "Sir William will be here shortly as Master of Ceremonies to make introductions, and you must all look your best."

Elizabeth made a face at Jane, who hid a smile and gave her sister a look of chastisement. Mary, too, hid a smile, and they did their best to appear to advantage as their neighbor made his way over with the two single gentlemen from Netherfield.

Introductions to Bingley were performed, and the gentleman immediately asked to be added to Jane's dance card. The eldest and tallest Bennet daughter gave a shy smile of acceptance, and Mrs. Bennet burst forth with such effusive gratitude that her eldest three daughters were put to blush.

"And does your friend also like to dance?" Mrs. Bennet inquired, looking past Bingley to peer at Darcy standing behind him.

Bingley quickly introduced his friend, who gave a curt bow and walked away without saying anything. The jovial Bingley flushed, then offered his arm to escort Jane to the dance floor.

"Have you ever met a more disagreeable man?" Mrs. Bennet

humphed in annoyance.

Elizabeth merely shrugged a shoulder, then found a place to sit and watch the dancing. As there were far more ladies than gentlemen, it was not unusual for the girls to sit out and watch unless they were standing up with one another, as Kitty and Lydia were doing now.

When the song ended, Bingley crossed the room to Darcy and urged him to dance. Darcy protested, declaring that Bingley's partner was the only handsome girl in the room.

"Darcy, she's an angel," Bingley enthused.

Darcy raised an eyebrow. "Didn't you say that about the tallest Bonnet Family Singer?"

Elizabeth, who had been attempting to *not* eavesdrop, could not help but start in alarm. Had they been recognized? This was the first time hearing Mr. Darcy speak, and his voice sounded suspiciously familiar.

"That woman's *voice* was angelic, but that was all I knew. Miss Bennet's voice is just as celestial, but her smile and beauty add so much more."

Relaxing at this evidence that their identity remained concealed, Elizabeth was about to stand and leave when she saw Bingley gesture towards herself. "Look, there is one of her sisters now. I daresay she is quite pretty too. Come, I will introduce you so that you may dance."

Darcy looked at her coldly and met her eye before deliberately turning away. "She is tolerable, I suppose, but not handsome enough to tempt me. I will not be badgered into giving consequence to a young woman who is slighted by other men."

Elizabeth gasped, not just at the words, but at the recognition of his voice—it was the man who had been shouting at the theater, demanding to be let back!

Springing to her feet, Elizabeth made her way across the room to her father, who was standing with Sir William. Shifting her weight from foot to foot, she impatiently waited until he acknowledged her. "Papa, I must have a word with you."

She pulled him to the side and, in a whisper, quickly related everything she had discovered. "What if he knows it is us?" she asked in fear after finishing.

With a frown on his face, Mr. Bennet slowly shook his head. "As the gentleman did not actually make it to the back to see any of you, I'm confident your identities have not been revealed. After all, not even the prince regent has heard your name—or even seen your face, although he did offer quite a pretty penny for that."

Elizabeth gaped. "He did what?"

Laughing softly, Mr. Bennet said, "He offered your uncle an additional five thousand pounds to see you girls without those bonnets and masks. It terrified your uncle to decline, but he did so."

"My word," breathed Elizabeth in awe and fear. "I shudder to think what would have happened had he seen Jane."

"Or you," Mr. Bennet replied. "He seemed most taken with your, uh... form."

Flushing scarlet, Elizabeth changed the subject back to Darcy. "You think we are safe, then?"

Patting her shoulder, her father replied, "I do indeed, my dear. There is almost no possible way for the gentlemen to realize that the Bennet sisters are, in fact, the Bonnet Family Singers."

Chapter 4

Darcy looked out the window of the Netherfield drawing room and scowled at the pouring rain. It was the second day in a row he was unable to escape, and not just from Miss Bingley.

No, Elizabeth Bennet had suddenly appeared on foot to tend to her sister, and Bingley insisted on inviting the girl to remain until the elder had made a full recovery. Her presence greatly disturbed Darcy's equilibrium. He couldn't put his finger on it, but there was something about her that seemed familiar.

Darcy spent the next several days trying to both avoid Elizabeth and spend time with her to see what it was about her that pricked his memory. During his observations, he realized just how lovely she was, both inside and out. Her wit and knowledge were impressive as well, and he found himself stating opinions that were not his own in order to provoke a debate.

It was with both relief and disappointment that he watched the two eldest Bennet daughters drive away in Bingley's carriage once Jane had recovered. He realized the danger of paying Elizabeth too much attention, and he did not want to raise her hopes. Her family had no connections to speak of nor dowry, and the behavior of the youngest was deplorable. There was no way he could lower his family status by marrying someone so far beneath him.

The next several days passed slowly. Bingley could speak of nothing else but the angelic Miss Bennet, and Miss Bingley could speak of nothing else but disdain for the hoydenish Miss Elizabeth. Darcy found himself anticipating the next event—a dinner party at the Lucases—as a way to break up the monotony.

As expected, the Bennets were present at the occasion. He watched as Elizabeth teased Colonel Forster about giving a ball, before she turned and caught him listening in to her conversations. Her face tightened somewhat, and she asked him what he thought of her opinions.

He responded with something he thought was wit, but it clearly did not give the reaction he anticipated, as she returned her attention to her friend, Miss Lucas.

After a few moments, the plain spinster told her friend that she would be opening the piano. "And you know what comes next, Eliza."

Elizabeth flushed and looked around the room. "Truly, Charlotte, there is no need for me to sing today. After all, there are so many guests who have not yet performed for our local society. Surely, one of them would be a better choice?"

"You know you have the most beautiful voice of anyone in the county," Miss Lucas replied. "My father would never allow you to deny him the opportunity of hearing you perform."

"My throat has been a bit sore today—"

"Nonsense," Miss Lucas interrupted. "I heard you singing this morning at your home, and even now, your speaking voice sounds perfectly adequate. Besides, as you said yourself, there are those present who have never heard you perform; you cannot turn down the opportunity to make such an advantageous appearance to them."

Elizabeth hesitated, and her friend pushed further. "Eliza, as the saying goes, keep your breath to cool your porridge. You should keep yours to swell your song, as I cannot allow you to reject me."

Giving a sigh, Elizabeth nodded in acquiescence and crossed the room to the piano. Along the way, she stopped to have a few words with her father. Darcy moved closer to catch her conversation, curious as to why she would be so adamant about not showcasing her talents.

"Papa, Charlotte Lucas is insisting that I sing tonight," she whispered to Mr. Bennet.

"She does every time we have a gathering," he replied.

"Yes, but we've never had guests present who have heard such"—she paused and looked around furtively—"beautiful voices like those in London, such as the Bonnet Family Singers."

Mr. Bennet's eyes widened as he looked around the room, taking in the Bingleys, Darcy, and the soldiers.

Why is she so hesitant? Surely her voice cannot be all that bad if her friend is encouraging her so strongly, Darcy thought in confusion. *And why would our presence cause her father to be uneasy?*

Finally, Mr. Bennet's gaze came back to his daughter. "If you don't perform, however, it would raise more suspicions. You know Sir William would never be quiet with his entreaties. You cannot alter your voice too much or risk your neighbors wondering why. You must simply do your best to—"

His final words were cut off when Miss Lucas beckoned her friend over to the piano and said to the quieting guests, "We will now be privileged to hear from our very own Miss Elizabeth Bennet, who will sing my father's favorite song, 'Voi Che Sapete Che Cosa E Amor.'"

Elizabeth's steps faltered at the title.

"Well, she'll certainly never do it justice, will she?" Miss Bingley remarked snidely at Darcy's side.

He jumped, not having heard the woman approach him. "What do you mean?"

"Well, after hearing it performed in London by one of the Bonnet Family Singers, there is no possible way that Miss Eliza of Nowhere could even come close!"

Perhaps that might help me get rid of this awful infatuation, Darcy thought desperately.

Elizabeth took a seat at the piano and spent several quiet seconds arranging her dress and the sheet music. She then opened her mouth and began to sing as she played.

Darcy was immediately transported back to London. Her voice was exquisite, and he was just as caught up in her song as he was that night at the Theatre Royale.

He listened in silence, eyes closed, as he basked in the tones washing over him. While there were a few differences between her performance and the one he heard, he could hear nothing lacking in technique.

Opening his eyes once again, he caught a glimpse of her tilting her head to one side. His fingers ached to stroke the delicate curve of her neck, creating a trail his lips would soon follow.

When the last note died out, strong applause filled the room. Elizabeth politely denied requests for a second performance, and instead she was replaced on the bench by her younger sister Mary, who eagerly played a dance.

After leaving the piano, Elizabeth crossed the room to her elder sister, who was standing with Bingley near the fireplace.

"I was correct, was I not?" Miss Bingley asked in a quietly smug voice, leaning in close to whisper into Darcy's ear.

He pulled away. "It was different, yes. Nonetheless, we should still offer our congratulations."

Darcy moved to join his friend and the two elder Bennet girls. "You did very well, Miss Elizabeth," he said with a bow, his heart pounding in his chest.

"Thank you," she responded quietly.

"It was just incredible!" Bingley enthused. "The only time I've heard anything like it was when I heard the Bonnet Family Singers in London."

"Oh?" Elizabeth asked in a strangled voice before taking a sip of her glass of wine.

"Yes, they were wonderful! There was a shorter woman who sang the very song you did. Right before her, however, another of the group performed the most beautiful aria I have ever heard. Her voice was positively angelic! She was much taller, however, than her fellow soloist. In fact, the difference in height is very similar to the two of you."

He gestured at the two sisters, both of whom turned white. The elder Miss Bennet looked frantically at her younger sister, who closed her eyes in dismay.

Good Lord, Darcy thought, *they* are *the Bonnet Family Singers!*

It was all Darcy could do to keep himself from gasping.

The moment passed, however, and Elizabeth's eyes flew open. She gave a false laugh. "Oh, Mr. Bingley, that was a very good joke on your part!"

Bingley laughed, and Jane joined in, her giggles sounding a bit close to hysterical. When their laughter died down, Bingley shook his head. "What a moment of fancy. Thank you, ladies, for indulging me in that bit of speculation."

Both of the Misses Bennets sighed in relief, and Elizabeth excused herself to speak with her father, unaware of Darcy's eyes following her, his mind in complete turmoil.

Chapter 5

Elizabeth walked briskly along her favorite path towards Oakham Mount, eyes focused on her boots. The events at Lucas Lodge the night before greatly troubled her. Mr. Bennet had been dismissive of her concerns that they had been discovered.

"After all, Lizzy," he had said, "Mr. Bingley is much too artless to think that you and Jane would not immediately confess when he made his jest."

"It's not Mr. Bingley I'm worried about," Elizabeth muttered to herself, kicking a stone on the path in her ire. "It's Mr. Darcy."

"Yes?"

Elizabeth looked up, startled to see Mr. Darcy in front of her on his horse. She gasped, and he dismounted.

"My apologies for startling you, Miss Elizabeth," he said with a bow. "I assumed you had heard my approach."

She took a step back and eyed him warily. "I am surprised to see you this early in the morning, particularly as this path is not as well-known as some."

He looked a bit sheepish as he replied. "I was searching for you, and I knew this to be one of your favorites."

Elizabeth took another step back from him. "What, pray tell, would cause you to seek me out unaccompanied? Surely you have no wish to be thought of in a compromising situation with one such as myself."

"A Bonnet Family Singer, you mean?"

"Quiet!" she hissed at him, glancing around to make sure no one was around. "Are you mad, or are you trying to ruin my family to keep Jane away from your friend? In any case, I referred to the fact that you think I am merely *tolerable* and would therefore not wish to be compromised with me."

Darcy's brows knit together in confusion; then he flushed deeply and looked away. "I owe you my sincerest apologies for that statement. I was in a foul mood that evening. I wished only to be left alone. It has been many weeks now since I have considered you to be the handsomest woman of my acquaintance. I have no desire to ruin you or your family."

"Then what do you want?"

"While it is true that being a performer could ruin your reputation if it were known, the fact that you have received the approbation of the prince regent is nothing to sneeze at. I imagine you also have more dowry than as put about by the locals."

Elizabeth merely looked at him, neither confirming nor denying his suppositions.

"None of it matters to me, however. I can look past your family and their behavior, as well as their connections to trade. I have struggled against it all in vain, but my feelings will not be repressed. I love and admire you, most ardently, and I beg you to relieve my suffering and become my wife."

She froze and stared at him uncomprehendingly. After an agonizingly long silence, during which the confident look on Darcy's face began to subside, she replied, "I suppose I must thank you for the honor of your proposal, but I must decline it, no matter the obligation you have placed on me by expressing your feelings. I do not intend to cause you pain, but perhaps my abhorrent situation in life—both a performer *and* without connections—will cause any genuine feeling you have to soon fade."

With that, she turned and strode away.

Darcy stared at her back, then ran forward to catch up. "Is this the only reply I am to receive? I suppose it is of little importance as to the reason you have rejected me with such incivility."

Elizabeth spun to face him, her eyes flashing with an anger so fierce his steps faltered. "Mr. Darcy," she seethed, "the manner in which you offended and insulted me while proclaiming your love would cause *any* lady to be uncivil, if indeed I was so. I have watched you these last weeks, staring at me with disdain and doing your best to assist Miss Bingley in her desire to separate Jane and Mr. Bingley. I am not so stupid as to be unaware of your plans.

She took a deep breath. "I also heard you that night we performed in London, demanding to be let backstage because of whoever your uncle is. You thought aught then of the wishes of those around who. Nothing could tempt me to accept a man so proud and conceited as yourself—indeed, you are the last man whom I could ever be prevailed on to marry."

The last words were said with a shout, and Elizabeth ran away, tears filling her eyes as she sprinted towards Longbourn.

Fortunately for her, Darcy did not choose to follow.

***

Darcy mentally kicked himself the entire way to Netherfield. The conversation had *not* gone as he had wished in the slightest. Who did the foolish girl thing she was rejecting him that way?

Upon arriving back at his friend's estate, he took to his rooms, claiming to be under the weather. He spent the entire day and into the night alternating between railing at an imaginary Elizabeth and castigating himself. It ended with him falling into bed in the wee hours of the morning and having a terrible nightmare where Georgiana had heard of his behavior towards the people of Meryton, causing her to choose to live permanently with their uncle the earl.

He awoke in a cold sweat, realizing just how poorly he had behaved—not just in his proposal, but for the last several months. The memory of demanding to be let backstage at the Theatre Royale caused him to lower his head in shame. When had he turned into such an arrogant clod? He acted just like the pompous fools of the Peerage who felt them above everyone else.

He needed to change. Not just for Elizabeth, but for himself as well.

***

Three days later, Elizabeth followed behind Bingley and Jane as they took a walk through the gardens. She did her best to be an invisible chaperon by paying close attention to the plants or the clouds. As she pointedly directed her face towards a bare rose bush, out of the corner of her eye, she spied Bingley kneel and take Jane's hand.

Tears filled her eyes as she watched her elder sister's face break out into a beautiful smile. Bingley stood and embraced his new fiancée.

"I do hope congratulations are in order?" Elizabeth teased as the couple approached her. "Otherwise I might have to speak with my sister about proper behavior with a gentleman."

Jane blushed, but Bingley laughed. Elizabeth continued. "I believe, before the news is announced to the family, that you should speak with my father first."

He gave her a puzzled look, then blushed as realization hit him. After he went inside, Elizabeth turned to Jane, who asked, "Do you think he will change his mind once Papa tells him about my real dowry and where the money came from?"

"I think when he finds out you're the 'angelic singer' he was describing, he'll want to move up the wedding date!"

Jane beamed and went inside the house, leaving Elizabeth to contemplate her own circumstances. Darcy's proposal still troubled her, and she felt ashamed at having responded to him so harshly. What had he thought about her family and her singing that she had not thought herself a thousand times over?

Granted, Darcy *was* arrogant, but there was no need for her to be so cruel. The crumpled look on his face when she told him he was the last man she would ever marry was her fault, and it wasn't as if the words were true.

As if her thoughts had summoned him by magic, Elizabeth turned towards the house and spied Darcy dismounting from his horse. When he saw her, he changed direction from the front door to the garden where she waited.

Upon reaching her side, he stopped. "Miss Elizabeth, I must beg your apologies for my abhorrent behavior three days ago. I have thought of nothing else. You are completely in the right; I was given good principles as a child, but I was left to follow them in pride and conceit. I have been a selfish being all my life, and you have been the only one to confront me. I will forever be in your debt."

He bowed and turned away, but stopped when she cried out, "Wait!"

Darcy's back remained to her as she said, "I wholeheartedly accept your apologies for your conduct, and I can only be ashamed for my own. You did not deserve such ire, and I truly am sorry for the manner of my declarations. I hope... I hope we can part as friends."

He spun around to her. "Friends? Of course, Miss Elizabeth. You will always have my friendship."

With that, he offered her his arm and escorted her into the house.

Epilogue

The friendship Darcy and Elizabeth had formed rapidly developed into a courtship. Jane and Bingley's relationship had thrust the pair into one another's proximity, allowing them to come to know one another better.

Eventually, Darcy realized he couldn't imagine living without Elizabeth in his life. He requested and was granted a courtship that slowly made way to an engagement almost a full year later.

Georgiana was delighted to learn that her new sister was one of the famous Bonnet Singers. The girl and her sister-in-law were often found in the music room at Pemberley, singing and playing together all the daylong. The sounds of their duets often brought Darcy from his study to enjoy the masterpieces they created.

Fortunately, no one in the ton ever discovered the identities of the Bonnet Family Singers, and they were allowed to fade away into obscurity. On occasion, someone would remark at how Elizabeth's voice sounded familiar, but no one could ever decide how.

Thus, Darcy and Elizabeth were able to live happily ever after.

But Then the Dragons Came

Rumors that dragons have been spotted in the north have hit Meryton, but Elizabeth Bennet is sure that the sightings are nothing more than hysteria. Plagued with migraines since her eighteenth birthday, she is struck down by one at the Meryton assembly, preventing her from dancing. This is cruelly remarked on by Mr. Darcy, a newcomer to the neighborhood. Before she can confront him about his behavior, a dragon is spotted flying over the town and everyone panics. How will the arrival of dragons change *Pride & Prejudice?*

Chapter 1

It is a truth universally acknowledged that a single man in possession of a good fortune must be in want of a wife.

However little known the feelings or views of such a man may be on his first entering a neighborhood, this truth is so well fixed in the minds of the surrounding families, that he is considered as the rightful property of some one or other of their daughters.

But then the dragons came.

Dragons, as everyone knows, are creatures of mythical origin. They stem from stories about King Arthur, Beowulf, Sir Guy, and Saint George, but these are simply stories told at bedtime by mothers who are enticing children to stay in their beds.

So said Elizabeth Bennet to her friend, Charlotte Lucas, one day as they visited in the drawing room at Longbourn.

"Now Charlotte, you can't possibly believe these fairy tales are real!"

"They aren't just stories, Elizabeth," Charlotte insisted. "My cousin lives in Northumberland and wrote to say there has been a dragon that is destroying the barns that contain the harvest."

"And he has seen this dragon for himself?"

"Well, no, but what else could burn down a barn without leaving a single footprint?"

"A very slim arsonist?" replied Elizabeth with a smile. "Or a careless servant? After all, the barn had to have had *some* footprints around it, else it would mean no one was caring for the animals."

Charlotte gave a small huff of exasperation. "Mark my words, Lizzy Bennet. One day, that wit of yours will get you into real trouble."

The two girls exchanged a long look before bursting into giggles. The noise commandeered the attention of the rest of the room.

"What are you laughing at?" Mrs. Bennet screeched as Lady Lucas nodded in agreement. "Didn't Charlotte tell you the news? Dragons have returned to England, and we are all going to be burned alive in our beds!"

"Mama, no one we know has actually *seen* any dragons," Elizabeth replied patiently, "and in any case, Northumberland is very far away. I imagine a lizard that has fire in its belly would prefer the cold north of England rather than coming all the way down here."

This stopped Mrs. Bennet's hysterics as she pondered the words. "Yes, well... that's very sensible of you, Lizzy. I think you must be right. If dragons even did exist, they wouldn't come here."

Elizabeth gave a sigh of relief, which was echoed closely by Charlotte. The two girls were unable to finish any conversation, however, because Lady Lucas insisted they leave in order to prepare for the assembly that evening in Meryton.

"Now don't forget Mr. Bingley will be there, and he is bringing a large party from London!" Mrs. Bennet told her daughters once the Lucases had departed. "You must all look your very best, for he may fall in love with one of you, you know."

Mrs. Bennet and her five daughters arrived at the assembly without Mr. Bennet, who had chosen to remain at home with his port and book. "If Mr. Bingley decides to marry one of our daughters tonight, you may give him the permission on my behalf," he teased his wife, who scoffed and walked out the door with her nose in the air.

It seemed that everyone that evening was discussing the reports of dragons. Every guest seemed to know someone whose grandson or brother-in-law or third cousin twice removed had seen the devastation in the north caused by fires of unknown origin.

"I cannot believe so many people are gullible enough to be convinced that there really are dragons in this day and age," Elizabeth complained to Jane. "I mean, I can understand accepting that the folklore is all true—we have Stonehenge to thank for that—but the idea that dragons have existed in silence for centuries without our knowledge and then just suddenly reappear is ludicrous."

Just as Elizabeth finished her tirade, a wave of nausea came over her, along with a tremendous ache in her skull. "Oh, no," she moaned, her face white as she swayed slightly.

Charlotte and Jane each grabbed her arm. "Another one of your headaches?" Charlotte asked.

Elizabeth nodded mutely. "That's the second one this week."

"They're definitely more frequent now than when they started two years ago," Jane said. "I really wish you would allow Papa to send you to a specialist in London."

"It would just be a waste of money," Elizabeth grumbled. "You've heard the replies to Mr. Jones's inquiries on my behalf; I am prone to megrims and must not behave like a hysterical female." Her voice was laced with bitterness.

Jane and Charlotte helped Elizabeth to a nearby chair, and Charlotte went to fetch a cup of punch. At that moment, the doors opened to admit a group of people whom Elizabeth had never seen before in her life.

"That must be the Netherfield party," Jane whispered as Charlotte joined them, carrying three glasses of lemonade.

"My brother slipped alcohol into the punch again," the older girl whispered, rolling her eyes. "It's probably best to stick with lemonade this evening, especially for you, Lizzy."

Elizabeth nodded her thanks, still fighting the urge to vomit or pass out. She looked around the room and saw Mrs. Bennet and Lady Lucas both waving frantically at their eldest daughters, beckoning them to join their families.

Nodding towards their mothers, Elizabeth said, "I don't think I can stand right now, let alone walk across the room. Will you please give my excuses to Mama? I'm sure she would prefer I eschew an invitation in lieu of making a spectacle of myself."

"Are you certain you'll be all right?" Jane asked anxiously.

"Of course, Jane. Now, both of you go and make the gentlemen fall madly in love with you."

The two older girls laughed and returned to their mothers. Elizabeth watched as introductions were performed, and she was able to make out the names of the newcomers as Sir William circulated them around the room: Mr. Bingley, Mr. Darcy, Mr. Hurst, Mrs. Hurst, Miss Bingley, and Colonel Fitzwilliam.

She was delighted to observe that Bingley was obviously interested in Jane's beauty. After he had finished standing up with Charlotte, he then led Jane to the floor. The colonel stood up with Charlotte, and the Hursts joined in the dancing as well.

Elizabeth watched with amusement as Darcy stood stoically to the side with a face like stone. Next to him was Miss Bingley, whose look of hauteur made Elizabeth want to stick her tongue out or do something likewise childish, but she did not wish to be compared to Lydia.

Instead, Elizabeth closed her eyes and leaned back in the chair, sipping her lemonade in an attempt to ease the pounding in her temples. A short while later, she heard a tense conversation begin with voices she did not recognize. Opening her eyes, she saw that Darcy was now standing only a few feet away with Bingley and Fitzwilliam next to him.

"Darcy, why do you insist on standing around in such a stupid manner?" the colonel drawled in a voice tinged with amusement. "You had better dance, else you'll give offense to the entire room."

"I've already stood up with both of Bingley's sisters. To ask anyone else would be unbearable."

"But Darcy, there are so many lovely ladies here!" exclaimed Bingley, unperturbed by the ice in Darcy's tone.

"You have been dancing with the only handsome woman in the room," Darcy retorted.

"She is the most beautiful creature I have ever seen," Bingley said eagerly. "And look, there is one of her sisters, I believe, and she is quite pretty as well. Let me have Miss Bennet introduce the two of you."

Elizabeth had smiled at this evidence of Bingley's admiration of her sister, and she blushed and looked down when she realized that she was now the topic of conversation. She peered at the trio from the corner of her eyes to know if they chose to head her way.

Darcy looked over at her, his piercing dark eyes looking her over from toe to head. When his eyes met hers, it felt as though she had been struck by lightning. Heat and energy coursed through her entire body, and it was as if every hair on her body was standing on its end.

It was obvious that Darcy had been similarly affected. It was as if time had frozen, and they were the only two people in the room.

Then the moment passed. Darcy blinked at her several times and gave his head a small shake. Then he turned back to his friends. "She is tolerable, I suppose, but not handsome enough to tempt me. She hasn't danced once this evening but is instead ensconced in a corner like a wallflower. I am in no humor to give consequence to ladies who are slighted by other men, no matter how attractive you find their sisters. Now leave me be."

Anger flared in Elizabeth's chest, and had it not been for her headache, she would have marched over to the arrogant man to give him a piece of her mind. Before she could decide to push through the pain and do just that, someone let out a terrified scream.

"Dragon!"

Chapter 2

"Dragon! Run! There's a dragon!"

Pandemonium ensued as everyone rushed towards the doors. Elizabeth stood from her chair, and a flash of blinding, white pain struck her head. She cried out and collapsed to the ground.

"Good Lord! Miss, miss, are you all right?"

She looked up through the tears and saw one of the Netherfield party at her side. "Colonel Fitzwilliam?" she asked in confusion.

He gave her a confused look. "I'm sorry, have we met before?"

"No, I just heard you being introduced by Sir William when you arrived. I believe you met my mother and sisters. I am Elizabeth Bennet, the *tolerable* one of the family."

Colonel Fitzwilliam looked at her with a mixture of amusement and dismay. "I'm glad to see you find some humor in the situation, Miss Elizabeth. Are you all right though?"

"Yes, I just have a megrim that came on shortly after we arrived. The noise has only aggravated things; it is a bit loud."

That was an understatement. People were screaming and running around the room, looking for loved ones. The commotion increased the pressure behind Elizabeth's eyes, and she fought to keep conscious.

"I can see that you are truly unwell. Let me find out exactly what is going on out there. Darcy, Bingley!"

The two men, who had gathered the Hursts and Miss Bingley, were standing nearby. Colonel Fitzwilliam said in a commanding voice, "Darcy, stay here with Miss Elizabeth. I am going outside to see what exactly the devil is going on. Bingley, can you find the Bennets?"

"No!" shrieked Miss Bingley, clutching her brother's arm. "We must get away! Didn't you hear there's a dragon? Charles, you cannot abandon me. We need to get to London immediately!"

Bingley shrugged his sister off. "Hurst, get Caroline and Louisa into your carriage. Go to Netherfield, then send the coach back for us."

Hurst nodded and hauled the two sisters away by their arms, ignoring Miss Bingley's shouts. Bingley then made his way through the crowd while Darcy knelt where Elizabeth was partially collapsed on the ground.

Once assured that Darcy had taken over watching Elizabeth, Colonel Fitzwilliam dashed towards the doors, one hand on the saber at his side.

"You do not need to remain with me, Mr. Darcy," she said, her teeth gritted in pain. "I am sure that my family will be collecting me shortly."

"A gentleman does not leave a lady in distress, especially if there is danger," he replied stiffly.

"I'm glad to see your disdain for my tolerable appearance and lack of partners doesn't extend towards total abandonment," she replied acerbically.

His face flushed a deep red, but there was no time for a response as Bingley came rushing up with Jane behind him.

"Oh, Lizzy, I was so worried! Mama was frantic and insisted everyone depart immediately. I refused to get in the carriage until I found you, and she just left!"

"What?" Elizabeth gasped in shock. "Mama just… abandoned us here?"

"What are we going to do?" Jane cried, wringing her hands.

"You'll come with us to Netherfield," replied Bingley firmly, "until everything can be sorted out."

"Could you not just take us home?" begged Elizabeth.

"Unfortunately not," Colonel Fitzwilliam answered as he rejoined the group. "It appears that a group of coachmen outside claimed to see a dragon flying over the town. Now, they had been enjoying some ale, so the verity of their story could be called into question, but a shop is burning. It would be safest if we all go to one place, and Netherfield is closer."

Elizabeth bit her lip. She hated going to an estate with complete strangers, but she would hate it more if someone were to be injured because of their foolish mother. "Very well," she sighed, "but only because Mrs. Hurst will be there to preserve our reputations."

"Has the carriage returned yet?" Darcy asked Bingley, who dashed off to check.

Within moments, he was back, breathing heavily. "Yes, it's there. The horses are behaving oddly though. I think we need to leave immediately."

Elizabeth tried to stand, but the pain in her head increased. Without a word, Darcy scooped her up in his arms, and the five of them made their way to the carriage.

Once they were all inside, Bingley forcefully rapped on the roof, and off they went. Elizabeth had never ridden with such speed in a carriage, and she wondered at the need. "Do you all really believe there are dragons?"

Bingley laughed as Darcy and Colonel Fitzwilliam exchanged a serious look.

"I don't," the jovial young man replied, "but you can't deny that something strange is going on. I simply wished to get us to safety as soon as possible."

"That was very wise," Jane said quietly, and Bingley beamed at her in response.

Suddenly, the speed of the carriage picked up. The horses snorted and squealed as they raced along the path towards Netherfield at a rate that caused Elizabeth to cling to the side of the carriage to keep her balance.

"What the devil?" cried Colonel Fitzwilliam as he pounded on the roof of the carriage.

Instead of slowing down, as everyone expected, the speed only increased, as if the coach were careening out of control without a driver. As they took the last turn of the road that led into the Netherfield drive, the wheels lifted off the ground. Jane cried out and wrapped her arms tightly around Elizabeth.

Fortunately, the coach did not topple over. The wheels came down with a thud and a sharp crack as the wood splintered, throwing the occupants of the carriage about, Elizabeth landing on Darcy's lap. The sudden movements increased the pain in her head to heights she had never before experienced. It felt as though her brain was trying to simultaneously implode and explode, and the conundrum was tearing it apart.

The carriage didn't stop with the broken wheel, however. The horses were shrieking in terror as they continued towards the stables. Their progress was slow, and each step caused the carriage to sway unbalanced.

Finally Colonel Fitzwilliam threw the door open. "We need to jump! Bingley and I will go first to catch the ladies. Darcy, you help them out, then follow!"

Before Bingley could object, Colonel Fitzwilliam grabbed him by the arm and thrust them both out of the door. They rolled to safety, then immediately took to their feet and sprinted along the carriage.

"Go, Jane!" Elizabeth shouted, shoving her sister out the door. Bingley caught her, but the force of her fall knocked the two of them to the ground, where they tumbled for a few seconds.

Elizabeth moved towards the door to jump herself, but a sharp jolt flung her back into Darcy's arms. Instead of helping her regain her feet, he wrapped his arms around her and leaped from the carriage, holding her tightly.

They rolled together for a few feet before coming to a stop. The pain in her head was agonizing, and she leaned over to expel all of her stomach's contents. To her very great surprise, Darcy stayed by her side, holding her disheveled hair out of the way. Once her stomach calmed, she sat up and offered him a small smile of gratitude.

"Watch out!"

Elizabeth and Darcy turned towards the voice, only to see a large, winged creature drop from the sky to swoop over their heads. They instinctively ducked, Darcy throwing himself on top of Elizabeth to protect her.

The wind from the creature told Elizabeth it had missed them only by inches. She and Darcy straightened to see the silhouette of a dragon, barely visible in the moon's dim light, soar away over the trees. A burst of flame shot from its mouth, barely missing the barn by inches.

"Inside!" cried Colonel Fitzwilliam, who was helping Jane support Bingley.

The younger man limped along, arms draped across the shoulders of Fitzwilliam and Jane. Elizabeth stood to help but collapsed as lightning shot once again through her head.

"I've got you," she heard Darcy say just moments before sweeping her off her feet and sprinting with her to the house.

"No! Jane!" she cried, fighting to get down so she could help her sister.

Darcy ignored her pleas and continued running. They reached the front door, which was opened by a large footman.

"Go help them!" Darcy demanded breathlessly, pointing a finger towards the struggling trio.

Elizabeth's eyes were closed tightly against the pain in her head. She felt Darcy open a door and lay her gently on an overstuffed sofa. Miss Bingley was there, as evidenced by the hysterical shrieks in the background.

"Jane," Elizabeth murmured, cradling her head with her hands.

"She's inside now," Darcy whispered. "It's going to be all right, Miss Elizabeth."

He went to stand, but she grabbed his arm. "Please, get her."

Darcy placed his hand over hers in reassurance, but when his bare fingers touched her gloveless hand, time stopped.

Chapter 3

A warmth spread up from Darcy and Elizabeth's connected fingers to her shoulder and throughout her entire body. Her headache was instantly alleviated, and a glow surrounded the pair.

At first, Elizabeth thought it was just her imagination, perhaps a reaction from the trauma they had all experienced. Then Jane gasped, and Miss Bingley cried out in alarm.

Unable to pull her hand away from his, Elizabeth locked eyes with Darcy. His dark gaze pierced deep into her soul, and she felt as though he could see her every thought. The intensity with which he looked at her was unlike anything she had ever experienced.

After an eternity—which was really only a few seconds—the glow faded, and Elizabeth felt mobility return to her limbs. She hesitantly began to withdraw her hand, only to have him grasp it tighter.

"What… what was that?" she asked in a breathless whisper.

"A bonding."

All eyes turned towards Colonel Fitzwilliam, who stood near the door, watching the entire scene with narrowed eyes.

"What do you mean a bonding?" Miss Bingley exclaimed. "They only just met this evening!"

Darcy sighed and finally released Elizabeth's hand. She winced at the disconnect, expecting the migraine's sudden return, but there was nothing. Nothing other than the warmth that still flowed through her veins, that is.

He pinched the bridge of his nose with his fingers. "There is too much to explain right now. We've all had a shock, and it is well past two in the morning. I propose we each retire to our rooms and take some willow bark tea, then have a good night's rest."

"Excellent plan," said Bingley, who had been deposited on a chair near the fire, Jane at his side. His foot was propped up on a cushion, boot off, and Elizabeth could see the swelling around his ankle. "Caroline, please show Miss Bennet and Miss Elizabeth to the two remaining rooms in the family wing."

"The family wing?" Miss Bingley sputtered. "But that is for family."

"Yes, well, you put Darcy and Fitzwilliam in there, and they're not family. Besides, the guest wing hasn't been made presentable yet."

The mistress of Netherfield turned an ugly shade of puce that clashed horribly with her red hair and orange dress. "Very well," she said through gritted teeth.

Unceremoniously, she stalked out of the room. Elizabeth and Jane hurried after their hostess. Behind them, Elizabeth could hear the gentlemen help Bingley to his feet and follow at a slower pace.

Miss Bingley gave instructions to the housekeeper about preparing the rooms and assigning maids to light fires.

"Don't forget the tea Mr. Darcy requested for everyone," Jane said in her soft voice.

Scowling, Miss Bingley also ordered willow bark tea to be served in each room. The housekeeper bobbed a curtsy and sent a maid to relay the instructions. Then all four women made their way up the stairs and into the guest wing.

Elizabeth had been to Netherfield once as a child when it was leased for the summer by a family in York, but she had never been upstairs before. They were quickly shown to separate rooms, and Jane looked at Elizabeth uncomfortably before going into hers.

The two girls had shared a room at Longbourn for a long time, and even as adults, they preferred to sleep in the same bed more often than not. It allowed them to not only keep warmer during the winter months, but to have privacy to visit and share confidences.

Elizabeth removed her outer clothing and stays, then looked

around upon realizing that she didn't actually have any clothes to sleep in. Hoping rather than believing that Miss Bingley would send anything, Elizabeth crawled under the blankets in just her shift. Had a nightgown been provided, she would have gone to Jane's room; without any covering, however, she did not feel comfortable wandering the halls in a strange home.

A maid knocked on the door and entered with a tray of willow bark tea. The girl seemed surprised to discover Elizabeth in her shift, but as any servant with a difficult mistress, she remained silent. Elizabeth smiled with gratitude and took a long drink of the tea. Within minutes, the brew had worked its magic, and she fell into a dreamless sleep.

It was almost noon when Elizabeth awoke to a bright ray of sunshine on her face through the open curtains. She groaned. "Jane, why didn't you pull them shut?"

When there was no response, she sat up and looked around at the unfamiliar furnishings, blinking in confusion. Her entire body ached, except for her head, which was unusual the day after a severe megrim. It took a few moments for her to recall where she was, and then all of her memories from the night before came flooding back to her.

Assembly. Dragons. Netherfield. Darcy.

Suddenly wide-awake and eager to speak to the man who had belittled her and then saved her life the night before, Elizabeth threw back the covers and put on her ball gown. She grimaced at the idea of having to put on dirty clothes that were meant for dancing, not breakfast, but there was no other option.

Upon leaving her room, Elizabeth knocked on Jane's door, but there was no answer. Hoping that her sister was already downstairs, she quickly made her way towards the breakfast room. Fortunately, everyone at Netherfield had awakened late that day, and the table was filled with all four gentlemen, Jane, and Mrs. Hurst.

Elizabeth exchanged greetings with everyone, then made her way to the sideboard to fetch a plate.

"Please, allow me."

She looked up in surprise at Darcy, whom she had not heard approach. Instead of declining—which she normally would have done—she wordlessly handed him her plate. To her great astonishment, he filled it with all the items she would have chosen for herself.

It wasn't until she was seated at the table that Elizabeth realized how hungry she was. Doing her best to eat in a ladylike fashion, she quickly inhaled everything that had been placed before her. As she ate, she watched Jane and Bingley speak quietly to one another at one end of the table, then Darcy and Fitzwilliam at the other. The Hursts sat in silence, ignoring each other, until Mr. Hurst gave a loud belch before excusing himself from the room. His wife accompanied him, and then only the five remained.

"Caroline took a breakfast tray in her room, I believe," Bingley said decisively. "As Miss Elizabeth has now joined us, I think it would be the perfect opportunity to discuss the events of last night."

Elizabeth raised an eyebrow at the unyielding tone coming from the affable gentleman. The night before, she would have considered him to be more like a puppy who is always following behind its master, eager for approval.

Darcy and Colonel Fitzwilliam looked at one another. "It's your story," the colonel said. "You would be the best one to tell it."

Letting out a sigh, Darcy said, "Very well. I have kept this secret for so long it seems odd speaking about it with strangers."

"Keeping what secret?" Elizabeth asked anxiously.

"Lizzy, let him speak," Jane said in a soft, yet firm, voice.

She sat back in her chair. "My apologies, Mr. Darcy. Please continue."

"As you witnessed last night, dragons are real, and they have returned to England. Most people assume that the Darcy family came

111

from Normandy and were called the family D'arcy. While that is true for one branch of my line, the reality is that the majority of my lineage stemmed from Ireland. Darcy is the Gaelic form of the surname O'Dorchaidhe, which comes from the Gaelic word *dorcha*, meaning dark."

Elizabeth's eyes widened at this, and she gave a light scoff. "Are you saying you had an ancestor who practiced dark magic?"

He hesitated, then said, "Whether or not he did is debatable, but we have ancient family histories in the library at Pemberley that describe the battles my ancestors fought with dragons. As they had a higher success rate than many other dragon slayers of the time, they were often accused of using magic of some kind to aid them."

"I'm afraid I find this all rather difficult to believe," she said, "but I cannot deny what I saw last night with my own two eyes."

He nodded. "I've never believed the stories either, until two years ago. There is lore that says when the time of the dragons returns, the fated two will be cursed with demons on the top of the slope from the time the younger is of age until they are merged as with the sun's rays. Then the magic will be restored, but only as lovers will the couple be able to confront and conquer the ancient foe. Only then will peace be restored to the land."

Everyone looked at each other in confusion. "I don't get it," Bingley finally said.

"Well, apparently, in ancient times, the head was called the top of the slope. They also believed headaches to be caused by demons and often attempted to alleviate the pain of migraines by trepanation."

"What's that?" Elizabeth asked warily.

Darcy grimaced. "Boring holes or cutting into the skull to release the trapped demons."

Turning white, she replied, "Well, I'm grateful all Mr. Jones wants to do is bleed me for a while when it happens."

"Do you get migraines, then?" Colonel Fitzwilliam asked with an intense gaze.

"Yes, since I turned eighteen."

"When you came of age!" Colonel Fitzwilliam exclaimed.

"When was that?" Darcy asked. "My migraines began on the eleventh of August, two years ago."

"That's my birthday," Elizabeth gasped. "I was eighteen then."

"So then what does it mean, united as one with the rays of the sun?" Bingley asked.

Elizabeth looked at Darcy. "When I grabbed your hand last night, my migraine immediately went away. I thought it was just the panic of the moment. But then the glow began, and when I let go, the pain was still gone. It hasn't returned since."

"But what about the last part?" Jane whispered. "Where it talks about... lovers. And battle."

Chapter 4

"I think that part is the most clear out of the entire prophecy," Colonel Fitzwilliam said.

"It means we must marry if we are to have any hope of defeating the dragons and keeping England safe," Darcy said, not meeting Elizabeth's eyes.

At Jane's horrified gasp, Elizabeth shook her head fervently. "Absolutely not. This is insane! I insist on returning to Longbourn at once. You have all lost your minds, and I will not spend one minute more entertaining this ludicrousness of a prophecy deciding to whom I must be wed."

Rising to her feet, Elizabeth urged Jane to join her, and the two left the room as quickly as possible. As soon as the door closed, however, her migraine returned in full force. She let out a cry and collapsed, the dizziness from the pain overwhelming her senses. The pain blinded her, and she gagged as she attempted to not lose her breakfast.

At her shout, both servants and the occupants of the breakfast room came rushing. Darcy knelt at her side and reached for her hand. The moment their flesh touched, the pain in her head disappeared. In astonishment, she looked at their joined hands, then up into his concerned face.

"I know it hurts," he said. "I've had them as well. At first, we thought I was ill. I consulted various doctors and was never able to find any relief. It wasn't until a dragon actually arrived that I realized the true source of my problem. I didn't believe it at first either. I've only told my cousin, as the rest of my family would simply think I was mad."

Tears filled Elizabeth's eyes. "I feel as if I'm caught in a bad dream. I just want to wake up, with all of this simply a figment of my imagination."

"I know," he said soothingly. "Believe me, an arranged match is not something I ever wanted. My parents married for love, and I'd always hoped for the same."

"I've seen my parents' unequal alliance, and I vowed that only the deepest love would induce me into matrimony."

"But this would be love, Lizzy."

Elizabeth looked at her elder sister, astonished. With the pain in her head disappearing like magic, she had quite forgotten that she and Darcy weren't alone. "How, Jane?" she begged. "How can I do this?"

"You would do it because you love us. You love your family, your town, and England in general. You love your fellow man. If you marry Mr. Darcy, you save all of us. If you don't, then we are all at risk of suffering death."

"You believe this, then?" Elizabeth asked her sister in surprise.

"I didn't at first, but I saw the golden light around you last night. I saw your migraine return when you rejected the story and its alleviation the moment Mr. Darcy touched your hand. There's no way to fabricate those reactions, Lizzy."

Elizabeth let out a small moan of despair, and Darcy's hand tightened its hold on hers. "Miss Elizabeth, please look at me."

She lifted her eyes to meet his dark, intense gaze.

"I cannot promise you a great love match," he said gently, "but I give you my word as a gentleman that I would always treat you with the utmost respect. I would be making vows before God, and I take that commitment seriously. You would want for nothing as my wife."

"Except for love," she said, a touch of bitterness in her voice.

"Perhaps not a grand passionate love as is read about in novels," he said, "but I think we could be friends, and love can always grow when there is mutual respect."

"And I can vouch for my friend," Bingley joined in. "He is one of the best men I have ever met, and I am grateful for his kindness towards myself. The nephew of an earl has no reason to be friends with the son of a tradesman, especially when said son is as hopeless at estate management as I am!"

This small jest lifted the tension in the air somewhat, and Darcy rolled his eyes and said dryly, "Bingley is one of those people who puts himself down with false modesty in order to receive praise about things he is secretly proud of."

Once the giggles had subsided, Colonel Fitzwilliam added, "Miss Elizabeth, I can give you my oath as an officer in Her Majesty's infantry that I will protect you with my life, even against my own cousin. Should you ever be in need of any assistance, my family and I are at the ready. My father is an earl, you see. As much as I vouch for the goodness of my cousin, I can promise you that should he ever betray the vows he would make to you, I would hold him accountable in society and with my sword."

Elizabeth looked at the earnest faces of the gentlemen gathered around her, then looked at Jane, who gave her an encouraging nod.

"Very well, then. I will marry you, Mr. Darcy."

The weight of her statement hung over the group, causing them to fall silent for a few moments. Then Darcy said, "I think we had better do it as quickly as possible. I do not think it was a coincidence that the dragon chose to follow our carriage home last night as opposed to another guest's."

"Nor I," said Colonel Fitzwilliam. "We must act with all speed."

Hesitating, Darcy said, "I took the liberty of purchasing a special license in London when the migraines began, just in case the prophesy proved to be true. The archbishop is my godfather, and he has known me all my life. When I told him I needed one that had left the bride's name blank, he was hesitant, but he gave it to me."

Elizabeth raised both eyebrows. "My goodness, that is a great deal of trust."

"Darcy is well known in the ton for his integrity," Bingley said effusively. "He doesn't gamble, he has no debts, and he writes to his steward at least four times a week when he is away from Pemberley."

"As much as I'd love to hear more about myself," Darcy said with a wry smile, "I think I should fetch Mr. Bennet and the parson immediately. You are not yet of age to be married without permission, even if you are of age to be considered an adult."

"How am I ever going to explain this to Papa?" Elizabeth groaned.

It was clear when Mr. Bennet arrived at Netherfield that her apprehension was not without merit. Mr. Bennet was already in a foul mood, having spent the entire night and a good part of the morning berating his wife for having abandoned her two eldest daughters.

The note he sent to Lucas Lodge revealed that his daughters hadn't gone to their friends for shelter, and he was just about to send out a search party when Darcy arrived to collect him.

The frown never left Mr. Bennet's face throughout his daughter's recitation, and when he heard the prophecy, his quick mind processed it before Elizabeth could interpret the meaning.

With a ferocious scowl, he turned to Darcy. "I absolutely forbid it. My daughter will not be marrying a stranger who claims to have access to magic. This is preposterous at best and criminal at worst. Jane, Lizzy, we are leaving now."

"Papa," Jane began in a gentle voice, but he cut her off with a harsh look.

Just as before, as soon as Elizabeth attempted to leave the room, she was struck by a migraine beyond anything she had ever experienced. She cried out in agony and thrashed on the floor. When Darcy touched her cheek, the relief was instantaneous, and a warm golden glow emanated around the two of them.

Mr. Bennet watched with his mouth ajar. When the glow ebbed, he said with a hoarse voice, "Well, I guess we'll be having a wedding today."

Chapter 5

The ceremony went so quickly that Elizabeth was still in shock by the time she'd said her vows and signed the register that the local parson had brought with him. It had taken a rather large donation to the church—from Darcy, of course—for the man to accept the special license with a filled-in name for the bride.

Miss Bingley had gone into hysterics when she'd heard the news that Darcy was being married to a stranger he'd met only the day before. She took to her rooms for the remainder of the day, much to everyone's relief. Jane and Mrs. Hurst did their best to make it a special day for Elizabeth. Jane gathered flowers while Mrs. Hurst loaned Elizabeth a beautiful gown and arranged a special luncheon.

Mr. Bennet's eyes were teary as he gave away his favorite daughter. Once the ceremony was complete and everyone had enjoyed the simple yet tasteful meal, he stated his need to return to the house and ensure the safety of the residents there.

"There was a dragon circling over the home last night," he told them. "It is gone now, but I have to say, it was quite terrifying. Hopefully, my dear, you will be able to put an end to this madness."

Mr. Bennet originally insisted Jane go with him, but Elizabeth was in such distress over the changes in her life that Jane begged to be able to remain to comfort her sister. Mr. Bennet reluctantly acquiesced once Mrs. Hurst assured him that she would watch over both girls and ensure all proprieties were observed.

"I dread telling your mother about this," he said with a groan. "She will be insufferable to live with once she learns Elizabeth is married after having been abandoned."

Everyone chuckled lightly, and Mr. Bennet bid the girls farewell. He gave Elizabeth a gentle kiss on the brow and said, "I always knew you were destined for great things, my Lizzy. If anyone can figure out how to keep us all safe, it's you."

With tears in her eyes, Elizabeth watched her father's carriage drive off, knowing she would never return to Longbourn except as a visitor. Darcy placed a comforting hand on her shoulder, but she turned away and buried herself in her sister's arms to weep.

"Come, let us allow the ladies some privacy," Colonel Fitzwilliam said quietly. "We should take some time to discuss combat tactics. It will be different with a dragon than with Napoleon's armies, but perhaps there's something in those books of yours that you brought, Darcy."

"How did you know to bring them here?" Bingley asked. "I mean, it's not as if you knew you'd meet Elizabeth here or anything."

"The decision to come to Hertfordshire, as well as to bring the books, was something I felt strongly compelled to do." Darcy shrugged. "I cannot describe it any other way, other than a gut feeling that was far beyond any I had ever felt before."

Once the gentlemen had left, Mrs. Hurst invited Elizabeth and Jane to her private sitting room. "Now, I know this conversation is going to be very uncomfortable for both of you, but as your mother isn't present, it's important to know what to expect tonight, Elizabeth."

Jane flushed a brilliant red and stammered, "M-maybe I should go to my rooms."

Shaking her head, Mrs. Hurst said, "You are old enough to be married soon, and your sister will need your support."

The next half hour proved to be very uncomfortable for Jane; Elizabeth could see it on her sister's face each time their new friend explained another detail of intimacy and the marriage bed. Elizabeth, for her part, was grateful for all the information. The only knowledge she had was her mother's complaints to Aunt Phillips and what she had seen animals do on the farm. This presentation eased much of her concern about what to expect.

Mrs. Hurst finished her explanation by saying, "I know you do not know Mr. Darcy very well at all, but he has been my brother's friend for several years. He is one of the most honorable men I have ever met, and I truly believe he will treat you kindly and with gentleness. If I thought otherwise, I would tell you so."

These words rang in Elizabeth's ears that night as she waited alone in her chambers. Rooms had been rearranged so that Darcy and Elizabeth had adjoining accommodations in the guest wing to give them some privacy. Her hands shook at the unknown that was to come, but she fought to keep her courage.

Darcy knocked on the adjoining door and entered the room, dressed only in a nightshirt. Elizabeth swallowed hard, and his face softened. "Here, a glass of wine might help."

She drank it quickly, and he said in a gentle voice, "I know this is very different from how you expected your life to go. If circumstances were any different, I would recommend waiting until we know one another better, but the prophecy refers to us as lovers. I do not wish to take any chances."

"I understand," she said in a quavering voice, the sound making her straighten her shoulders in determination.

Darcy proved to be true to his word, and the night was filled with tenderness and passion.

Elizabeth woke the next morning and looked at her sleeping husband with a small smile. She had never once thought she could ever feel the way she did when Darcy touched her, but it was much better than anything she could have possibly expected.

Suddenly a scream pierced the air, and Darcy shot up in the bed. Within seconds, there was frantic pounding on their door.

"Darcy, Elizabeth, come quickly!" shouted Colonel Fitzwilliam. "There are a half-dozen dragons circling Netherfield!"

They dressed with all speed and ran out of the room and to the front foyer. From the windows in a nearby drawing room, they could see large shadows on the ground from the great beasts overhead.

"What do we do?" Jane whispered.

Darcy and Elizabeth looked at one another, determination on both their faces. "We're going out there," Elizabeth said grimly.

"No!" Jane cried. "Lizzy, do you even know what to do?"

"No," Elizabeth replied, "but so far everything about the prophecy has come true. All that's left is for the lovers to confront and conquer the foe. We can't confront them unless we go out there."

Jane collapsed to the ground, weeping, and Bingley crouched next to her.

Colonel Fitzwilliam stepped forward, a hand on his saber. "I will go with you. I may not have whatever magic on my side, but I vowed to protect you with my life, and I will do that."

Darcy shook his head. "If the worst does happen, I'll need you to protect Georgiana and keep Pemberley safe by any means necessary."

Elizabeth could see the internal battle play out on the colonel's face. After several long moments, he embraced Darcy. "God be with you."

Darcy turned towards Elizabeth and extended a hand. "Are you ready?"

She gave a silent nod and took his hand, the now-familiar warmth spreading throughout her body at the contact. Together, as one, they walked out the front door and into the sunlight.

By the time they had reached the front lawn, all six bright jewel-colored dragons were circling directly above their heads, each a different color. Smoke and fire emanated from their snouts, and the breeze from their wings caused Elizabeth's dress to swirl wildly around her legs.

Darcy raised his hand, and to Elizabeth's surprise, a jet of blue fire shot from his palm towards the sapphire dragon directly above his head. It dodged effortlessly, breaking up the circular formation.

"How did you do that?" she gasped.

"I have no idea," he said, eyes wide with shock. "It just felt like the right thing to do."

The dragons then began to swoop down at them: ruby, emerald, onyx, aquamarine, amethyst, and then the sapphire again. Darcy met each approach with blasts of blue fire, shielding Elizabeth with his body.

"Why aren't they fighting back?" she shouted at him over the noise of roaring, fire, and flapping wings.

"I don't know!" he yelled, shooting another burst of blue flame from his palm, which struck the ruby dragon directly on the left wing.

A howl of pain came from the dragon, and it dropped from the air, hitting the ground with a loud crash. It remained motionless, and Elizabeth impulsively sprinted towards it. Even as she ran, the logical side of her brain was screaming at her to stop, but her legs refused to obey.

"Elizabeth, what are you doing?" Darcy yelled after her.

Before he could follow, however, the remaining five dragons landed in between the couple, preventing him from passing. He held up his hands, which were enveloped in blue fire, readying himself for the next strike.

Oblivious to the danger to her husband, Elizabeth's only thought was of the dragon. She reached the spot where it lay, the painful whimpering tearing at her heart. Without thinking, she placed a comforting hand on its snout.

The same golden glow that appeared the first time she touched Darcy began to emanate from where her hand touched the dragon's scales. Darcy and the dragons all stopped and stared as the light grew brighter and radiated farther.

Thank you.

Elizabeth heard a relieved voice in her head and gasped in shock, pulling her hand away. Even with the broken contact, the mental connection remained.

That feels so much better. I didn't think I could bear it any longer.

In her mind, Elizabeth saw brief flashes of a dragon emerging from an egg and growing up. When it reached adulthood, there was agonizing pain in its head that was only relieved by blasting fire. The noise from barns and shouts of people only intensified the anguish, causing the dragon to lash out.

Elizabeth's touch, however, had removed the torment entirely. In its place was a deep sense of loyalty towards the human woman and her mate.

Touch the others. Heal them.

Looking back, Elizabeth gasped at the sight of five dragons encircling her husband. She rushed forward, causing Darcy to shout in alarm. The dragons reared back and opened their mouths, but they hesitated when the ruby dragon growled.

One by one, Elizabeth walked to each dragon and stroked their faces with a comforting hand. Just has before, a golden glow radiated from each connection, and she could feel their relief and gratitude.

Once each dragon had been touched, they lowered their wings and settled themselves around her, much as a tired dog lies down at the feet of its master.

"Elizabeth?" Darcy's confused voice broke through the tumult of six dragons' thoughts and emotions in her mind. Wordlessly, she extended a hand to him, and he gasped.

"Their thoughts," he marveled. "I can hear them. They... they want to *serve* us."

And the two lovers stood in the midst of the conquered dragons, having brought peace to England at last.

Epilogue

Ten years later…

Elizabeth Darcy looked around the lands of Pemberley, smiling as Emerald and Aquamarine playfully spit small streams of fire at one another.

After the dragons had been conquered at Netherfield, they became as docile and friendly as a puppy. It was the agony and lack of master that had caused them to act out in fear and pain. Once both issues had been dealt with, they obeyed Darcy and Elizabeth without question.

The mental connection remained even after the battle, and Elizabeth was able to communicate with them. Darcy could as well, but only when he was holding Elizabeth's hand.

A sanctuary for the six dragons was established at Pemberley, and they were each named for the bright jeweled tones of their scales. Onyx was male, and the other five were females, and a few eggs had been laid and stored in a special place.

Due to her unique connection with the dragons, Elizabeth learned that the eggs didn't have a set incubation time. They only hatched when England was in great danger. Unfortunately, the knowledge about the unique relationship between a couple and the dragons fighting together to save England had been lost over the centuries.

Once Darcy understood the purpose of dragons—to protect England during times of great danger—he reached out to Colonel Fitzwilliam, who was promoted to general by the king. The dragons were more than happy to be trained with select soldiers and were vital in bringing a swift end to the war against Napoleon, who had nearly successfully invaded England with a secret naval attack.

At the end of the war, the dragons returned to their home at Pemberley. The Darcys raised their children to respect the dragons, and the children could often be found playing games like fetch and hide-and-seek.

Special care was given to preserve the story of the events for future generations to have when the dragons were needed again and the eggs hatched.

While all of England was grateful for the help in the war, no one was happier than Darcy and Elizabeth that the dragons came.

Nothing But Officers in Her Head

Catherine Bennet, aka Kitty, is known as being her younger sister's shadow. But what if that is all a disguise to hide who she truly is—one of the most renowned cryptographers of the Napoleonic Wars?

Chapter 1

Catherine Bennet—known as Kitty to her friends and family—rolled her eyes as she watched her sister Lydia tug down the bodice of her dress right before the officers were announced at the front door of Longbourn. It was calling hours the day after their Aunt Phillips's card party.

Typical Lydia, always focusing on the wrong things. Not only was it wrong to attract a man based solely on her figure, but officers were most definitely not the sort of man she should wish to marry.

The door opened, and Lieutenants Chamberlayne, Pratt, Denny, and Wickham entered. Kitty gave an inward sigh and put on a vacant expression of delight.

"Look who has come, Lydia," she squealed, inwardly wincing at the earsplitting tone of her voice, but she kept her bright, empty-headed smile pinned on her face.

She and Lydia were swarmed by the officers, who paid false compliments and made phony protests over which man most wished for the honor of escorting the girls on a walk in the gardens. The next half hour outside made Kitty want to pull her hair from her head.

How had she allowed the Home Secretary to talk her into this? Henry Addington, Viscount Sidmouth, had told her that her participation was of vital national importance, but she couldn't see how. The soldiers, save Colonel Forster and Lieutenant Wickham, didn't share an ounce of sense between them.

For as long as Kitty could remember, her father had been impressed by her deduction and puzzle-solving skills. From a young age, she was able to disassemble and reassemble small puzzle toys, which eventually led to her finding patterns in letters and teaching herself to read.

When Kitty was eight years old, her father sent her to the Gardiners in London on the pretext of visiting a special doctor to help Kitty recover from a cold that had left a lingering cough. In reality, Mr. Bennet had contacted an old schoolmate of his who worked for the Home Office and insisted that his daughter be tested.

Her scores were so high that the Viscount Sidmouth himself had undertaken to train her. For six months as she "recuperated" at the Gardiners with special doctors, she was trained in French and other languages, as well as code-breaking and even espionage.

Once she returned to Longbourn, she was regularly sent documents and letters to translate and decode, if necessary. The money the British government paid to her father on her behalf was carefully deposited into a separate account for her that was managed by Mr. Gardiner, who invested it to improve its growth.

Mr. Bennet was able to explain Kitty's regular visits to his study as her handwriting was the neatest of all her sisters, and he often wanted her to transcribe pamphlets and other tracts he found interesting. When in public, she wore a facade of being her younger sister Lydia's shadow.

No one would suspect birdbrained Kitty Bennet of really being *Le Chaton*, one of the most famous cryptographers during the Napoleonic Wars.

Her code name always made her smile. In French, "chaton" can be translated as either *stone* or *kitten*. Everyone who heard her code name assumed her to be male (hence, *le* chaton) and referred to the Rosetta Stone that had been discovered in Egypt, which unlocked the key to translating hieroglyphics.

Only Viscount Sidmouth knew that *Le Chaton* was picked specifically to refer to her nickname, Kitty. The knowledge that she was fooling some of the most intelligent men in England and France always gave her a renewed sense of purpose when she felt frustrated with the role she was forced to play to hide her identity and have a somewhat normal life.

The soldiers were taking turns pushing Lydia on the swing. Kitty had been thinking about her work while watching, with a fake look of jealousy for not being the center of attention.

Flirting with immature men, such as the officers, was more than her poor nerves could take. *Good Lord, I sound like Mama*, she thought to herself. *I have got to get out of this situation.*

As if by magic, Mr. Bennet appeared at the door to the garden, meaning he needed her in the study.

Mary stepped out past her father, scowling at having to come outside with all the frivolity. "I don't know why Papa has you do his writing when I could do just as well," she grumbled as she took a seat near the fence with her book. She was there to act as a chaperon so Kitty could go inside.

She made a childish face and forced herself to pout as she walked back to the house, repressing the urge to run with glee for having escaped. When she reached the door, her father said, "Come, Kitty, I have a special project that I need you to transcribe. I know you're disappointed at leaving the officers, but this cannot wait."

This time, Kitty's frown was real. Mr. Bennet's pointed words caused her to realize that it would have drawn less notice had she been allowed to continue outside until the men had left.

What could be so urgent that it's worth risking my cover?

Trying not to let the foreboding she felt show on her face, she walked sedately behind her father into his book room. Once the door was closed behind them—and she verified the window was closed—she allowed all traces of deception to fade from her body.

Shoulders no longer slouched, and eyes sharp and alert, she asked in a rigid voice, "What news from Sidmouth?"

Mr. Bennet passed her a paper, which contained a letter from the Home Office director.

Mf Dibupo,

Ju ibt dpnf up pvs buufoujpo uibu uifsf jt b dpnqboz pg njmjujb ofxmz bss-jwfe bu zpvs mpdbujpo. Xf ibwf dsfejcmf joufmmjhfodf uibu bu mfbtu pof nfncfs jt b tqz gps uif Gsfodi.

Bt uifjs gjobm eftujobujpo xjmm cf Csjhiupo, ofbs uif ujnf uif Qsjodf Sfhfou jt bmtp jo uibu bsfb, ju jt wjubm xf ejtdpwfs uif jefoujuz pg uif jogpsnbou. Xf bsf dpogjefou ju jt fjuifs Mjfvufobou Hfpshf Xjdlibn ps Dpmpofm Gpstufs ijntfmg, cvu xf offe efgjojujwf qsppg.

Up ifmq bje zpvs tfbsdi, b Dpmpofm pg Ijt Nbkftuz't Esbhppot xjmm cf bssjwjoh voefs uif qsfufyu pg wjtjujoh ijt dpvtjo bu Ofuifsgjfme. Uijt gbnjmz dpoofdujpo jt joeffe sfbm, xijdi nblft ju uif qsgfdu dpwfs. Dpmpofm Sjdibse Gjuaxjmmjbn jt bmtp bmsfbez lopxo up cpui tvtqfdut, tp if xjmm cf bcmf up fohbhf fbtjmz xjui uifn.

Zpvs njttjpo xjmm cf up johsbujbuf zpvstfmg xjui cpui nfo jo bo fggpsu up hfu uifn up dpogjef jo zpv. Xf ibwf uif vunptu dpogjefodf jo zpvs bcjmjujft.

Dpmpofm Gjuaxjmmjbn ibt cffo nbef bxbsf pg uif gbdu uibu zpv bsf ifmqjoh ijn, cvu if epft opu lopx pg zpvs usvf jefoujuz bt Mf Dibupo, boe ju jt jnqfsbujwf zpv lffq uibu tfdsf.

Mfu zpvs tvqfswjtps lopx jg uifsf bsf boz jttvft, boe if xjmm tfoe xpse up vt.

Tjenpvui

Quickly translating and decoding the message in her head, she read aloud:

Le Chaton,

It has come to our attention that there is a company of militia newly arrived at your location. We have credible intelligence that at least one member is a spy for the French.

As their final destination will be Brighton, near the time the prince regent is also in that area, it is vital we discover the identity of the informant. We are confident it is either *Lieutenant George Wickham* or *Colonel Forster himself*, but we need definitive proof.

To help aid your search, a colonel of His Majesty's Dragoons will be arriving under the pretext of visiting his cousin at Netherfield. This family connection is indeed real, which makes it the perfect cover. Colonel Richard Fitzwilliam is also already known to both suspects, so he will be able to engage easily with them.

Your mission will be to ingratiate yourself with both men in an effort to get them to confide in you. We have the utmost confidence in your abilities.

Colonel Fitzwilliam has been made aware of the fact that you are helping him, but he does not know of your true identity as Le Chaton, and it is imperative you keep that secret.

Let your supervisor know if there are any issues, and he will send word to us.

Sidmouth

Chapter 2

Kitty wordlessly put the paper down on her father's desk and stared out the window, a frown on her face.

"Well?" he prompted when she remained silent for several minutes.

"Well, what?" she replied, her voice tinged with bitterness. "It's not as though I have a choice in the matter, is it? I cannot reject an assignment, especially when someone could have access to the prince regent and his movements."

"This is your first assignment that isn't on paper," Mr. Bennet said with a frown. "I must admit to some trepidation about the situation."

"Isn't this what I was trained for?" she asked in reply, her voice now devoid of any emotion.

"I meant for you to use your brain to solve puzzles and break codes!" he exclaimed. "I never had any notion that you would have to put yourself out there and possibly be in danger."

"I hardly doubt I will be in any danger, Papa," she answered. "Besides, the orders have come, and there's nothing more for it. Will the payment be more?"

"Yes, it's actually quite a substantial addition to your dowry."

"That's something, at least. Maybe I can even retire with the amount."

Mr. Bennet's frown deepened, and he suddenly appeared much older than he usually did to her. "Kitty, I will tell him that after this, there can be no more in-person missions. It is one thing to translate and decode a letter; it is quite another to interact with the enemy."

She nodded in agreement. "In this scenario, I would be interacting with them in any case, only I wouldn't be aware of the danger. I'm grateful to at least be informed of the situation."

Mr. Bennet grumbled, but he couldn't find any other reason to object. It was true that with the knowledge of enemies in their midst, he would be better able to protect his family. Waving his hand, she was summarily dismissed from the room.

As Kitty left the room, she couldn't help but feel some small stirrings of excitement well up inside her. Finally, things were going to be interesting! Even if she continued to play the same part she always did, it was with a more tangible purpose than simply maintaining cover.

She, Catherine Bennet, was going to take down a spy!

Making her way towards the front door, she was disappointed to see Lydia once again in the drawing room without a redcoat in sight. Apparently, in the time she was in conference with her father, the officers had excused themselves and returned to the barracks.

The pout on Kitty's face was genuine as she flounced into the drawing room and plopped herself lazily onto a settee. "It's so unfair that I missed the time with the officers!" she wailed. "I don't know why Papa keeps insisting I'm the only one who can help him."

"It's not like you missed out on much," Lydia said with a smirk. "They all paid much more attention to me than they ever did to you. I daresay no one even missed your presence."

Kitty petulantly stuck her tongue out at her younger sister. "Had I been able to stay longer, I daresay they would have been more in love with me than you. After all, I'm two years older!"

"But I'm taller! And more fun to be around."

This turned into a squabble that allowed Kitty to vent some of her pent-up emotions, which she desperately needed. It was difficult to be seventeen years old and to have kept a secret of such magnitude for as long as she had. Even though her father knew who she

135

really was, he also did not seem to care much about her sentiments. She was achingly lonely, and it was made worse when Elizabeth was decried as the family wit throughout the neighborhood.

Although Kitty tried to be mature, it rankled that she not only had to give way to her younger sister, but she was also forced to keep her talents hidden and allow another Elizabeth to take the spotlight in wit and intelligence. She was bright and well informed, it was true, but she also allowed her emotions and prejudice to rule her insights.

Take Darcy and Wickham, for example. It was plain to Kitty that poor Darcy was half in love with Elizabeth from just the first time he saw her at the Meryton assembly. His objection that her elder sister wasn't handsome enough to tempt him was the perfect example of someone protesting too much.

Elizabeth's constant complaints of Darcy's arrogance and of how he only looked at her to find fault caused Kitty to roll her eyes so much she thought they would fall from their sockets.

The coup de grâce was when Wickham approached Elizabeth with his sad tale of being used by Darcy. Kitty could see straight through the man's ploy, even before she had received the letter from Sidmouth informing her of his perfidy. Wickham saw Elizabeth as an easy target because she publicized her feelings of antagonism towards the wealthy young man Wickham despised.

It was this kind of behavior that frustrated Kitty. For all of Elizabeth's wit and intelligence, she lacked the ability to perform self-examinations and to see things objectively.

Well, she would just have to learn the hard way. Kitty did not envy her sister for having to face the hard lesson that was to come. Whether or not Wickham was a spy, he was definitely a scoundrel.

Kitty kept up her complaints about not having bid farewell to the officers for the rest of the day. Finally, Lydia suggested the two of them walk to Meryton in the morning to see if they could go early enough to catch the men before they were dressed.

Their plans were interrupted, however, when the Netherfield party came to call upon them. As much as she was eager to begin ingratiating herself with Forster and Wickham, she knew she could not miss this opportunity to be introduced to Colonel Fitzwilliam.

"I think we should stay just for a few minutes," she responded to Lydia, who had suggested they sneak out before they were caught and forced to sit for a quarter hour while visiting.

"Lord, what on earth for? Mr. Bingley only has eyes for Jane, and I can't stand that awful Mr. Darcy."

"Perhaps Miss Bingley will be with them. She could tell us of the latest fashions in London," suggested Kitty. "We can catch the officers undressed any morning."

Lydia gave an exaggerated sigh of annoyance but eventually agreed. The two sisters came into the drawing room just as Bingley was introducing the latest arrival to Netherfield, Colonel Richard Fitzwilliam of the fifty-first infantry and cousin to Mr. Darcy.

The eyes of the youngest Bennet daughter lit up at the sight of a colonel from the regulars. "Oh, Colonel Fitzwilliam, it is *such* a pleasure to make your acquaintance!" she squealed.

Kitty rolled her eyes towards the colonel, who looked at her with a barely perceptible nod. She then echoed Lydia's cry and made her way over to the gentleman and took his arm. "It must be so interesting to go overseas and fight the enemy," she said in a breathless voice. "I do hope you'll tell me all about it."

Lydia attached herself to his other arm and batted her eyes. "Oh, yes! Please tell us about the French, Colonel. Is it true they really eat frog legs?"

From the corner of her eye, Kitty could see Jane and Elizabeth wince and exchange looks. Darcy gave a severe frown in the direction of the flirtatious scene before walking towards the window and staring out in silence. Bingley, as oblivious as ever, sat next to Jane and engaged her in conversation.

The next quarter hour was spent with Lydia flirting and Kitty copying, although she was ever aware of Elizabeth's and Darcy's increasing discomfort. She noted with a sly smile that Darcy's place at the window was perfectly situated to allow him to see Elizabeth's reflection in the glass.

At the end of the call, Kitty batted her eyes at Colonel Fitzwilliam. "Colonel, I was about to walk towards Meryton. Would you be willing to escort me?"

Elizabeth gave a small gasp at this forwardness, and Lydia's face grew red with anger. Colonel Fitzwilliam, on the other hand, gave a dashing grin. "I would be most delighted, Miss Kitty. Darcy, what say you to taking Miss Lydia and Miss Elizabeth on your arm?"

Kitty almost burst into laughter. She couldn't tell who was more upset about the situation: Lydia, Darcy, or Elizabeth! "What an excellent idea," she cooed at the colonel. "I think Lydia would enjoy your cousin's company very much."

Nearly apoplectic, Lydia almost flew into a tantrum of epic proportions. It was only Colonel Fitzwilliam's presence that kept her from venting her spleen to Kitty.

"I hope you're satisfied. You'll pay for this," Lydia seethed as the girls put on their boots and fetched their bonnets.

Kitty knew that she could expect ink on her best gown or her favorite bonnet torn to shreds, but that paled in comparison to the thrill of consorting with another secret member of the Home Office.

Yes, Kitty was indeed satisfied.

Chapter 3

Kitty wore a satisfied smile as she walked arm in arm with Colonel Fitzwilliam down the road towards Meryton. Lydia, Elizabeth, and Darcy were several feet ahead.

"We had better speak quickly, as I wouldn't put it past Lydia to find a way to join us," Kitty said, giving Colonel Fitzwilliam a flirtatious look that belied the seriousness of her words.

He chuckled. "I must admit, you aren't quite what I expected when I was told a young lady would be assisting me on this mission."

"You expected someone more like my sister Elizabeth?"

He looked forward to where Elizabeth was deliberately ignoring the arm Darcy gave her, then gave her a teasing grin. "Honestly, yes, based on how my cousin has described her in his letters."

"Do you think he realizes yet that he's in love with her?"

He stumbled at this blunt question, then threw back his head in laughter, causing the three in front of them to look back. Lydia's face was nearly purple. "You are very astute to have noticed it in my reticent cousin. I think he's in denial."

"It doesn't help that he told Bingley that she wasn't tolerable enough to tempt him, and in her hearing."

Colonel Fitzwilliam's eyes widened, but he maintained his flirtatious grin. "Well, that would explain why she is trying to avoid him."

"She also believes Mr. Wickham's tale of having a living that was left in Mr. Darcy's father's will denied to him."

A low growl came from the colonel's throat, which was at odds with the congenial expression on his face. "Allow me to tell you a story about George Wickham and my cousin Georgiana…"

At the end of his tale, he said, "I only shared this with you because we are partners in this mission and you have Sidmouth's approval. I am sure I need not request your discretion, else my poor young cousin would be ruined by the rumors."

Kitty scowled briefly before remembering her company and turned it into a playful smile. "My dear Colonel, I would no sooner betray Miss Darcy's secret than my own. It appears that whether or not Mr. Wickham is the spy we seek, he is quite the blackguard."

"That he is."

"Well, no matter what his lies have been, we must discover if it is he or Colonel Forster who is the traitor. Do you know what information has narrowed it down to the two of them?"

"Both men were in possession of information about the prince regent's upcoming trip to Brighton, and both men were absent from camp when the leak occurred. We gave each regiment different dates about the trip so that when the leak occurred, we would have a general idea of its source."

"That was... quite brilliant."

He gave a roguish smile that made her heart flutter. "Why, thank you."

Kitty let out a genuine laugh at his response, her first in probably years. "How did you even discover what information was actually leaked?"

"We have our own sources of spies within Napoleon's ranks, just as he has spies in ours. We're able to ascertain *what* information he hears, but we're unable to determine *who* sent it. This is our first clue in months."

She opened her mouth to say something about having translated the notes, but at the last minute, she remembered Sidmouth's warning that she should keep her identity private.

"I am glad you were able to discover the leak in the first place," she said lamely.

"Yes, well, only thanks to the cryptographer who deciphered the new code that was adopted by Napoleon. The men at the Home Office spent weeks working on it before finally sending it on to *Le Chaton*, who was able to crack it within two days. You called my idea brilliant, but that man is a genius."

Kitty's face flushed with warmth at this rather large bit of praise coming from an experienced member of Britain's security force. She forced her voice to remain calm as she said, "That is certainly quite the talent, then. But that does not help us now. I hate to change the subject, as I would love to hear more, but I'm afraid Lydia's patience is almost worn out."

Indeed, Lydia was now looking back and scowling at the couple at least every minute, which Kitty knew to be a sign that she would soon come up with a reason to interrupt. It had happened in the past whenever any gentleman paid more attention to herself than her younger sister.

"Very well. Perhaps I will be able to speak with you more about it in the future. For now, we need to formulate a plan to discover where both men were when the leak occurred."

"This is where I come in, I believe," she said. "As a single, eligible woman, it is nothing for me to spend some time getting to know both men. Colonel Forster is in a courtship, I believe, but it is not an engagement yet. He is in a good enough situation that no one would think twice of me attempting to turn his attentions towards myself."

"And Wickham?"

She giggled and batted her eyes, realizing that even Darcy and Elizabeth were occasionally looking back at them. "He is even easier. Mr. Wickham is an extremely handsome officer with whom half the town is madly in love. Even better, he is aware of it, and his ego makes him more likely to ignore any hints of suspicion he might have towards me."

Colonel Fitzwilliam grinned wolfishly. "It seems my old friend's immoral behavior may end up being the cause of his downfall."

"Oh, we're out of time," Kitty said as Lydia walked towards them. "I will plan on putting myself in their company as much as possible. I will report anything I learn to my father, who can pass it on to you without suspicion. Now quick, give me a flirtatious smile and tell me how I'm the most enchanting girl you've ever met."

The colonel followed her orders with alacrity, just in time for Lydia to hear the final words. "Oh, Colonel Fitzwilliam, you only think that because you haven't yet spent any time with *me*. I'm a lot more interesting than my sister is."

Lydia forcefully took his arm and leaned into his side, allowing her breasts to brush up against him. Kitty did her best to keep the look of disgust and reproach from her face at her younger sister's scandalous behavior. Her ire was mollified when Colonel Fitzwilliam gave her a small wink before turning his attention away.

Kitty spent the rest of the walk into Meryton making plans on how she would engage with Forster and Wickham. Her thoughts were frequently interrupted, however, by the sight of Colonel Fitzwilliam's charming smile.

He's really not that handsome, she thought to herself, *so then why do I find him so compelling?*

As she pondered the question, she came to realize that he was the first man—other than her father—with whom she could completely be herself. Well, yes, her Uncle Gardiner and Viscount Sidmouth both knew of her identity, but she never really spent time with them.

The conversation Kitty had just engaged in with the colonel was the first honest one she'd had with a young man in... well, probably in her entire life. She was so young when she began to keep secrets, and they'd been a part of her for so long that she didn't even know how freeing it was to speak candidly.

Well, he doesn't know everything *about me,* she thought ruefully. *But he's seen more of me than any other person in my life. Perhaps someday...*

She shook her head to clear her mind. Thoughts of the future and sharing her secrets were dangerous. She could lower her guard and put herself and her family in real danger. No, as much as she yearned to completely unburden herself with someone, that was probably not going to happen anytime soon.

At least, not until she could complete this mission and retire.

Chapter 4

Over the next several days, Kitty laid the foundation for her plan. She subtly manipulated Lydia into visiting the soldiers regularly, only in such a way that Lydia always thought the idea was hers. She flirted and batted her eyes at Wickham and Forster every chance she got, hoping to compel them to speak with her.

"So what have you been up to lately, Colonel Forster?" she asked, gazing at him with adoration and leaning forward to give him a peak of her décolletage.

The man's eyes remained fixed on her chest while he answered, "Training up these soldiers, Miss Kitty. It's a time-consuming business, and we're at war! Men like myself have to be constantly working to keep our lands safe from our enemies."

"Oh, I quite agree," she said, leaning in a little further. "I imagine there is so much that takes up your time. It must be quite... lonely."

"That it is, my dear. We soldiers don't often find as warm a welcome everywhere as we have here in Meryton."

"That's just silly!" she cried, putting her hand on her bosom in dismay. "Where on earth were you before? I must know which towns have been so traitorous!"

She held a similar conversation with Lieutenant Wickham.

"I understand you have recently taken orders, Lieutenant. How exciting!"

He immediately agreed. "I cannot think of a finer calling than to protect our land from those who would destroy us. It can be a bit dull at times though. I'm already proficient at the saber and rifle thanks to my education as a gentleman, so Colonel Forster uses me as an example to the others and asks me to teach them."

"I believe Captain Denny said he met you in London? I've only been a few times, and that was to visit my uncle Gardiner before I came out. What is it like?"

"Oh, you should see it! The theater, the entertainment, Covent Garden—it's all quite incredible. I know if you were to ever go, you would take it by storm."

Kitty widened her eyes, pretending to be enthralled. "Really? I would imagine someone like Lydia would do better in a place like that."

"Oh, nonsense! Your sister is a bit too young, I think. You are just the sort of intelligent, beautiful woman who would know how to take advantage of the opportunities there. Perhaps one day I can show you."

"That would be wonderful," she sighed, "but I doubt I will ever be able to do it."

"There are many other things I could show you instead until then," he replied suggestively as he placed his hand on her leg.

Kitty froze for a brief moment, then forced herself to give him a winning smile. "I would love to sometime, but not here. Why don't you tell me more about London and the other places you've been and the things you've done?"

With both men, Kitty did her best to steer the conversations towards their whereabouts during the time the information was leaked. Forster claimed to have been visiting a sister, and Wickham said he was on leave to see an ailing aunt who might leave him some money when she passes.

Kitty believed neither of them.

Colonel Fitzwilliam didn't believe the stories, either, when she related them to him one morning while those from Netherfield called on Longbourn.

"Wickham doesn't have an aunt. His mother was an only child, and his father had one brother who never married. All of them are dead, in any case; he literally has no living family."

"What about Colonel Forster?" she asked.

Pressing his lips together, he said, "That one is a little different. He does actually have a sister, but our research shows that she lives north near the Scottish border. His leave was only for a few days, so there would not have been time for him to go there and return. We have no records of her coming south to visit either."

"But it cannot be disproved entirely?"

"No, but I am inclined to believe he was visiting the young woman he has been courting and did not want to tell you about it. You have been quite… forward in your attentions."

She gave a false laugh, aware of their location in her mother's crowded drawing room, but her eyes flashed angrily. "I believe that was what I was requested to do. Besides, with a sister like Lydia, I need to do something to command their attention to me instead of her."

He held his hands up. "I meant no offense, Miss Kitty. You are doing an admirable job. It must be difficult to be a lady in this type of situation. Propriety can make it difficult for a young, unmarried girl. If you were married, you could easily speak to men without causing too much of a scandal."

Mollified by his words, she said, "I wish there was a way to know better which one has a genuine alibi. I haven't been able to detect a hint of deceit on the matter from either of them."

"Time is running out too," Colonel Fitzwilliam said. "Bingley will be holding his ball soon, and after that, we will be leaving Meryton."

"You are leaving?" she asked, her heart sinking inside of her chest.

"I'm afraid I must. Darcy is adamant that we leave by December so we can spend Christmas with Georgiana at Matlock. With them going to my own parents' home, I will have no believable excuse for remaining, especially if a certain happy event occurs," he said, his eyes darting to the corner where Jane and Bingley sat in quiet conversation.

"Do you think Bingley will truly propose?" she asked, forgetting for a moment all her worries about Britain and national security.

"Well, I wouldn't like to speak out of turn, but Darcy was trying to tell Bingley that your sister had no more interest in him than any other man she smiles at. Thankfully, I was there to tell my cousin what a stupid prat he was."

"Jane is very shy, and she had a bad experience when she was younger than I am now," Kitty said. "With our mother the way she is, my eldest sister is hesitant to reveal her feelings with a sure commitment."

"I figured as much. I think Darcy was more trying to protect himself from Miss Elizabeth than anything. He is more attracted to her than he has been to any other woman, but he thinks she is below him. I do not agree," he added hastily as Kitty's eyes flashed again. "He could do much worse than your sister. She may not have the connections or dowry he could get in another match, but she is superior in every other way."

"Well, he should worry more about having to overcome her hatred of him before he worries that she is below him!"

The colonel grinned. "Either way, we will be leaving after the ball to spend Christmas with family. I know the militia will not go to Brighton until the spring, but you will have to continue without my assistance if we cannot solve this before then."

Tears filled Kitty's eyes, but she grinned widely. "I will take your words under consideration. Perhaps we can orchestrate something to occur at the ball."

"What do you have in mind?" he asked.

"Just an idea at the moment. Give me a few days to work it out, and I will let you know."

Once the Netherfield party had left, Kitty ran to her room and flung herself onto her bed. The tears she had been holding back wet her pillow as she imagined what it would be like without Colonel Fitzwilliam's presence.

For the first time in her life, she had felt a connection with someone who saw her for who she truly was. Even though he had no idea of her identity as *Le Chaton*, he had frequently complimented Kitty on her intelligence without seeming offended by it.

Her first inclination was to not discover the spy so that Colonel Fitzwilliam would have to return after Christmas, but she realized the selfishness of that decision. He had a life and career outside of this time in Meryton, and it was not fair to make him stay behind because she was lonely.

No, she *would* complete this mission and allow him to live his life. It was the kindest thing to do, even if it broke her heart.

Chapter 5

The Bennet carriage arrived at Netherfield on the night of November the twenty-sixth for the ball that Bingley was hosting. Everyone was dressed in their finest clothing, and Jane had received a new gown entirely for the event, as Mrs. Bennet was sure there would be an important announcement.

While Bingley had not yet requested an official courtship from Mr. Bennet for Jane, he had paid his attentions so frequently that there could be little question of his intentions. Doubtlessly, he wished for a romantic gesture for a proposal, and the ball was the perfect setting. It also would prevent his sisters from making a scene, a plan of which Kitty heartily approved.

Descending from the carriage in one of Jane's gowns—as Lydia had pilfered all of hers—Kitty made her way towards the house and receiving line with her family. When she spied Colonel Fitzwilliam in his regimentals, she gasped at the handsome figure he made.

Kitty greeted the Bingleys and the Hursts before moving on to Darcy and Fitzwilliam. When she reached the colonel, he bowed low and requested the honor of her first two dances. Darcy raised an eyebrow at this and pursed his lips, but otherwise he remained silent.

She accepted with alacrity and had to sternly remind her heart that his only reason for asking her was to finalize their plans for the evening, not because he was interested in making a statement. No, he would leave Hertfordshire in a few days, never to return again.

Forcing herself to pay attention to her tasks at hand, she giggled loudly as she looked around for her targets. Both Wickham and

Forster had requested to dance with her: Wickham the third set and Forster the fourth. During those dances, she would set the trap.

The fifth set—the supper set—was when the trap would be sprung, and they would discover once and for all who the traitor was.

Kitty downed her champagne, then took another glass. It was important to appear as if she were in her cups. Colonel Fitzwilliam had pulled aside a footman and told him to only give her glasses that had been severely watered down. This would allow her the appearance of drunkenness without actually losing control of her faculties.

The musicians finally began, and Colonel Fitzwilliam escorted her to the floor, causing a few gasps and titters amongst the matrons. Lydia, who had been asked by Denny at the last minute, was giving her sister a ferocious glare. Kitty smirked at her before batting her eyes at her partner, who was trying not to laugh.

"I'm afraid you've made an enemy of your younger sister these past weeks in taking up so much of my time," Colonel Fitzwilliam said.

"She'll be impossible to live with once you've gone," Kitty replied, the grim tone of voice at odds with the flirtatious look on her face. "Lydia will crow at my having been jilted by you for probably the next decade or so."

"Jilted?" he looked down at her, startled. "Surely, you don't think—"

"Me? Certainly not!" she protested quickly, interrupting him. "But my mother has begun to hint at your attentions towards me to the exclusion of all others. My father knows the truth, of course, but no one else will."

"I'm very sorry," he said. "I hadn't fully considered your situation after I left."

She tried to maintain an indifferent tone as she responded. "Yes, well, it won't be much different from what it always is. To everyone here, I am simply an empty-headed girl of loose standards who is one of the silliest girls in England, as my father says frequently. This will only reinforce that reputation."

"It must be difficult to have everyone assume you are the opposite of your character," he said.

Kitty forced a bright smile and a tinkling laugh. "Come, the second dance is nearly done, and we have yet to finalize our plans. Is the room I requested in readiness?"

"Yes, the fourth door on the right as you leave the ballroom is the green room. I will be waiting in the adjoining room. Once you have gained a confession from Wickham—"

"Or Forster," she interjected. "I know you have reason to hate Wickham, but we have yet to prove the guilt or innocence of either."

"Forster is too much of a fool, and Wickham is too much of a scoundrel." When she opened her mouth to protest, he sighed. "Have it your way. When *whichever* gentleman arrives and confesses, I will be on hand to apprehend him once I hear you say *it's done*."

The dance ended, and Kitty curtsied to her partner. She danced the next with her father, which again caused murmurs from those watching, as Mr. Bennet rarely danced. He simply wanted to reassure himself that she was willing to go forward with her plan.

"Colonel Fitzwilliam will be right in the other room, and you can follow behind whichever man comes during the supper set, if you'd like."

Mr. Bennet frowned. "I would, but I have a suspicion that Bingley will be looking for me at some point during or after the dance."

"Don't worry, Papa. The colonel will keep me safe."

The dance ended, and her father kept a tight hand on her arm as Wickham approached for their dance. She gently tugged herself free from her father's grip and allowed Wickham to escort her to the floor. "I was beginning to think you had chosen to not come tonight," she said with a flirtatious smile, allowing her words to slur.

"And how could I not, when I promised a dance to the most beautiful girl in all of Meryton?" Wickham replied with a roguish grin.

Noting that he had not actually specified herself as that girl, she nonetheless giggled loudly and tripped over her feet. "Oh goodness, that champagne really does go to one's head! But no, I thought maybe your feud with Darcy would prevent you from coming."

His face darkened but almost immediately reverted to its flirtatious mien. "Nonsense. Darcy cannot scare me. If it is he who wishes to avoid a scene, it is he who must go."

"Not even if he knows your secret?" she asked in a loud whisper.

"Secret? What secret?" he asked, a hint of alarm in his voice. "I mean, I have no secrets."

"Now we both know that's not true, is it? I know your secret," she slurred out. "I know all about your plans with France and Brighton and the prince regent."

He forced a laugh. "I think you may have had too much to drink, Miss Kitty! Perhaps I should take you back to your father."

"No, not too much to drink. I know about your plans, and I'll keep silent... for a price. Meet me during the supper set in the green room. Fourth door on the right."

Kitty had an identical conversation with Colonel Forster, who reacted in much the same way as Wickham. Both men protested their innocence but fell silent when she told them to meet her later.

At the end of the dancing, she stumbled her way through the guests and into the hall, along the way laughing at how much she'd had to drink. A few matrons shook their heads in dismay, but most of them were focused on Bingley and Jane, who had gone over to speak to Mr. Bennet.

Once in the hall and out of sight, she quickly righted her gait and rushed to the small sitting room decorated in various shades of green. She knocked twice on the adjoining door, paused, then twice again. Colonel Fitzwilliam responded with the same pattern.

The moment was here. All Kitty had to do was sit and wait.

After about five minutes, the door opened. She stood from her chair and turned to face…

Colonel Forster!

Like Fitzwilliam, Kitty had thought Wickham would be the traitor, although she had done her best to be impartial. "It was you?" she asked uncertainly.

"How did you know?" he growled. "I was so careful to make that idiot Lieutenant Wickham appear to be the spy. It was all perfect too. How did you know?"

He crossed the room in long strides and grabbed her by the throat before she could answer. "I will *not* allow you to ruin all my hard work! Tell me how you found out, and I'll let you live."

Kitty gasped for breath and pulled at the fingers on her neck, but he was too strong. She struggled to free herself, but that only made him lift her into the air, her feet swinging helplessly.

Just as everything began to fade to black, she remembered something from her training. Using the last of her energy, she swung her foot forward to kick him directly between the legs.

Colonel Forster let out a shout and released her before falling to the ground and clutching himself. He moaned in agony, and she scrambled back from him. "It's done," she yelled, but all that came out was a hoarse whisper.

Gasping and attempting to shout, she made her way to the door behind which Fitzwilliam hid. Once there, she pounded on it with one hand and leaned on it with the other as she croaked out, "It's done, it's done, it's done."

The door flew open in front of her, which caused her to tumble forward and into Fitzwilliam's chest. "My God!" he cried out in horror, taking in her wheezing breaths and red neck.

He thrust her behind his back and moved forward towards the man writhing on the floor. "Forster?" he asked incredulously.

She nodded, unable to speak. Fitzwilliam quickly bound Forster's legs and arms, then roughly deposited him in a chair and tied him to it. Once complete, he raced back to Kitty's side and inspected her neck for damage. In spite of the pain, she felt a thrill go through her at the touch of his fingers on his skin.

"Oh Lord, you could have been killed," he groaned, then pulled her into his arms.

She leaned into his chest and allowed the embrace, oblivious to the fact that the door had opened to the hallway behind them. It wasn't until she heard her mother's shriek that she came to her senses.

"Kitty! What have you done? We are ruined! Mr. Bennet!"

Never mind the fact that Kitty was injured and Forster was tied up; a compromise was a compromise.

Mrs. Bennet ran wailing towards the ballroom, and Kitty looked at Fitzwilliam in dismay. "What do we do?" she asked fearfully.

"We marry," he said, giving her a tender smile.

"What?" she exclaimed.

"We get married," he repeated. "Isn't that usually what happens after a compromise?"

"Well, yes, but… I don't want to force you… that is, I know you are leaving…"

He looked down and gently brushed a lock of hair from her face. "You didn't think I wanted to leave you behind, did you? I was always going to return for you. I love you, Catherine Bennet."

Hope and warmth filled her chest as he leaned down and kissed her, the promise of forever on his lips.

Epilogue

No one was more surprised than Miss Caroline Bingley when two engagements were announced the night of the Netherfield Ball: Bingley and Jane's, and Fitzwilliam and Kitty's.

Mrs. Bennet was beside herself with joy over having two daughters so successfully engaged. She wasn't sure if she was more excited about a son-in-law with five thousand a year, or a son-in-law who wore a red coat and was the son of an earl.

"Perhaps his older brother might become very ill or something," she said one day in delight. "These things do happen."

Kitty was only grateful that Fitzwilliam wasn't there to hear her mother wish for his older brother's death. His absence was due to two reasons, both of them equally important.

Firstly, Fitzwilliam decided to personally accompany Forster to London, where he would be interrogated by the Home Office and then sentenced to death by a firing squad for treason.

Apparently, Forster had been aware of Wickham's penchant for gaming and debts, and he had determined that the steward's son would be the perfect patsy, which was why there was so much confusion as to which man was the guilty party.

Wickham did not escape unscathed, however. Kitty's "drunken ramblings" had sent the scoundrel into a panic, as he *was* a thief; he had stolen many valuable items from his fellow soldiers. Afraid any investigation would uncover his larceny, he abandoned his post and attempted to escape. As this meant he was a deserter during wartime, he, too, was sentenced to death.

Forster's reasons for becoming a spy for France had to do with his hatred for the upper classes. He'd had a fiancée, but the year prior, she'd been the victim of a lord who would not accept her rejection of his attentions. His attack on her left her weak, as well as with child. Both mother and baby died when her confinement came at only six months. The lord walked away from the situation without any repercussions.

Kitty felt very sorry for poor Colonel Forster, but her pleas for leniency were rebuffed, and even she could not deny that the man had tried to end her life to maintain his clandestine conspiracy against England.

The second reason Fitzwilliam was away was to declare his engagement to both the Home Office and his parents. Lord and Lady Matlock were surprised and concerned that he had been taken in by a fortune hunter, but when they heard how their son had rescued his sweetheart from a vicious attack, they chose to give their support by gifting the couple a small estate in Derbyshire between Matlock and Pemberley.

Lord Sidmouth was dumbfounded at the announcement that his two best spies would be marrying one another, but he gave his consent, as the alternative was to risk Kitty's identity becoming known. He did, however, inform Fitzwilliam that Kitty was *Le Chaton*, and said he would expect the Colonel to allow his wife to continue her work.

Fitzwilliam already knew his soon-to-be wife was brilliant, but the news that she was considered the best cryptographer on both sides of the Channel nearly knocked him over. He then told Sidmouth that she could continue her work only *if* she wanted to; he would leave the decision entirely in her hands.

Second only to Kitty's joy at being married was her satisfaction with her sisters' faces when they were finally allowed to know her identity at the end of the war and the role she had played in its success. Elizabeth—who had long been married to Darcy—had laughed for a good while before she realized Kitty's assertion was

156

truth, not jest. It certainly put a different perspective on Mr. Bennet's lament that his most intelligent daughter had abandoned him for Derbyshire.

As for her part, Kitty was extremely grateful that her husband knew everything about her and loved her for who she was. It had always been a fear of hers, and now her loneliness was gone.

She often joked, however, that she fell in love with her husband because, at that time in her life, she only had flirtation and officers in her head.

In His Nightcap and Powdering Gown

Mr. Bennet falls and bumps his head after teasing his wife about not visiting Mr. Bingley. When he awakens, he is just as flighty and unstable as Mrs. Bennet! Dressing in his nightcap and powdering gown while calling for his salts, how will Mr. Bennet's new personality affect the behavior of his wife and daughters?

Chapter 1

"Oh, Mr. Bennet!" wailed his wife, fluttering around the drawing room as her five daughters watched on in silence. "How can you be so cruel to our girls? I insist you go this instant and call on Mr. Bingley!"

"And go through all that trouble?" he replied with a sardonic grin. Rising from his chair, he added, "I would much rather sit in my library, in my nightcap and powdering gown, and give as much trouble as I can."

On that note, Mr. Bennet spun around dramatically and turned to leave the room. Unfortunately, he did not take into account the small step into the hallway. He tripped over the elevated lip of the floor and fell forward, head colliding into the doorframe with a terrible noise before collapsing on the ground, motionless.

Everyone stared at him in silent horror before Mrs. Bennet let out a tremendous scream. "He's dead!" she wailed and crumpled sideways on the settee in what was probably the first genuine faint in her life.

Elizabeth rushed to her father's side. "Jane, check on Mama. Mary, ring for a servant," she barked. Then she turned to Kitty and Lydia, who were frozen speechless on their chairs. "Girls, go to your room."

The room burst into life, each girl hastening to follow Elizabeth's orders. She knelt by her father's side and was relieved to see his chest rising and falling. There was a large lump forming on the side of his head, but it was not bleeding.

Hill came down the hallway to answer the bell and gasped at the sight in front of her.

"Hill," Elizabeth said, "please send a servant to fetch Mr. Jones, then help Mama to her room. Jane will accompany you."

Just as before, her instructions were obeyed without question. Mary joined Elizabeth at their father's side. "Is he alive?" she whispered, eyes large behind her spectacles.

"Yes, I can see him breathing," Elizabeth whispered.

"Should we get him to the sofa or his room?"

"No, we'll wait until Mr. Jones arrives to determine what would be the best. I don't know enough about head wounds, and I don't want to make anything worse."

Mary nodded and placed her hand gently on their father's shoulder. "Please wake up, Papa," she whispered.

Elizabeth pushed back the tears that filled her eyes. After what seemed to be an eternity, Mr. Jones was announced at the door. He quickly made his way to Mr. Bennet's side and examined him.

"I think we had best get him upstairs and into his bed," Mr. Jones said finally. "There's not much that can be done here, and I don't notice any damage to the spine or neck, so careful movement shouldn't make things worse."

Together, with a footman, Mr. Jones and Elizabeth helped carry Mr. Bennet up the stairs and into the master's chambers. Elizabeth hadn't been in her father's private rooms in many years—if ever—and she looked around curiously.

There were books laid carelessly about the furniture, along with some candles to allow for nighttime reading. The room and its contents were decorated to please a simple, masculine taste, and Elizabeth noted just how much the decor went with her father's personality.

Once he was laid out on his bed, Elizabeth and Mary were sent outside while the servant changed Mr. Bennet into nightclothes and Mr. Jones performed a more thorough examination.

Mary absentmindedly hummed the tune of the new song she was learning on the pianoforte, and Elizabeth paced anxiously up and down the corridor. After just a few minutes that felt more like hours, the door opened, and she was readmitted to the room.

"Your father still has not regained consciousness," Mr. Jones said, "although he did display some discomfort when I felt the lump on his head. That is a good sign. I am going to use smelling salts to see if I can get him to awaken."

Elizabeth held her breath as the apothecary waved a small bottle of the foul-smelling substance underneath Mr. Bennet's nose. She waited eagerly to see him flinch and groan the way her mother always did, but he remained still. Her shoulders sank, and she let out a disappointed sigh.

"Now there, Miss Lizzy, it is as I expected. Your father took quite a knock to the head. Sometimes sleep is the body's way of repairing itself and preventing movement from causing any further damage. He has a very good chance of awakening in the next twenty-four to forty-eight hours."

"What if he doesn't?"

Mr. Jones's face furrowed with concern. "Then I'm afraid his chances of ever awakening become quite slim."

"What can we do?"

"Unfortunately, not much can be done to actually awaken him. As for caring for him while he is unconscious, there are things you can do to help him maintain his strength. Spoon-feed him broth and weak tea every two hours so his body can receive some nourishment. Go slowly though so he does not choke or breathe it into the lungs."

She nodded fervently. "Anything else?"

"He will need to have a manservant with him at all times to help care for him and keep him clean. I would normally discuss this with the patient's wife or mother, however..." Mr. Jones's voice trailed off.

"We all know how Mama is," Elizabeth replied. "You may speak plainly with me, Mr. Jones. I will not take offense at anything that may seem indelicate."

He nodded approvingly. "You've always been a strong one, Miss Lizzy, and your family will need that strength. The waiting is the most difficult. Well, as I was saying, a manservant will be needed to help to keep your father clean. Even though he is sleeping, his body will still continue to perform its automatic necessary functions. Much like a child with a dirty nappy that is left on for too long, if your father is not kept clean, it can cause bedsores that will be uncomfortable. If they become infected, they could prove to be more dangerous than the head trauma."

Elizabeth blushed faintly at this, but she pushed forward past her embarrassment to say, "Of course, Mr. Jones. We will make sure all of Papa's needs are met."

Suddenly, a keen wailing filled the air. Both Elizabeth and Mr. Jones turned towards the sound's direction—toward her mother's chambers. Jane and Hill must have managed to get Mama upstairs.

"It appears Mama has regained consciousness," Elizabeth said with a tight smile.

He gave her a sympathetic look. "I have some calming herbs with me, as well as some laudanum. Perhaps I should offer some to her? I know this is a difficult time."

Elizabeth gave a sigh of relief and led him towards her mother's chambers. "Mama? Mr. Jones has some medicine for you," she called through the door.

"Send him in! I must know everything!"

Elizabeth opened the door and gestured for the apothecary to enter. She left the door open, as Hill, Mary, and Jane were all present, and went in search of Lydia and Kitty.

She found both girls in their room, huddled together on the bed and speaking in whispers. Their red-rimmed eyes made the evidence clear that although they were both frivolous and thoughtless at times—most of the time—they truly did love their father.

"What did Mr. Jones say?" Lydia demanded the moment Elizabeth entered. "Is Papa going to be all right? Is he alive?"

"Yes, he is alive."

Elizabeth sat next to her two youngest sisters and pulled them into her arms. They both burst into noisy sobs and burrowed into her shoulders as they had once done when they were children. She felt a swell of tenderness rise within her as she patted their backs.

"Now, girls, I won't lie to you; there is some concern. Mr. Jones says that if Papa does not wake in the next forty-eight hours, the chances are that he will not awake at all. There is nothing we can do to change that, but there *are* things we can do to help Papa keep up his strength while he is unconscious."

Elizabeth explained everything Mr. Jones had said, including the part about keeping their father clean. Lydia wrinkled her nose at this reminder of their father's humanity, but she volunteered to sit with him and feed him broths.

"And I can help too!" cried Kitty, eager to be of use as well.

"Perhaps you would each like to take turns reading to him?" Elizabeth suggested. "Not one of your novels, but there are some good books that Papa enjoys that I think you would both like as well, like *Robinson Crusoe*."

Both Kitty and Lydia agreed with alacrity, and Elizabeth left them to sort out the finer details. Her heart was lighter at how they were behaving in a more mature manner; she had been quite concerned they would be as much a burden as Mama.

Knocking softly on her mother's door and with a heavy heart, Elizabeth waited for Jane or Mary to answer. The door being closed indicated that Mr. Jones had left, and as there were no hysterics emanating from the room, Elizabeth was hopeful it meant her mother was asleep—or at least resting quietly with help from Mr. Jones's herbs and tonics.

Mary opened the door slightly and whispered, "Mr. Jones just left, and Mama is asleep. I was just coming out to find you. Jane will remain as long as needed."

Closing the door softly behind them, Elizabeth quickly explained the plan she had worked out with Kitty and Lydia. "It will keep them out of our way and also remove some of the burden."

The middle Bennet daughter nodded. "Now all we must do is wait."

Chapter 2

Elizabeth awoke two days later to the sound of hysterical shrieking. She threw on her dressing gown and raced for the door, terrified that Mrs. Bennet had awakened to find her husband dead.

"What is it, Mama?" she cried as she burst into the master's chambers and rushed to her father's bedside.

"He is awake! He let out a groan and opened his eyes! Oh, we are saved! He is not dead!"

Elizabeth looked at her father with a mixture of hope and fear. To her great relief, his eyes were opened, and he looked around the room in some confusion.

"What... what happened?" he asked hoarsely.

"You took a fall and hit your head, Papa," she replied with a smile. "We were all quite worried about you."

The rest of the Bennet daughters—also summoned by the noise of their mother's histrionics—piled into the room in varying stages of alertness. At hearing his voice, grins broke out around the room, and they all began to chatter at once.

"Stop!" he bellowed. "Too much noise for my nerves!"

Everyone fell silent, and Elizabeth frowned at her father before chuckling lightly. "Good joke, Papa. First, we all think you're dying, and now you prove you're well enough to tease us!"

A relieved giggle spread throughout the room, but it faded when Mr. Bennet tried to sit up. He fell back against his pillows with a groan of pain. "Dying? Was it that serious? Then it's a miracle I am still here! After all, I do not know who would be able to maintain you when I am gone. Your mother has too small a dowry, and none

167

of you are married. You would be out in the hedgerows before I was cold in the ground!" His eyes widened dramatically, and he looked around the room frantically.

Elizabeth's smile faltered, and she looked at him concern. "Papa? Surely you are jesting."

"Certainly not! I would never joke about something so serious! How long have I been unconscious?"

"Two days," Elizabeth answered hesitatingly.

"Two entire days? But what about Mr. Bingley? How can one of you marry him if I did not go to call on him? Now Sir William Lucas will have made the first impression! No, we cannot have that! I must go to Netherfield immediately, or you will all die old maids!" His voice was hysterical and high-pitched, which was quite the opposite of his normal manner of speaking.

He once again tried to sit up, but as before, he was unable to remain upright. The room was silent as everyone stared at him anxiously and attempted to judge his sincerity in what he had spoken.

Finally, Elizabeth placed a hand on her father's head. "Now, Papa, there will be plenty of time for that later. You do not feel warm, but perhaps you are a bit confused from the blow. Let's have you rest, and we will send for Mr. Jones to come check on you."

Elizabeth placed a kiss on her father's head and ushered the rest of the family out the door, which she closed behind her. Everyone began to speak at once, but she raised her hand. "Not here. Let us go downstairs to the parlor, where Papa will not be disturbed."

The room was eerily silent in spite of all six Bennet women being present at once as they waited for Mr. Jones to call. Each lady was lost in her own thoughts of what their father's change in behavior meant.

Mr. Jones arrived shortly and immediately went upstairs. After performing a thorough examination of his patient, Mr. Jones came to join the ladies. "Was Mr. Bennet this… altered when he awoke?"

"Yes," Elizabeth replied. "I was hoping it was merely the confusion of waking and that he would be set to rights by the time you arrived."

Mr. Jones shook his head. "I'm afraid your father seems to be just as altered as he was before, if not more so. He seemed extremely preoccupied with the need to visit Netherfield and order all of you new gowns for the assembly in a few days."

"Normally that would be something Mama would say," Kitty burst out before darting a glance at her mother, who had remained unusually silent.

"It's as though he's awoken with a new personality," Elizabeth added. "Is it temporary? Do you know how long it will last?"

The apothecary scratched his head. "I can't rightly say. I know of one man, years ago, who fell off the roof of his home while attempting to repair it. The blow completely addled his senses, and he was unable to remember anything after awakening. This is completely different, however, as your father is very aware of *who* he is."

"So you don't know?" Jane asked in a small voice.

"I'm afraid I have no idea. I can send some letters of inquiry, but it's very possible your father is put to rights on his own before I even receive a response. On the other hand, it could also be a permanent change."

"Permanent?" Mrs. Bennet burst out. "Mr. Bennet was out of his senses! What was he thinking, trying to discuss lace and gowns with you? Who is going to tend to the estate and look at the accounts and manage everything?"

"Is there a family member you can call on to help you? Perhaps Mr. Bennet's heir?"

"No," Mrs. Bennet replied sharply. "We are *not* contacting the Collinses. Old Mr. Collins was a miserly, awful man, and I can't imagine his son is any better. I absolutely forbid anyone from breathing a word of this to anyone, or they might come to take over Longbourn and drive us out before it's our time."

"Perhaps Uncle Phillips or Uncle Gardiner..." Jane began, but

Mrs. Bennet again shook her head firmly.

"My brothers are in trade; they do not own estates. Their skills would not be of much use. No, my dears, I'm afraid it's going to be up to us until your father regains his senses."

Elizabeth blinked at her mother. *Did they switch places during the night? This is the most sensible my mother has sounded in... well, in forever, I daresay.*

"Mr. Jones," Mrs. Bennet said, "do I have your assurances that you won't speak a word of this? To anyone?"

He gave a solemn vow and punctuated it with a hand over his heart. Mrs. Bennet then turned to her daughters. "Not a word, girls, *not one word.* Not even to my sister Phillips. If anyone asks, your father bumped his head, but it is not serious and he is recovering nicely. Is that understood?"

All five Bennet daughters nodded mutely, and Mrs. Bennet continued. "If any of you break this confidence, you will be returned to the nursery and all your pin money forfeited for the next two quarters."

Gasps came from the youngest Bennet girls, and Elizabeth raised an eyebrow. "What will we do, then, Mama? Do you know how to run the estate?"

"I will take that as my cue to leave," interrupted Mr. Jones.

Everyone bid their farewells, and once the front door had been closed behind him, all eyes returned to Mrs. Bennet, who gave a little sigh.

"When your father and I were married, he tried teaching me about the things he did to manage the estate. I never thought it very important at the time; I focused more on decorating the house and preparing to have a son. Eventually, your father stopped trying to teach me, and I never asked him."

Elizabeth sat back in her seat in disappointment. "Then it's quite hopeless, isn't it? There isn't a steward who can guide us, and none of us really knows what to do."

"I do remember a few things he showed me," Mrs. Bennet said, "and your father has always kept excellent records. Elizabeth, your father has always said you're his most intelligent child. I think you and I can figure things out."

"Could I help, too?" Mary asked timidly. "I am quite good with sums, and Papa would frequently ask me to figure out where he'd made a mistake when the numbers weren't balanced."

"I didn't know that," Elizabeth said with some surprise.

"Mary, dear, that would be wonderful, as arithmetic was something I struggled with even as a child," Mrs. Bennet said with a rare smile at her middle daughter, who blushed with pride at the compliment.

"What shall we do, Mama?" Lydia asked. "Now that Papa is awake, he doesn't need us to read to him or feed him anymore."

"I was hoping Jane could take over running the household; she can teach the two of you how to do it," Mrs. Bennet replied. "She was your age when she came out, and I began to prepare her for marriage. I'm afraid I haven't done the same for you two because it was so easy to just let Jane do it all."

"That's all right, Mama," Kitty said graciously. "I'm sure I would have found it boring, in any case, and not wished to do it. But now I want to help."

Elizabeth looked around at her family, in awe of the changes that were happening around her. When Mr. Bennet had awoken with such a transformation, she had been terrified of having two silly parents. This conversation, however, gave her some much-needed hope for the future.

Chapter 3

Elizabeth entered the assembly room at Meryton at an eager pace. It had been a long, difficult week at Longbourn. Mr. Bennet's mental state only seemed to deteriorate with each passing day.

Just as he had proclaimed before his fall, he spent the entire day in his bedroom, in his nightcap and dressing gown, causing as much trouble as possible. His food was never good enough, his pillows constantly needed fluffing, and all he wished to do was go visit his friends to hear the latest gossip about Mr. Bingley.

"After all, the more we know about him, the more our girls can help him fall in love with one of them!"

Mrs. Bennet, Elizabeth, and Mary spent hours every day in the study, poring over ledgers and reading notes. Thankfully, the harvest was already in for the year, so there was little that needed to be done other than prepare for the winter.

"I can't imagine what this would have been like if it were spring," groaned Elizabeth one day as she sat up and arched her back to work out the kinks. "Planting would be a nightmare to figure out on our own."

"We may very well need to do it if your father continues this way," Mrs. Bennet had replied. After a moment's hesitation, she said, "Do I... do I often sound like that?"

"Sound like what?"

"Well, sound like how your father is now."

Elizabeth and Mary had exchanged alarmed looks, and Mrs. Bennet had given a heavy sigh. "No need to answer, girls. Your expressions say it all."

Nothing more had been said on the subject—something for which Elizabeth was extremely grateful—but Mrs. Bennet had been quieter than usual the past few days. They had all been working very hard, however, and the assembly was just the sort of break everyone needed.

"Oh, Elizabeth!"

She turned her head and saw Charlotte Lucas headed her way. The two girls grasped hands and exchanged a kiss on the cheek. "It feels as though it's been ages since I saw you!" cried Elizabeth.

"I heard about your poor father, Lizzy," said Charlotte with sympathy. "How is he faring?"

"What have you heard?" Elizabeth asked, trying to feign a casual tone.

"Only that he was injured and is now recuperating. Why? Is something else the matter?"

Elizabeth shook her head, sighing inwardly with relief. Charlotte, as the daughter of Lady Lucas, could always be relied upon to know the latest gossip. "Not at all. It has simply been exhausting, that's all. He is not happy to be confined to his bed, and we are doing the best we can to make up for his needed convalescence."

All of that was true, and Elizabeth only felt a twinge of guilt for misleading her friend. Had the situation not been so dire—had there been a son who could be an heir—the need for secrecy about the truth of Mr. Bennet's condition would not have been so crucial.

"So tell me all about this Mr. Bingley," Elizabeth said, changing the subject. "With Papa ill and all of us so occupied, we know nothing!"

Charlotte began to speak, but almost immediately, the doors opened, and the Netherfield party entered the room, consisting of three gentlemen and two ladies. They were announced as "Mr. Bingley, Mr. Darcy, Mr. Hurst, Mrs. Hurst, and Miss Bingley."

"Which is which?" Elizabeth whispered, as the entire room had fallen silent.

Quickly pointing out each person, Charlotte efficiently summed up each person's marital status and position—the Misters Darcy and Bingley being the single available gentlemen, with the former being a head taller than the latter.

Before Elizabeth could ask another question, she noticed her mother discreetly beckoning her from across the room. Elizabeth promised Charlotte to find her again later, then went and joined her family.

Within a few minutes, Sir Lucas—the master of ceremonies—approached the Bennets with Misters Bingley and Darcy. "Mr. Bingley has expressed a desire to become acquainted with you and your daughters," he said with a jovial grin.

Introductions were made, and Bingley, a broad smile on his face, explained that he was leasing Netherfield with the intention of learning how to run an estate. "My father wished for me to purchase one someday, but Darcy here told me I should learn on a leased property first. He's here to give me advice."

Without pausing for breath, he then turned to Jane and requested the next two dances with her. Jane agreed with a blush, and the two moved towards the dance floor. Darcy stood awkwardly with the remainder of the women, looking pointedly at a spot above their heads.

"You are here to advise your friend, then, Mr. Darcy?" Mrs. Bennet asked.

"I am."

"You have an estate of your own, then, I presume?"

He eyed the matron warily. "I have," he replied shortly.

"Excellent. Would you be willing to advise me on estate matters whilst you are here?"

"Mama," hissed Elizabeth, her face turning red with mortification as Darcy finally turned his eyes to actually look at the women, the shock evident in his face. "We do not even know Mr. Darcy. It would be impertinent to make such a personal request with so little acquaintance!"

"Now is not the time for pride, Elizabeth," replied Mrs. Bennet firmly. "The worst he can do is say no, and nothing will have changed for us. But if he agrees, then that will help ease our burden tremendously."

Darcy watched the exchange with bewilderment and curiosity warring on his face. "What exactly do you mean, advise you on estate matters?"

Elizabeth opened her mouth to object, but a sharp look from Mrs. Bennet caused her to remain silent. The matron answered, "My husband was recently injured with a blow to the head. He did not have a steward, and my daughters and I have been attempting to understand how to manage things until he recovers. Elizabeth is especially intelligent, and with her help, we have managed to muddle through things so far. We have many questions, however, and unfortunately, there are not many estate owners around us from whom we can petition aid."

"Is your eldest daughter not the heir? Why is she not helping?"

"No, the estate is entailed away from the female line to a very distant cousin. The family has been estranged for many years, and from what I remember from our last meeting, they were extremely cruel and unpleasant. I would not wish for my husband to be waylaid in his own home when he is not yet dead."

Darcy looked between a mortified Elizabeth and a determined Mrs. Bennet. After several long minutes of silence, he finally said, "I would be happy to offer whatever assistance I can. I cannot guarantee to be able to answer all of your questions, but I have been managing my own estate for the last five years since my father's passing."

"I'm sorry for your loss," Elizabeth said quietly. "I know how I felt when we thought we might lose Papa; I cannot imagine the sorrow of him actually being gone."

Darcy peered at her more closely. "Thank you. My father was the best of men, and while time has eased the pain, I do miss him."

The pair locked eyes for a moment before Mrs. Bennet quietly cleared her throat. Darcy jerked his eyes away as Elizabeth lowered hers to the ground.

"I would be happy to call on you and your family with Bingley next week, if that works for you?"

"Thank you very much, Mr. Darcy," said Mrs. Bennet, giving a deep curtsy. "It is very kind of you to take pity on us in our situation."

"Yes, we are quite grateful for your kindness. I know we are strangers to you," Elizabeth added.

He nodded solemnly, and the group fell into an awkward silence. Elizabeth finally said, "Well, I don't know about you, Mama, but I think I have had enough talk about estate business for the day! We are at an assembly, and we should be dancing and forgetting our cares for a while. So if you will excuse me, I will go and find Charlotte again."

Without waiting for a response, Elizabeth dipped a curtsy to her mother and Darcy, then practically skipped away to rejoin her friend, not aware that the tall gentleman's eyes followed her for the rest of the evening.

Chapter 4

Elizabeth sighed in frustration as she looked over the ledger in front of her. She had been able to interpret the majority of her father's notes, but there were a few letters and symbols that she could make neither heads nor tails of.

"You're going to give yourself a headache if you keep staring at those papers, Lizzy," Mrs. Bennet said. "Why not have a break and take a cup of tea with us?"

"I just wish I knew what it all meant. I think we could actually save quite a bit of money every year with some economizing, but without knowing how important some of these expenses are, there's no way of telling what can actually be put aside."

"Really?" Mary said with interest. "That would be quite a relief to add to our dowries in case something were to occur to Papa before we were all married."

"What kind of economizing?" Mrs. Bennet asked, her voice laced with suspicion. "I do hope you do not mean retrenching and letting some of the servants go."

"Oh, no, Mama, nothing like that," Elizabeth hastened to assure her mother. "We *do* spend quite a bit above our pin money on dresses, lace, and other fripperies that aren't really all that necessary. We could also spend less at the butcher's, too, if we had fish less often—or if we could encourage Papa to go fishing more often."

"You know he hates it," Mary said.

"Maybe if one of us accompanied him and read to him aloud or something. Then he wouldn't find it quite as boring," suggested Elizabeth.

"Just as long as it's not Kitty or Lydia. They'd make too much noise and scare away all the fish!"

Elizabeth chuckled but tried to put on a stern face. "Now, Mary, you know they have quite improved since Papa's fall."

"Oh, they weren't all *that* bad," Mrs. Bennet replied in defense of her youngest. "They were just lively, that's all."

Elizabeth gave Mary a small shake of her head. "Either way, I have appreciated the efforts they have made in caring for Papa, as well as helping Jane with the household."

A knock came at the door, interrupting their conversation. Hill entered the room. "Mr. Darcy and Mr. Bingley have come to pay a call, madam."

"Very good, Hill. We shall see them in the drawing room," Mrs. Bennet replied.

"Are we not going to have them come to the study?" Elizabeth asked in surprise.

"Well, I'm not entirely certain Mr. Darcy was sincere in his offer to help us with estate matters. Besides, I want Mr. Bingley to be able to spend some time with Jane."

"Mama!" Mary cried in shock.

"Lydia and Kitty will remain there," protested Mrs. Bennet.

"Then I shall as well," Mary replied firmly.

"Oh, very well, do as you like." Mrs. Bennet sniffed at her middle daughter and marched out of the room.

Elizabeth put an arm around her younger sister. "For all the improvements she has made these last few weeks, Mama is still Mama."

"Which is honestly a bit of a relief," Mary said with a sigh. "I don't know if I could handle *both* of our parents gaining completely opposite personalities."

"How was Papa this morning when you saw him?" Elizabeth had taken to avoiding her father, as his behavior became increasingly more erratic and hysterical.

Mary rolled her eyes. "He keeps demanding to visit Uncle Phillips to get more details on how much he can spend for Jane's wedding trousseau. He waxed on and on about the need to import lace and brandy from France."

"He does realize Jane isn't even being courted, let alone engaged, right?"

"Yes, but he keeps insisting she is so beautiful that it will happen any day now, and he wants to be prepared."

Elizabeth frowned. "Perhaps we should call for Mr. Jones again."

Mary shrugged. "Oh, Lizzy, you should see him waving around a handkerchief and calling for smelling salts at the slightest provocation, still in his dressing gown. If I didn't know any better, I'd say he was mocking Mama as a joke."

"And that is why I haven't seen him recently. I don't think I could prevent myself from releasing my tongue against him," Elizabeth said. "I can't bear to see him acting that way and not feel angry about it, even if it is out of his control."

The girls were silent, then Mary said, "Perhaps we should join our guests now."

"Oh, good heavens, I completely forgot. Yes, let's go into the parlor."

They hadn't taken more than a few steps down the hall when they saw Mrs. Bennet coming towards them, Darcy immediately behind her.

"I'm sorry, Mama, Mr. Darcy," Elizabeth said. "We weren't meaning to be rude, we were just…"

"No matter, girls." Mrs. Bennet waved a hand at them airily. "Mr. Darcy has graciously agreed to come take a look at the parts that have been giving us trouble. Jane and the other girls have gone for a walk in the garden with Mr. Bingley. Jane was looking quite pale after managing the house all day, so I sent her out for some fresh air."

Elizabeth groaned within herself at her mother's obvious

matchmaking ploy but kept her opinions to herself. Instead, she led the way towards the study and sat at her father's desk. "We are very grateful for your assistance, Mr. Darcy. Here, let me show you what we have been able to discover thus far."

He took a seat across the desk from her, and she did her best to ignore the fluttering in her chest as she took in his handsome features and broad shoulders. Shaking her head slightly, she opened the book on the top and turned it his direction.

She spent the next half hour showing him the current ledger, along with her notes for what the entries meant. Next, she showed him how she had read through everything done over the past year to ensure they weren't forgetting things they needed to do to prepare for the winter and get everything in readiness for planting in the spring.

When she finished, Mr. Darcy looked at her with a raised eyebrow. "And you were able to figure all of this out yourself, Miss Elizabeth? You have had no training in estate management?"

Elizabeth blushed. "Well, Mama knew a few things, and Mary has been going over the numbers, so I have not done it entirely on my own. But, no, until these last few weeks, I had never even looked at a page like this, let alone known what things meant."

Darcy raised both eyebrows. "This is quite impressive work, Miss Bennet. Most men would not even be able to figure out what you have, let alone a woman."

"I hope you are not saying women are inferior to men in intelligence, Mr. Darcy," she said with a touch of ice in her voice.

"No, not at all," he said with surprise and a hint of offense. "Only that most women have not received an education that would allow them to begin to make these kinds of deductions. My sister, Georgiana, might be able to, but that is because I had her given extra tutoring in math and Latin."

Mollified, Elizabeth replied, "I have often enjoyed learning, and I believe I have read every book in my father's library, including those on crop rotation and sheep breeding."

"That is very well done of you," he said, admiration clear in his voice. "It has done you much good under the circumstances. Is your father still so unwell that he cannot help you?"

"Well," Elizabeth hesitated, looking at her mother, "the blow to the head has left him a bit confused. I do not wish to be given misinformation that ruins preparations for the future."

"Very wise of you. Has a doctor seen him?"

"No, only Mr. Jones, the apothecary. He sent out some letters of inquiry, but he has yet to receive a response."

Darcy was quiet for a moment. "If you wish, I would be happy to send for my personal doctor from London."

"Oh, but the expense—" Elizabeth cried out.

Darcy shook his head. "There would be no expense charged, I assure you." When she bit her lip in confusion, he said, "I would do nothing less for any of my tenants or neighbors in Derbyshire. I have often been of the mind that I have been blessed to be born into wealth, and in turn I should use that fortune to help others who are hardworking but have not the same fortune of birth as I."

Elizabeth was stunned. "That is... that is very good of you, Mr. Darcy. In any other circumstances, I would decline your offer, but with my father and my family's situation at stake, I will gratefully accept. I only hope to return the favor someday."

"No need to return anything, Miss Elizabeth. Only pass it forward when you can to someone less fortunate than yourself."

With that, the conversation returned to the ledgers. Darcy was able to explain all the remaining letters and symbols, which were a type of shorthand that was taught in most universities and were a mix of Latin and English. They then spent the next several hours in conversation about the steps Elizabeth would need to take over the following weeks and months to prepare the house and the land for winter and planting.

By the time they were finished, it was just approaching the dinner hour. Bingley and Darcy graciously declined the offer to stay, as Miss Bingley was sure to have prepared for their return.

That night, as Elizabeth thought back on the day, she was amazed at the sense of relief she felt in Darcy's presence nearby. On meeting at the assembly, she thought him to be proud and above his company. His help today, however, revealed him to be one of the best of men she had ever met.

Chapter 5

Darcy led the way on horseback towards Longbourn. It had been a week since he had last visited, and his personal physician had just arrived at Netherfield the night prior. Darcy, Dr. McKay, and Bingley were on their way to pay a call on the Bennets.

Bingley had been at Longbourn nearly every day since Darcy had helped Elizabeth in the study, and it was clear that he was growing quite fond of his Miss Bennet. With the delicate health of their father, however, Darcy worried that the woman might encourage him for reasons other than love or affection.

Once at Longbourn, Bingley immediately suggested a walk in the garden. Darcy watched Miss Bennet carefully as she blushed and lowered her eyes. At first, he thought she was unaffected by his friend's attentions, but then he saw the sparkle in her eyes and winning smile she flashed at her beau before donning a calmer face. This insight into her hidden feelings caused Darcy to feel great relief about the matter.

Mrs. Bennet showed the doctor upstairs to her husband's chambers while Darcy was escorted by a maid to the study, where Elizabeth and Mary were hard at work.

"We'll have to make sure to visit each tenant's home before the winter cold sets in," he heard Elizabeth say. "I will not have anyone starve or freeze because of our lack of competence."

Admiration filled him as he thought about how much his mother would have respected this woman. She seemed to be a lady who—in addition to being intelligent, witty, and beautiful—had genuine care for those beneath her.

He cleared his throat and knocked on the door. "I have brought the doctor, as promised," he said when the two girls looked up at him.

Elizabeth, for her part, felt flustered upon seeing Darcy standing in the doorway. Had he always been so tall and handsome? Her feelings for him certainly had grown over the last week, even in his absence. The fact that he had kept his word in sending for his own physician from town only added to the attraction she had for him.

"Thank you so much, Mr. Darcy," she said with feeling. "I cannot begin to express how much this means to us."

"Think nothing of it," he replied. "When my father was ill, it helped to know we were doing everything we could for him. Even though he eventually passed on, we never had to wonder if it was for lack of effort on our part. That hasn't been the case with other people I have met. I never want someone to have to choose between necessities and medical help."

"That is very good of you," she whispered.

Their eyes met and held for a long moment before Mary cleared her throat and shuffled a few papers. They broke contact, and Elizabeth looked down shyly at the papers on her desk.

"How are your estate matters progressing?" he asked.

"Well, I think. The only problem is a letter I discovered on my father's desk that he never opened. Apparently, our distant cousin and my father's heir presumes to arrive tomorrow for a visit."

"What?" exclaimed Mary. "You never said a word!"

"Yes, well, I'd only just found it a few minutes ago," Elizabeth explained. "I must admit that I do not feel comfortable having him in our home, especially with Papa's condition. But it is too late for us to deny him now."

"What is his situation?" asked Mr. Darcy.

"He is a parson," she said. "His name is Mr. William Collins, and he has a living in Kent."

"Would that be Hunsford, by any chance?"

"Why… yes, yes it is. Do you know him?" Elizabeth asked.

Darcy gave her a grim smile. "His patroness is my aunt, Lady Catherine de Bourgh. I think your instincts to not have him in your home are wise. She tends to hire sycophants who have an odd combination of pride and servility."

Elizabeth stifled a giggle. "Based on his letter, I think you are right." Her face then sobered. "But what do we do? What if he refuses to go to the inn? Or worse, insists on taking charge while my father is indisposed?"

"I can be here when he arrives," Darcy replied. "My being Lady Catherine's nephew may help strengthen your position."

Just as Darcy predicted, his high status had the most effect on Mr. Collins, who had arrived with pomp and arrogance. Upon hearing that he hadn't been expected and that his cousin was injured, he immediately insisted on taking control of the estate before even entering the house.

"After all, I am to be your guardian and manage things when your father dies, which may be very soon," he said in a haughty tone. "It is only reasonable that I should quickly marry my fairest cousin Miss Bennet—as is her due as the eldest and my due as heir—and take up permanent management of Longbourn and its inhabitants."

Elizabeth practically growled in outrage as Jane went pale. Mrs. Bennet gaped at the foolish man, and Darcy rolled his eyes at the typical behavior of one of his aunt's lackeys. It was Bingley's response, however, that proved to be the most surprising.

"I'm afraid marriage to Miss Bennet is quite impossible," he said, face almost purple in rage, "as I will be marrying her myself."

Everyone gasped at this announcement. "Oh, Jane dear, I had no idea!" squealed Mrs. Bennet.

Jane turned pink and looked a bit confused.

"That is, if she will accept my hand," Bingley said, looking at her with loving eyes.

"Yes, yes, I will marry you, Mr. Bingley," Jane whispered, her eyes shimmering with happy tears, a broad grin on her face.

"I see. My felicitations," Mr. Collins said awkwardly. "No matter, I will marry the second eldest, then."

"Absolutely not!" cried Elizabeth. "Sir, you are completely out of order. My father, although in his bed, is under the care of an excellent physician and will be making a full recovery. He is not close to death. And until this moment, I have never laid eyes on you before in my life! I certainly would not consider marriage to someone who is a stranger!"

"You must consider, my dear cousin, that it is very unlikely that another offer of marriage shall ever be made to you. Even with your many charms, which I'm certain you possess in abundance," this was said with a look towards her bosom, "your lack of dowry means you are unlikely to attract the attentions of anyone of significance."

"How dare you, sir," Darcy interrupted with a voice as cold and calm as ice. "I will not stand by and allow you to denigrate this lady."

"This is a family matter," replied Mr. Collins, sticking his nose in the air. "As I know none of my fair cousins are married, and there is not a Bennet son, you have no business being here."

"I am a friend of the family, and my presence has been requested. Furthermore, my aunt is Lady Catherine, and I believe she will be most displeased to hear about your words and actions today."

The change in Mr. Collins's countenance occurred so quickly that Elizabeth almost giggled aloud. Gone was the arrogant, pig-headed man, and in his place was a stuttering, obsequious oaf.

Darcy refused to allow any apologies nor would he permit Mr. Collins to enter the home. Instead, he was told to find a room at the inn or to return to Hunsford.

"Although, should you choose to remain in Meryton," Darcy said, "I will send a letter to my aunt informing her of your every behavior whilst here."

The cringing parson quickly left, waddling towards the buggy on which he'd arrived as fast as his large frame would allow. Had tensions not been so high, Elizabeth would have laughed at the spectacle. As it was, the confrontation had drained her so completely of energy that she sagged against Mary.

"I daresay that was the most unpleasant man I have ever had the misfortune to meet," Darcy said, turning to Elizabeth.

When he saw her pale face and exhausted form, he immediately offered his arm to escort her into the house. The rest of the group followed, and they all sat in the drawing room to partake of a strong cup of restorative tea.

Elizabeth took a grateful sip from her cup, then looked around the room. Bingley and Jane were in quiet conversation, and she could not make out everything that was said. She turned to Darcy and remarked, "I had no idea Mr. Bingley planned to propose today. He has good timing."

"Er, I don't believe he had actually asked your sister to marry him before the debacle. Mr. Collins's declaration of intent must have spurred him to action."

She bit her lip and looked at her sister with concern. "Oh, dear. I hope she doesn't feel forced to accept him now. I have so wanted her to be able to marry for love, not convenience or comfort."

He looked at her curiously. "Do you doubt her affection for my friend?"

"No, I know she greatly esteems and admires him. I just had hoped marriage would never feel forced up on her."

Darcy nodded. "I understand what you are saying. For what it's worth, I believe they will be very happy together."

"Now I shall just have to find a way to avoid Mr. Collins for the rest of my life, or at least until I find someone to marry who *isn't* such a fool!" chuckled Elizabeth. "But he did make a valid point—who would have me?"

"I would."

The laugh died in her throat, and she turned to stare at him, not daring to hope he was saying what she thought he meant. "You... you would?"

"Yes, I would marry you, if you'd let me."

"But... why?"

He gave her a tender smile. "Between your care of your father and family, and your dedication to learning your estate, you have enthralled me the way no other woman ever has. I see your genuine desire to care for others, and it's caused me to fall in love with you."

Ignoring the rest of the room, Darcy knelt at Elizabeth's feet. "Will you marry me, Elizabeth Bennet?"

She stared into the eyes of the kind, honorable man she had come to know so well. "Yes, I will."

Epilogue

Mr. Bennet smirked to himself as he watched from the window of his bedroom his two eldest daughters and their beaus walk in the garden.

When he had first awoken from the lump on his head, he had been genuinely confused. His wife's lamentations had brought him to his senses almost immediately, but he was so frustrated with her self-centered concern for herself that he lost all control and gave into the impulse to behave as she did.

Initially, he had planned to let them in on the joke once he finished enjoying their astonishment. To his surprise, however, none of them behaved in a way that he had anticipated! Mrs. Bennet seemed to regain some of her lost nerves, and his two youngest began to think of someone other than themselves.

Curious to see how far it could go, Mr. Bennet kept up the pretense of having developed a personality like his dear wife at her worst. It was quite liberating, actually, to act in such a carefree, unconstrained way. He could say and do whatever he liked, and no one took him to task for it or thought ill of him.

It wasn't until a doctor arrived from town at Mr. Darcy's request did Mr. Bennet finally begin to wonder if he'd gone too far. He never meant to cause worry or concern for his elder daughters; he'd only wanted to continue the improvement of his wife, Kitty, and Lydia. He hadn't the slightest notion on how to get out of the situation without confessing the truth, which could cause him to lose the trust and love of his favorite children.

He was selfish, and he knew it. He'd always been indolent with

regard to his family, but he did love them in his own way. He simply loved peace, quiet, and a good book more.

When Dr. Mckay had arrived, Mr. Bennet asked the man if he
could be trusted to not betray a patient's confidence. The man, rather offended, had stiffly replied that he took his client's privacy as
a sacred duty. No one, not even Mr. Darcy—who was paying his
fee—would hear the private details of the case.

Mr. Bennet took the doctor into his confidence, explaining how
the whole situation was at first meant to be a joke. He'd wanted to
lighten the mood a little when he first awoke, as everyone was so
somber and worried. Then when it had the effect of improving his
family, he wanted to help make that be a permanent change.

Fortunately, Dr. McKay—who did not necessarily approve of
the situation—was willing to help smooth things over without
wounding any of the ladies' tender feelings. He informed the family,
in a very grave manner, that he had a tonic he could prescribe to
Mr. Bennet.

"This is by no means a guarantee, however. It has the effect of
lowering inflammation in some cases, but I do not know if it will
make a difference on a head trauma. The swelling on the outside
has gone down, but there may be swelling in the brain. *If* that's the
case, then this medicine *might* be able to help. I cannot make any
promises, you understand."

Mr. Bennet drank the tonic—which was really a nip of good
brandy in a bit of tea—every day for three days. On the third morning, he awoke as his old self once more, pretending to have little
recollection of everything that had occurred.

His permission to marry the elder two Bennet daughters was
immediately requested, and that request was just as quickly granted.
As sad as Mr. Bennet was to part with his daughters, he felt a small
bit of relief in not having to keep up a pretense in front of those
whom he respected the most.

As he watched the girls walk with their betrotheds below his window, he smirked to himself again. Perhaps he should lie around in his nightcap and powdering gown more regularly after all.

Punish Him for Such a Speech

Elizabeth Bennet is stuck at Netherfield, tending to her elder sister. Tired of being the object of disdain for both Mr. Darcy and Miss Bingley, Elizabeth gets her revenge in a unique manner—flirting brazenly with Mr. Darcy one evening as she and Miss Bingley take a turn about the room. How will Mr. Darcy react?

Chapter 1

Elizabeth paused before entering the drawing room at Netherfield. Having just left Jane in her sickbed upstairs, she had gone down to join the Netherfield party in their evening socialization. She'd heard her name mentioned, and she wanted to know what she was about to walk into.

"She has nothing, in short, to recommend her, but being an excellent walker," Mrs. Hurst was saying. "I shall never forget her appearance this morning. She really looked almost wild."

"She did indeed, Louisa," agreed Miss Bingley. "I could hardly keep my countenance. Very nonsensical to come at all! Why must she be scampering about the country because her sister had a cold? Her hair, so untidy, so blowsy!"

"Yes, and her petticoat; I hope you saw her petticoat, six inches deep in mud, I am absolutely certain, and the gown which had been let down to hide it not doing its office."

"Your picture may be very exact, Louisa," said Bingley, "but this was all lost upon me. I thought Miss Elizabeth Bennet looked remarkably well when she came into the room this morning. Her dirty petticoat quite escaped my notice. Besides, her willingness to come all this way to tend her sister shows her to have great affection for Miss Bennet, which I find very pleasing."

Elizabeth smiled at this kind defense from Bingley, whom she had thought very well of since the beginning.

"That may be so, but I just don't know what I think of Miss Elizabeth," replied Miss Bingley. "Now, I have an excessive regard for Jane Bennet—she is really a very sweet girl—and I wish with all my heart she were well settled. But with such a father and mother, and such low connections, I am afraid there is no chance of it."

"I think I have heard you say that their uncle is an attorney in Meryton?" Mrs. Hurst asked her sister.

"Yes, and they have another, who lives somewhere near Cheapside." Both ladies laughed heartily, causing Elizabeth to clench her fists in anger.

"If they had uncles enough to fill all Cheapside," cried Bingley, "it would not make them one jot less agreeable."

"But it must very materially lessen their chance of marrying men of any consideration in the world," replied Darcy.

Unable to bear it any longer, Elizabeth made several loud stomps in place, causing the room to fall quiet other than a few titters from the ladies. She opened the door, entered, and sat on a chair near a small table, which contained a book. Mr. Hurst invited her to join in with cards, but she instead begged his forgiveness for desiring to read instead.

She was mocked somewhat for this preference, but eventually the conversation turned back to those at the table. Miss Bingley asked after Miss Darcy several times, and Darcy answered in as few words as possible.

It was all Elizabeth could do to keep from snickering at the scene. It was clear that poor Darcy had no desire to entertain Miss Bingley's attentions, and it was equally clear that Miss Bingley was oblivious to that fact.

The following evening passed much the same way, only this time at dinner, Elizabeth drank several glasses of wine to brace herself for the evening ahead. She did not usually imbibe, and the alcohol made her feel strange, but she worried she would lash out in anger otherwise.

Within a few minutes of the sexes rejoining one another in the music room, Miss Bingley—in an attempt to call Darcy's attention to herself—interrupted Elizabeth's readings with a request to join

Miss Bingley in taking a turn about the room.

Elizabeth was surprised, but she immediately agreed. As they walked, Darcy's eyes finally raised from the letter he had been writing to fix them on the two ladies. He was directly invited to join them, but he demurred.

"There can only be two motives for your walk," he said, "and my joining you would render either of them irrelevant."

"What on earth could you mean, Mr. Darcy?" exclaimed Miss Bingley. "Miss Eliza, pray tell me, do you understand Mr. Darcy in his making this statement?"

"Not at all," was her answer, "but depend upon it, he means to be severe on us, and our surest way of disappointing him will be to ask nothing about it."

Miss Bingley, however, was incapable of disappointing Mr. Darcy with anything, and persevered, therefore, in requiring an explanation of his two motives.

"I have not the smallest objection to explaining them," said he, as soon as she allowed him to speak. "You either choose this method of passing the evening because you are in each other's confidence and have secret affairs to discuss, or because you are conscious that your figures appear to the greatest advantage in walking: if the first, I should be completely in your way; and if the second, I can admire you much better as I sit by the fire."

Elizabeth felt a fury rise up in her unlike any she had ever known. How dare this man mock her appearance at the Meryton assembly, then choose to do so again—this time to her face? To pretend that he admired her? The rage was also directed towards Miss Bingley, who had been nothing but condescending and disdainful.

"Oh, shocking!" cried Miss Bingley. "I never heard anything so abominable. How shall we punish him for such a speech?"

Before Darcy could respond, Elizabeth lost control of her tightly held manners. *Two can play at this game*, she thought angrily. *Since Mr.*

Darcy appears to despise fawning attentions, I shall give him all I can whilst in residence. See how he feels to be made as uncomfortable as he makes me.

Releasing Miss Bingley's arm, she slowly walked over to Darcy, slightly swaying her hips with each step, much as Lydia would do. Frozen in his seat, Darcy kept his eyes fixed upon Elizabeth.

"Why, Mr. Darcy," she purred as she approached his chair. "I had no idea you looked at me to admire. I admit, I have seen your eyes on me frequently since I have been in residence, but I assumed it was to find fault with my... country manners. I'm so glad to know I was wrong."

As she spoke, she let her hand trail along her neck and down the swell of her bosom to her waist. Darcy's eyes flared with an emotion she didn't fully recognize, but she knew that it was anything but equanimity.

"What should we do now, Miss Bingley, to further entice Mr. Darcy?" she said, turning back towards the woman, who was gaping at her guest. "Perhaps another turn about the room, this time more slowly? We must, after all, give Mr. Darcy plenty to appreciate and admire about our figures."

Once again, she swayed her hips as she walked back to where a frozen Miss Bingley stood. Taking the taller woman's arm, Elizabeth said, "Now, shall we discuss our secret affairs as we walk?"

It was all Elizabeth could do to keep from bursting into laughter at the unflattering shade of purple that had come across Miss Bingley's face. She then looked over at Bingley, who was staring at her with uncertainty. She gave him a tiny wink, which shocked him somewhat, and then slowly understanding crept across his face, and he gave her a small nod in return.

"Mr. Bingley, I do believe I am quite tired," she said, pretending to smother a yawn. "I cannot even remember where my room is. Would you be willing to point me in the right direction?"

Mrs. Hurst let out a small gasp, but before any other response could be made, Bingley stood with a broad grin. "It would be my pleasure, Miss Elizabeth," and the two left the room.

Once they were most of the way up the staircase, Elizabeth was no longer able to contain her laughter. "Oh, do forgive me, Mr. Bingley!" she said, wiping her eyes. "I don't know what came over me. I don't usually behave in such a manner!"

"You certainly surprised everyone," he agreed with a chuckle. "What on earth compelled you to behave that way?"

"I was just so frustrated with both your sister and friend. I know they belittle Jane and myself behind our backs—I heard them last night—and Mr. Darcy proclaimed me only *tolerable* the first night we met. I did the one thing I knew would upset them both the most: pretend an interest in the man."

The humor on Bingley's face was replaced with mortification. "Good Lord, Miss Elizabeth, I must apologize at once for the unkind remarks made by those of my household. Please, do not think that their opinions reflect the one that I hold for your sister—and you, of course."

She waved a hand at him and smiled gently. "I know, Mr. Bingley. You have a good heart. I can see why Jane admires you so."

Slapping a hand to her mouth, she giggled. What was wrong with her? "Oh, please forget I said that. Jane would absolutely kill me; she's so shy, you see."

He merely blinked at her. "She admires me? Really?"

Elizabeth shook her head frantically. "Do not make me repeat it. I feel terrible enough as it is for letting her feelings slip. I don't know why I did it. I don't know why I'm doing anything that I am tonight. It must be the drink; I had far too many glasses of wine at dinner than I should have."

"Ah, yes, I've had that happen to myself before too."

"Then please excuse me. We have reached my door, and I will go in and get a good night's sleep. I shall certainly be mortified about all of this tomorrow. Good night, Mr. Bingley."

"Good night, Miss Elizabeth," he said.

With a wobbling curtsy, she entered her chamber, closed the door, and collapsed on the bed with the world swirling around her.

Chapter 2

Elizabeth awoke late the next morning with a terrible headache. She tried to sit up in bed, but the movements made her stomach roil. Not eager to cast up her accounts in a chamber pot, she lay back on the pillows, trying to shut out the sunlight and noise.

Some while later, a soft knock came on the door that adjoined her room to Jane's.

"Come in," she called, her head pounding with the mere effort of speaking.

A maid entered and dipped a quick curtsy. "Forgive me, Miss Lizzy, but Miss Jane has awakened and was concerned that you were not yet out of bed."

Recognizing the voice as that of Sally, the daughter of a Longbourn tenant, Elizabeth gave a small sigh of relief. "Good morning, Sally. I believe I had a bit too much wine last night, and I am mortified. I would claim to be sick, but I know you won't spread any gossip."

"Of course not, Miss Lizzy! I know my duty," the young girl said primly. "Shall I fetch you some plain toast and weak tea?"

"Yes, that would be most appreciated. And perhaps a clean bowl to keep by the bedside?"

"Of course. I'll inform everyone downstairs that you've come down with the same illness as your sister. That should keep any talk at bay."

"Thank you so much, Sally. You're an angel."

The girl laughed. "Well, I don't know about that, Miss Lizzy, but I'll thank you for the compliment all the same… but what should I tell your sister?"

"Oh, she can know the truth. Otherwise she'll feel terribly guilty for having gotten me sick or some other such nonsense."

"Very well. I'll pull the curtains closed for you as well."

Elizabeth said a prayer of gratitude for her great fortune in having Sally to tend to her that morning, then did her best to fall back to sleep.

After another hour or so, she once again awoke, but this time, the headache had lessened significantly. As Sally had promised, there was a bowl by the bed, and on the table lay a tray with dry toast and tea that was fortunately still quite warm.

Elizabeth forced herself to eat the toast and drink the tea in spite of her nausea. Within about ten minutes, the ill feelings began to ease enough that she felt she could get out of bed and check on Jane.

She found her elder sister also having tea in her bed, looking a bit peaked, but much improved since the day prior.

"Lizzy," Jane said, the relief evident on her face, "how are you doing? I was so concerned about you."

"Oh, Jane," Elizabeth said, collapsing onto the bed next to her sister, "I am absolutely mortified. Miss Bingley was being horrid during dinner, so I kept drinking wine to keep my mouth closed, and I ended up doing something very foolish."

Elizabeth told Jane the entire story of what she'd overheard the first night there, Miss Bingley's snide tone, and Darcy's condescending attitude. Jane's eyes widened when Elizabeth explained how she'd flirted with Darcy, then rambled on at Bingley before going to bed.

"And I don't know how I can bear to face any of them ever again," she cried dramatically, burying her face in her hands.

"Poor Miss Bingley."

"Poor Miss Bingley?" cried Elizabeth in mock outrage, flinging her pillow at her sister. "You mean, poor Elizabeth! Is that honestly all you can say?"

"Well, it's clear she so desperately wishes for Mr. Darcy's attention, but he isn't interested in her. That must be so difficult."

"Jane, are you not upset with me for telling Mr. Bingley how much you admire him?"

Jane flushed a brilliant red. "Oh, Lizzy, of course not. I know you didn't mean to. I feel embarrassed about having to see him again; he may not feel the same in return."

"Well then, we can both be mortified together. Perhaps we shall simply remain in our rooms until we can go home."

"Lizzy! You cannot be so rude!"

"They won't know the truth; after all, Sally is putting it out that I have come down with whatever is afflicting you."

Elizabeth rolled her eyes at the stern look Jane gave her. "I know it's dishonest, *Mary*," Elizabeth said, thinking of her younger sister's self-righteous attitudes and her judgments should she have been there, "and I shall do my best to repair any damage I've caused before we leave." She sighed. "Dinner this evening is going to be miserable."

She was not the only person to dread the upcoming evening.

***

Darcy gave a great sigh as he descended the staircase for dinner. The evening before had not been at all what he expected, and he dreaded a repeat of the performance.

He knew when he accepted the invitation to Netherfield that he would have to put up with the cloying attentions of Miss Bingley, but he did not anticipate another lady in residence who would do the same.

He was supremely disappointed with Miss Elizabeth. She had caught his eye at the Meryton assembly as being a miss of pert opinions and fine eyes. In all their subsequent interactions, he'd enjoyed her witty bantering and lack of pretensions and artfulness. The more she'd ignored him or debated with him, the more intrigued he'd become.

Until last night.

It was as if she had been replaced by a simpering girl freshly come out in the ton. Her swaying form and husky tone were captivating, but at the same time, he felt repulsed by how brazenly she had flirted with him, only to wink at and then disappear with Bingley!

His friend had been quite tight-lipped about what had occurred when he returned to the parlor after escorting Elizabeth to her chambers, which alarmed Darcy even more.

Had he been fooled by her nature? Was she just as mercenary as every other grasping young lady in London?

The idea of the Miss Bennets remaining in Netherfield any longer filled him with more dread than it had the day prior. Previously, the worst thing that could have happened was that he and Bingley would fall for the girls' charms. Now it seemed they were doomed to be actually chased.

He paused at the door of the drawing room and swallowed, straightening—and loosening—his cravat before entering.

Thankfully, the entire party was already in the room, meaning he would avoid any awkward tête-à-têtes with any of the ladies. He crossed the room and accepted a brandy from Bingley to fortify himself.

After moving to the window, he gazed out on the darkening landscape, hoping to escape being forced into conversation with anyone.

He was not so fortunate.

Miss Elizabeth left her seat on the sofa where she had been reading and crossed the room to join him at the window. He sighed to himself, then turned and politely inquired, "Miss Elizabeth, I hope you have recovered since your imposition this morning."

She blushed. "Yes, well, I'm afraid I had a bit too much wine at dinner last night. In fact, that is why I wished to speak with you. Mr. Darcy, I sincerely apologize for my appalling behavior yesterday evening. I can only blame the wine for my lack of decorum."

He gaped at her. "Then why...?"

Wincing, she replied, "To be very honest, sir, I know you and Miss Bingley hold my sister and I in much disdain. I grew tired of the barbs and unfriendly looks, and I decided to make the two of you feel as uncomfortable as you were making me. It was very unladylike and inexcusable. I promise, you are quite safe from me. You are the last man in the world whom I would wish to pursue, so you needn't fear anything on that score. I have arranged with Mr. Bingley for my sister and I to return to Longbourn tomorrow."

She spoke all of this in a rush, then dipped a small curtsy and returned to her seat before he could get in a word edgewise.

Miss Bingley, who had watched the scene with alarm on her face, immediately joined him. "I am so sorry, Mr. Darcy, that you have been forced to bear that dreadful girl's attentions once more. Do not worry. I will see to it that she and her grasping sister are returned home immediately. Charles will be forced to see things my way. Then we can return to the intimate family party we have always been."

She ran her hand along his arm as she made this last statement. Fortunately, the butler arrived at that moment to call them in to dinner. Bingley asked Darcy to take Mrs. Hurst into the room, which caused Darcy to give his friend a smile of gratitude.

It was some hours later before Darcy could begin to ponder everything that had occurred that evening. True to her word, Elizabeth had kept her distance from him the entire evening, not saying a word in his direction.

In fact, she only spoke when spoken to, other than when she requested Bingley's carriage the next morning. The confused expression on Miss Bingley's face was almost enough to make Darcy laugh, and it was clear evidence that Elizabeth's assertions were true.

Darcy was awake long into the night, puzzling over the unique character that was Elizabeth Bennet. What did she mean that he held her in disdain? He had been endeavoring to hide his attraction to her!

Perhaps he had succeeded too well in maintaining a facade of indifference? But there was quite a difference between apathy and disdain. No, she must have had a reason for saying so.

Resolving to ask Bingley the next time they spoke, Darcy finally fell into a restless sleep.

Chapter 3

Elizabeth gave a deep sigh of relief as the Bingley carriage pulled away from Netherfield.

"I daresay, I have never been more happy to leave a place in my life," she said.

Jane just gazed out the window, saying nothing in response. It was clear her mind was elsewhere.

Hoping to shock her sister, Elizabeth said, "I then told Miss Bingley that I preferred her above all others, even Charlotte. She then informed me that she would only return the sentiment if I would agree with her that the sky was purple. Of course, since it's green…"

She couldn't keep up the ridiculous monologue for any longer and began to giggle at herself.

Jane startled at the noise, then turned blank eyes towards her sister. "Hmm? What did you say, Lizzy?"

"Nothing of any note, Jane," Elizabeth replied, the laughter still in her voice. "Where was your mind just now? Perhaps you left it back at Netherfield?"

Jane flushed. "This morning, before we left, Mr. Bingley asked if he might call on me at Longbourn."

Elizabeth squealed, then winced at having sounded exactly like their youngest sister. "Oh, Jane, I am so happy for you!"

"It is just a courtship, Lizzy. There might not be anything that comes of it."

"We shall see," Elizabeth said with a sly smile. "It's fortunate I was in my cups the other night, then, wasn't it?"

Jane's face turned even more red, and she refused to acknowledge her sister's assertion, choosing instead to gaze out the window and ignore her sister's laughter for the remainder of the ride.

Once home, Jane went into her father's book room and shared the good news with him. He cautioned her to not inform Mrs. Bennet until Bingley had actually come, made the request, and left again. Elizabeth wholeheartedly agreed with that warning, which comforted Jane, who felt guilty for keeping a secret from her mother.

As promised, Bingley arrived the next day. His eagerness was apparent in the fact that he had paced in the front drive with his pocket watch for ten minutes until the appropriate hour for making calls arrived. He knocked on the door and was brought to Mr. Bennet's study immediately to bypass Mrs. Bennet's histrionics.

Permission was granted with only a *minimal* amount of teasing on Mr. Bennet's part, as it was clear Bingley was too amiable and oblivious for the father to derive any real enjoyment from the situation.

While Mr. Bennet had counseled Bingley to allow Jane to make the announcement after he had left for the day, the good-humored young man was incapable of keeping his emotions to himself. As soon as he entered the drawing room, he exclaimed, "Mr. Bennet has given me permission to court the lovely Miss Jane Bennet."

The room fell silent, then Mrs. Bennet burst into effusions. "Oh, my dear, dear Jane, I am so happy! I was sure you could not be so beautiful for nothing! Oh, he is the handsomest young man that ever was seen! What a lovely couple the pair of you shall make!"

The genial Bingley stood next to Jane, beaming and nodding in agreement as Mrs. Bennet prattled on for the next ten minutes about what a jewel Jane was, so kind and gentle, the perfect wife for a gentleman in search of a marriage partner.

At last, the matron bustled off to find Hill to prepare a special dinner in honor of the formal courtship. Bingley made use of the distraction to ask Jane if she would like to walk outside, and Elizabeth hastily offered to accompany them as chaperon.

The next hour passed in a relaxing manner; Elizabeth ambled about on the other side of the garden while Bingley and Jane spoke in hushed conversation. She wanted to give them as much privacy as possible so they could come to know one another better.

At the end of the visit, Bingley said, "I am sure once I deliver the good news to my sisters, they will wish to call on you to offer their own congratulations. You can expect them in the next few days."

Elizabeth bit her tongue to keep from making a witty retort as Jane expressed her pleasure at receiving their felicitations. The second Bennet daughter was under no delusions that Miss Bingley and Mrs. Hurst would think that this announcement would be good news of any kind.

Their upset over the circumstance was made clear when they finally paid a visit three days later, stayed barely the requisite fifteen minutes that good manners dictated, and continually spoke about how fickle their brother was, always falling in and out of love, and even their going so far as suggesting that there was an *arrangement* between Bingley and Miss Darcy.

It was all Elizabeth could do to keep from dragging the two harpies out of the Longbourn parlor by their ears and tossing them into the mud. Jane was in tears, having taken every word to heart as a kindly meant warning to protect her feelings. It took most of the night for Elizabeth to convince her sister to not break off the courtship entirely via letter.

The following day, when Bingley called, Jane was extremely reticent, only answering with monosyllables. Darcy had called along with his friend, which upset Elizabeth's composure somewhat as it was her first time seeing him since her apology at Netherfield.

Darcy spent the first part of the visit watching Jane closely, a frown on his face. Even Bingley looked disturbed by Jane's hesitancy. Finally, unable to bear the situation any longer, Elizabeth suggested the four of them walk out together.

Once outside, Elizabeth said, "Now, I'm afraid I am going to once again do something that all of society would dictate that I should not, but I cannot allow this to go on any longer."

Jane turned a deep red and said quietly, "No, Lizzy, please don't."

"I'm sorry, Jane, but I must."

Bingley and Darcy looked between the two women, confusion on the face of the former, and wariness on the face of the latter.

"I think, Mr. Bingley, that you deserve to know exactly what your sisters said yesterday."

In spite of Jane's protestations, Elizabeth told Bingley everything. The man's face grew more and more upset as he listened to the disparaging remarks his own kin had made against him. When Elizabeth mentioned the part where Miss Bingley had strongly suggested that Miss Darcy and Bingley had an arrangement, Darcy's grew pale with fury.

"Are you quite certain about this, Miss Elizabeth?" Darcy snapped. "I can assure you that no such match has ever been spoken of between myself, my sister, or Mr. Bingley. Georgiana is not even out into society. As much as I esteem Bingley, and I could entertain the idea of him being a brother, that would not be for several years yet and only if both parties were in agreement."

"If you doubt my word, Mr. Darcy," Elizabeth replied coolly, "then may I suggest you ask my mother what was said in her drawing room? Or maybe you could ask Hill, as she was the one comforting my mother for most of the evening as she bewailed the idea that my sister would be jilted?"

Darcy turned red. "Forgive me. I was not intending to question your integrity, only to ensure that the situation hadn't been misinterpreted."

"No, it was not," she said shortly. "This is why Jane has been so quiet today. She is convinced that your sisters, being true friends, were only concerned for her heart and were telling her the truth so she could prevent herself from any worse heartbreak when you left, Mr. Bingley."

"Miss Bennet, is this true? Did my sisters lead you to believe that I would desert you?" Bingley took Jane's hand in his and looked into her eyes intently.

The tears that had filled the eldest Bennet daughter's eyes during the conversation streamed down her cheeks. Unable to speak, Jane could only nod.

"Oh, my poor dear," Bingley said, grasping her hand and raising it to his lips. "I would never be so callous as to leave you if I thought there was any hope of your returning my affections."

"That is part of why I called with Bingley today," Darcy added grimly. "Miss Bingley and Mrs. Hurst returned yesterday to inform us that Miss Bennet had taken them into her confidence, saying that she was only accepting their brother because of pressure from her mother."

Elizabeth gasped in outrage. "Why, those little—" she seethed, but paused when unable to think of a word that was sufficient enough to express her outrage but ladylike enough to be uttered aloud.

"I quite agree," Darcy replied.

"That is why I asked Darcy to come with me today," Bingley said. "I knew from your words, Miss Elizabeth, that your sister had genuine fondness for me. Her actions and smiles have also proved it, and I wished for Darcy to be able to witness it and to help me explain to my sisters that they were wrong."

"Which is why you were frowning at Jane so much this morning," Elizabeth said in understanding. "I thought perhaps you disapproved of the match due to our lack of fortune and connection. It does make it difficult for us to marry anyone of consideration in the world."

Darcy gave her a quizzical look. "I assure you, my only concern was that of my friend's heart. He would be miserable in a loveless match."

"As would Jane," Elizabeth replied fiercely.

The two stared at one another, then Darcy nodded. "I bow to your superior knowledge of your sister's feelings. I am glad to hear that my friend's admiration is returned."

"But what are we to do now?" Bingley asked. "I mean, what do we do about my sisters?"

Chapter 4

Darcy and Bingley rode back to Netherfield, both still furious after their illuminating visit at Longbourn.

"I am so glad Miss Elizabeth had the courage to say something," Bingley said. "I was beginning to worry that Jane had changed her mind about me but was too kind to say anything."

"Yes, Miss Elizabeth's lack of decorum does seem to be useful at times," Darcy said. "It does, however, give her a certain air of conceited independence that is rather difficult to tolerate."

Bingley gaped at his friend. "Good Lord, man! What a snob you are. Well, no matter; she knows your opinion of her anyway."

"What do you mean?" Darcy asked, ignoring the ringing in his head of her words during her apology when she spoke of his disdain for her. "I daresay I've treated her just as I have any other lady of my acquaintance."

Snorting, Bingley gave his friend a look and said in a mock deep voice, "She is tolerable, I suppose, but not handsome enough to tempt me."

Darcy turned a bit pale. "She heard me?"

"Of *course* she heard you, you idiot. She was sitting not three chairs away from where we were standing, and you looked straight at her when you said it. You're only lucky she laughed at you with her friends instead of running away in tears."

Desperately, Darcy tried to justify himself. "It's not as if I actually meant it when I said it. I barely noticed her appearance; I was only trying to get you to leave me alone."

"Yes, and that's what you were doing when she overheard you

and Caroline denigrate her family her first night in Netherfield," Bingley replied dryly.

"What?"

"You don't even remember? She quoted it to you back there, saying she and her sisters have little chance of marrying anyone of any consideration in the world."

Darcy's first reaction to this was akin to that of a child's reaction after having been caught for sneaking a pie left on the table. "She shouldn't have been eavesdropping on a private conversation!"

Bingley laughed in disbelief. "You? A private conversation with my sister? In a drawing room filled with the house's inhabitants *and* a maid? Honestly, Darcy, when did you become the stupid one in our friendship?"

Stiffening, Darcy urged his horse forward without responding, eventually breaking into a hard gallop. Bingley followed behind, shaking his head. When they arrived at Netherfield, Bingley dismounted and tossed the reins to a servant.

"Darcy, you need to understand that my courtship of Miss Bennet means my priorities are changing. I will be informing my sisters tonight that they have broken my trust and must return to town. I'll have my aunt Gertrude from Scarborough come be my hostess."

"Good for you, Bingley. It's about time you took a stand against them."

"This goes for you as well though. As much as I appreciate your willingness to come here and help me learn about running an estate, I will not tolerate disrespect to anyone in the Bennet family, no matter how much you think it might be deserved. Miss Elizabeth is due an apology—more than one—and if you cannot offer that and then be civil, I will ask you to leave as well."

Before his friend could reply, Bingley spun on his heel and marched inside, leaving a gaping Darcy behind him.

It took a full thirty seconds for Darcy to recover his shock at having been spoken to in such a way by his usually affable friend.

When the words sunk in, he was overcome with anger. He threw his riding crop to the ground and stormed his way into Netherfield and up to his rooms.

"Harcourt, I need a bath," he growled at his valet. "And once I am done, start packing my things. We're going to London tomorrow."

The servant looked up at his master, startled. "Tomorrow, sir?"

"Did I stutter?" Darcy barked.

"No, sir," Harcourt replied, his stoic countenance back on his face. The only sign of his surprise at his master's unusual harshness was a widening of his eyes. "Right away, sir."

Fuming, Darcy paced the room as he waited for the servants to heat the water and bring it upstairs to fill the tub. It was quite a lengthy process, and he felt a twinge of guilt worm its way through the anger at how he'd behaved towards those who were dependent on him.

Once filled, he pressed a coin into each servant's hand. "Thank you for the bath on short notice."

Then, turning to Harcourt, he pressed three coins into the valet's hand. "And this is for you, for putting up with my foul mood."

Harcourt nodded in return. "Would you like assistance with your bath, sir?"

"No, I think I need some time to finish ridding myself of my petulance. I'll let you know when I'm through."

"Very good, sir."

Darcy watched as Harcourt left the room and closed the door behind him. Sinking into the hot water, Darcy allowed his mind to go over Bingley's words down in the stables.

"How could he think I would behave in any way less than a gentlemanlike manner? I have been nothing but polite to Miss Elizabeth. It's not as if it's my fault she keeps overhearing conversations that upset her. Besides, I've only spoken the truth."

Grumbling, he washed himself, as if he could wipe away the remorse that was overpowering his anger. By the time he had completed his bath, he admitted that he did owe Bingley—and Miss Bennet—an apology.

Telling Harcourt to stop packing for London, as he couldn't leave before making amends, he went down to the drawing room where everyone was gathering for dinner. He took a quick minute to offer his apology to Bingley, who accepted it with a grin and a clap on his friend's back. "I knew Caroline couldn't have rubbed off on you *too* much."

Darcy winced at the idea that he had behaved anywhere close to Miss Bingley's level of deception and arrogance. After all, he was the grandson and nephew of an earl, and he never once sought to deceive his friend.

Thankfully, Bingley waited until Darcy had retired for the evening before speaking to his sisters. From his rooms, Darcy could hear Miss Bingley's muffled—but shrill—shrieks of indignation about the Bennets, which lasted long into the night and only ended when Darcy fell asleep with a pillow over his ears.

It was with great relief that Darcy awoke to discover that the Hursts and Miss Bingley had already departed for London, in spite of the fact that it was Sunday. "I knew I wouldn't be able to bear it another minute longer," Bingley explained at breakfast. "Can you believe that Caroline tried to tell me that it had all been a misunderstanding, and that Jane must have made the entire story up?"

"But it was Miss Elizabeth who even told us what had occurred." Darcy frowned as he spread jam over his toast.

"Precisely. I know I'm not the smartest man around, but even I can figure out who's telling the truth in this situation."

The two men left for church and arrived just as the service was about to begin. Bingley led his friend into the Netherfield pew, which was directly across the aisle from the Bennets. By sitting in the seat closest to the aisle, Bingley and Jane could see one another clearly and exchange fond looks.

Darcy did his best to ignore the Bennets, especially the beguiling Miss Elizabeth. From the corner of his eye, however, he could see her attempt to hush her youngest sisters and nudge her father awake from time to time. Each time Darcy's eyes moved towards hers, he would shake his head and refocus his attention on the sermon.

The elderly parson put his withered hand on the Bible as he spoke. "Now, let us remember what the Good Book tells us in Matthew chapter 25, verse 40. *Inasmuch as ye have done it unto the least of these my brethren, ye have done it unto me.*"

For some reason, the words rang in Darcy's head, and he shifted uncomfortably. The parson continued. "The next time you go to speak gossip, or the next time you argue with a neighbor, or the next time you disdain someone because their life is different from yours, remember that it's as if you were doing it to Jesus Himself."

The sermon continued about the importance of treating one's neighbor with kindness, but Darcy sat on the bench, the verse of scripture ringing in his ear. Suddenly, all of his justifications over what he'd said about Miss Elizabeth and how he'd treated the Meryton residents faded away and he was left with the glaring truth.

He was no better than the Pharisees who mocked the Son of God.

This woman, these people, had done him no harm. Yes, many of them only saw him for his money, but did that even matter in the long run? He had forgiven Wickham countless times over the years for behavior far more abhorrent than simply being a gossip or a matchmaking mother.

And as for Miss Elizabeth, all she had done was laugh at his foolishness and ignore him. But even before that, she simply had the misfortune of being the woman Bingley had singled out at the assembly. She literally had done nothing but sit there, and he spoke as if she was the dirt under his boots, not good enough to even dance with.

The enormity of his arrogance, his conceit, and his selfish disdain for the feelings of others felt like a boulder had landed on his shoulders.

Yes, he was a Pharisee.

Chapter 5

Elizabeth followed her family out of the church, her heart troubled by the sermon she had just heard. She had apologized to Mr. Darcy for her behavior at Netherfield, but the fact that she had slandered his character to the entire county after his ill-judged remarks at Meryton made her feel ashamed.

The weather was fine, so Elizabeth told her parents she would walk home. Not only would it allow her time to think in private, but it would also free her from an overcrowded carriage with squabbling younger sisters.

She hadn't gone more than a few yards down the road when she heard her name being called. Turning, she spied Darcy walking quickly towards her. She groaned. *Great, the last man I wish to see right now.*

Pausing to allow the gentleman time to catch up, Elizabeth wrestled with the decision about what to do once he arrived. She had already been so forthright with him over their last several encounters that she wanted to show she could carry on an appropriate conversation, perhaps about the weather.

On the other hand, the message from that day's sermon made her wish to unburden herself by apologizing to him yet again. *But does he even know that I've been speaking poorly about him? An apology might only make things worse for him, even if it does alleviate my own guilt.*

Prudence won over selfishness, and she decided to stick to general pleasantries. Just as she came to this conclusion, he arrived at her side, slightly breathless.

"May I escort you home to Longbourn?" he asked, lifting his elbow.

She blinked at him in surprise—she was only expecting a short conversation, after all—and unthinkingly took him loosely by the arm.

The pair walked in silence for some moments before she said, "The weather is very fine today."

"What?" he asked, startled. "Oh, yes, very fine indeed."

They fell once again into quiet; the only sounds that were heard were from the birds in the trees and the leaves under their boots.

Unable to bear the quiet any longer, Elizabeth gave in to her remorse. "Mr. Darcy—"

"Miss Elizabeth—"

Darcy had spoken at the same time. They both paused, then Elizabeth giggled. "Please, you go first, sir."

"No, no, ladies first. I insist."

She sighed. "Very well. I cannot go any longer without apologizing to you for something that I'm afraid may cause you some pain."

He looked at her in alarm. "Pain?"

"Well, distress, perhaps. You see, I heard your comment at the Meryton assembly about my appearance. I'm afraid it wounded my vanity, in spite of the comment's veracity, and I took great delight in recounting the tale to many of my acquaintance. Today's sermon has quite humbled me, and I wish to once again ask for your forgiveness. I'm afraid that most of Meryton does not think very highly of you, and I contributed to that. I should have kept the situation to myself, as you were having a private conversation."

Darcy stopped and stared at her. "You have to be one of the most incredible women I have ever met."

"I beg your pardon?" Elizabeth dropped his arm, surprised at his response to her admission of guilt.

He paced in front of her. "You see, all my adult life I have been surrounded by women who are looking for marriage. They present their best selves to me, seeking to hide all of their flaws. They flatter and simper, and they agree with everything I say, even if I contradict myself."

The pacing stopped, and he looked her straight in the eyes. "You are the first young lady I have ever met who not only admits to her mistakes and apologizes for them, but has never avoided sharing her true opinions with me. It is rare, indeed."

Elizabeth blushed furiously and shifted her weight on her feet. "It was not my intent—"

"And that's precisely what makes it so incredible."

Realizing he had stopped walking, he once again offered her his arm in escort, and she took it without hesitation. As they continued towards Longbourn, Darcy spoke again.

"You see, Miss Elizabeth, my purpose in escorting you home was to gain the privacy and time required to apologize to *you*. Bingley told me that you had heard not only my words at the assembly—which I will explain in a moment—but also what Miss Bingley and I discussed on your first evening at Netherfield."

The genuine remorse on his face caused her heart to soften.

He then said, "At first, I was quite angry that you would dare to be upset over statements I felt were true and that weren't meant for your ears. As I thought on it, however, I knew I had behaved ungentlemanly, and last night I came to the decision to apologize to you as soon as possible."

She raised an eyebrow at his candor over his belief that his words had been natural and just. "I appreciate your apology, Mr. Darcy," she said with a frosty voice.

"No, you mistake me! That was how I felt prior to services today, but so much has changed since then. If the Son of God had been a guest at Netherfield, would I have spoken about Him in that way? Would I have allowed others to do so? Would I have refused to be seen standing up with Him—er, if He were female, that is."

Elizabeth laughed at this statement, and Darcy's ears turned pink, but he persevered. "I realized then that I treat my tenants and servants better than I treated you. Not that you deserve better than

221

them because of your station, but you *do* deserve equal compassion and civility. I felt guilty last night for snapping at my valet and causing the servants extra work, but where was my remorse for how I disdained you, both in public and in private."

He took a deep breath, his voice trembling with the last sentence. "I think my parents and my God would be very dissatisfied with my behavior and the pride I exhibited. I was raised with good principles, but I've been conceited in thinking I have followed them. I may be above my peers in how well I treat those of the lower classes, true, but that does not excuse how I treated you."

At a bend in the road, Longbourn came into view in the distance. Darcy stopped and took one of her hands. "So please, Miss Elizabeth, allow me to sincerely apologize to you. Not just for speaking unkindly where you could hear it, but for thinking so poorly of you when you did absolutely nothing other than not be born into high society."

A burst of surprised laughter came from her lips. "You are not who I thought you were, Mr. Darcy, I must admit. It makes me feel even more shame for treating you as I have."

"I was exactly who you thought I was," he countered, dropping her hand, "until last night and today. Knowing you has turned me into a better man, and I thank you for it. Please, forgive me for the discomfort and pain I have caused you."

"Only if you forgive me as well," she replied.

"But of course," he said immediately. "Your perceived sins are much less than my own."

"Oh, this will not do!" she cried out with a hint of laughter. "We will not be able to agree on who is more at fault. I think we ought to forget the matter entirely and move forward. For my part, I forgive you for everything, and I will think only of the past as its remembrance gives me pleasure."

He smiled. "Very well, then. I will remember with pleasure the debates we have shared and the way you give your pert opinions."

"Now that I will accept," she said with amusement. "Now come, Mr. Darcy, let us shake hands and go into Longbourn as friends."

"Yes, friends," he said huskily as he took her small hand in his large one.

Epilogue

Darcy and Elizabeth did indeed become the best of friends. Bingley and Jane's courtship led the way to marriage, which threw Elizabeth and Darcy in one another's paths quite often over the next six months.

It wasn't until Mr. Bennet's cousin, a certain Mr. Collins, came to visit Longbourn that Darcy realized his friendship with Elizabeth had blossomed into love.

Mr. Collins—who was quite upset at not being able to visit Longbourn when he had planned due to Jane's wedding and poor roads—arrived in the spring of the following year. He was offended by the fact that the most beautiful of his fair cousins had chosen to marry without waiting for his visit, but he did his best to hide his upset.

His eyes immediately settled on Miss Elizabeth as his future partner in life, but her impertinent attitude towards Darcy was extremely unsettling. Being the nephew of the great Lady Catherine de Bourgh meant—to Mr. Collins, at least—that Darcy should be treated with all civility and respect that his rank demanded.

The oafish man's attempts to counsel his cousin and temper her brazen nature led to frequent confrontations, especially when such suggestions were made in the presence of Darcy himself. It finally took Mr. Bennet leaving his study to forbid Mr. Collins from even speaking to Elizabeth at all for the conflict to end.

Highly offended, Mr. Collins turned his attention towards Mary, who was happy to receive them. She thought her sister to be quite foolish in not paying heed to a man of the cloth who would also be the master of their home someday. A proposal was quickly made—within two days—and Mary looked forward to the prestige above her sister that her married state would create.

Sadly for Mary, her triumph did not last long. Darcy was so horrified by the fact that he could have lost Elizabeth to a bumbling parson if not for her father's interference that he immediately resolved on marrying her himself.

"I cannot imagine life without my best friend, Elizabeth. The idea that you could be tied to another man, lost to me forever, is abhorrent. I beg you to relieve my suffering and consent to marry me."

Elizabeth, who had not dared hope that her budding feelings of love towards Darcy would be returned, accepted his proposal with alacrity. Knowing that his family—especially Lady Catherine—would try to interfere, a special license was purchased and the wedding was held.

The entire family attended, except for Mary, who was kept in the dark about the entire affair. Elizabeth knew that if her sister discovered the engagement, she would write to Mr. Collins at Hunsford, who would then inform Lady Catherine.

When Mr. Collins heard about the wedding, he was so irate that he attempted to call off his engagement with Mary. Mr. Bennet was furious about the man's cowardice and threatened to take him to court over the broken contract; the papers had been signed already, after all.

Mary was able to pacify Mr. Collins with a reminder that if he married her, he would then be brother to Darcy, which was a much higher position than simply the parson to Lady Catherine. This appeal to Mr. Collins's vanity allowed the union to proceed.

For her part, Mary never did forgive Elizabeth for what happened, which gave Elizabeth no cause to repine. The two sisters had never been close, and Elizabeth refused to base her happiness on someone whose foremost thought was selfishness.

Darcy and Elizabeth's marriage was one full of happiness and laughter. There were times when Darcy reverted to his former, prideful self, which usually resulted in a row. It never lasted long, however, because Elizabeth always knew the best way to punish him for such speeches.

To Yield Readily

Mr. Bingley is a man who is easily persuaded by the strong opinions of his friend and sisters. When he leaves Netherfield Park after hosting a ball, Miss Bingley sends Jane Bennet a letter, which Mrs. Bennet insists is read aloud at breakfast. Upon hearing that his fairest cousin has been abandoned, Mr. Collins offers a proposal of marriage. Mr. Bingley's return six months later has him discovering a very different Longbourn than the one he saw before. What will he do now that he's realized he yields too readily to others?

Chapter 1

Elizabeth watched as her elder sister fought back tears. She and her sisters, father and mother, and the loathsome Mr. Collins were taking breakfast, and Jane had just received a letter saying that the entire party had left Netherfield less than forty-eight hours after the ball they'd hosted.

The elegant, hot-pressed paper had arrived as they were dining. Mrs. Bennet insisted on Jane's reading it immediately. It was clear from Jane's face that she was loath to share the contents, but Mrs. Bennet would brook no opposition. Jane hung her head and read in a whisper.

When my brother left us yesterday, he imagined that the business which took him to London might be concluded in three or four days, but as we are certain it cannot be so, and at the same time convinced that when Charles gets to town, he will be in no hurry to leave it again, we have determined on following him thither, that he may not be obliged to spend his vacant hours in a comfortless hotel...

Mr. Darcy is impatient to see his sister, and to confess the truth, we are scarcely less eager to meet her again. I really do not think Georgiana Darcy has her equal for beauty, elegance, and accomplishments, and the affection she inspires in Louisa and myself is heightened into something still more interesting from the hope we dare to entertain of her being hereafter our sister.

I do not know whether I ever before mentioned to you my feelings on this subject, but I will not leave the country without confiding them, and I trust you will not esteem them unreasonable. My brother admires her greatly already; he will have frequent opportunity now of seeing her on the most intimate footing; her relations all wish the connection as much as his own; and a sister's partiality is not misleading me, I think, when I call Charles most capable of engaging any woman's heart.

With all these circumstances to favor an attachment and nothing to prevent it, am I wrong, my dearest Jane, in indulging the hope of an event which will secure the happiness of so many?

Upon hearing these last words, Mrs. Bennet flew into hysterics the likes of which her family had never seen before. The matron had consoled herself when Elizabeth rejected Mr. Collins the day prior that at least Jane would marry Bingley and provide for her after her husband's death.

The idea that *both* of her daughters—in whom she'd had such high hopes the day of the ball—had now been foolish enough to lose their chances of a good match was more than she could take. Her breath came faster and faster, as did her harsh, shrill words.

"Jane, what did you do to drive him away? How could you do this to your poor Mama? You and Lizzy, ungrateful girls, the both of you! Oh, what will become of me when your father is dead and gone?"

And with that, she fell into a motionless heap atop her breakfast table.

The reactions at the table were mixed. Jane gave a horrified gasp, and Elizabeth jumped from her seat and ran to her mother. Lydia laughed at the sight of their mother face down in her plate of eggs and jam, which caused Kitty to join in. Mary lectured all of her sisters on the importance of honoring their mother and father.

Mr. Bennet merely rolled his eyes and excused himself from the table, only stopping to call for Hill to send a servant for Mr. Jones as he left. Elizabeth stared in dismay at her father's callous reaction to her mother's genuine faint, and she began to rub Mrs. Bennet's hands and fan her face while awaiting Hill's arrival.

Looking around at the chaos, Elizabeth was dismayed to see Mr. Collins watching Jane with a slight leer on his face. Horror struck, she realized that Bingley's departure and Miss Bingley's hints in her letter had informed the odious parson that the most beautiful Bennet daughter was no longer likely to become engaged shortly.

Hill arrived at that moment, and she and Elizabeth guided a somewhat cognizant Mrs. Bennet up the stairs and into her bed. After ensuring that all was well in that quarter, she rushed down the stairs to join Jane.

It was too late.

Flying through the door and into the breakfast room, Elizabeth arrived just in time to see Mr. Collins place a kiss on Jane's hand, then walk smugly towards the exit. "Excuse me, Cousin Elizabeth," he said haughtily, "but I must go and speak to your father."

With that, he left the room.

"Jane, what have you done?" Elizabeth asked in a horrified whisper. "Please, please don't tell me you've accepted an offer of marriage."

Jane's face was whiter than Elizabeth had ever seen. "Yes, Lizzy, I have."

"But why?"

"Mr. Bingley is not going to return. This offer is the only one I have ever received, and I am twenty-two years old. This will save our family, and I will be of great comfort to my parents."

Elizabeth grasped her emotionless sister's shoulders. "No, Jane, I cannot allow this. I will go to Mr. Collins and tell him I have changed my mind and will accept his offer from yesterday. That will make you free to find love. I have never trusted Miss Bingley. What if she is lying? What if Mr. Bingley does return in a few days, only to find you engaged to someone else?"

"But what if he doesn't?" Jane cried out, shocking Elizabeth with her outburst. "What if I turn down Mr. Collins, and Mr. Bingley never returns? What then, Lizzy? I've only had one suitor in my entire life, and that was seven years ago. No, I will not risk it. A bird in the hand is worth two in the bush, they say."

"But we always swore we'd marry for love," Elizabeth whispered.

Jane shook her head. "But don't you see? I *am* marrying for love—for the love of my family. I will be able to care for my mother and sisters for their entire lives."

Tears filled Elizabeth's eyes. "How can you bear it? He is ridiculous."

Jane straightened her shoulders. "Mr. Collins may not be the most intelligent of gentlemen, but he is not vicious. He has a comfortable home, and I will one day be mistress of the home in which I grew up. In any case, I have given my word, and I shall not break it."

The firm resolve on Jane's face was a look Elizabeth had never seen before. "Very well, Jane. I will argue with you no longer."

The eldest Bennet daughter's shoulders dropped in relief. "I shall depend upon you, dear Lizzy, to write to me frequently and visit me in Hunsford."

"Of course," Elizabeth said, hugging her sister tightly.

Their embrace was interrupted several moments later when Mr. Collins returned to the room. "My dear Jane—as I may now call you—your father has given his consent. Is it not wonderful? You have made me the happiest of men!"

Mr. Collins waxed on at length about the infinite pleasures that awaited himself and Jane as a married couple, including the attentions that Lady Catherine would pay once he returned with a wife. Elizabeth bore it for as long as she could before excusing herself and fleeing into the hallway.

She ran down the corridor and entered her father's study without knocking first. He looked up, startled at the intrusion. "Lizzy, what on earth?"

"How could you, Papa? How could you give that horrible man your permission to marry Jane?"

He sighed and put down his book. "I take it you mean Mr. Collins? Unless another man whom I do not remember has requested permission?"

"Papa, this is no time for sarcasm," she scolded. "This is Jane's *entire life* that's being affected, not just Lydia's happiness for a day over a new bonnet or ribbon."

"What would you have me do, Lizzy?"

"Rescind your permission! Write to Mr. Bingley and bring him back. Let Jane go to London with the Gardiners and have a season."

"Lizzy, you know as well as I do that none of those options are possible. Jane is of age; my permission and blessing are not required. Mr. Bingley will do what he likes, regardless of whether I send him a letter. Jane has been with the Gardiners several times now."

"That is only because we have small dowries and little but our charms to recommend us."

"I know I should have put aside a certain amount every year to persuade worthless young men to marry my daughters," he said, the creases in his face becoming more pronounced. "Your mother and I always intended to have a son. When it was clear that wouldn't happen, it seemed too late to do anything about it."

"And now Jane will pay the price for your negligence," Elizabeth said bitterly.

"Enough, Elizabeth," her father replied sharply. "It is done, and there is nothing more to be said on the matter. Your sister will have a ridiculous husband, but she won't be the first to have to deal with a foolish spouse. She'll bear it as well as any of the rest of us have."

She gave her father a look of disdain. "I will never forgive you for this." And she walked out of the room, slamming the door behind her.

Chapter 2

"Oh, Lizzy, I am so glad you are here!" Jane came rushing forward from the front step of the Hunsford parsonage and embraced her sister, with Mr. Collins trailing behind.

The two hadn't seen one another since Jane's wedding day, when Elizabeth had held her sister after the wedding. Jane had sobbed for a quarter hour after repeating her vows, then pinched her cheeks and joined the wedding breakfast with a smile.

Four months had passed since that day, and Elizabeth had grown concerned about the letters she was receiving from Jane. Although the words were all that was correct, there was a melancholy tone that grew progressively worse with each missive.

Jane never expressed any private emotions in her letters either. They were all discussions about chickens, members of the parish, Lady Catherine's recent advice, and other mundane details. Elizabeth only wished to know what her sister's true feelings were, and everything she read revealed nothing about Jane's state of mind.

"Come, my dear," said Mr. Collins. "Let us bring your sister inside and show her your new home."

"Oh, yes, of course," Jane agreed immediately.

Elizabeth was ushered into the home and given a thorough tour of each room, including the shelves in the closet of each bedroom.

"Lady Catherine herself recommended I do this before your sister arrived," Mr. Collins said. "Nothing is beneath her notice. Is that not right, my dear?"

"She is a very attentive neighbor," Jane said evenly, without a hint of emotion.

Eventually Mr. Collins left the sisters alone in the guest room so Elizabeth could unpack her clothes. As she did so, she watched Jane carefully, who was avoiding eye contact by hanging the dresses in the small wardrobe.

Unable to bear the silence any longer, Elizabeth walked over and embraced her sister once more. Jane turned and sobbed into her sister's arms. The two remained there for a long time before Jane pulled back and wiped her eyes.

"I'm sorry, Lizzy. I don't know what came over me. I am happy, truly I am. I have a kind husband, a comfortable home, and good friends in the parish."

"Of course," Elizabeth murmured in agreement, not knowing what else she could say.

The deed was done, after all. Jane was married, and there was no changing the situation. All Elizabeth could do now was provide support to her sister in any way she could.

"There may be something else causing my emotions to be a bit overwrought. I think... I think I may be with child."

Elizabeth's jaw dropped open. "Jane, oh my goodness!"

Jane blushed and lowered her eyes. "I have missed my courses the last two months, and I have been feeling ill in the mornings. The midwife says that is all typical for someone in the family way."

Doing her best to block any images from her mind about how exactly her sister had entered into such a state, Elizabeth once again gave her sister a hug.

"This is wonderful news!"

"I only hope it is a boy," Jane said. "Then all of Longbourn's future is secure."

"I pray it may be so. Now, tell me how I can best help you while I am here."

Elizabeth spent the next fortnight helping her sister with her regular duties, including feeding the chickens and helping Cook in the kitchen. It was labor that had once been beneath Jane in Meryton, but Lady Catherine apparently had strong opinions about the proper roles of a parson's wife.

They were invited to dine at Rosings twice—an experience Elizabeth found brought her more sorrow than joy. She had prepared to find great amusement in the lady, as she sounded quite ridiculous when quoted by Mr. Collins, but the condescending way with which her ladyship spoke to Jane quite infuriated Elizabeth. It was all she could do to hold her tongue.

It was with great relief that Elizabeth received the news that Lady Catherine would not require their presence for several weeks, as her ladyship's nephews were expected to arrive shortly for their annual Easter visit. Mr. Collins was quite distraught at the idea, but Elizabeth relished the freedom for both herself and her sister.

Jane's stomach had begun to swell gently, and the midwife informed her that she would soon feel the quickening within the following month or so. At Elizabeth's private suggestion, the elderly woman also told Jane that Mr. Collins ought to be told to avoid performing his husbandly duties until six months after the babe came. Jane had turned a furious red at this, but she accepted the counsel gratefully.

Elizabeth kept herself quite occupied with helping her sister around the parsonage, but Jane made sure that her younger sister took time each day for a private walk to regain her spirits after being in close proximity to Mr. Collins for lengthy periods of time.

One day, as Elizabeth walked through her favorite grove of trees, she came upon a gentleman who was inspecting a tree.

"Mr. Darcy!" she cried.

He turned around quickly and looked at her in astonishment. "Miss Elizabeth? Whatever are you doing in Kent?"

"Visiting my sister, sir," she replied stiffly. "And it's Miss Bennet now."

"I was unaware you had family in this part of the country."

"My elder sister Jane married our cousin Mr. Collins in December.

His patron is Lady Catherine de Bourgh."

"Ah, I see. Lady Catherine is my aunt," he replied stiffly.

Elizabeth simply nodded. "Well, I shall not intrude on you any longer. Good day, Mr. Darcy."

She walked away as swiftly as she could, leaving the tall man to gape after her.

All the emotions she'd suppressed since arriving in Hunsford and witnessing Jane's unhappiness for herself rose to the surface upon seeing the man whose friend had abandoned her sister so cruelly. She sat on a nearby log and burst into tears.

Only a few moments later, she heard a deep voice calling her name. "Miss Elizabeth, wait!"

She groaned to herself and stood, mopping the tears from her face with a handkerchief in her pocket. Before she could turn and run, Darcy came through the trees.

"Please forgive me for being so abrupt just now. I was surprised to see you here, that's all."

She forced a smile as he approached her, continuing to speak. "I wanted to—Is everything all right, Miss Eliz... Bennet? You look unwell."

Elizabeth gave a light laugh, trying to mask her emotions. "That is the second time you have spoken poorly about my appearance, Mr. Darcy. I do hope that will be the end of it now."

"That was not my intention! I merely meant to inquire after you, as you seem to have been crying. Wait, the second time? I do not recall..."

"She is tolerable, but not handsome enough to tempt me," she quoted in a deep voice meant to be a mockery of his own.

He paled. "Who told you about that?"

"I heard it myself! I was sitting no more than a few feet away from you!"

"It wasn't meant for anyone but Bingley. I was in a foul mood that night and wished for nothing more than to be left alone."

"Yes, that seems to be your standard, doesn't it? Simply ignore the people in the room whom you feel are beneath you."

Darcy's brow furrowed. "I don't understand your meaning."

Elizabeth sighed. "Mr. Darcy, from the very first moment we met, you displayed your clear disdain for all others around you. Like Miss Bingley, your actions and conversation led everyone to believe that you felt yourself far above them."

"To be quite frank, Miss Elizabeth, I *was* far above everyone in Meryton."

"In wealth, certainly," she agreed, "but that does not mean you have more value than anyone else who attempted to befriend you."

"I do not feel very comfortable amongst strangers and large groups. I would have thought that you, of all people, would have understood me."

Eyes widening, Elizabeth arched an eyebrow. "And why would I?"

"Because of all our time spent together! Surely you noticed all the attentions I paid you when you stayed at Netherfield and again at the ball. It was agony to force myself away from you, but I had to do it, for mine and Charles's sakes."

"I don't understand what you mean," she replied coldly.

He took two steps forward and grasped her hands in his. "I love you, Elizabeth. I know I shouldn't, what with your station in life so below my own. Your mother threw your sister at my friend, and it is clear now that she married someone else so quickly that her heart was untouched. With no dowry and no connections, I knew there was no future for us, so I left. Can you ever forgive me for abandoning you?"

He released one hand and touched her cheek. This contact startled her out of her shock, and she jerked away from him.

"Love me? *Love me?* You must be joking! Mr. Darcy, if you were paying me attentions in Meryton, I assure you that I never was made aware of it. You spoke poorly about me, you broke Jane's heart, and now you denigrate the people I love most in the world!"

"You... you didn't know?"

"Of course not, you daft man! All you did was stare at me to find fault, call me tolerable, ignore my friends and family, and dance once while remaining silent! If that is your idea of a courtship, I would hate to be on the receiving end of your indifference!"

"But I—"

"And even if you *had* been paying your attentions to me, how could I ever accept them when you consigned my most beloved sister to a lifetime of heartbreak and misery?"

"I don't—"

"She *loved* your friend, Mr. Darcy. Jane accepted all of his affections and attentions because she felt the same way in return! When we received Miss Bingley's note that her brother had all but abandoned Jane without a word or any chance of return, it devastated her. It also caused Mr. Collins to propose to my elder sister the day after he asked *me* to marry him! In her misery, she accepted. Had I known that was to occur, I would have accepted him myself to spare her the suffering she now endures on a daily basis!"

"I had no idea—"

"Of course you didn't! You have absolutely no connection with my sister whatsoever, yet you deemed yourself the proper person to speak on her behalf to your friend? To decide the feelings of someone so wholly unconnected with yourself? Your pride knows no bounds, Mr. Darcy, and I shall never forgive you for this."

With that, she whirled around and sprinted back towards the Parsonage, deaf to the calls of the man behind her.

Chapter 3

Darcy drummed his fingers impatiently on the surface of his table at White's. He was meeting Bingley at the club for dinner, and it was the first time the two men had seen each other since Netherfield.

Once Bingley had returned to town, his sisters kept him occupied with event after event to help him forget his latest angel, now Mrs. Collins. Once the season ended, Bingley had gone to Staffordshire to visit an uncle, while Darcy had gone to Rosings.

It was now mid-summer, and Bingley was only just returning from his trip. Darcy had debated confessing his sins to Bingley in a letter, but he knew his friend deserved the truth face-to-face. As Miss Bennet was already married, there was nothing either of them could do.

At first, Darcy had decided against even telling Bingley anything about what he had learned from Elizabeth. But disguise was every sort of his abhorrence, and the truth weighed on his conscience like an anvil.

Bingley arrived at last and settled himself down in the chair across from Darcy.

"Hey there, old chum! How are you doing?"

Darcy gave a small smile. "Tolerably well, I suppose. And yourself?"

"Tired. I only just arrived from Staffordshire, but I was eager to see you—and get away from Caroline. I've only been back for two days and already she's nagging me about the ladies I should meet, the debutantes I should dance with, and the places I should escort her. I'm about to go mad. You're lucky Miss Darcy still has a few years before her coming out."

Darcy nodded and opened his mouth to reply, but Bingley continued. "I've been thinking I might return to Netherfield. There are still several months left on the lease, and I did leave rather abruptly. I enjoyed my time there and the people I met, and the fishing would be good this time of year. What do you think?"

Remorse filled Darcy with this evidence that Bingley had not overcome his attraction to Miss Bennet. He sighed. "I think that would be a good idea. I imagine it was quite difficult for the servants to be let off so suddenly and by letter."

Bingley's eyes widened. "I didn't even think of that. I imagine Caroline would have taken care of that, don't you?"

"While your sister has some admirable hostessing skills," Darcy said delicately, "she may not be aware of the usual protocols that gentlewomen follow when things like this occur. Usually the servants are paid for the time they were hired for, not just the time they worked. Letters of reference are provided as well."

"Oh," Bingley faltered. "I don't think that happened. I mean, I pay the bills, and I think I would have remembered something like that."

Darcy's eyebrows raised. "The servants weren't paid *at all?*"

"Erm… maybe? I mean, Caroline wouldn't not pay them their wages, right?"

Darcy sighed. "I think your sister may simply be untrained in how to run an estate. It doesn't matter the *why* for now, but you had best find out what happened immediately and make it right."

"Will you come with me? Help me sort it all out? I have many amends to make, not just to the servants but also to the neighbors."

"I'm afraid I am needed at Pemberley," Darcy replied. "I have been away for far too long, and there are situations needing my attention."

When Bingley looked deflated at this information, Darcy added, "I will be available via letter to answer any questions you may have."

His friend brightened somewhat. "Thank you, Darcy. I appreciate your friendship and guidance more than words can say. I think I will enjoy returning to Netherfield. Some of my happiest memories are there, like the ball we had. It was the twenty-sixth of November, and I will always cherish it."

Darcy winced, wondering how on earth he was going to bring it up. "You may find that some of the neighborhood has changed since you went away."

"Nonsense!" Bingley laughed, waving a hand. "It has only been half a year; what could have changed in such a small town in that short amount of time?"

The grandfather clock at the side of the room chimed, and Bingley looked at it with surprise. "Oh no, I am late meeting with my solicitor! Well, it was good to see you, Darcy. I'll be riding out first thing tomorrow morning, so this will probably be the last time we see each other for a while. Farewell, my friend!"

With that, Bingley dashed out of the club before Darcy could get his friend to listen. Groaning, he realized that he would need to send a note that night to Bingley's home, or else his friend would show up in Hertfordshire thinking the eldest Bennet daughter was still available.

***

Bingley rode his horse up the drive to Longbourn, happiness brimming in his chest. He had arrived at Netherfield the day before, surprising the few servants that were kept on the permanent staff.

To his horror, he discovered that not only had Caroline declined to pay the servants until the end of the initial contract, but she also refused to release any wages at all or sign any letters of recommendation, declaring that the services rendered had been below standard.

Infuriated, Bingley immediately authorized his bank to give each servant triple what they were owed, taking it out of Caroline's allowance. He then promised double wages to any servants who were willing to return, promising to give the full amount of the wages to the housekeeper in advance.

This has gone too far, he thought grimly. *It is one thing to act like a snob around others of her social standing, but to withhold someone's livelihood... it defies all reason.*

He then wrote a letter to his solicitors to discover the exact terms of his father's will with regard to Caroline's guardianship. Perhaps he had the ability to force her into a marriage with someone who could control her.

By the time it was all resolved, it was well past calling hours. A few questions to the housekeeper informed Bingley that there were no public events that evening either. He resigned himself to a long evening on his own.

Bingley hadn't informed his sisters he was going to Netherfield or even that he was leaving town. As far as he was concerned, they could stay where they were at. He owed them nothing, not after they did all they could to take him away from the woman he loved.

He wished Darcy had accompanied him, but he supposed it was for the best. If only the note Darcy had sent hadn't fallen into a puddle on the way. Bingley was unable to decipher any of it, but he figured if it were urgent, Darcy would send another one on to him.

Realizing he had arrived at Longbourn, he dismounted and knocked on the door. The housekeeper admitted him to the drawing room, where Mrs. Bennet was sitting with Elizabeth, Mary, and Kitty.

"Oh, Mr. Bingley!" The matron began waving her handkerchief and speaking very quickly. "We had no idea you had returned to Netherfield! It has been so long since we've last seen you. What brings you here?"

Looking desperately around the room for Jane, Bingley finally replied, "Well... er... that is, I completed my business in town and in the north, and I am looking to have some peace and quiet for the next several months."

"And do you come alone, sir?" Elizabeth asked, giving him a curious look.

"I do. My sisters are remaining in the Hurst townhouse, and Darcy has returned to Derbyshire for the time being."

Elizabeth merely raised an eyebrow. "And none of them had any objections to your return?"

Bingley blushed. "My sisters are… unaware of my presence here. As for Darcy, it was he who encouraged me to be a good master of an estate. I was unaware that my sisters had left things so haphazard. I had only intended to be gone a few days, you see."

"Yes, well, when one has a temperament that yields readily to others' opinions, it is easy for a few days to turn into six months."

Her stare was beginning to unnerve Bingley, so he turned back to Mrs. Bennet—who had been watching the discussion with wide eyes—and asked, "Pray, Mrs. Bennet, how has *everyone* in the family been these last months?"

Mrs. Bennet just continued to gape at him, and Elizabeth replied icily, "Papa is in his study, Lydia has gone to Brighton with the regiment, and my elder sister, *Mrs. Collins*, is in Kent with her *husband*."

Bingley felt as if he had been punched in the stomach. His face turned pale and his hands felt shaky. "I… I see," he stammered. "I was unaware of Miss Bennet's marriage. Is she… is she well?"

"As well as can be expected for someone in her delicate condition," Elizabeth answered. "My cousin proposed to her the same day we received your sister's letter about your leaving Netherfield permanently. It was just two days after your ball, I believe, and your sister was quite eager to follow you to town. Which puts me to mind. How is your courtship with Miss Darcy progressing?"

"Courtship? Of Miss Darcy?" Bingley asked in bewilderment.

"That is what your sister said in her letter." Elizabeth's voice was like steel, anger in her eyes. "It was not twenty minutes after Jane learned of your permanent departure and attachment to someone else that she accepted Mr. Collins's offer."

Had Bingley been standing, he would have collapsed. Jane... *his* Jane... was married to someone else because she'd thought he'd abandoned her?

Unable to think of anything to say, Bingley simply stammered out a few words of congratulations. While Mrs. Bennet prattled on about her hopes for dear Mrs. Collins's future, Bingley felt Elizabeth's eyes boring into him. After several minutes, he could bear it no longer.

"Excuse me," he interrupted, standing quickly. "I believe I must be going now."

"Oh, but you must stay for dinner!" exclaimed Mrs. Bennet, unaffected by having her words cut short. "You are quite in our debt; I have not forgotten, you know."

"Another time, perhaps," he said, struggling to breathe. Why was the air suddenly so thick? His cravat so tight?

He gave a cursory bow, then dashed out the door. Once outside, he leaned against the doorframe, his chest heaving as he fought to inhale.

"Mr. Bingley?"

Chapter 4

Bingley looked up, still struggling to breathe. The world seemed to be spinning, and he was barely able to focus on the young lady in front of him.

"Mr. Bingley, are you quite all right? Shall I have someone fetch Papa, or perhaps Mr. Jones?"

Through the haze, he was able to make out Catherine Bennet, standing in front of him, with his forgotten hat in her hands.

"No," he gasped, "I just need a moment to calm myself."

"You're upset about Jane being married," she said. "I imagine it came as quite the shock. We were all surprised when she accepted him."

His distress fading, Bingley looked up at Kitty. The kind expression on her face reminded him so much of Jane that he almost gasped. "You look just like her," he said.

She smiled. "You and Lizzy are the only two who have ever said that. I don't think I'll ever be as pretty as she was, but our hair and eyes are the same." Looking down, she startled. "Oh! Your hat! That is, you left it inside, and I was just bringing it out to you. Here." She thrust it into his hands. "I'll let you have your solitude now."

"No, please stay," he said without thinking. At her shocked face, he added, "That is, I would like to know more about how all of this happened. Did Caroline really send a letter that said I wouldn't return because I was courting Miss Darcy?"

Kitty's face fell. "Yes, it was really quite awful. The letter arrived at breakfast, and Mama forced her to read it out loud. Once she—

Mama, that is—realized what it all meant, she began to chastise Jane for not having done more to entice you to a formal arrangement. Mr. Collins proposed just after Mama collapsed, and I think Jane was desperate to secure our future."

"It is all my fault," he said. "I have doomed the kindest woman I have ever met to a lifetime of misery with a pompous fool."

She giggled; then her face grew solemn. "I know Lizzy thinks it's your fault," she said matter-of-factly, "and Mr. Darcy's and Miss Bingley's too."

"What do you think?"

"I think you're a good man who is young and easily led."

The astonishment Bingley felt must have shown on his face, because Kitty's eyes widened slightly. "Oh dear, I do apologize," she said. "I've gotten into a dreadful habit lately of just saying what I think all the time."

"That isn't necessarily a bad thing," he replied.

"It is if it causes hurt and pain. That wasn't my intention; you see, I think I've been a lot like you have. I used to do everything Lydia told me to do because I wanted her to like me, and I didn't feel confident in my own preferences and decisions. It's taken her departure—and Lizzy's help—for me to see that I can be myself and have my own opinions."

"That is very wise of you," he said. "I think you are correct; I allowed myself to be too easily swayed. Your sister—the current Miss Bennet, Miss Elizabeth as was—confronted me about it at Netherfield when your eldest sister was ill. I didn't think much of it at the time, but she and Darcy had a debate about this aspect of my character one evening."

"What was their conclusion?"

"I don't think there was one; I felt so uncomfortable with the contention that I made some sort of joke about always listening to Darcy's advice because of his height, then I begged them to desist."

She gave a small laugh. "Maybe it is for the best that you and

Jane didn't marry. She is of the same character, and Papa always joked that if the two of you were to marry, every servant would cheat you and you would never resolve on anything as you would each wish to give way to the other."

This comment took Bingley aback; he had never really considered what married life with Jane would be like other than the bliss of having her gentleness and beauty as a constant presence in his life.

The conversation was interrupted by Mary coming to the door. "Kitty, honestly! How long does it take to give a man his hat? Mama is wanting you."

Kitty blushed and handed Bingley his forgotten item. He bowed in gratitude. "Thank you for your kindness, Miss Kitty. I hope we will be able to speak again sometime."

With that, he rode away towards Netherfield, having much to ponder on. Those musings continued for the next week, during which time he fished, hunted, and sorted out his household.

Upon discovering that he still had guardianship of his younger sister and could arrange a marriage for her, he instructed his solicitor to find someone of strong will but kind character—it would not do to have her mistreated, after all—who was in need of a wife with a dowry.

He then wrote to Caroline and the Hursts, informing them that if Caroline had not settled upon an engagement by the end of the year, he would choose a husband for her. He further explained about deducting the servants' extra wages from her pin money and informed her that he would no longer cover any bills that exceeded her quarterly income.

In between those duties, Bingley met daily with the steward to try to understand how the estate was run. He also paid calls on all the neighbors, going out of his way to make amends for having left without so much as a note before.

In the back of his mind, however, was the comment Kitty had

made about his and Jane's compatibility. He had been drawn to her gentle nature and truly loved her, but he never once thought about what it would be like with two such obliging people as marriage partners.

The more he thought on it, the more Bingley realized that his lack of tenacity could have caused many difficulties in their future, had there been one. Would he have always given way to Caroline and Darcy? Would he have defended his wife against their cruelty? Would he have even noticed it happening?

A week after his initial call to Longbourn, Bingley realized he wished to speak to Kitty again about all of his musings. She had given good insight before, and he wanted to know more of her thoughts on the matter.

His call the following day at Longbourn turned into what would become a daily ritual of walking in the garden with the fourth Bennet daughter. Elizabeth and Mary took turns accompanying them, but that usually consisted of the chaperon sitting on a bench with a book. Bingley was grateful for that habit, as both women usually fixed him with stern glares each time he arrived at the house. He had hoped Elizabeth would go to the Lakes with her aunt and uncle as had been discussed.

Bingley and Kitty eventually moved on from debating the defects of his character—and hers—to general topics of conversation. They discovered they had a mutual interest in plants and their different uses, as well as art.

One July afternoon, about a month after his return to Netherfield, his daily call to speak with Kitty began in an unusual manner. She was more subdued than usual, and her face was marred with heavy worry lines etched deep into her skin.

"What is the matter?" he finally asked after having to repeat a question for the third time with no response.

She hesitated, then said, "I've received a letter from Lydia that has me greatly concerned. A month or two ago, I would not have thought much of it other than it being a grand adventure, but now…"

A sense of foreboding came over him. "What did she say?"

"I think… I think she might be planning to elope with Lieutenant Wickham."

"What?" Bingley gasped out. Wickham—the horrible prat who had cheated Darcy and nearly destroyed Georgiana—had his grasping claws on Kitty's sister?

"She mentioned being the next to marry out of all her sisters and expressed her delight at being able to sign her next letter as Mrs. Wickham. She swore me to secrecy, but I do not feel right about it."

"You did the exact right thing," Bingley assured her. "With your permission, I will speak with your father. I think you need to tell your Elizabeth."

Kitty nodded, not meeting his eyes. Without thinking, Bingley took one of her hands in his and lifted it to his lips. "Don't worry," he said reassuringly, "I will take care of everything."

Tears filled her eyes, and she gently squeezed the hand that held hers before going to join Elizabeth on the bench. He watched the younger girl withdraw a piece of paper from her pocket and show it to her elder sister, who read it and gasped in alarm. Satisfied that the situation with the ladies was under control, Bingley entered Longbourn and asked to see Mr. Bennet immediately.

He could hear Mrs. Bennet's effusions from the drawing room about the fact that he was speaking with Mr. Bennet, but it could not be helped. Closing the door muffled the sounds, and Bingley took a seat across the desk from Mr. Bennet.

"Well, Mr. Bingley. I had expected this conversation to happen last year. As it so happens, Jane is now married and no longer available. Now that we've got that settled, you may go."

Bingley gaped at Mr. Bennet, then said, "Mr. Bennet, I am not here to discuss Mrs. Collins. My appointment is in regard to Miss Lydia."

"Lydia, eh?" Mr. Bennet raised his eyebrows. "I had not expected you to be the sort of man to wish for such a silly wife, but I've been wrong about your character before. Very well, you may have her."

This was spoken with a smirk on Mr. Bennet's face, which enraged Bingley in a way that he had never before felt. Did the man not know the very real danger that was facing his family, or did he simply not care?

"Mr. Bennet," he said severely, "I am here because Miss Kitty received a letter from her younger sister stating that she had intentions to elope with Mr. Wickham. Knowing the man as I do, I can absolutely guarantee you that he has no designs on marrying her. Instead, she will be ruined, as will her remaining unmarried sisters."

The older man sat up straight in his seat, all traces of amusement gone from his face. "Lydia told Kitty this?"

Bingley nodded.

"And Kitty told you? Why would she confide in you and not in her family?"

"I cannot answer that for her, but I am glad she did. I am here to offer my help. I would like to request Miss Kitty's hand in marriage; then I can go to Brighton and act on your behalf to bring Lydia home for the wedding without any hint of scandal."

Chapter 5

Elizabeth watched with tears in her eyes from the front of the church as Kitty walked up the aisle to join Bingley at the altar. She had been honored that Kitty had requested Elizabeth be the sister to stand up with her rather than Lydia.

No one was more surprised than Elizabeth on that fateful day when Kitty revealed Lydia's letter. Bingley had left his meeting with Mr. Bennet to come outside and request a private interview with the younger Bennet daughter. After the tête-à-tête, he raced away towards Netherfield on his horse.

"Kitty, are you out of your senses to be accepting this man?" Elizabeth had exclaimed when Kitty shared the news of the engagement. "Only seven months ago he was courting Jane, only to abandon her!"

"I know," Kitty replied in an even tone, "but I think he has changed quite a lot since then. In November, he was dependent on his sisters and Mr. Darcy to guide him in all things. Since that time, he has taken Miss Bingley in hand—he arranged a marriage for her since she refused to obey him in not exceeding her pin money! Furthermore, he…"

Elizabeth listened as Kitty rambled on about all the things she and Bingley had discussed during their frequent walks. Unable to help but be impressed at Bingley's reform, Elizabeth also agreed that the reason for Bingley's retrieval of Lydia was the perfect cover to squelch gossip.

The main concern was Jane; how would she feel upon hearing that the man she once loved was now to marry her younger sister?

Elizabeth wrote to Mrs. Collins, begging her to share her true feelings. Jane's letter in return spoke only of her hopes for the future happiness of Mr. and Mrs. Bingley. Nothing was said about her own emotions.

As Jane was too close to her confinement to travel for the wedding, Elizabeth resolved to travel to Kent to assist her sister as soon as Jane came to term. This meant that only Lydia or Mary would be available to accompany Kitty on her wedding trip, and to everyone's astonishment, she wanted Mary.

Lydia had thrown a conniption of epic proportions upon being returned to Longbourn. She blamed Kitty for ruining all of her fun—and that was before she realized everyone now knew about her intended elopement. This betrayal sent Lydia into a tantrum far beyond anything that had been done by a child over the age of five.

The commotion roused the normally indolent Mr. Bennet to action. He declared Lydia to no longer be considered out, and she was sent back to the nursery. To everyone's surprise, Mrs. Bennet was in complete agreement with this decision. No one except Kitty—who told Elizabeth—knew that Bingley had made a few comments about his hopes that Lydia's wild behavior wouldn't affect her remaining sisters' chances of a good marriage.

It was all of this information that caused Elizabeth to feel as she did on the wedding day. She hoped desperately for Kitty's sake that Bingley had indeed changed, and her heart ached for Jane, the woman for whom Bingley was not willing to step up and take control.

Wiping away a tear, Elizabeth looked across from her at Darcy, who had come from Derbyshire to attend the wedding and stand up with his friend. He and his sister had arrived late the day before, and she hadn't had a chance to speak to him other than in greeting.

Elizabeth was mortified to discover from Bingley that not only had Darcy encouraged the return to Meryton, but he also had done much to protect Lydia from Wickham's charms. Lydia had repeatedly assured everyone that Wickham would come for her, but

Bingley privately told them that Darcy had bought up the scoundrel's debts and called them in, forcing him into debtor's prison.

The day before the wedding, another letter had arrived from Jane for Elizabeth, this one expressing her gratitude for two additional servants and the nursemaid that Bingley had hired for the Hunsford parsonage.

When Elizabeth asked Kitty, the soon-to-be bride confided that it wasn't Bingley at all who was doing it, but rather Darcy. Apparently he felt tremendous guilt over Jane's situation, Kitty had explained, and was doing what he could to make her life as comfortable as possible. As he was unrelated to Jane, his involvement needed to go through someone who was family, and Bingley was being forced to take the credit of it all without actually being of use.

As she watched Darcy stare determinedly at the wedding ceremony that was being performed, Elizabeth could not help but feel desperate to speak with him privately. She had so much gratitude for what he had done for her family. He truly was a good man, and she owed him an apology for the appalling way she had treated him the last time they'd spoken.

Within minutes, the wedding was over and everyone was headed to the breakfast, which was being held at Netherfield. Bingley's sisters had refused to come to the wedding, so Mrs. Bennet was acting as hostess for the event. As Netherfield was much larger than Longbourn, it seemed the more logical place to celebrate.

Elizabeth was introduced to many of Bingley's acquaintances from town, but none of them held her interest. She was only desirous to find Darcy and speak with him before he could leave. As fate would have it, she spied him and his sister gathering their wraps and departing the room.

She rushed through the crowd and followed the siblings to the front door. "Wait!" she called when she saw them about to go through.

The pair turned around, giving Elizabeth time to reach them.

"Mr. Darcy, might I have a word with you, please?"

He looked at her with a mixture of surprise and trepidation. "Here in the foyer, of course," she added hastily.

Darcy looked at his sister, who was eyeing the scene with a hint of curiosity. "Dearest, do you mind delaying for a few moments?"

She immediately acquiesced, and Darcy followed Elizabeth a few steps away. He looked at her expectantly, and she took a deep breath. "I'm sorry, Mr. Darcy, but I could not allow you to leave without offering you my deepest thanks for all you have done for my sisters, especially Jane and Lydia. I also need to apologize most sincerely for the abhorrent things I said to you when we last spoke in Hunsford."

His eyes widened. "I had hoped my involvement to remain private. I am disappointed Bingley was so little to be trusted."

She shook her head. "It was Kitty who told me, but Jane had written to ask that I thank Bingley for the extra servants. I was concerned about what his generosity could mean, which forced Kitty to confide in me."

"I see. Well, if you must thank me, let it be for yourself alone," he said. "As much as I respect your elder sister, I believe I thought only of you."

A feeling of warmth spread from her stomach and up through her chest. "Truly?" she whispered. "I would have thought you had hated me after I accused you so abominably to your face."

"What did you say that I did not deserve?" he replied. "You spoke rightly of my interference in your sister's happiness; your words were nothing but the truth, and I am heartily ashamed of my behavior when I was last here."

"I hope… I hope this won't be the last time we see you," she said daringly. "Otherwise I fear I shall regret the loss of your friendship my entire life."

Darcy's eyes lit up at this statement, but he said cautiously, "You have been, and always shall be, my friend… and perhaps more, someday?"

This last bit was stated more as a question, to which Elizabeth eagerly replied, "Yes, I think I would greatly enjoy coming to know you better, even though I already think of you as one of the best men of my acquaintance."

"Well then, perhaps we had best accept Bingley on his invitation to remain at Netherfield a bit longer."

With that, Darcy took Elizabeth's arm, and together they went back into the celebration.

Epilogue

Jane Collins sat in the rocking chair of the Longbourn nursery and looked at the tiny six-month-old boy she held in her arms. The black of her mourning gown contrasted with the little white outfit he was wearing.

"You fell asleep quickly today, didn't you, Tommy?"

She laid the baby in the crib and stroked his cheek before walking away to check on her three-year-old twins, William Collins Bennet and Elizabeth Colleen Bennet. They were also fast asleep in their small beds, likely dreaming of the adventures they would have the next day.

She left the nursery and went to her bedroom, which was the same one she had shared with Elizabeth only five years before. It was difficult to believe that she was already a widow before she had even reached the age of thirty.

Everyone in the family had rejoiced when Jane gave birth to both the heir and his twin sister. The pregnancy and labor had been quite traumatic for her body, and it was some time before the midwife allowed Mr. Collins to resume his scheduled, weekly visits to his wife. Tommy was the result of one such visit, providing even more joy at the security of Longbourn.

Although she was never truly happy in her marriage to Mr. Collins, she had to admit that he was a caring husband. When she expressed her sorrow during her first pregnancy that Longbourn would be lost to the Bennet name—which it had held for over two hundred years—he immediately offered to allow their sons to be christened with their mother's maiden name as their surname.

Jane had felt more sorrow than she anticipated when her husband had caught a chill that turned into pneumonia the previous winter. He eventually succumbed to the ailment, leaving her seven months with child.

Lady Catherine had attempted to oust Jane from the Parsonage in spite of her advanced condition, an act which brought the Darcys to Rosings for the first time since their wedding. Infuriated over the treatment of his sister-by-marriage, Darcy turned the tables on Lady Catherine with the help of the Earl of Matlock, the great lady's brother.

Now Anne was the mistress of Rosings, and Lady Catherine was banished to the dower house with only a few servants to attend her.

After delivering Thomas Colin Bennet, Jane removed to Longbourn so her eldest son could grow up learning to care for the estate. While she knew her father wouldn't bother to teach his grandson anything about management, she knew she could rely on her brothers-in-law to assist.

At first, she was terrified about seeing Bingley and Kitty together—as they had purchased Netherfield—but to her very great surprise, her heart was completely untouched the first time she laid eyes on them. Instead of heartbreak, she felt only sisterly affection, and she was relieved that time truly did heal all wounds.

Now having been at Longbourn for five months, Jane was finally beginning to feel as if it was home again. It helped that General Fitzwilliam—cousin to Darcy—had taken up residence in a leased home nearby. He had visited Rosings quite often, and he and Jane had found much to discuss over the last five years.

Nothing improper had ever happened, of course. Jane would never allow herself to stray in her thoughts or break her vows. His friendship, however, was much appreciated during some of the loneliest months of her young life with a husband who cared for her but did not understand her.

As she was about to move into half-mourning in a few weeks,

she allowed herself to dream once again. Perhaps there would be a happily ever after for her after all, the way there had been for Kitty and Elizabeth.

Even if not, she had no cause to repine. She found great joy in her children, and watching her sisters' bliss made Jane feel content in a way she never would have with Bingley. After all, had she married him when he was still so easily swayed, she would never have felt secure or confident. Now, having been mistress of a home and wife to a parson, she knew exactly who she was and what she was worth.

Indeed, Jane would always be grateful that Mr. Bingley was willing to yield so readily to his friend and sisters all those years ago.

And Then the Murders Began

Netherfield has a reputation for being a haunted manor house. The rumors stem from two centuries of unnatural deaths and horror for each tenant who has resided there. When Elizabeth is invited to stay to tend to her sister Jane, she discovers a murder most foul. Will she and Darcy be able to solve the murder and break the curse? Or are they doomed to suffer the same fate as all the previous inhabitants?

Chapter 1

It is a truth universally acknowledged that a single man in possession of a good fortune must be in want of a wife.

However little known the feelings or views of such a man may be on his first entering a neighborhood, this truth is so well fixed in the minds of the surrounding families, that he is considered as the rightful property of some one or other of their daughters.

And then the murders began.

Mr. Charles Bingley, a young man of large fortune from the north, had leased an estate in Hertfordshire near the small town of Meryton. Netherfield, as the estate was called, had been empty for quite some time due to a horrific slew of murders and deaths that occurred each time it was occupied over the prior century.

Netherfield had not been let in at least four decades, so only a few people remained who were old enough to remember the events that had occurred when Lord Sedwick, the Earl of Kilmorey, had let the estate with his young family. Within a week, the entire family had been killed by nefarious means, but no one was ever apprehended.

All the members of the gentry who lived in Netherfield had met with untimely ends or tragic accidents; whether they were the owners or merely tenants, it was immaterial.

So when news spread in Meryton that Netherfield was let at last, the gossip flew quickly. Those of the older generations—such as the senior Mrs. Goulding, who lived in the dowager house behind Haye Park—predicted the first death would occur within a fortnight.

Those who were more middle-aged, like Mrs. Bennet, were torn between hoping the wealthy gentleman would bring a large party of friends to marry their daughters and being terrified that the stories they heard as children would once again repeat themselves.

As for the younger generation who were currently on the marriage mart—such as the Bennet sisters and Charlotte and Maria Lucas—how much belief they put into those stories was in direct proportion to their sense and intellect. Kitty, Lydia, and Maria were in raptures over the drama that was to befall their new acquaintances, whereas Charlotte and Elizabeth were more inclined to hope Mr. Bingley did not have a distant heir who was jealous of his fortune.

It was with this mix of emotions that the entire neighborhood came together for the Meryton assembly shortly after Bingley and his guests were established in the house. The young man had promised Sir William that they would be attending, and everyone was eager to make their acquaintance.

The assembly had already begun when the doors opened to admit Bingley, along with two ladies and two gentlemen. Everyone began murmuring with one another as rumors and gossip made their rounds. Sir William approached the group and took them around to make introductions.

Mrs. Bennet was in a near state of hysteria by the time it was her family's turn to be introduced to the newcomers. It was clear that Bingley only had eyes for Jane, from whom he immediately requested a dance. He then introduced his friend Darcy, who stood silently nearby.

"Have you come as eager to dance as your friend?" Mrs. Bennet asked, her gleaming eyes taking in his tall stature, handsome face, and expensive clothing.

"I rarely dance," Darcy replied shortly before turning and striding away.

"Well, I never!" Mrs. Bennet pulled out her fan and waved at her face in indignation. "With any luck, he will be the first of the group gone."

Elizabeth let out a burst of surprised laughter, then hastily covered her mouth. "Mama!" she scolded, torn between horror and amusement.

Her mother merely raised her nose into the air and sniffed. Elizabeth shook her head, then excused herself to join Charlotte across the room, who was just completing a dance with her brother. She related what her mother had said, and the two girls giggled and discussed the ludicrousness of there being an actual curse on a house.

Their conversation was interrupted when Charlotte's father asked her if she would like to stand up with him. She beamed, unaccustomed to this attention from a parent who considered her to be an old maid. Elizabeth watched with delight as her friend once again took a place on the dance floor.

As she tapped her foot in time with the music, Elizabeth spied some movement next to her. Bingley had approached Darcy and was telling the man to dance instead of standing around in such a stupid manner. She smirked at this, but the smile faded from her lips a few moments later as she heard the taller gentleman declare her not handsome enough to tempt him.

Well, she thought with a huff, *perhaps the curse should take him after all!*

This thought brought the cheer back into her face, and she was able to soothe her wounded pride by imagining some irate ghost taking its displeasure out on the tall, wealthy man.

After she mentally allowed her wit to flow long, she felt a bit of guilt. After all, while she did not precisely believe in a curse, there was no denying that terrible things had occurred at Netherfield in the past, and those victims were real people.

No matter how much he may have insulted me, he would not deserve such a cruel end.

She resolved to not think too harshly of Darcy and to give him the benefit of the doubt the next time they were in company with one another.

Her opportunity to do so came much quicker than Elizabeth thought. Several days after the assembly—and after multiple calls had been made between the ladies of Longbourn and Netherfield— a note arrived for Jane, inviting her to dine at Netherfield, as the gentlemen would be supping with the officers of the newly arrived militia and the ladies of the house would need an occupation for the evening.

Mrs. Bennet refused to allow her daughter to take the carriage, as she hoped Jane might be delayed at Netherfield until she could see the gentlemen return. What no one anticipated, however, was Jane's ride on horseback being interrupted by a torrential downpour that resulted in her falling ill and having to remain overnight.

Lydia and Kitty were both thrilled and terrified that their eldest sister was in residence at the haunted manor home. Mary spouted a few scriptures concerning evil spirits, but she was largely ignored. The idea that Jane may be in danger sent Mrs. Bennet into hysterics that Elizabeth had never witnessed before.

"If she is murdered, what is to become of us all?" wailed the matron. "Jane's beauty was to secure us a future for when your father is dead!"

A note arrived from Jane to say that she was still unwell and that Mr. Jones had been sent for. Elizabeth immediately departed for Netherfield on foot, anxious to check on her sister's well-being.

She was dismayed to find Jane much more ill than she expected. The young woman was feverish, with a dreadful cough. Mr. Jones declared it to be a particularly bad cold and insisted she stay abed at least three days. Bingley urged Elizabeth to remain to care for her sister, and Elizabeth agreed with alacrity.

Her trunk arrived shortly after dinner, which had been a tedious affair, as Miss Bingley alternated between directing snide remarks to Elizabeth and cloying bits of flattery to Darcy. Elizabeth was grateful for the excuse to remove herself for the evening to tend to her sister and unpack her things.

Once Jane was asleep and a maid was installed in a comfortable seat near the window, Elizabeth made her way to her bed in the adjoining room. Whether it was the stress of the day or the memories of the haunted tales that Lydia had repeated frequently that morning, Elizabeth was unable to sleep. Every noise startled her out of a light slumber, and after a full hour of tossing and turning, she decided to seek out a book.

After lighting a candle, she made her way down to the library that Bingley had shown her earlier—which was woefully neglected and had very few volumes on the shelves. She browsed them, finding only books about crop rotation or other more masculine pursuits. A copy of *Fordyce's Sermons* caused her to make a face; she wasn't that desperate.

Frustrated, she ran her hands over the top shelf, where she was unable to see. Thick dust rained down on her, but she ignored it in the hope that a forgotten novel would be found on the top shelf.

Just as Elizabeth was about to give up and take one of the farming books, her hand brushed against a slim volume. She pulled it down and wiped the grime from a blank cover. After turning to the first page, she found an elegant handwritten script on faded yellow paper—it was a diary!

Confident that it could not belong to any of the newly arrived Netherfield party, she tucked it into a pocket on her dressing gown. Eagerness to read the timeworn writings replaced any fear she'd had. She brushed her hands off before once again picking up her candlestick.

When she turned back towards the door to head to her room, the light from Elizabeth's lamp shone on a woman's slipper peeking out from behind a settee. Not wishing for it to become lost under the furniture, she moved forward to pick it up and place it on a small table.

As she approached, Elizabeth noticed the shoe was actually on a foot, which was attached to a leg. A sense of dread welled within her, and her mind shouted at her to stop, but her body refused to obey. She peered around the sofa and let out a horrified scream.

Miss Bingley lay on the floor, open eyes staring blankly ahead, blood covering her face and dress.

Chapter 2

A scream echoed through the halls of Netherfield, and Darcy sat up in bed, alarmed. He had only just sent his valet away after spending the previous half hour being prepared for bed.

A second scream followed the first, and Darcy leaped out of bed. He threw on his dressing gown and sprinted towards the door. Down the hallway, both Bingley and Hurst were sticking their heads out of their respective doors.

Someone screamed for the third time, causing Darcy to rush down the hall in the direction of the sound. Several footmen had gathered near the library, and he pushed his way through the crowd.

There stood Elizabeth, looking down at something on the other side of the sofa.

"Miss Elizabeth? Was that you screaming?" he asked.

She looked at him with wide eyes and pointed towards the ground. He came around the corner of the sofa and let out a shocked gasp.

"What is it, Darcy?" Bingley asked from behind him.

"Don't look, Bingley," he warned. "This is not something you will want to see."

"What is it?" his friend repeated, craning his head to look.

Gently moving Bingley backwards, Darcy turned to the room in general. "That's it. Everyone out of here immediately. You!" he snapped at the butler, "make sure not a single person leaves this house. That includes servants and residents both. Have at least three servants stand guard at each entrance."

The butler nodded and, straightening his shoulders, began to give everyone assignments. Darcy turned to his valet, who had followed him from where he slept in the dressing room. "Roberts, I need you to ride immediately for the doctor and bring him here as quickly as you can."

"There's only an apothecary, but he also has training as a coroner."

Darcy spun around at Elizabeth's voice, which cracked as she spoke. She cleared her throat. "Mr. Jones, the apothecary, is whom you should fetch. His house is in Meryton, the blue one across from the haberdashery."

"I know the one," Roberts said. He gave a brief bow, then left the room at nearly a run. Had Elizabeth been in a different frame of mind, she might have giggled at the posh servant moving like a tenant child at play.

"Darcy, I demand to know what on earth is going on," Bingley cried.

Darcy hesitated and looked at Elizabeth, who met his gaze with tear-filled eyes. He heaved a great sigh, then said, "Bingley, I think we should adjourn to the study."

"Please, don't leave me on my own," Elizabeth's voice broke. "Jane is sound asleep—the apothecary gave her some laudanum—and I do not want to return to my room. I know there's no such thing as a curse, which is why I didn't mind staying here with my sister, but now—"

Her voice trailed off, and Darcy felt his empathy stirring inside of his chest. The poor thing was probably witnessing a traumatic death for the first time. As magistrate in Derbyshire, Darcy had experience in these sorts of things, but a sheltered young woman would not have seen injuries like this before.

"Of course," Darcy said softly. "Why don't we head to the drawing room next door instead?"

Bingley opened his mouth to object, but Darcy gave his friend a sharp look. "Bingley, let's make sure there is some brandy in the room. I think even Miss Elizabeth will be wanting some."

The sharp tone of his voice compelled Bingley to obey without complaint. When they were settled, Darcy poured three glasses. He pressed one into Elizabeth's hand. "It will help, but just sip it."

"Now, will you please tell me what the devil is going on?" Bingley cried in agitation once Darcy had taken his seat.

"I am so sorry, my friend. I wished to wait until we were all settled before I informed you. The servants needed to be dealt with, as well as the coroner."

Bingley went a bit pale. "Is someone injured? What happened? Who?"

Darcy swallowed hard. "On the other side of the sofa was a body. It appears someone had been bludgeoned to death. There was quite a bit of blood."

"Who was it? One of the footmen? Has there been a robbery?"

"No, it was..." Here Darcy's voice trailed off, and he looked down at his glass, unable to form the words.

"It was Miss Bingley," Elizabeth said in a whisper.

Bingley looked at her in bewilderment. "What? Caroline? No, that's not possible. There must be a misunderstanding, a mistake of some kind. She's upstairs in bed, asleep, like the rest of the household."

"I'm sorry, my friend, but it was your younger sister. That is why I did not wish you to come around and see. It was... quite the gruesome sight. It is little wonder Miss Elizabeth did not faint at the very sight."

Bingley slammed his glass down on the table, and Elizabeth winced, expecting it to shatter from the force. "No," he said firmly, rising to his feet. "You're wrong. There has been a misidentification, that's all. Here, let me go show you."

He took two steps towards the door, but Darcy grabbed his friend's shoulder from behind. "There is no mistake," he said in a quiet voice. "It was a tall woman with red hair and an expensive dress that was identical to the one your sister wore at dinner tonight."

"I recognized her necklace," Elizabeth said in a quiet voice. "I'm afraid there is no confusion, Mr. Bingley. I am so dreadfully sorry."

Bingley let out a wail and dropped to his knees, sobbing. At that moment, the Hursts came into the room, Mrs. Hurst clearly having been fetched by her husband. Elizabeth noted that in her loose dressing gown, it was clear she was with child. Elizabeth blushed at having noticed something so private.

"Charles, what on earth?" she asked with concern as she rushed over and knelt beside him.

"She's dead, Louisa," he said, crying into her arms. "Caroline is dead."

"What?" she exclaimed, looking around at Darcy for an explanation.

"I'm afraid it's true." Darcy briefly related the events thus far. "We must also fetch the local magistrate, but I'm not entirely certain who that is."

"That would be my father," Elizabeth said. "It's an office that he rarely has to perform in our quiet town."

"And how have you come to be involved in this?" Mrs. Hurst asked Elizabeth in an accusatory tone. She paused with a coughing fit, then continued. "I thought you were upstairs with your sister this evening."

Elizabeth's eyes widened, and she began to ramble. "After I got Jane settled for the night, I was struggling to sleep. The noises in the house, you see, are so different from Longbourn's. Between that and the rumors of the curse, I was wide awake. I thought I'd come to find a book, hoping to distract my mind and fall asleep. That's when... that's when I found her, and I screamed."

Mrs. Hurst looked hardly mollified by this explanation, but Darcy interjected before the grief-stricken woman could say anything further she might regret later. "That's the second time you've mentioned this curse, Miss Elizabeth. What do you mean?"

She looked in surprise at him. "Did no one tell you or Mr.

Bingley about it? I would have imagined the attorneys at least might have mentioned it at the lease signing."

"No one said anything other than that it had been empty for a long time," Bingley said in a hoarse voice from where he knelt on the ground.

Elizabeth bit her lip. "I see. Well, allow me to tell you the history of Netherfield."

After she finished reciting the macabre history of the manor's prior residents, there was silence in the room for several moments, interrupted only by a few coughs from Mrs. Hurst.

Perhaps she has caught Jane's cold, Elizabeth thought.

Mrs. Hurst erupted from the couch and shouted at her brother. "How could you have brought us here, Charles?" She ran out of the room, Mr. Hurst following close behind her.

Once again, the room fell into a silence that was broken only by Mr. Bingley's sobs. The poor man shook his head and wailed. "What have I done? I've killed my sister!"

Chapter 3

"I hope, young man, that that was not a confession."

All eyes turned to see Mr. Bennet and Mr. Jones standing at the door, both with grim looks on their faces. Behind them, Roberts said, "Mr. Jones recommended we collect Mr. Bennet on our way here, as he is the magistrate."

"Very good," Darcy said. "Thank you, Roberts. If you could please report to the butler and receive an assignment. I don't want a single servant alone until inquiries have been made."

Mr. Bennet raised an eyebrow. "Mr. Darcy, you have experience with this type of situation?"

Darcy flushed. "I am the magistrate in Derbyshire. While never with the upper classes, we have had a few situations similar to this one. I did my best to follow protocols as I understand them."

The master of Longbourn nodded slowly. "I would much appreciate your insights while we look into this. That is, of course, only after we are able to determine your guilt or innocence."

Elizabeth gave a slight gasp, which called attention towards her. "Lizzy?" Mr. Bennet asked, dismay on his face. "What are you doing in here so late at night, unchaperoned, with two gentlemen?" He crossed to the room and took her glass from her. "And drinking brandy?!"

Anger flashed across his face as he turned towards the two young men. "I trust there is a reasonable explanation for this."

"Miss Elizabeth is the one who discovered Miss Bingley's body," Darcy said stiffly. "She was in quite the shock, so we brought her in here to explain the situation to Bingley. The Hursts were with us until only a few moments ago when Mrs. Hurst fled the room in tears. Her husband gave chase to try to calm her, I imagine."

"And Jane?"

"She is in her room, asleep," Elizabeth whispered. "A maid is there. I couldn't sleep; Lydia's wild talk of the cursed manor and all that." She gave a bitter laugh. "I went in search of a book. It seems there is more to this curse than I gave credence."

Mr. Bennet frowned at his daughter, but it quickly softened. "Now, now, Lizzy, none of that. You are not my most intelligent daughter for nothing. As tragic as this experience is, there is a logical explanation, not a supernatural one."

She sighed. "I know, Papa, but you must admit the coincidence is somewhat disconcerting, especially given that no one has been caught before."

"That was before your intelligent father was the one investigating," he said with a forced smile. "Now, I need everyone to return to their rooms until we have had a chance to interview them— including you, my dear."

"Please, Papa," she begged, "I'd rather not be alone right now. Could I wait here while you question everyone? I swear I won't speak a word."

Sighing, Mr. Bennet reluctantly agreed on the condition that she sit in a chair behind the door so as not to be seen by those being interviewed.

"Mr. Darcy, as you and Mr. Bingley are currently present, I will speak with you first. But before that, Jones and I need to see the body. Mr. Bingley, could you—"

"Allow me to show you," Darcy said quickly. As they left the room, Darcy explained, "I didn't actually allow Bingley to see his sister's body. It was quite gruesome, and I didn't want that image in his mind."

"Very thoughtful of you," Mr. Jones said, speaking for the first time.

They arrived at the library, and Darcy gestured for the two men to go behind the couch. "I'm not entirely certain how Miss Elizabeth even noticed the body. She is quite hidden."

"I'll have to ask her." Mr. Bennet sighed and rubbed a hand over his weary face. "I hate that she has been exposed to such an atrocity, though I daresay that of all my daughters, she is the most equipped to handle it. God forbid it had been Jane."

Mr. Jones had knelt near Miss Bingley's body and was examining it. The other two gentlemen watched as the apothecary-coroner examined the deep wounds in the lady's abdomen, chest, and arms. Finally he sat back on his haunches. "I believe she has been dead for at least two hours but no more than three. Her body is quite cool, but she is only beginning to stiffen."

Mr. Bennet turned to Darcy. "What was going on at that time?"

He looked at the grandfather clock near the door, which stated the time was five minutes to midnight. "Miss Elizabeth was already in her room, having excused herself to tend to her sister after dinner ended. I believe a maid was present the entire time, so that should excuse her."

The lady's father raised an eyebrow at Darcy's first information being about his daughter and her innocence, but he chose to keep his observation to himself for the time being. "And the rest of you?"

"We were in the music room until about nine-thirty, which was when Bingley and I expressed a desire to retire. We have—had, now, I imagine—an early morning inspecting tenant homes and the stream on the southern border."

"That one tends to flood each spring," Mr. Jones said, having joined the other two men.

"Were you alone after retiring?"

Darcy thought back, then shook his head. "No, Bingley and I parted ways at the doors to our rooms. My valet was already present when I entered, and after I retired for the night, he took his place on the cot in the dressing room."

"He doesn't have his own room in the servants' quarters?"

Darcy shifted uncomfortably and said after a moment's pause, "I have made it my habit to have him present throughout the night whenever I stay under the same roof as an unmarried lady."

"Probably very wise of you," Mr. Bennet replied. "Very well, provided your servant independently confirms your story, I believe you can be cleared of any suspicion."

Some of the tension eased from Darcy's shoulders. Mr. Bennet continued. "Until I can speak with him, however, I would prefer you remain in my sight so that you cannot influence his testimony."

"Understood," Darcy said with a nod. "With your permission, I would like to return to Miss Elizabeth and Bingley and see to their welfare."

Without waiting for a response, he turned and strode out of the room, anxious to return to those who were suffering the most.

Mr. Bennet and Mr. Jones followed directly behind Darcy. They entered the room and discovered that the Hursts had returned and were ensconced on a sofa in the corner, Mr. Hurst patting his wife's back soothingly.

Elizabeth was sitting on the floor next to Bingley, who was still on his knees in the same place he had collapsed. A few quick questions from Mr. Bennet revealed that Bingley had also been in his room with his valet.

"Let's send for both men quickly to confirm these stories and get it out of the way," Mr. Bennet said.

Darcy rang the bell and ordered the maid who answered it to fetch the two servants. It took several minutes for them to be found, as the butler had assigned them to guard the doors to the outside along with some of the footmen. Each man independently told the same story their master had told, and all four—the valets, Bingley, and Darcy—were deemed innocent.

"Now that we have that resolved," Mr. Bennet said to the

Hursts, "I'm afraid I must ask the two of you where you were after the gentlemen retired for the night."

The married couple exchanged a look, then Mr. Hurst said, "Caroline was complaining about how Darcy wasn't paying her the attentions she wanted. We quickly tired of it and excused ourselves to bed. With no one else to speak with, I assumed she had gone to her own rooms for the night as well."

"And the two of you were together the entire time?" Bennet confirmed.

"Well, we have separate chambers, but they do connect with a door," Hurst said, glancing at his wife. "We both were in them the entire time."

"Can any servants vouch for the fact that you did not leave your rooms?"

Mrs. Hurst shook her head. "I dismissed my maid immediately after she loosened my stays. I simply wanted to go to bed." She stroked the swell of her stomach as she spoke, causing Mr. Jones to give Mr. Bennet a significant look.

"Completely understandable," Mr. Bennet said in a kind voice. "My wife was much the same with each of our children." He turned to Mr. Hurst. "And you, sir?"

"I'm afraid I don't quite remember," Mr. Hurst said, a sheepish look on his face. "I was quite a bit into my cups at that point. I vaguely remember falling into bed after my valet got my shoes and coat off."

Another look was exchanged between Mr. Bennet and Mr. Jones. "Very well," Mr. Bennet finally said. "I shall ask that both of you remain at Netherfield, but for now, you are both clear of suspicion."

The couple sighed in relief. "Then I will take my wife and myself back to our rooms," Mr. Hurst said, standing and offering his arm to Mrs. Hurst. "It has been an extremely difficult night."

Throughout the conversation with the Hursts, Darcy and Elizabeth had helped Bingley to a chair. Mr. Jones went to the young man and offered him a tonic to help him sleep, which was gratefully accepted.

Darcy looked at Elizabeth. "I will return to you in a few minutes after I get Bingley to his room and in the care of his manservant."

She looked at him in surprise. "As you'd like," she said, a bit of indifference in her tone.

Once the gentlemen had left, Mr. Bennet gave a sigh and said to his daughter and Mr. Jones in a dry voice, "Now all we have to do is interview the entire staff. That shouldn't be too much trouble, should it?"

Chapter 4

The interrogation of the servants at Netherfield proved to be an arduous ordeal. Elizabeth was amazed at how many people were in residence at the estate to help it function smoothly. As she took notes behind the door, eager to help her father discover the killer and prove the curse to be false, she marveled at how large a household it was compared to Longbourn.

At last, just as the sun was rising, Mr. Bennet finished speaking with the last member of the household. He stood from his chair and let out a groan as his joints cracked. "I need to sleep for a few hours before I can process all the information I was given."

He then turned to Darcy, who had remained at Elizabeth's side throughout the entire ordeal, offering her tea and fetching her fresh ink and paper. "I know you are not the master of the estate, but might I trouble you for a guest room? Not only am I so tired that I would fall off my horse trying to ride back, but I wish to avoid the interrogation that awaits me from my wife and daughters."

"Oh, Papa," Elizabeth said, "you can hardly blame them, given the circumstances."

Mr. Bennet grimaced. "You are quite right, my dear, but I am not in any sort of state to treat them with kindness and patience. Besides, Jones tells me that Jane is still too unwell to move, and I refuse to allow the two of you to remain here without my presence."

"It will be easier for you to conduct your investigation as well," Darcy responded. "Yes, I can have the housekeeper set up a room for you. I know Miss Bingley always kept several in readiness in case of last-minute visitors. For all her flaws, she was an excellent hostess."

"Her flaws?" Mr. Bennet raised an eyebrow. When Darcy blushed and opened his mouth to reply, Mr. Bennet waved a hand. "Never mind. I need sleep more than I need you to explain something you said in exhaustion. I recommend we all retire."

"What about Mr. Jones?" Elizabeth asked. "Will he need a room as well?"

Mr. Bennet shook his head. "He will oversee the removal of the body before he returns home. He may be my age, but as the primary medical man in town, he is more accustomed than I to being aroused from his bed and working throughout the night."

With that, all conversation came to a stop, exhaustion taking over. Darcy and Mr. Bennet first escorted Elizabeth to her room, then the two moved on to find Mr. Bennet a place to rest.

After checking on Jane—who was still sleeping soundly and had not awoken once, according to the maid—Elizabeth splashed some water on her face and collapsed onto the bed. She didn't think she would be able to sleep with the image of Miss Bingley's bloodied body etched into her memory. The sleep deprivation was more powerful than her mind, however, and she was asleep within seconds.

Several hours later, Elizabeth awoke to a knock at the door. "Would you like some breakfast, miss?" a young maid asked, holding a tray as she entered the room.

Realizing she was famished, Elizabeth gratefully agreed. A look at the window told her that it was long past luncheon. "What time is it?" she asked, blinking the sleep away from her eyes.

The maid informed her that it was one o'clock in the afternoon, and that Mr. Bennet had given strict instructions for Elizabeth to remain there until dinnertime. Jane had awoken, eaten her lunch, and returned to sleep already, so there was no need to check on her; Mr. Bennet had done so himself not half an hour before.

At first, Elizabeth chafed at this restriction. She wanted nothing more than to go for a long walk and clear her head of the horrors she had seen, so she put on her dressing gown, which was heavier than expected. The memory of brushing dust off a diary flooded back into her mind, and she eagerly pulled it out of her pocket.

It was a worn book and still looked filthy in spite of her wiping away dirt the night before. She carefully opened the front cover and turned to the first page, which she had briefly seen the night before.

A fine script covered the page, and it was dated fifty years prior, the same year the former tenants were so gruesomely murdered.

Well, at last my husband has returned to England. I thought he would never arrive after having been so long away in the New World. My dearest wish is that his wanderlust will ease and we can be a proper family once more.

He brought me this journal as a surprise, along with the news that we will be residing in Hertfordshire for the time being. I have loved being here thus far. The country is quite pretty, and I have a favorite walk that takes me to a nearby view. The locals call it Oakham Mount, and I struggle to not laugh at the name. If they could see the beauties of the mountains and peaks in the north, they would recognize their hill for what it is!

Elizabeth smiled as she read the words of a woman who enjoyed walking as much as she did. The hours passed and the death from the night before faded away as she dove into the life of a young wife and mother not many years older than her friend Charlotte Lucas.

In her journal, the woman—Lady Sedwick, Elizabeth presumed—expressed her love for her husband and children, and how she wished he were home more often. Although he had promised that his journeys were over, she expressed her melancholy during the times he was away when the children were merely infants. He had missed more than one childbirth because of his travels.

She spoke of her favorite foods and activities, including spending frequent time with her children. One entry gave a detailed account of playing hide-and-seek with them in the garden, where she had discovered a tall plant with beautiful flowers.

The gardener informed her that his grandfather—who had been

a young man when he was hired as a gardener for the first owner of Netherfield when it was built a century before Elizabeth's time—told him that the plant came from the New World and was supposed to ease coughing. It was so precious and rare, however, that strict instructions were given that it should only be used by the residents of the house, not the servants.

Lady Sedwick expressed her gratitude for the plant when she contracted a severe cold—most likely influenza—that caused her to expel blood from her lungs. Although the flowers had such a horrible scent within ten feet, none of the usual tonics and herbs could ease her cough. In desperation, she asked the housekeeper to brew a pot of tea with a couple of the leaves from the strange plant. To everyone's surprise, the plant was successful, but only when she drank a dose each morning.

Elizabeth's brow furrowed as the handwriting progressively became sloppier and the words more frantic. The faint worry that he might want to leave her slowly turned into a frantic obsession that he no longer loved her. *The children and I will be left all alone,* she wrote in an uneven hand, *and he will stop loving us. I cannot allow that to happen. I must keep our family safe, no matter what the cost.*

That was the last time Lady Sedwick wrote, as far as Elizabeth could tell. She thumbed through the pages, then stopped at one that was crumbled and stained brown. Straining her eyes to see through the splotches, she read the woman's last words.

It is done. They are all gone. My dear Robert will never be allowed to leave, and I have put the boys with him so they can be together for eternity. It was easier than I thought it would be; the knife was sharp, and their passing was relatively quick and painless. Now it is time for me to join them. May God forgive me, but He knows I could not let us be separated.

Elizabeth stared at the page in horror, and it struck her that the dark brown stains must be dried blood. She gasped and dropped the journal, frantically shaking her hands as if they, too, had been stained with the contact.

"She must have gone mad," Elizabeth said aloud. "Her life was perfectly normal until she became ill. Could the plant have made her lose her mind?"

She then gasped, realizing that if the plant was, indeed, the cause, then someone in the household must have ingested the leaves as well, and that person murdered Miss Bingley.

Throwing on a robe over her clothes and ignoring her hair, Elizabeth ran out of the room, determined to find the plant to inspect it.

Chapter 5

Fortunately for Elizabeth, there were no servants to prevent her from leaving the house. She ran into the extensive gardens and began to look around. She had never explored them before, so she was unsure of what she was looking for other than the description of its height and flower colors.

In her haste, she rushed around the corner of a hedge and ran directly into someone.

"Oomph!" she cried, falling backwards onto the damp grass.

"Oh, Miss Elizabeth!" Mr. Hurst extended one hand to help her up, the other holding a fistful of leaves. "I do apologize for knocking you down."

"No, no, it was quite my fault. I was in a rush and did not expect to see anyone else in the garden."

"Is everything well?" he asked, taking in her disheveled state of hair and lack of formal clothing.

Blushing, Elizabeth crossed her robe tightly across her frame. "I am merely looking for... something. I think it might be a clue to Miss Bingley's death."

Mr. Hurst's face tightened. "Such a terrible tragedy. Perhaps I could be of help? I am only out here to collect a few leaves from a plant. The housekeeper said the cook found a recipe for it in the household cookbook, and it helps with coughing."

Elizabeth froze and looked at him with concern. "Mr. Hurst, has your wife used these leaves before?"

"Why, yes, but only a few times. I must admit that I added a few extra in her tea yesterday evening, as I was concerned the coughing would harm the baby."

"Mr. Hurst," Elizabeth gasped, "you must drop those immediately! I have reason to believe they are poisonous!"

The gentleman froze and looked at her in confusion. She reached out to pull the leaves away, but as she did so, a shriek came from behind the shrubbery.

"I knew it!" Mrs. Hurst exploded from the bush, brandishing a fire poker. "I knew you were after my husband!"

The pregnant woman swung the poker at Elizabeth, who dodged out of the way just in time.

"Louisa, what on earth?" Mr. Hurst yelled, dropping the leaves and reaching for the weapon. "Give that to me before you injure yourself or someone else."

"Oh, I will definitely be causing injury, but it won't be to myself—it will be to this trollop!"

Mrs. Hurst advanced towards Elizabeth again, who backed up as quickly as she could. "Mrs. Hurst, I don't know what you think you saw, but I promise that I do not have designs of any sort on your husband in the slightest."

"Liar!"

She swung again, and this time Elizabeth was not quite fast enough. The poker crashed hard into Elizabeth's right arm, causing a horrible crunch. She cried out and collapsed to the ground. Cradling her injured arm with the other, she attempted to stand, but Mrs. Hurst was bearing down on her again.

"No, please!" Elizabeth cried out, desperately trying to get out of range.

"Louisa, stop!"

Mr. Hurst lunged forward and, from behind, grabbed his wife around the waist above her swelling belly, but not before the poker made contact with Elizabeth's ankle. Elizabeth yelped as Mrs. Hurst twisted in her husband's grip, trying to free herself.

"I won't let you take him from me!" the madwoman howled.

"First Caroline, now you! I won't let you have my husband, not when I finally can provide him with an heir!"

Elizabeth gasped, remembering that Mrs. Hurst was with child. No wonder poor Mr. Hurst hadn't just tackled the woman to the ground. He was afraid for his unborn child's safety too.

"Run, Miss Elizabeth!" he shouted, his portly frame struggling to control his wife as she thrashed about in his arms, trying to get to Elizabeth.

Finally able to make her way to her feet, Elizabeth stumbled in the direction of Netherfield. She wound her way through the garden paths, praying desperately that she was going the right way. As she went, she called for help at the top of her voice.

After what seemed like hours, she tripped onto the gravel that led from Netherfield's front drive along the garden and down to the stables. She stopped and panted for breath, fighting against the blackness on the edges of her vision. A manic shriek pierced the air behind her.

"Help me!" Elizabeth screamed, staggering down the lane.

She heard footsteps running along the rocks, but she couldn't tell if it was Mrs. Hurst from behind her or someone coming from Netherfield to help. To be safe, she picked up her pace, terrified that the drug-crazed pregnant woman had escaped her husband's hold.

"My God, Elizabeth!"

At the sound of Darcy's voice, she burst into tears and collapsed, unable to go another step. Strong arms encircled her, preventing her from plunging onto the sharp stones. She cried out in pain when he put pressure on her arm, and he immediately pulled back.

"Your arm—it's broken! Good Lord, what happened?"

"Mrs... Hurst," she choked out in between broken gasps. "Not... her fault... Drugged... poison... went mad."

Another eerie shriek echoed from the gardens, much closer this time.

"She... must have... escaped... her husband. Hurry... we must... stop her."

Darcy swept Elizabeth in his arms and sprinted towards the manor house, doing his best to not jostle Elizabeth any more than necessary. She gave no thought to the propriety of the situation; it was all she could do to remain conscious through the agony.

"Mr. Darcy, I demand you explain yourself this instant."

Elizabeth heard her father's bellow just as they entered the house, Darcy slamming the door closed behind them. "Quickly, we must get her somewhere safe until we can apprehend Mrs. Hurst," Darcy panted. "The woman attacked Elizabeth in the gardens!"

Bingley, who had come running towards the door along with the others at the sounds of commotion outside, turned white. "Louisa? But... why?"

"We can sort that out later," Mr. Bennet commanded. "You there," he snapped his fingers at the butler, who was watching the proceedings with wide eyes, "get the three strongest manservants you have and summon them here now. We must find Mrs. Hurst immediately."

"That shouldn't be too difficult," Darcy said, his breathing finally slowing. "She was coming out of the gardens just as we came up the steps."

As if to emphasize his ever-present accuracy, someone pounded on the front door. "Let me in!" shrieked Mrs. Hurst from outside.

Elizabeth shrank back against Darcy, not fully realizing she was in his arms. He gently tightened his grip and brushed a kiss on her forehead before whispering, "Don't worry, Elizabeth. I won't let her harm you anymore. She'll have to go through me first."

She was too dazed with pain and the shock of it all to fully realize the intimacy in his manner. All she knew was that his soothing tone and warm embrace wiped away her fears, and she felt safe, in spite of the danger.

Mr. Bennet was giving directions to three burly servants who had answered the butler's call. On the magistrate's command, the door was opened, and Mrs. Hurst flew into the room, brandishing the fire poker. One of the men caught it and pulled it from her grasp, while the other two gripped her arms and pulled her to the ground, forcing her arms behind her.

Mrs. Hurst began wailing, kicking, and even biting at the men, but they maintained their hold until her arms and legs were tied.

"Don't hurt her! Please, the baby!" Hurst came in through the door, blood dripping down his face from a cut above his eye that was rapidly swelling.

"It's not her fault!" Elizabeth cried out weakly. "She's been poisoned! It's not her fault!"

"Shh," soothed Darcy. "I will ensure she gets the best care. For now, though, we must get you looked at."

The next few hours passed in a blur. Darcy sent for his doctor from town to come look not only at Elizabeth but also Mrs. Hurst. He refused to leave Elizabeth's side, however, even in her chambers, despite Mr. Bennet's protests. It was only when Elizabeth gripped Darcy's hand as he was about to acquiesce that Mr. Bennet relented, but only until she was asleep.

Mr. Jones prepared to set her arm, but before she was dosed with laudanum, she shoved the journal at her father. "It's the plant. The curse is the plant."

He took it with some confusion but promised to read it. Mr. Jones forced a cup of bitter liquid down her throat, then began to move her arm. The pain was so intense she lost all consciousness.

Elizabeth awoke to a darkened room several hours later. She made to sit up but cried out from the pain of trying to use her broken arm to move herself. Jane, who had been sitting on the chair next to the bed, jumped up. "Lizzy, no, you must lie down!"

"Water," Elizabeth rasped, and Jane fetched a cup from the table, stopping to ring the bell on her way back to her sister.

Once the terrible dryness of her throat had been soothed, Elizabeth asked, "What has happened? How long have I been asleep?"

"About twelve hours, but—" Jane attempted to explain further, but the door flew open with a bang. Darcy strode in, followed closely behind by Mr. Bennet, Mr. Jones, and Bingley.

Darcy knelt at the floor beside Elizabeth and placed his hand on hers. "How do you feel?" he asked, his dark eyes intent on hers.

"A bit muddled," she said.

"That would be the laudanum," Mr. Jones answered. "It is almost time for another dose."

"I'd rather have the pain and a clear head," she replied.

Mr. Bennet said, "I understand, my dear. Perhaps you take some after we leave."

Elizabeth reluctantly agreed on the condition that she be told everything she had missed. "How is Mrs. Hurst?" she inquired.

"Always thinking of others," Darcy said.

The fond expression on his face caused her to blush, and she pulled her hand away from his. Only twenty-four hours ago, she was sure he was one of the most rude and arrogant men she had ever met. Since she found Miss Bingley's body, however, she had seen a tender side of him in his care for her, and it made her unsettled.

Although, everything else has been unsettling, too, she admitted to herself.

Mr. Bennet explained that he had read the journal, and he, too, was able to determine the true cause of Mrs. Hurst's actions. The plant had been found and destroyed, along with the recipe the housekeeper had discovered.

"Then it's all over," Elizabeth replied when his story ended, sighing in relief. "The curse was really the plant, and it cannot hurt anyone ever again."

"Exactly," Mr. Bennet said. "Leave it to my Lizzy to solve a mystery that no one else could."

"Her quick mind helped her piece it together," Darcy said, causing Lizzy to blush. "And while it's the end of the curse, I hope it's the beginning of something much happier."

And so it was.

Epilogue

Mr. Hurst had been relieved to discover the reason for his wife's actions. Apparently, he had suspected Mrs. Hurst of killing her sister. The night before, she'd accused Miss Bingley of attempting to have an affair with Mr. Hurst. He had then heard Mrs. Hurst leave the room shortly before the murder was determined to have occurred, but he was too afraid to tell anyone his fears, lest something happen to the baby.

Fortunately for the Hursts, Mr. Bennet was an intelligent, understanding man. He would not press charges against either of them, on the condition that they retire to the countryside for a full year under the care of two doctors. Hurst agreed with alacrity, and the couple was already on their way to the Hurst estate in York.

"Miss Elizabeth, you must allow me to apologize on behalf of my family. I—" Bingley's voice was too choked with tears for him to continue.

"It is absolutely no one's fault," Elizabeth assured him. "Had I not stumbled onto the journal, it could have ended much worse, and who knows what would have happened in the future."

The conversation was stopped when Elizabeth groaned with pain, the ache in her arm turning into an intense throbbing.

"I think that it's time we allow Elizabeth to take some laudanum and rest more," Mr. Bennet said firmly. "Jane, I will have you stay, as you are mostly recovered from your cold, but I insist that everyone else leave. Except you, Jones, of course."

Thus began the pattern of Elizabeth taking laudanum, sleeping, and then awakening only for a short period. This lasted for a week until she could move without the severe agony she once experienced.

Every time she awoke, she would discover Darcy at her bedside. At first, she was indignant at his compromising presence, but he assured her that a maid was in the hall with the door open at all times.

As she recovered, he read her poetry and engaged her in debates. They spoke of books and philosophy, as well as his sister and responsibilities at Pemberley.

Their time together blossomed into a true romance, which eventually led to marriage, beautiful children, and a lifetime of happiness together.

Thus, the new story in Meryton about events at Netherfield was the claim that true love broke the curse of the haunted manor.

Author's note: the plant described in this story that caused Mrs. Hurst (and others) to lose their minds is called Jimsonweed. It is a weedy annual plant with striking white tubular flowers and spiky seedpods. The leaves and seeds contain alkaloids that cause hallucinations.

Jimsonweed is native to North and South America, and it was used by indigenous peoples to produce intense spiritual visions with terrifying hallucinations and paranoid delusions. In small doses and prepared properly, however, it was used to treat asthma, coughs, and flu. That is why the first gentleman brought it back.

I *have* taken a few liberties with its properties to help it fit the story better. You can learn more about Jimson Weed on WebMD.

If Only They'd Had a Son

What if Lydia had been born a boy? Lyndon Bennet has turned out quite wild, having been spoiled by his parents for being the heir who would save them all. What difference will his cruelty and indifference to his elder sisters make in their lives?

Chapter 1

"Lyndon, come back here right now!"

Fourteen-year-old Elizabeth Bennet was about ready to strangle her ten-year-old brother. He had dipped poor Kitty's braids in the inkwell of the schoolroom, and the girl was in tears over her ruined hair.

"Elizabeth Bennet, I will not have you speak to your brother in such a tone of voice."

Mrs. Bennet's stern tones echoed down the hallway from the drawing room, where the woman was sitting with Jane, preparing for the young girl's come out.

Elizabeth sighed in frustration. It just wasn't fair. Lyndon was allowed to get away with anything, all because he was the heir. It didn't matter that she, Jane, and Mary were older, or even that Kitty was his twin. The boy had no care for anyone besides himself.

Mr. Bennet rarely took a hand in raising his son, other than giving him the occasional instruction in estate management. This was in part due to the fact that the man himself was of an indolent nature and rarely stirred himself from his study to guide his family.

For a time, Mr. Bennet had planned on sending his son away to school, perhaps Harrow or Eton, but Mrs. Bennet could not bear to be parted from her precious son. "What if he were to meet some misfortune away from home and die? What would become of us all?"

The small surge of hope that had accompanied Mr. Bennet's announcement was dashed by Mrs. Bennet's fears about her future. Thus Lyndon was allowed to run wild, ignore the governess who had been hired to teach him, and wreak havoc amongst the household without any recriminations.

This latest catastrophe—and catastrophe it was, as it would take weeks for the ink stain to wash from Kitty's fair hair—was merely one in a long line of misbehaviors that went well beyond usual childhood antics.

Oh, if only there was a way to get Lyndon to a school! Elizabeth thought. *Then perhaps he would have some sort of discipline.*

Eager to avoid the chaos of the house, Elizabeth chose to go for a long walk. Along the way, she thought hard about how she could make changes in her home. The only reason she even had the ability to think so rationally was because the governess had taken pity on her.

The woman's original mandate was to teach Lyndon, but as he refused to obey and Mrs. Bennet would not allow discipline, Miss Stewart had taken to instructing the Bennet daughters. Jane learned to sing and embroider very well, Mary was making decent progress on the piano, and Kitty's drawings improved every day.

It was Elizabeth, however, who was the governess's best pupil. She devoured every book that was given to her, and her father had even given permission for her to borrow from his private library—not even Lyndon was allowed to touch those books!

Mathematics, French, piano, Latin, history, and other subjects were all offered to any of the girls who wished them, but Elizabeth was usually the only one who took the governess up on her offer. The others occasionally listened in and were passably educated, but without parents who were willing to instill the importance of education into their children, the three girls tended towards being idle.

Elizabeth kicked at a rock as she walked along in an attempt to relieve her frustrations with the circumstances. Eventually her rambles led her to Lucas Lodge, where she visited for a few minutes with her friend Charlotte.

"Are your parents planning to send your brother to school next

298

year?" Elizabeth asked her friend, who was the oldest of several siblings.

"Yes, as soon as he turns eight. They want him to have a gentleman's education, as he will be inheriting. Mama says it's necessary for him to be able to move about in polite society."

Sir William had been in trade before his elevation to knighthood due to some service he performed for the king. He was considered gentry, but he did not have a gentleman's education as a child.

That sparked an idea in Elizabeth, and when she arrived back at Longbourn for dinner, she put her plan into action. "Mama, did you hear that Sir William and Lady Lucas will be sending Robbie to school next year?"

"Robbie's leaving?" Lyndon's voice was outraged at the idea of his closest friend going away.

"Yes. Apparently they are concerned that if he doesn't receive a gentleman's education at a well-known school, he will not be able to move about the gentry in London due to his parents' history in trade."

Mr. Bennet raised an eyebrow at this comment, and Elizabeth determinedly avoided his gaze.

Mrs. Bennet sniffed. "I can certainly see why they would want to do that. Sir William is barely a gentleman."

"But, Mama, wasn't your father in trade?" Mary asked innocently.

Elizabeth would have thought Mary's comment to be guiltless had Mary not sent her next elder sister a small wink after speaking.

"But Lyndon's father is a gentleman, which makes him born to be a gentleman!" Mrs. Bennet cried out defensively.

"Both your brother and brother-in-law are still in trade however," Elizabeth pointed out. "As much as I love my uncles, you must admit that they have just as few connections as the Lucases did before their elevation. And Sir William even has a title!"

"I don't want Robbie to leave!" Lyndon cried angrily, interrupting the conversation.

Protocol would dictate that the younger children would dine in the nursery until they had come out, but for regular dinners at home, Mr. Bennet preferred to have his children present. It was not that he gained any sort of satisfaction by having them there—indeed, there was little affection—but it prevented him from being the only person available for his wife to speak to.

When Mary was deemed old enough to join the family, Lyndon put up such a fuss—followed by Kitty, who always mimicked her brother's tantrums—that they were allowed downstairs for dinner as well, for the sake of peace in the household.

"Do you really think my dear boy would be snubbed in London?" Mrs. Bennet gasped, the thought never having entered her mind.

"All I know is that Charlotte told me her father—after having been to St. James's Court—is adamant his son receive a proper gentleman's education so as to not be any more ostracized."

"Oh my heavens! Oh, I never thought about it that way! That my own family could be the cause of my son's rejection and shame! We would be ruined!"

Mrs. Bennet's laments were so fierce that it took several rounds of smelling salts and a full ten minutes before order could be restored at the dinner table.

Once she was at peace, Mrs. Bennet then demanded that her son immediately begin school—preferably at Eton or Harrow, the two most well-known schools. She was extremely distraught to discover that once the school year had begun, he could not be enrolled until the following year, and that was only if there was space.

Fortunately for the Bennet girls, a letter arrived a fortnight later to inform them that a pupil had dropped out of the boys' school Eton. There would now be room to accept Master Lyndon, provided he could arrive within the week, else they would be forced to move to the next person on the waiting list.

It was with mixed emotions that the Bennet girls gathered together to wave farewell to Lyndon and Mr. Bennet, who had been vociferously encouraged by his wife to escort their son to London. It wasn't until they drove away that she shrieked, "But what if there is an accident and they *both* die? We will be cast out of Longbourn!"

Her wails refused to cease until Mr. Bennet returned safely two days later.

Chapter 2

Five years later...

"Mr. Bennet, have you heard? Netherfield Park is let at last!"

The gentleman ignored his wife in favor of the newspaper in front of him, but she kept fluttering about the room and rambling on in such a manner that he was forced to set it aside and pay her some attention.

"Well, what has it to do with us?" he asked impatiently.

"It has been taken by a single man of fortune from the north! Lady Lucas said that Sir William paid a call on the young man already, and he was thought to be all that was amiable and charming! Is this not a fine thing for our girls?"

"How can it affect them?" Mr. Bennet asked with a sly grin directed towards Elizabeth, who smiled briefly in return before returning her focus to her book.

"Why, I am thinking of him marrying one of them! We cannot expect poor Lyndon to always care for his sisters once we are gone. He will have his own family to think about then."

As Mrs. Bennet chattered on about the importance of her husband paying a call on Netherfield, Kitty leaned over to Elizabeth and whispered, "I do not think it is a good idea to expect Lyndon to care for any of us. He was quite horrid last time he was home."

Elizabeth grimaced at the truth of Kitty's statement. Five years ago, she had nothing but hope for her brother's improvement outside of Longbourn. The sad truth, however, was that he had turned even more selfish and spoiled than before. While he did learn discipline and received an education, he also was surrounded by heirs to other estates who also had inflated egos and a high sense of their own self-importance.

Every holiday—usually summer and Christmas—Lyndon would return home for a brief time. He would complain about the quality of the food at Longbourn, how small the estate was, and how dull it was to be the only boy. As he grew older, his dissatisfaction grew even more pointed. He would remind the girls that they would have to be kind to him, as he would one day be their guardian unless they married quickly.

The only person Lyndon listened to was his mother, and that was only because she never criticized or corrected him. Thankfully, he had formed friendships that meant he often traveled to stay with friends over breaks, rather than spending the entire time at Longbourn. When he was in residence, the girls did all they could to avoid his presence.

"Perhaps we will be very lucky and the new tenant of Netherfield *will* fall in love with one of us," Elizabeth whispered to Kitty. "We should not marry without love, but even a strong affection or mutual respect would be preferable to becoming dependent on Lyndon."

"He is not all *that* bad," Jane said quietly, joining in the conversation.

"You only say that because he's never mean to you," Kitty retorted. "I've had so many people tell me how twins are supposed to be the best of friends because they spent nine months in the womb together, but that couldn't be further from the truth."

"You were close once," Mary chimed in, having recently left the piano to sit with her sisters as Mrs. Bennet's chattering had interrupted her playing.

"That was before he left," Elizabeth answered for Kitty. "She has improved much and come to know her own mind and worth in the time that he's been away. I am quite proud of her for that."

The conversation ended when Mrs. Bennet dramatically exited the room, sobbing loudly about how her daughters would all end up old maids because their father couldn't take the trouble to pay a call on a new neighbor.

"I had better see to her," Jane said, laying down her embroidery.

"Better you than me," Kitty muttered.

Mary returned to her place at the piano, and Kitty offered to turn the pages for her. Elizabeth returned to her book, but she was immediately interrupted by her father demanding her attention.

"Well, Lizzy, what say you of this new neighbor we're to have, eh?"

Elizabeth bit her tongue to prevent herself from divulging her true feelings and simply said, "It is always good to have different people in the neighborhood. A character study of new neighbors should bring some enjoyment."

Thankfully, Mr. Bennet was satisfied with this answer, and he left the room in search of privacy in his library.

Watching her father leave, Elizabeth sighed with relief. Her relationship with her father was a strange one. When Lyndon was born, Mr. Bennet spoke frequently of all the things they would do together. He expected his son to be a younger version of himself. To his dismay, however, the boy took after his mother with regard to intelligence and temperament.

By the time it was clear that the lad had no desire to read and study like his father, Elizabeth was old enough to have been hurt by her father's neglect over the years. After Lyndon's departure, Mr. Bennet used Elizabeth as a surrogate of sorts. She was someone with whom her father could display his wit and be intellectually challenged.

At the very beginning, Elizabeth was flattered and touched by her father's attention. It became clear, however, that some of Lyndon's cruelty at the expense of others was inherited from both parents, not just Mrs. Bennet. Mr. Bennet liked to make sport of

others in spite of their feelings, which was something that Elizabeth—having been on the receiving end of such treatment by both
her parents and her younger brother—struggled to approve of.

She now simply managed her father by saying something witty
enough to pacify him without joining in his mockery. Each time he
spoke, however, she ached with the desire to tell him exactly what
she thought of his parenting style and the manner in which he cared
for his family.

No, as much as Elizabeth admired her father's wit and intelligence, she desperately wished he would use it in a kinder and more
thoughtful manner.

*How on earth both of our parents managed to create a child as sweet as
Jane, I'll never know,* she thought. *It's as if she got so much goodness when
God created her that He ran out of any to give to Lyndon.*

Elizabeth could only hope that her father would actually make
the call on the new neighbors. While she loathed to agree with her
mother on anything with regard to courtships and making matches,
she did admit that it would help her and her sisters make a good
impression towards the young gentleman.

Please, God, let him be amiable and kind. We so desperately need that here.

An entire week passed before Elizabeth would come to know if
her prayers were answered or not. Mr. Bennet did pay a call on Mr.
Bingley—that was the name of the new resident at Netherfield—
but he had little to say of his character other than, "He seemed a bit
like a puppy."

Fortunately, time flew quickly, and soon the Bennets were at the
Meryton assembly. The party was in full swing when the group
from Netherfield arrived. Rumors had flown rampant that week
about how many people Bingley would be bringing—twelve ladies
and seven gentlemen, or else five sisters and a cousin.

When the group arrived, however, it was with much relief that
only two ladies were present, in addition to three gentlemen. Sir
William began introductions, and the Bennets soon learned—along

with everyone else—that the company consisted of Bingley, his two sisters, his brother-in-law, and a friend.

Once Bingley had gotten sight of Jane, he immediately asked to be introduced and then requested the next dance. Elizabeth was happy with the man's pleasant manners at the introduction, as the rest of his group appeared to be quite above their company with their sneers and giggles.

Elizabeth did feel a bit of pity for the friend. Mr. Darcy was much spoken of due to his owning an estate that brought in ten thousand pounds per year. She could only imagine what it would be like to be the center of such attentions and gossip.

Her pity faded somewhat later in the evening when she chanced to overhear a conversation between Bingley and Darcy, in which Bingley urged his friend to dance with someone.

"You are dancing with the only handsome girl in the room," Darcy said.

Elizabeth smiled at this frank appraisal of her sister, but this turned to a blush when Bingley said, "Look, there is one of her sisters now. She is very pretty, and I daresay she is also very agreeable. Come, let me introduce you."

Darcy looked over and caught Elizabeth's eye before saying coldly, "She is tolerable, I suppose, but not handsome enough to tempt me."

The rest of his words faded away, replaced with a faint ringing in her ears. She had always known that she was not as beautiful as Jane or Kitty—indeed, her mother had made that very clear—but she had never thought of herself as merely tolerable either.

Tears filled her eyes, and she quickly stood from her chair. Eager to not be noticed, she bit her lip and made her way as unobtrusively as possible to the doors to the balcony, which was thankfully empty.

Once in the cool air, she moved to the corner and leaned against a pillar and looked out over the small town. At last alone, she allowed the tears to fall freely down her cheeks, counting on the shadows to keep her safe from observation.

Was it not enough that her parents and brother thought very little of her? To be sure, Jane, Mary, and Kitty appreciated Elizabeth, but then again, they'd formed a close bond over the years. Having a stranger—and a man of the world at that—proclaim her not good enough was more than she could bear.

The ache that was always present in her chest became agonizingly tight, and she wrapped her arms around herself as if to prevent the hole from growing larger. Her silent weeping turned into sobs that she did her best to keep as quiet as possible.

A creak came from the door opening, and she hastily wiped her face, expecting Jane or Charlotte to have followed her. She turned around, forcing a smile, when she gave a gasp upon discovering who had joined her.

It was Darcy.

Chapter 3

Darcy winced at the sight of the girl he had just insulted making her way across the room to the balcony. He was in a foul temper, and he shouldn't have taken it out on some stranger. Attempting to alleviate his guilt, he told himself that she couldn't possibly have heard him.

When she exited the room, however, and moved out of sight from the windows, he accepted that his hopes were lost. She *had* heard his thoughtless and cruel words, and it was very badly done of him.

What if someone had spoken of Georgiana that way?

He winced as he thought back to the summer at Ramsgate. The look on his dear sister's face when she'd heard Wickham say he was relieved to not have to be bound to such an ugly, pathetic creature for all his life still caused Darcy to clench his fists with anger.

You must always be a gentleman, Fitzwilliam. A lady should never be treated with disrespect.

The voice of Darcy's father echoed in his ears. As a foolish young man trying to fit in with the world, he had once made a derogatory remark to another young man about a woman's hat at one of his first assemblies in Lambton. He had never seen his father as furious as he had been at that moment. Fortunately, the woman had not heard him, and the friend had never repeated the remark.

That was not this case this time. Groaning to himself, Darcy knew he would need to apologize to the girl. How he would explain himself, he didn't know, but there was nothing to be done for it. He watched the door for several minutes, waiting for her return. When she did not come, he knew he must have caused some true damage, so he went after her.

She was leaning against a pillar with her back towards him, but upon hearing his footsteps, she spun around. Her eyes were wet and her face was splotchy from her tears. The fake smile she'd forced on her lips disappeared when she realized who he was.

Darcy bowed. "Please forgive me for speaking to you without an introduction, but I felt it imperative that I speak to you now. I want you to know that I am very sorry you heard my words to Bingley a few minutes ago. I should not have spoken so of any lady, and I ask your forgiveness."

"Why?" Her voice was hoarse.

"Why am I apologizing?" The confusion was evident in his voice. "I should have thought that obvious."

She shook her head. "No, why did you say it? Did you mean it?"

Taken a bit aback at the fact that she did not immediately accept his apology, he simply stared for a moment before saying, "To be quite honest with you, I'm not sure if I did or not. You see, I didn't really even look at you. I simply wanted to say anything to get Bingley to leave me alone and stop pressuring me to dance."

"But you *did* look at me," she replied, her voice stronger. "You looked me straight in the eye and declared me unhandsome and intolerable."

He winced at this characterization of his words. "I know I looked in your direction, but I looked without really seeing, if that makes any sense at all. Again, I sincerely do apologize. It was very wrong of me."

"If you didn't mean it either way, then why did you say it?"

Darcy gave an impatient huff. "As I already explained, I simply wanted Bingley to stop pressuring me to dance."

"I see," she said. "Then it was nothing personal."

"Precisely," he said with a small sigh of relief.

"Then I accept your apology. It was very kind of you to make it, even if it does bend propriety somewhat, not having been properly introduced. Or rather, Mr. Bingley presented you to us earlier, but I do not believe you waited for us to be introduced to you in turn."

Darcy winced at another piece of evidence for his incivility that evening. "Then I must ask your forgiveness for that as well. It has been a very difficult day, and I was in no mood for socializing with strangers."

"Then why did you come?"

Darcy stared at the girl in disbelief. Not once in all of his time in society had a young lady spoken with him in such a frank manner. "I do not believe that is any business of yours," he replied stiffly.

The cheerful expression that had been slowly creeping onto her face immediately disappeared. "My apologies, Mr. Darcy. It was not my intent to speak so familiarly. As you have rightly pointed out, we have not even been introduced. In fact, this entire situation is most inappropriate, and I should return to my party."

Before he could object—or even say anything—she gave a swift curtsy and brushed past him to once more go through the doors and into the assembly room.

Darcy was still thinking about the entire conversation as they finally left the dance and rode in their carriage back to Netherfield. He had never been questioned about his behavior or motives before from a young woman. Usually, they just simpered and fawned, agreeing with his every word, even when he contradicted himself on purpose.

Her unusual nature lingered with him over the next several days. He was aware that the ladies at Netherfield had exchanged calls with those at Longbourn, but he never actually saw the girl again. He was usually with Bingley, occupied with hunting or estate matters, and didn't hear of the calls until after they were over.

That is, until she arrived on foot one day to check on her sister, who had taken ill the night before, having ridden in the rain for a dinner invitation from Miss Bingley.

As Miss Elizabeth—for that was her name, he had discovered—came into view around the path, he was struck by the brightness of her eyes, the flush of her cheeks, and her light and pleasing figure. This was the woman he had decried as barely tolerable?

How could he have been so blind?

She blushed fiercely upon encountering him so suddenly, but she raised her chin. "I have come to inquire after my sister. Would you be so good as to take me to her?"

Now it was his turn to blush at having been caught staring at her. While she didn't have the classic beauty of her elder sister, there was something about the wildness of her hair and dress that called to him.

"Y-yes, of course," he stammered out, extending his arm as an offer to escort her.

Darcy led Elizabeth to the breakfast room, where Bingley, Mrs. Hurst, and Miss Bingley were finally rising from their bed to eat. They still kept to town hours, even though they were in the country.

Once Miss Bingley had given Elizabeth the information she'd requested, she rang the bell to have the housekeeper escort the new arrival to her sister. Once the door closed behind Elizabeth, the two Bingley sisters immediately began to disparage the state of her petticoat, the wildness of her hair, and the conceit of her independence in walking so far alone without an escort.

"I thought it showed an affection to her sister that was very pleasing!" Bingley cried out, unable to stand the injustice of such discussion any further.

"It just goes to show her lack of breeding," Miss Bingley replied snidely. "She has an uncle here in Meryton that is an attorney, and another who is in trade and lives in Cheapside. Besides, with all those girls, who knows what will happen to their estate when their father is dead."

"As it just so happens, they have a younger brother who is in school in Eton," Bingley replied sharply.

Darcy raised an eyebrow at this evidence that Bingley had learned quite a bit about his latest angel of beauty. "That does make a difference in their status," Darcy said, joining in on the conversation for the first time. "Whatever their mother was, their father is a gentleman, as is their brother, which does improve their chances of marrying men of any consideration in the world."

Miss Bingley flushed at Darcy's subtle hint towards the fact that her own father and brother were not gentlemen in the truest sense of the word. While Bingley had quite the fortune, that fortune was made in trade, and Bingley was merely leasing an estate, not owning it.

With that being the end of the conversation, and Darcy being disinclined to have a new variation of the same topic once again rehearsed, he reminded Bingley of their prior engagement with Mr. Hurst for some hunting, and the three gentlemen made their escape.

In the week that Elizabeth resided at Netherfield to care for Jane, she was struck by the kindness and solicitude from both Darcy (towards herself) and Bingley (towards Jane). She told herself that Darcy's mannerisms were due to his guilt over how he'd treated her at the assembly.

They enjoyed lively debates in the evenings when the entire company came together after dinner and the separation of the sexes. At first, poor Bingley was distressed at what he viewed as genuine antagonisms between the two, but with Jane giving the couple faint smiles of approval—once she had improved enough to join them downstairs—his anxiety eased.

For her part, Elizabeth reveled in the feeling of having a gentleman listen to her opinions with attention and respect. Her brother never took notice of anything she had to say, and her father only accepted opinions that he either agreed with or thought were exceptionally witty.

With Darcy, however, she didn't feel the need to perform or temper her thoughts. Their conversations grew spirited, of course, but it was always with mutual respect and an open mind.

In short, he was just the sort of man she hoped to marry some-day.

Oh, she knew it wasn't realistic to think she could marry *this* man. His income alone put him high above her reach. Furthermore, his attitude towards her at the Meryton assembly when she pried into his personal reasons for attendance showed he had a boundary he did not want her to cross. It was one thing to discuss philosophy and debate about generalities, but quite another to involve personal feelings.

After all, the distinction of rank must be preserved.

Chapter 4

It was with mixed emotions that she left Netherfield and went back to Longbourn with Jane, who had made a complete recovery. Elizabeth's confusion, however, did not last. Along the journey, Jane hummed a happy tune as she looked out the window with a secret smile.

"Jane, tell me," Elizabeth demanded.

"Oh, Lizzy! Mr. Bingley has asked to call on me when we return to Longbourn! Can you believe it?"

Elizabeth grinned at her sister. "Of course I can! It was clear to anyone who watched you converse that he is halfway to being in love with you already. But the important thing, Jane, is how do *you* feel about *him?*"

Jane blushed. "I find him to be the most amiable man of my acquaintance. He is so kind, Lizzy, and so gentle. I don't believe I've ever met anyone more considerate of others than Mr. Bingley."

"Do you love him?"

After looking out the window for a long moment, Jane finally said, "I do not believe so, but I think it would be easy to grow to love him. It would only with time."

"Well, fortunately time is something that is on your side. He has asked to call on you, which will give you time to come to know him better."

"You do not think it dishonest to allow him to call when I am unsure of my feelings?" Jane asked her sister anxiously.

Elizabeth paused briefly, then shook her head. "No, I think the only thing dishonest would be to show him more affection than you feel.

The purpose of a courtship is to acknowledge an attraction and spend time investigating those feelings to see if they could lead to marriage, which is what you are doing. If you accepted his courtship when you knew you could not love him ever, that would be dishonest."

Jane's shoulders sank in relief. "I truly do esteem him, Lizzy."

Leaning forward, Elizabeth took her sister's hands. "Then that is all that matters. You will have the time to come to know him, and hopefully our mother's effusions will not frighten him away."

At her sister's startled look, Elizabeth laughed. "He has already met her, Jane, and still requested to call. I don't believe anything she does will surprise him any more than already. Let us just be grateful Lyndon is not at home; I'd worry more about his wild behavior than Mama's attempts to matchmake."

The conversation came to a halt as the Bingley carriage arrived at Longbourn. Mrs. Bennet's laments that the girls had not remained another se'ennight at Netherfield were only interrupted by dinner, in which Mr. Bennet expressed his relief that his most sensible daughters had returned home.

Has he always been this harsh and condescending? Elizabeth wondered.

As she pondered the question over the following days, she realized that her father was the same as he always was, but it was *she* who had changed. Her time in the company of gentlemen who were kind and respectful—not including Miss Bingley, of course—made her father's patronizing tone even more abrasive.

During her time of contemplation, Bingley called on Jane at Longbourn as promised. For an entire fortnight, he visited the Bennet family and walked with Jane in the garden, accompanied by Elizabeth and Darcy, and at times Mary and Kitty.

While Bingley made love to Jane with flowers and poetry, Elizabeth and Darcy discussed their opinions on books, the differences between their two estates, and the variations that occurred amongst the diverse counties in England.

Darcy was surprised to hear that Elizabeth's aunt, Mrs. Gardiner, was the daughter of the vicar at Lambton. He expressed a desire to meet her someday but hesitated when Elizabeth mentioned Mr. Gardiner's profession. Elizabeth could clearly see Darcy push his hesitation aside and reaffirm his interest in making their acquaintance again one day.

"I believe they will be coming for Christmas," Elizabeth said. "Do you plan to remain in Hertfordshire for the holiday?"

He faltered, then replied, "I usually spend Christmas with my sister Georgiana. She is but fifteen years old, and I am her guardian, along with my cousin."

"Oh!" Elizabeth said in surprise. "I quite forgot that you had a sister; I never knew her age, only that Miss Bingley is enraptured by her talent at the pianoforte. She is only a year older than Kitty, then."

"Yes, but unlike your sister, she is quite shy by nature. She had an unfortunate encounter this past summer with someone whom she once considered a friend that has made her more timid than usual. I do not wish to abandon her for the holiday."

A bit saddened at the idea of Darcy leaving the neighborhood, she couldn't help but admire his devotion to his sister. "If only my brother gave such care to his own sisters' feelings," she said wistfully.

"He is at school, is he not? What is he like?" Darcy asked.

Now it was Elizabeth's turn to hesitate. She did not wish to speak poorly about Lyndon, but neither did she wish to tell a falsehood. "He is sixteen years old; he and Kitty are twins, although their personalities are quite different. Being the only son and heir, Lyndon is... well, he is allowed many more freedoms than his elder sisters, and that has not yet been tempered with age," she finished delicately.

"Will he be coming for Christmas?" Darcy asked.

"Yes, I believe the Gardiners will bring him down when they come," she replied.

The conversation then turned towards other topics, and Elizabeth was grateful for the reprieve. If she were to be honest with herself, she hoped Darcy and Lyndon would never cross paths. She couldn't imagine how each would react to the other, being such opposites of character.

After several weeks, Bingley came with an invitation to a ball at Netherfield for the following week. Jane blushed furiously when he solicited her hand for the first two dances as well as the supper set. Elizabeth raised an eyebrow at these particular attentions and Jane's corresponding response.

She had the intent on asking her elder sister about her feelings, as Elizabeth expected Bingley would most likely propose at the ball and wish to announce the engagement during the dinner. Unfortunately, such a thing didn't occur, as the peace at Longbourn was interrupted that day with an unexpected arrival.

Lyndon returned home from school three weeks early and in disgrace. He had been sent down for gambling and fighting, and the entire house was in chaos. The young man convinced his mother he had been set up and wrongfully accused, which caused her to wail and moan about the injustices her "dear boy" had experienced.

Mr. Bennet took to his book room even more frequently than usual. Elizabeth's attempts to get her father to get his son to take the situations seriously only caused Mr. Bennet to sigh and shake his head. "We will have no peace at Longbourn until your brother has learned things the hard way, as is his wont. Nothing I say will matter to a lad his age. All boys go through this, and it will pass."

For his part, Lyndon relished in his mother's attentions and affirmations. His arrival coincided with that of a militia under the command of Colonel Forster. While the girls attempted to avoid the soldiers, who were a rowdy and uncouth lot, Lyndon befriended many of them.

Each night, the young man went to the barracks to drink and gamble, only to return home in the early hours of the morning, drunk and stumbling, having lost everything in his pockets.

Even the unflappable Bingley, who had attempted to befriend his beloved's brother, did not know what to make of such a wasteful and disrespectful young man. Upon meeting Bingley, Lyndon's only response was, "Ah, excellent! At last one of my sisters will make a match that will keep them from being a burden on me when my father is dead."

Darcy, who had accompanied his friend, raised an eyebrow at this response, which made Elizabeth blush uncomfortably. The tall gentleman's face became impassive and stonelike, and he spent the remainder of the visit with his lips pressed together and speaking only monosyllables. He had not returned since.

Elizabeth had only seen Darcy once since then, and it was in Meryton when Lyndon insisted on introducing his sisters to his friends Denny and Saunderson, who were officers in the militia. Among them was a handsome young man named Wickham who had just purchased a lieutenancy.

Bingley and Darcy had approached the group to greet the Bennets, but upon seeing the group of men, Darcy had turned red with fury. He immediately turned his horse around and rode away without saying a word. Elizabeth's heart had sunk, certain that he was rejecting her brother, but then she spied Wickham's white face as he watched Darcy ride away.

She did not have much time to contemplate the situation, however, as they were all to go to a card party at the Phillipses' home. Wickham sat by her and told her a scandalous tale involving Darcy and a denied living, but Elizabeth was hesitant to trust the story. After all, Darcy had never been anything but honorable and kind, even when in error.

At the end of the card party, Lyndon left with the officers. Elizabeth's discomfort over Wickham and his character grew as she watched him befriend her brother, who had to be at least a decade and a half younger than the officer, if he had truly grown up with Darcy.

Her father brushed away her concerns, but six hours later, a pounding on the door awoke the household. Mrs. Bennet shrieked about how they would all be murdered in their beds. Mr. Bennet pulled the door open with a revolver in hand as the girls huddled on the stairs in their nightclothes.

To their surprise, the family discovered Darcy standing in the rain, supporting a bloodied, shivering Lyndon.

Chapter 5

Elizabeth let out a shocked gasp at the state of the two men drenched and shivering. Mrs. Bennet screamed and fainted, thankfully caught by Jane and Mary.

Darcy stumbled into the house under the weight of the young man. Mr. Bennet gaped at the scene in a frozen stupor, unable to move. Elizabeth rushed forward past her father to help lower her brother to the floor. To her horror, she could barely make out his face under the swelling, and his arm hung at an unnatural angle.

"Papa, send for Mr. Jones!" she cried, cradling her brother's head in her lap.

"Allow me," Darcy gasped. "My horse is already saddled outside."

Before she could protest, Darcy was out the door, his footsteps muffled by the freezing rain that was increasing in intensity every second. She turned back to her frozen family. "Jane, get Mama to her room!"

The Bennet family awakened under her command. Mary and Kitty were both needed to help Jane carry their unconscious mother up the stairs. Elizabeth absentmindedly wondered if this was the first time in Mrs. Bennet's life that she had legitimately fainted.

"Should we take him to his room? He's freezing," Elizabeth said to her father, who had shaken himself out of his stupefaction and knelt at his son's side.

"No, he might have more injuries than just the arm," he answered, gesturing towards the awkwardly placed limb.

"But surely it can't be any worse than Mr. Darcy bringing him on horseback?"

Mr. Bennet grimaced. "Fair point. Let me call for Mr. Hill, and we can take him upstairs."

While her father and his manservant carried her lethargic brother upstairs, Elizabeth ran to the kitchens and ordered the cook and maids—who were groggily stirring themselves from bed at Hill's urging—to prepare a hot bath and warm broth. She then took the first pot of steaming water upstairs along with clean cloths and towels.

To her relief, Mr. Jones had already arrived and was checking on Lyndon. She deposited the linens and water before leaving to allow them privacy. As she made her way downstairs to the kitchen, a sound in the drawing room caught her attention.

Much to Elizabeth's astonishment, a soaking wet Darcy stood by the fire, warming himself. "Oh, Mr. Darcy! I had no idea you were still here! Please, allow me to fetch you some dry clothes."

Before the man could protest, Elizabeth rushed to her father's room and pulled out some clothing that was too long for him. She blushed briefly at the idea of helping Darcy with such a personal matter, but she refused to allow him to fall ill because of maidenly sensibilities.

"Here, these should hopefully fit somewhat," she said as she returned to his side, trying not to admire his body through the damp clothing that was practically translucent. "Allow me to show you to the guest room. Mama always keeps it in readiness, and I hope you won't mind if I insist you remain for the night. The rain is only getting worse, from the sound of it, and it is quite dark outside."

"I should protest, Miss Elizabeth, but I find I cannot muster the energy to do so," Darcy admitted, following behind her up the stairs. "I will gratefully accept your offer of a room and the dry clothes."

They made their way down the hall without speaking, but at the door to his room, she could no longer bear it and blurted out, "What on earth happened?"

Darcy scowled. "A scoundrel of the worst sort. If you will allow me to change and dry myself, I will be happy to explain everything to you."

She blushed. "Of course, Mr. Darcy. In fact, please do not trouble yourself tonight. I apologize for my selfishness; you should get your rest."

He ran a hand through his hair, his eyes moving from her face, down her body, and back up again. "To be honest, I am still quite worked up over the situation. A pot of tea, a warm fire, and good conversation with you would be much better for me than lying in bed, waiting for my mind to calm."

A feeling of warmth spread over her at the thought of him preferring her company when he was distraught. "I will wait for you downstairs, then."

Without waiting for a response, she hurried down the corridor and back to the drawing room, where she called for tea and stoked the fire to a warm blaze. When the maid brought the tray, Elizabeth asked that a fire be made in the guest room as well.

Darcy arrived just as the maid left, and he sank gratefully onto the overstuffed chair placed by the fire. Elizabeth poured him a cup of tea, making sure to prepare it the way she had noticed he requested it at Netherfield. He accepted the tea with gratitude, and she sat on the chair across from him.

"What happened?" she asked again after he took a long drink of tea.

He gave a sigh and looked at his cup. "When I realized that Mr. Wickham had taken orders here in Meryton, I wondered if perhaps he had followed me here. We have a history, you see. When I was a child—"

"Yes, he told me that he grew up at Pemberley as the son of your father's steward," she interrupted, anxious to hear about the present, not the past.

"Ah, I see." A bit discomposed, he gathered his thoughts and continued speaking. "I hired an investigator to keep an eye on him. Late this evening, the man came and told me Wickham had won an estate in a card game. It seems your brother attempted to gamble Longbourn away."

Elizabeth let out a horrified gasp. "I cannot believe he would be so foolish! Lyndon knows very well that the estate is entailed until he is eighteen, and that is if Father agrees to break it."

"Apparently that was part of the gamble. Your brother thought his roll at Faro would be the highest and no one would be the wiser. Unfortunately, either Wickham cheated or he is the luckiest man in the world to roll the main when your brother had rolled the chance."

"I have absolutely no idea what that even means," Elizabeth said with a small laugh.

Darcy smiled. "Perhaps one day I can teach you. For now, just know that your brother lost when all odds were that he should have won."

"So then what happened?" she asked breathlessly.

Darcy became solemn again. "When Wickham began crowing and celebrating about being an estate owner, your brother laughed. He mocked them for their gullibility and told them Longbourn was entailed; there was no way for Wickham to collect any winnings other than what was on the table."

Elizabeth closed her eyes. "Foolish boy," she whispered.

"Er, he may have also insulted the intelligence of militia officers in general, saying they were far below him as a gentleman. With tempers already running high at having been fooled, combined with the strong drink, it didn't take long for Wickham and some of the other officers to be pushed past their breaking point. When I arrived, there were four of them on top of your motionless brother."

She gasped and covered her mouth with both hands, eyes filling with tears. "How—how did you stop them?"

"When they heard my horse, they tried to run, but the investigator and myself were able to contain two of them. I had sent a servant to fetch Colonel Forster as soon as I knew what was happening, and he and his men arrived in time to round up the other two."

She let out a slow breath. "You saved my brother's life, Mr. Darcy. I do not know how I could ever thank you for that. Not only for his sake, but for that of all my sisters."

He leaned forward and took her hands in his. "You owe me no thanks; I would have done the same for anyone who fell victim to Wickham. But if you must thank me, let it only be for yourself. As much as I respect your sisters, I thought only of you."

The tears in her eyes slipped down her cheeks. "Do you, do you mean that?" she asked breathlessly.

"I do. I wish to marry you, Elizabeth, and not just because I have irreparably ruined you by spending time alone with you in only your nightclothes."

Elizabeth gasped and looked down. She was, indeed, in her nightdress with not even a dressing gown on! Heat spread across her face and neck. "I completely forgot! Oh, what you must think of me!" She buried her face in her hands.

Darcy gave a soft chuckle. "I had noticed it when you showed me to the room, but I was certain you would change. I... I hoped you would not, and when I came in and saw you, I couldn't bring myself to point it out. You are beautiful, and my greatest wish is to see you this way again for the rest of our lives."

She gave him a small smile. "Well, Mr. Darcy, this compromise is your doing, not mine. I'm afraid I have no choice but to accept the only man I could ever see myself marrying. There, your wish may come true after all."

And indeed, it did.

Epilogue

Darcy's wish did indeed come true, and much sooner than he dared hope for. Mr. Bennet had been informed by a maid that his daughter was undressed in Mr. Darcy's company, and that information was soon spread over the neighborhood. The banns were called, and Elizabeth and Darcy were married in less than a month.

Not to be outdone, Bingley proposed to Jane the day following Lyndon's attack, and they were married in a double ceremony with Darcy and Elizabeth. Bingley's sisters chose to attend, but the sour expression on Miss Bingley's face made her feelings about the matter clear—although it was anyone's guess which of the two couples she objected to the most.

As for Lyndon, Mr. Jones determined that he had suffered a broken arm, several cracked ribs, and severe bruising in his stomach from having been kicked repeatedly. It took several days for him to regain consciousness, most likely because of the blows he had sustained to his head.

Darcy had immediately sent for his private doctor from London, which turned out to be very fortunate. The thorough soaking and chill that both men received led to fevers. Darcy recovered quickly, but Lyndon suffered such a high temperature that he became delirious for almost a week. His injuries were such that he had to be strapped down to the bed lest he cause further damage to his arm and ribs in his frenzy.

When the fever finally broke—much to the relief of his mother and father—Lyndon was as weak as a newborn babe. A nurse was hired to care for him on the recommendation of the doctor and

Colonel Fitzwilliam, who had seen similar injuries in the war. The woman, Mrs. Bates, was a fifty-year-old battle-axe who had run a tight ship treating soldiers overseas.

Between Mrs. Bates's discipline and Lyndon's humbled state, he emerged from the entire adventure a completely different man. He never returned to Eton, as he needed a full year to recover his strength. Special masters were hired to tutor him so he could still go to Oxford. Elizabeth fretted that her brother would return to his former character, but he conducted himself with the utmost decorum, following in his brother-in-law Darcy's example.

The experience had changed Mr. and Mrs. Bennet as well. The near-loss of their son due to his own conceit and arrogance caused them to rethink how they were parenting their children. Although two were now married and the others almost full-grown, Mr. and Mrs. Bennet devoted themselves to improvement.

Mrs. Bennet's nerves calmed considerably, and she worked to understand Mary and Kitty better. The girls blossomed under their mother's attention and love. For his part, Mr. Bennet focused more fully on the estate, eventually increasing their annual income by half. When Lyndon came home from university, he joined his father in managing their holdings, determining crop rotations, and caring for tenants.

Eventually, Lyndon fell in love with Maria Lucas, and the two were married from Longbourn where all their friends could see. Elizabeth, and Kitty—who had married a landowner near Pemberley—traveled for the wedding with their husbands and children in tow. The Bingleys had purchased Netherfield, so there was no need to wait on them.

Mary, who had chosen to never marry, remained at Longbourn with her much-improved parents while Lyndon and Maria moved into the dower house. When Mr. and Mrs. Bennet passed away within a fortnight of one another, Lyndon and Maria actively encouraged Mary to stay with them, but she was just as adamant to not be a "burdensome old maid," a phrase that always put Lyndon to the blush, even when it was said in jest.

They finally compromised on Mary moving into the dower house with a companion, but she was invited to dine at Longbourn every night.

No one had ever dreamed of this ending for the Bennet family when Lyndon was born all those years ago, but Darcy and Elizabeth were grateful every day that Mr. and Mrs. Bennet had a son.

Overhearings More to the Purpose

Mrs. Bennet happens to overhear Wickham and the other officers discussing her youngest two daughters in the crudest of terms. When her demands to Colonel Forster are met with the harsh truth, and her insistence to Mr. Bennet that he challenge the officers to a duel is mocked, how will she react?

Chapter 1

"That Lydia is a looker, eh, Wickham?"

Mrs. Bennet smiled to herself in satisfaction at Captain Denny's words. She was in the back of the cobbler's shop to get her favorite pair of shoes repaired, and her daughters had been speaking with the soldiers in the street. Apparently, the group had parted ways, and now the soldiers had entered the same shop as herself.

"She's a good enough chit for a tumble, I daresay," Wickham replied nonchalantly. "With those necklines, you know she'll be begging for it. What does the face matter when there are other features that are more enjoyable?"

Mrs. Bennet let out a small cry in alarm, then pressed her hands over her mouth. Shock prevented her from doing anything more as the men continued uninterrupted.

Denny made an exaggerated gasp of dismay. "You would compromise a gentleman's daughter."

"Wouldn't be the first time," Wickham replied, a smirk in his voice. "Though I've never met one so willing as Lydia. She acts more like a tavern wench than a proper young lady. I'll have her before the end of the week."

Denny laughed and made a crude statement that involved Kitty, and the two soldiers left the store bantering.

Mrs. Bennet stood horrified behind the shelf, tears filling her eyes. *My Lydia, a tavern wench?*

A burst of anger surged forth from her chest. *How dare they! Well, they are no gentlemen at all to speak of a gently born young lady that way. I will speak with Colonel Forster about their appalling conduct!*

With the thought of retribution firmly in her mind, Mrs. Bennet strode determinedly towards the front of the store and made her exit. As she marched down the street towards the direction of the colonel's main lodgings, her mind raced with everything she was going to say to the colonel.

Fortunately for Mrs. Bennet—and perhaps unfortunately for Colonel Forster—the military man had just completed some training and was therefore available to speak with her in his study.

"Colonel Forster, I have a few words to say about the behavior of your officers!"

As Mrs. Bennet recounted the conversation she had overheard, she watched with satisfaction as the Colonel's lips tightened and his face turned red, confident that she had impressed upon him the grievous comportment of those under his command.

Her tirade finished, she sat back and waited for some moments for him to speak. Colonel Forster opened his mouth, then closed it again. When he repeated the same action without actually letting out a word, she decided she'd had enough.

"Well?" she snapped at him impatiently.

Colonel Forster heaved a tremendous sigh and leaned back in the chair behind his desk. "Mrs. Bennet, while I completely agree with you that no officer should speak about a gentlewoman in such a way, the very real fact is that we live in a country where our communications cannot be monitored in that way. Were I to punish every officer who ever spoke ill of a lady, they would spend more time in punishment than in training."

Mrs. Bennet's mouth dropped open in astonishment. "But Colonel Forster, this is more than speaking poorly of a woman! Are there not laws and such against slander and lies? I want these officers to face justice for what they said about my dear girls!"

The colonel let out another sigh and leaned forward, his brow furrowed. "Mrs. Bennet," he said quietly, "there are such laws, of course. But they must be proven to be absolutely false in a court of law to merit punishment. Based on my albeit limited acquaintance with your two youngest daughters, I'm afraid the remarks of my officers would be established more as truth rather than lie."

Now it was Mrs. Bennet's turn to fall silent as she struggled to understand just what Colonel Forster had meant.

He took advantage of the silence to press on. "Now, I know this may sound harsh to you, Mrs. Bennet, but I say this with the best of intentions. The behavior of your younger two daughters, coupled with their lack of dowry, is more likely to end up in their ruin rather than in marriage."

Mrs. Bennet leaped to her feet at this last remark. "I have never been so insulted in my entire life!" she wailed. "Just you wait until I tell my husband what you have said!"

She stomped out of the room, leaving Colonel Forster calling after her. Ignoring the servant who offered her a cloak, she flew down the steps towards where she had left her carriage, eager to return to Longbourn as quickly as she was able.

Upon arriving at Longbourn, Mrs. Bennet shoved her hat at Hill and stormed towards Mr. Bennet's study, where she threw the door open and marched in. Her husband looked up from his book, startled. "My dear Mrs. Bennet! What on earth is going on?"

Mrs. Bennet immediately launched into a diatribe, detailing everything that had happened thus far. She concluded by declaring, "And now, Mr. Bennet, you must go call him out! You cannot allow such slander to occur!"

Any visions she'd entertained of Mr. Bennet rushing out the door and calling for a horse were soon dashed when he began to laugh. "Call out a colonel in the militia? You must be mad!"

Seeing her confused face, he struggled to pull himself together to continue speaking. "Mrs. Bennet, as the good John Ray recited in his book of English proverbs, 'Listeners ne'er any good of themselves.' I suppose we can now apply that to daughters as well. Well, now you know why I've always said they are two of the silliest girls in England."

Mr. Bennet returned to his book, but a stomp and a shriek from Mrs. Bennet interrupted him. She glared furiously at him, which caused him to shrug. "What did he say that was not true? While I admit that the idea of them finding themselves ruined is troublesome, I trust that their sisters are wise enough to find men who won't concern themselves with such foolish trivialities. Besides, my dear, if I were to attempt to duel a military man, I would most likely be killed—in which case, you would be cast out into those hedgerows you are constantly lamenting."

Mrs. Bennet turned from red to white at that last remark. Upon being certain of having silenced her for good, Mr. Bennet said, "Now, my dear, it is almost time for dinner. Leave me to my book until I have to socialize with the... what were they called again? Oh, yes, tavern wenches."

She stood there in shock, and it wasn't until he cleared his throat and motioned with his hand towards the door that she was able to make her feet obey and leave the room. The door slamming closed behind her prompted her to keep moving, her wooden legs carrying her up to her bedroom.

Once inside, she collapsed onto her bed. For the first time in her life, she understood what a true attack of the nerves might actually be. In spite of her furiously pounding heart and the trembling of her hands, she was unable to find the strength to ring for Hill to bring smelling salts. Instead, she rolled onto her side and cried herself to sleep.

Chapter 2

Several hours later, a soft scratching on the door awoke Mrs. Bennet from a restless doze.

"Mrs. Bennet?"

When the lady gave no response, the door opened to admit Hill, who quietly walked towards the bed. The elderly servant laid a hand on Mrs. Bennet's shoulder and gave it a gentle shake. "Mrs. Bennet? It's time to dress for dinner."

Mrs. Bennet remained in her fetal position on the bed, knees tucked up towards her chin. "I am very ill tonight, Hill. Tell Jane she may take my place."

Hill made a small noise of surprise. "Would you like a tray sent up, madam? Perhaps some tea and toast?"

"No, I have no appetite tonight."

There was a moment of silence; then Hill noiselessly crept away from her mistress's bed and out the door. The soft click of the closing door did nothing to stir Mrs. Bennet from her prone position on the bed. Instead, her mind was once again racing with the events of the entire day.

How dare the militia denigrate my dear girls? They are quite lively, I suppose, but their spirits do not mean they have loose morals!

Her mind then turned towards Mr. Bennet and his cruel words. *I simply cannot understand how a man can speak so poorly of his own daughters! We all know that Lizzy is his favorite, but that doesn't give him the right to treat them so poorly!*

Mrs. Bennet's indignation eventually gave way to sleep for the night. She fell asleep with the satisfaction that on the morrow, her husband would have noticed her absence and would apologize for his behavior.

Unfortunately for Mrs. Bennet, her subconscious mind was far more troubled by the men's words than the rational part of her brain. Her sleep was severely troubled with dreams of her daughters.

"Lord, when did I become so fat?" whined Lydia, unable to pull her newly made dress over her stomach as the seamstress looked on with alarm.

Mrs. Bennet's eyes widened in alarm at the sight of her daughter's rounded belly. "Lydia, when did you last have your courses?" cried her mother.

"Not for these last several months, thank goodness," Lydia replied, trying to put on another gown. "It has been a great relief, that is for certain... I say, this dress is too small as well! Really, you must have sewn it wrong."

Mrs. Bennet looked frantically around the shop, hoping desperately that no one else would notice that her daughter was pregnant, not fat. Unfortunately, it seemed as if everyone in Meryton were there. Lady Lucas and Mrs. Long were whispering together in the corner, looking at Lydia with disdain.

She tugged on Lydia's arm, trying to discreetly get her daughter to cover herself. In response, Lydia yanked herself away. "La, Mama! Whatever is the matter with you? After I am married, you shan't be able to boss me around anymore!"

"Who are you marrying?" Mrs. Bennet asked in confusion.

Lydia pursed her lips before saying, "Well, the engagement is of a peculiar kind. You see, both Denny and Wickham have told me they're madly in love with me. And why wouldn't they be? Of all my sisters, I am the only one who is enticing enough to make the men wild for me."

"What do you mean wild for you?" Fear crept into Mrs. Bennet's voice.

"I'm the only one who could cause them to want me so badly they had to be inside me or they would die," Lydia replied smugly. "That's what they all told me."

"Oh!" cried Mrs. Bennet, faint with horror. "Lydia, you mean to say you have given your virtue to two men?"

"Why, of course, Mama. It would have hardly been fair to deny them when they were so tragically depressed without me. Besides, one of them will have to

marry me now, won't they?"

Mrs. Bennet looked around helplessly. She spied Colonel Forster with Captain Denny and Lieutenant Wickham. The two younger officers were smirking and laughing while Colonel Forster shook his head. "I warned you, Mrs. Bennet. No militia man can afford to marry for so little a dowry. You should have taken better care of your girls."

"No!

Mrs. Bennet spun around to see who had shouted, just in time to witness Jane collapse to the ground, weeping. Elizabeth bent down to console her while glaring up at her mother. "Mr. Bingley has left Netherfield, leaving Jane with a broken heart, all because of Lydia's foolishness. You have ruined us all, Mother. No man will want to marry us now."

The matron pressed her hand to her chest, searching frantically for her husband. When she spied him, his face was gray. "What has your daughter done, Mrs. Bennet?" he rasped out. "You were supposed to be teaching her better. It was your job as her mother to protect her. And now, the shock has killed me."

With that, Mr. Bennet fell down, dead. Mrs. Bennet shrieked and tried to run to his side, but a firm hand gripped her arm. "There is nothing you can do, madam. He is dead, and Longbourn is mine!"

The voice belonged to the elderly Mr. Collins, whom Mrs. Bennet had only met one time. He looked even more evil than he did all those years before, but now he cackled with glee. A sinister smile crossed his face as he said, "And unless you want to be removed from your only home, you will do everything I demand." He lifted a hand and caressed her cheek.

"Help me!" Mrs. Bennet cried out, tears pouring down her face. Spying her sister Phillips and brother Gardiner, she called to them. "Edward, Sister! Please, help me!"

Her two siblings looked at her in sorrow. "I'm sorry, Fanny," Mr. Gardiner said. "I cannot allow you and your daughters to have any contact with my family. I mustn't let the scandal carry over to my own children."

"You have made your own bed, and now you must lie in it," Mrs. Phillips said, a tinge of triumph in her voice. "You always thought you were above me because you married a gentleman instead of a man in trade. Well, now we see *which of us is the superior!"*

They both turned their backs to Mrs. Bennet. As she tried to pull away from Mr. Collins to run to them, he pulled her backwards. "Now, to Long-bourn!" he said with a leer. "I'm sure I can think of a way you and your daughters can repay me for allowing you to stay in my home."

"Thomas! Thomas!"

"Mrs. Bennet. Mrs. Bennet!"

Mrs. Bennet jerked awake, thrashing wildly. She shrieked when she felt the hand grasping her arm and tried to pull away, which only led to her falling off her bed. The crash shocked her into silence, and she looked around at her surroundings.

"Mrs. Bennet, are you quite all right?"

In the dim light, Mrs. Bennet could make out Hill holding a candle, her other hand reaching out to where Mrs. Bennet had been on the bed only moments before.

"Oh, Hill! I had the most terrible dream."

Mrs. Bennet burst into tears, her entire body shaking with the sobs that poured out of her.

"There, there, missus," Hill said soothingly as she helped her mistress back into the bed. "'Tis all right. You are safe at home. Whatever your bad dream was, you're not in it anymore."

This only caused Mrs. Bennet to sob harder. *If only you knew that the nightmare was at home.*

Eventually, however, exhaustion settled over her, and her weeping subsided. With Hill rubbing her back in a soothing way, Mrs. Bennet eventually fell back asleep.

Chapter 3

Mrs. Bennet awoke the next morning with an aching head and a fluttering in her chest. Whilst she had often claimed such symptoms in the past, this was the first time she actually experienced them for longer than a few moments.

She chose to have a tray sent up for breakfast, in spite of the fact that she had not dined with her family the evening prior. While she waited for the tray, she dressed with Hill's assistance.

Thankfully, the second half of her night had passed without any dreams. The dread she had felt, however, still lingered. She could not help but reflect on the horrid events that had occurred in her sleeping state. What was worse, she was finally beginning to suspect that her youngest might behave in such a loose way.

Nonsense, she told herself firmly. *Lydia is a good girl. She has high spirits, but she would never do anything truly improper.*

With that thought, she resolved to think on it no more and enjoy her breakfast, which had just arrived. The sustenance went a long way in restoring her to good humor and health, and it was with a lightened heart that she descended the stairs.

"Everyone is in the drawing room, missus," Hill informed her. "There are already some callers."

Hoping to see her sister and confide all her worries, Mrs. Bennet bustled into the room. To her very great surprise, Captain Denny and Lieutenant Wickham were sitting with her daughters.

"Oh!" she exclaimed in surprise. "I had not expected to see you young men today."

The two officers jumped to their feet and performed deep bows.

They only took their seats when she had taken hers, and Wickham gave a winsome smile. "I hope we are not intruding. We simply couldn't stay away from such lovely ladies and the fine hospitality that we receive here from our dear friends at Longbourn."

Mrs. Bennet gave him a sharp look, searching his face for deceit. To her very great astonishment, he appeared just as sincere and charming as he always did. *If I had not heard his words yesterday for myself, I never would have believed him capable of saying such a thing about those of whom he speaks so highly!*

Realizing he was waiting for her response, Mrs. Bennet belatedly said, "Well, a compliment is always welcome, is it not, girls?"

Lydia and Kitty giggled and batted their eyelashes, and Mary rolled her eyes at their antics. Elizabeth and Jane gave polite smiles from their side of the room, then began conversing in hushed tones once again.

Mrs. Bennet sat back quietly, intent on observing the interactions of her daughters with the two officers. She was certain that in the quarter-hour visit, she would find more than enough evidence to prove her dreams were nothing more than that fantasy of her mind.

To her dismay, she discovered quite the opposite.

Lydia and Kitty flirted incessantly with the officers, batting their eyelashes. Had this been all, Mrs. Bennet would have been consoled. Instead, she noticed that Lydia kept surreptitiously tugging her neckline down and pressing her bosoms against Wickham's arm. At one point, Mrs. Bennet was certain she could see her youngest's nipple peeking out above the lace!

Meanwhile, Mary gave her two younger sisters disgruntled looks each time one of them squealed with laughter. While this was not out of the ordinary, those glares were accompanied by winces from Jane and Elizabeth. Mrs. Bennet could count Elizabeth's behavior as jealousy, but not Jane's. The faint blush on her eldest daughter's cheeks each time Lydia let out a bark of laughter or scooted closer to Wickham was of great concern to Mrs. Bennet.

Just as she was about to say something, the doorbell rang, and Hill admitted Mr. and Miss Bingley. The young man immediately made his way to Jane's side, while Miss Bingley took a seat in the corner, a faint look of disdain on her face.

To Mrs. Bennet's mortification, Miss Bingley's look increased in severity each time Kitty or Lydia behaved boisterously. The matron could see Elizabeth try valiantly to distract the Bingleys from the youngest Bennet girls, but even the amiable Mr. Bingley couldn't hide his shock when Lydia demanded to know when the promised ball would be held. "I simply must dance with all the officers," she cried gaily, once again rubbing her breasts against Wickham.

While none of the other ladies in the room would understand Wickham's eyes widening, or the tightening of his breeches, Mrs. Bennet certainly did. His reaction to Lydia, along with his words from the day before, was the final piece of ample evidence that everyone—Denny, Wickham, Forster, and even Mr. Bennet—was correct.

Kitty and Lydia were hoydens.

The realization stunned Mrs. Bennet so thoroughly that she could barely think. When she came to herself, she realized the Bingleys and the officers were both making their adieus. She stammered out some sort of farewell, which she recognized as being far different from her usual entreaties for everyone to remain. Elizabeth, she noted, was giving her a strange look.

Once the guests had all left, Mrs. Bennet's second daughter turned to her. "Mama, are you feeling unwell?"

"Yes, Mama," Jane added, "you took neither dinner nor breakfast with us, and you were unusually quiet during the visits."

"Lord, who cares? We have more important things to discuss!" Lydia turned to her mother. "Mama, I simply must have a new gown for the ball. Denny and Wickham both promised to dance with me."

"And me," chimed in Kitty.

"Pooh, who cares about you? I'm the one the officers are all madly in love with."

This phrase, almost identical to the one from her dream, filled Mrs. Bennet with such dread that she could bear it no longer.

"Stop!"

Everyone in the room froze at the shout, unaccustomed to the serious tone of voice emanating from Mrs. Bennet.

"That. Is. Enough." Mrs. Bennet said through gritted teeth. She glared at her two youngest daughters. "There will be absolutely no balls for either of you. As of this moment, you are no longer considered out."

The entire room was silent for a full minute before Lydia burst into laughter and Kitty followed close behind. "La, what a good joke, Mama!"

Mrs. Bennet's chest was about to explode with rage. "I am most definitely serious about this matter. I am ashamed of you both, and I will not allow you to ruin the chances of your elder sisters making good matches, especially Jane. Your behavior today has shown me that neither of you care about anything other than being the worst sort of flirts, who will bring ruin on our family, and I will not have it!"

The last sentence left Mrs. Bennet's mouth as a shout. She nodded firmly to emphasize her point, then turned and marched up the stairs. Her daughters remained frozen in place for a few seconds before Lydia and Kitty scrambled after her, shouting questions. The three elder girls quickly followed behind their sisters.

"Mama, where are you going?"

"Mama? What are you talking about?"

"What are you doing?"

Mrs. Bennet called for Hill and ignored the questions being shouted behind her. Instead, she marched up the stairs and into the room that Kitty and Lydia shared. Throwing open their closet, she dragged out the largest trunk and furiously shoved dresses into it.

"Mama, have you gone mad?" Lydia screeched, running forwards and trying to tug a dress out of her mother's arms.

The girl was no match for a woman who had birthed five chil-dren, however. Lydia succeeded in tearing a bit of lace fringe off the dress, which caused her to fly backwards and land on her derrière on the floor. The shock caused her to wail at the top of her lungs.

Meanwhile, Mrs. Bennet had successfully cleared the closet and was now collecting the bonnets, ribbons, and lace that were strewn about the room. These, too, were added to the trunk.

"Mrs. Bennet?"

The matron spun around at Hill's tentative voice. "Ah, excellent. Hill, can you please send a note to the seamstress to make up some dresses for Kitty and Lydia at once? They will need a wardrobe more appropriate for young girls in the schoolroom, and I daresay they will have outgrown the last gowns they wore. Two dresses apiece should do it, and she may use the measurements that are on file."

Hill's eyes were wide as she looked around at the bare room. Bobbing a curtsy, she said, "At once," and scurried away.

"Mama, you simply cannot do this!" wailed Kitty, who had sat on the floor next to a sobbing Lydia.

Mrs. Bennet opened her mouth to respond, but she was inter-rupted before she could say anything. Mr. Bennet stood in the doorway, a grim look on his face. "What, pray tell, is going on here?"

Chapter 4

Mrs. Bennet looked up at her husband as she worked to force the trunk closed. Brushing aside a lock of hair that had come loose from her coiffure, she said calmly, "I have determined that you are quite right, Mr. Bennet. Our youngest daughters are as silly and immature as you have always said them to be. Only unlike yourself, I am not content to remain secluded and allow them to harm our family."

Mr. Bennet's eyes widened at this chastisement. "And what have you decided to do, then?"

Calmly locking the trunk before standing, Mrs. Bennet said, "The girls are now back in the schoolroom. I will ask my brother to send a governess who can train them in proper deportment."

"Where will you get the funds to do so?" he asked curiously.

"With their pin money, plus all the extras they are granted to keep them from whining. I'm sure that's more than enough to cover the cost of a governess. I will give up some of my own, if necessary."

Mr. Bennet's eyebrows raised high on his forehead at this. "Very well, then," he finally said after a long pause. "I must say I am quite surprised by this, but I cannot complain."

"Papa!" screeched Lydia. "She must have run mad! You cannot allow her to do this!"

"On the contrary," her father replied mildly. "I have never once interfered in your mother's decisions with regard to her youngest daughters, despite the fact that Lizzy has repeatedly begged me to do so."

At this, Mrs. Bennet looked at her second daughter, who blushed and looked uncomfortably at the floor. Mr. Bennet continued. "Furthermore, I daresay this is the most sensible thing your mother has done in probably the entirety of our marriage. Bravo, my dear."

With that, Mr. Bennet gave his wife a low bow, then left the room. The resulting stunned silence lasted only a few moments before Lydia and Kitty began to wail again.

"Good heavens," Mrs. Bennet said, covering her ears with her hands. "That is quite enough. I shall lock you in here until you can express your feelings at a more appropriate level as opposed to howling like fishwives."

Before either girl could react, Mrs. Bennet ushered her eldest daughters out of the room, pulling the full trunk behind her. Panting, she reached the hallway and slammed the door closed, turning the lock just before Lydia and Kitty rushed to the door. Their sobs increased, and Mrs. Bennet could hear them pounding on the door with their fists.

Mrs. Bennet let out a loud sigh and leaned against the trunk, the day's efforts having worn her out. She turned and looked at Jane, Elizabeth, and Mary, who were staring at her with wide eyes.

"Mama, are you sure you are well?" Elizabeth asked hesitantly.

The matron gave her second daughter a worn smile. "Not entirely, but I think I will be. It is going to be a difficult few days, I believe."

"Or months," Mary muttered quietly.

"Or months," Mrs. Bennet agreed.

Mary flushed and ducked her head at having been called out for disparaging her mother's former favorites.

Mrs. Bennet let out another sigh. "Girls, will you join me in the sitting room? I think I need to explain everything, and we will be able to hear one another much better there."

The three eldest Bennet daughters silently followed their mother down the stairs, the shouts and pounding in the younger girls' bedroom fading away. When they reached the sitting room, Mrs. Bennet rang for tea, which Hill had wisely already prepared in advance, knowing her mistress's habits.

After taking a bracing swallow of the hot liquid, Mrs. Bennet began her story. She told Jane, Elizabeth, and Mary about everything: from the conversation she'd overheard between Denny and Wickham, to her confrontations with Colonel Forster and Mr. Bennet, all the way to her horrible dreams from the night prior.

Once she had finished her recitation, Mrs. Bennet sat back in her seat, taking a long drink of the tea, which was now quite cool.

"Mama, I do not intend to correct you," Jane said hesitantly, "but do you think you were a bit too harsh on Kitty and Lydia? They are still young, after all, and they aren't really that poorly behaved."

Elizabeth snorted. "Jane, I have always said that you see too much of the good in others, and this confirms it. If even Mama is concerned enough about their behavior, how can you say otherwise?"

"I agree," Mary said quietly before ducking down as if preparing for a scolding.

Mrs. Bennet's heart sank within her as she looked at her ignored middle daughter. "Thank you, Mary," she said kindly. To her amazement, Mary straightened slightly, and the glow in her cheeks made her almost as pretty as her sisters.

Have I been the cause of Mary's difficulties all this time? Mrs. Bennet wondered to herself.

She filed the thought away to contemplate later, however, when Elizabeth said, "I don't mean to be cruel, Mama, but I am very concerned that you will quickly tire of Lydia and Kitty's complaints. In the past, you and Papa have always given in to them just to make them be quiet."

Mrs. Bennet shook her head firmly. "I plan on informing your father that he isn't to allow me to do that. I truly don't think that I will, but I understand why you're concerned. I will count on the three of you to make sure he doesn't give in to them or me."

The tension eased from Elizabeth's shoulders. "What happens

now, then?"

Sighing, Mrs. Bennet said, "I will write to my brother to have him find a governess who can have a firm hand, both with the girls and myself, should I revert back to former habits. He told me once when you girls were younger that a governess rarely receives a salary of more than twenty pounds per year; although most work for just room and board, and perhaps five pounds a year."

"So little?" whispered Jane.

Mrs. Bennet nodded. "That is part of why I have pushed you girls to marry well. A life in service is difficult, and just one well-settled brother-in-law can make the difference between happiness and misery for the remainder of your lives."

The girls sat quietly, contemplating the information their mother had shared. Hesitantly, Mary broke the silence and asked in a whisper, "How-how much would a music master cost?"

Everyone looked at her in surprise, and she turned bright pink. Once again, a pang of guilt struck Mrs. Bennet at the sight of her neglected middle daughter. "Would you like that, Mary, dear?"

Mary nodded fervently, and Mrs. Bennet said, "Then I will include a request for that information in my letter to my brother."

The timid girl beamed with happiness, and Mrs. Bennet once again noticed the potential beauty in her daughter's happy face. Thinking hard, Mrs. Bennet said, "Now, girls, as a way to express my gratitude for your forbearance with the difficulties we will all endure, I think each of you deserves a new gown for the Netherfield ball."

Elizabeth and Jane smiled, but Mary scowled. "Favor is deceitful, and beauty is vain. Proverbs, chapter 31."

"Are you saying that Jane is vain for wishing for a new gown?" Elizabeth asked, frowning.

Startled, Mary looked at her sister. "No... that is, I had not thought..." she stammered out.

"Proverbs 31 also says that a virtuous woman dresses in scarlet and purple, and that she makes fine linen," responded Mrs. Bennet.

In surprise, the three girls looked at their mother, who smiled sheepishly. "I may have memorized that section of verse when I found myself in love with a clergyman once."

Elizabeth let out a burst of laughter, then quickly covered her mouth with her hands. Mrs. Bennet laughed. "Don't worry, Lizzy. I agree that I would have made a terrible wife for a parson!"

Even Mary smiled at this self-disparagement from her mother. Elizabeth then looked at Mary. "I think there is no vanity in trying to look one's best to glorify the body God made for you, or to honor your parents and their love for you. Vanity only comes when you compare yourself to others and set yourself above them because of your looks. I think Jane is a perfect example of dressing well yet remaining humble."

Jane flushed scarlet red. "Oh, Lizzy."

Mary nodded slowly. "I think I understand. I just don't want as many ribbons and lace as Kitty and Lydia ask for."

Mrs. Bennet turned pink. "I promise, Mary, that I will do my best to not push those fripperies on you as I usually do."

"And Jane and I will be there to support you," Elizabeth said encouragingly.

As they finished making their plans to visit the dressmaker the following day, Mrs. Bennet added, "Now girls, we will probably see officers while we are out, and again at the ball. You may speak with them, and even dance if asked, but I utterly forbid you to be alone with them or flirt with any of them."

Mary rolled her eyes, causing Elizabeth to laugh. "I think Mary would preach at them, and Jane has eyes for no one but Mr. Bingley."

Jane protested, but Elizabeth overrode her sister. "As for myself, I am determined to never give another thought to Mr. Wickham or Mr. Denny. At the risk of sounding like Jane, I can scarcely believe Mr. Wickham capable of such deceit and indecency! He has such a pleasing countenance, and had the report come from anyone else, Mama, I daresay I wouldn't have entirely believed it."

"But you do believe me?" Mrs. Bennet asked anxiously.

"Of course! Nothing but something that severe by someone so trusted could have caused such an alteration in you, Mama," Elizabeth said frankly. "I shall greet them civilly, but otherwise, I hope to never see Mr. Wickham or his ilk again. Imagine, such a man thought he was fit for the church! I can well understand why Mr. Darcy might have denied him the living."

"Perhaps it makes you see Mr. Darcy isn't quite the villain that you have made him out to be?" Jane asked with a sly smile.

"Well, he did call me tolerable." Elizabeth laughed. "But other than that and his unsocial disposition, I know of no particular ill of him. He has always at least been polite."

"Perhaps we will come to know him better as we spend more time in his company," suggested Jane.

Elizabeth shrugged. "Perhaps. It will be interesting to attempt to make out his character."

Chapter 5

The twenty-sixth of November arrived, which was the day set for the ball at Netherfield. Along with the Bennets came a rather unpleasant guest in the form of their cousin and the heir presumptive to Longbourn, Mr. Collins.

The tall, heavy-looking young man of twenty-five years of age had formal manners and a grave air. He had not stopped speaking once since his arrival to Longbourn, and most of it was about his patroness, a certain Lady Catherine de Bourgh.

It was with great relief that the company arrived at Netherfield for the ball. Although the carriage was much less crowded than usual, due to Kitty and Lydia having to remain at home in the recently cleaned schoolroom (that the new governess forced them to clean themselves), the odor emanating from their cousin made the short trip of three miles almost unbearable.

Mr. Collins had originally set his sights on Jane, but Mrs. Bennet gently steered him away with the hint that there was a suitor on the horizon. When it became obvious that he had turned his attentions towards Elizabeth—who was quite horrified by them—Mrs. Bennet decided to have a talk with her second daughter.

Elizabeth made it clear that the idea of being mistress of Longbourn was not enough to outweigh her inability to marry such a ridiculous man. While Mrs. Bennet did not fully understand—after all, Mr. Collins seemed very kind and deferential, albeit a bit proud—she had learned enough over the prior weeks to not push the issue.

Mary, on the other hand, seemed to almost desire the strange man's company. She frequently asked him questions that she deemed to be of great doctrinal importance, and she did her best to sit with him. A brief conversation with her middle daughter confirmed Mrs. Bennet's suspicions, and she began to actively guide Mr. Collins towards Mary and away from Elizabeth.

The fact that Mary had allowed her mother and sisters to help with her hair and wardrobe was a key factor in Mr. Collins easily being steered towards a third Bennet daughter. At first, he chafed at Elizabeth not being for him—she was, after all, second only to her sister in beauty—but Mrs. Bennet wisely pointed out Elizabeth's impertinent wit several times as being a detriment. "After all, if her father cannot temper her, who can say that Lady Catherine would be able to? Is it worth the risk?"

Such talk was sufficient for Mr. Collins's simple understanding, and by the time the Netherfield ball had arrived, he and Mary were officially courting with Mr. Bennet's amused approval.

With Longbourn nearly secure and her youngest daughters in good hands, Mrs. Bennet felt better than she'd had in years—if not decades. When Lydia was born a girl and the midwife declared there was no possibility for more children, she had begun to worry about how her girls would be provided for in the future.

Mrs. Bennet had also never realized just how much her nerves had been affected by Lydia and her tantrums. With the governess keeping a firm hand on both girls, life at Longbourn had become quite calm and enjoyable. The music master had given Mary some advice on her playing, which also improved the atmosphere.

As the Bennet family entered Netherfield, the matriarch smiled to see Bingley's eyes locked on Jane, who looked very becoming in her new ball gown. The young man was speechless for a full ten seconds before he stammered out a greeting and solicited Jane's hand for the supper set, in addition to the first two dances he had requested earlier in the week. Mrs. Bennet smiled with satisfaction.

Miss Bingley greeted her guests with a cool, superior air. She exclaimed surprise over the absence of the younger two Bennet girls. "They provide such good entertainment; it is a shame to not have them in attendance."

Mouth agape at the woman's rudeness, Mrs. Bennet couldn't think of a single thing to say. Fortunately, Elizabeth was standing right next to her. "How kind of you, Miss Bingley. I had no idea you enjoyed the attentions of my younger sisters so much. Perhaps we shall arrange for them to pay a call on you; it certainly seems you have much in common, given your desire for their company."

Miss Bingley blanched, and Mrs. Bennet looked away to hide her smile. She moved forward in the receiving line and looped her arm around Elizabeth's. "Well done, my dear. It appears your inherited wit from your father is good for something after all."

Elizabeth gave a light laugh as they approached Mr. Darcy, who, as a current resident of Netherfield, was standing in the line at the end, greeting guests along with his friends. "Mrs. Bennet, Miss Elizabeth," he intoned in a deep, solemn voice.

For the first time, Mrs. Bennet was struck by how tall and handsome the young man was. "Mr. Darcy," she replied, dipping a curtsy.

Elizabeth echoed her mother's actions, then moved away from the receiving line, saying, "Mama, I wish to go and find Charlotte."

"Very well, my dear," Mrs. Bennet agreed. Out of the corner of her eye, she noticed Mr. Darcy's gaze follow Elizabeth intently through the crowd. He only looked away when Miss Bingley hissed something to him.

That could prove to be interesting, Mrs. Bennet murmured. *What pin money she would have as Mrs. Darcy!*

Her first inclination was to bustle off and find Lady Lucas to share this new revelation, but something the governess had been teaching the younger girls came to her mind. "The mark of a true lady is in how she speaks about others. Before sharing news about someone, you should ask yourself these three things: is it kind, is it true, and is it helpful?"

Well, it certainly would be true, and it would be helpful in furthering a match with Mr. Darcy, as gossip will bring about a marriage quicker than any courtship could. But... would that be kind to him or Elizabeth?

Deciding that she should probably keep her eyes open and her mouth shut for the time being, she joined Lady Lucas and Mrs. Long without speaking a word about what she had witnessed. Even when Mr. Darcy and Elizabeth joined the dance floor, causing gasps of surprise from most of the ballroom, Mrs. Bennet merely smiled. "It appears he finds her tolerable after all, but perhaps he just wished to dance with someone other than his own party and my Lizzy was the nearest to him."

Meanwhile, Elizabeth took her place in the set, ignoring the looks of surprise from her friends and neighbors. Charlotte sent her a wink, which Elizabeth chose to ignore. Instead, she focused her gaze on the ground and followed the steps of the dance in intense silence.

After several moments, she decided the best way to annoy Mr. Darcy—and indeed, she *did* wish to annoy him since her pride still smarted from his comment at the assembly about her beauty— would be to disoblige his wish for silence, so she made an observation about the dance.

When he made no more than a small reply, she then said, "It is *your* turn to say something now, Mr. Darcy. I talked about the dance, so perhaps you should remark on the size of the room or the number of couples. Or perhaps you might wish to observe that private balls are more pleasant than public ones."

"I shall say whatever you wish," he replied stoically.

Elizabeth laughed. "Now that won't do! It would be odd for our conversation to be entirely of my own opinions. No, you must say something of your own volition."

"Very well," he replied, then hesitated. "Do you and your sisters often walk to Meryton?"

"At times," she said. Then, unable to resist the temptation, she added, "When you met us the other day, we were forming a new acquaintance with someone who seems to be known to you—a Mr. Wickham?"

A deep look of disdain came across Darcy's features, and he stiffly replied, "Mr. Wickham is blessed with the happy manners of making friends easily, but it is uncertain if he is capable of retaining them."

"Oh, I know," Elizabeth blurted out. At Darcy's quizzical look, she blushed. "My mother—quite by accident—happened to overhear a conversation between Mr. Wickham and another officer that greatly disturbed her. In response, she has placed my two youngest sisters back into the schoolroom and forbidden us to spend any time speaking alone with any member of the militia, even in public, unless a dance has been requested."

Darcy's eyebrows rose high on his forehead. "I must admit, I had not thought your mother to be wise enough to understand Mr. Wickham's danger."

"Indeed, nor I," admitted Elizabeth. "I must admit to being heartily ashamed for having been so taken in by his good manners. It made me realize I hardly knew myself. I have always prided myself on being a good judge of character, but it appears I was greatly deceived by him, even going so far as to think ill of you and your sister."

"My sister?" The surprise on Darcy's face turned quickly to alarm. "What did he have to say about Georgiana?"

"Nothing terrible," Elizabeth answered with some confusion. "Only that she was sweet as a child and he devoted hours to her amusement, but since she has grown, she has become just as proud as yourself."

Darcy relaxed, but Elizabeth flushed at this inadvertent insult she had given him. "I beg your pardon," she muttered.

"It is quite all right," he assured her. "Georgiana is not proud, but extremely shy. I imagine it could come across as pride to those

354

who do not know her well, but that is not always a failing. After all, did we not discuss this one evening some weeks ago? We agreed that pride under good regulation would always be a virtue."

"I most certainly did *not* agree," she exclaimed indignantly.

A small twitch at the corner of Darcy's mouth almost caused Elizabeth to stumble. "You are… you are teasing me?" she asked in astonishment.

The sole trace of humor vanished from Darcy's face, replaced by an aloof stiffness. "I apologize if I caused offense."

Elizabeth shook her head. "No, no, not at all. I am not offended, merely surprised. I had not known you were capable of teasing someone."

Darcy's eyes widened in surprise. "Perhaps not in strange company, but with those whom I feel comfortable, I enjoy the diversion."

Elizabeth felt a warmth rise in her chest. "I am honored you feel comfortable with me, Mr. Darcy, especially when we have done nothing but argue for the entirety of our acquaintance."

"It is for that very reason that I do. You do not agree with every word I say, nor do you fall into silence. A genuinely intelligent debate is always preferable, and I find myself greatly enjoying speaking with you."

She felt as though her face were on fire. "I don't believe I was always so appealing to you." At Darcy's questioning glance, she added in a deep voice, "She is tolerable, I suppose, but not handsome enough to tempt me."

Darcy looked confused for several seconds, then his face turned ashen. "I beg you to forgive me. I uttered those words in haste, with a terrible headache, and did not even know about whom I was speaking. It was never intended to be overheard nor personal. I merely wished for Bingley to leave me be."

Elizabeth let out a light laugh. "Well, as my mother has learned recently, those who listen rarely hear good about themselves. Perhaps I should not have been listening in to your private conversation. Perhaps we can agree to both be at fault and begin anew."

At that moment, the music ended, causing everyone to stop dancing and bow to their partners. Darcy took Elizabeth's arm, but instead of returning her to her previous place beside Charlotte, he pulled her over to a quiet, secluded corner.

"I don't think I *can* begin anew," Darcy replied. When Elizabeth's brow furrowed, he continued. "I cannot forget our debates, our conversations, and the esteem with which I hold you. Indeed, it has been many weeks now that I have considered you one of the handsomest and kindest women of my acquaintance."

Elizabeth gasped. "What—what do you mean?"

"I mean, dearest Elizabeth, that my feelings will not be repressed. You must allow me to tell you how much I ardently admire and love you. I have fought against it, because of my pride, but I beg you to relieve my suffering and agree to be my wife."

From across the room, Mrs. Bennet watched with satisfaction as Mr. Darcy spoke privately to her second daughter in the corner. A broad grin crossed her face when Darcy smiled, gave Elizabeth his arm, and the two crossed the ballroom to speak to Mr. Bennet.

Perhaps my eavesdropping was more to the purpose than I originally anticipated.

Epilogue

15 years later...

Mrs. Bennet looked up at the holly adorning the mantelpiece and smiled. Everything was in readiness for Christmas at Pulvis Lodge, where she resided with her companion Mrs. Hayter.

No one was more surprised than she when Mrs. Bennet discovered she greatly enjoyed the company of her daughters' former governess. Although she knew it was what she wanted when she hired the stern women to control her youngest children, Mrs. Bennet had not expected to come to actually *like* and respect the woman.

But when the girls came out into society and no longer were in need of Mrs. Hayter, Mrs. Bennet offered the woman the position of companion, which was gratefully accepted. After Mr. Bennet passed last year, Mrs. Hayter's company was very welcome. It gave Mrs. Bennet the courage to turn down her daughters' offers to reside at Longbourn and Netherfield. Instead, with the financial support of her two eldest sons-in-law, she began to lease the very house whose attics she had once despised.

Well, they were quite dreadful, she told herself. *At least until dear Darcy hired that carpenter to make the repairs.*

Mrs. Bennet was especially excited for Christmas this year, as all of her daughters and their families would be coming to Meryton for the holidays.

After Mr. Bennet's death, Mary Collins came to Longbourn, along with her husband and their seven children. *I still don't know how that girl gave birth so many times in so few years.* Mrs. Bennet winced at the thought. Part of Mrs. Bennet's desire to leave Longbourn had more to do with the space and noise rather than a lack of love for her middle daughter.

Mr. Collins had improved greatly under his sensible wife's tutelage, and their children were well behaved and thankfully took more after their mother in appearance.

Mrs. Bennet was especially touched when Mr. Collins declared that his children would all have the surname of Bennet, so as to keep the estate in the same family line. Mr. Collins, Sr. had been quite miserly and cruel, and his son had little wish for the name to sully the estate of his wife's parents, who he had come to love as his own.

Jane, as expected, had become engaged to Mr. Bingley shortly after the Netherfield ball. His sisters, upon hearing the announcement, immediately quit the estate and returned to town in protest. As a result, Mr. Bingley spent more time at Longbourn than his own estate in the weeks leading up to his wedding. He decided to purchase Netherfield after the lease expired, and he, Jane, and their three children were quite content living next to Mr. and Mrs. Bennet.

Mr. Bingley might not have proposed so quickly had his friend not entered into a courtship with Elizabeth. Mr. Darcy had proposed at the Netherfield ball, but Elizabeth had not felt comfortable accepting such a commitment at that time. She offered a counter-proposal that he court her for three months so she could come to better know his character.

She only needed a month.

The two now lived happily in Derbyshire with their three sons and two daughters. The eldest son was also the eldest grandson, and he was named Bennet, following the Darcy tradition of giving the first boy his mother's maiden name as his Christian name.

Part of the reason for the courtship to move more quickly was the arrival of Georgiana Darcy and Colonel Fitzwilliam, whom Darcy summoned once the militia had moved away from Meryton. Elizabeth and Georgiana became such good friends that Elizabeth no longer felt as though Darcy's character were a mystery to her. It was with great confidence that she informed Georgiana one day on a walk that, should her brother care to repeat his question from the Netherfield ball, he would receive a more favorable answer this time.

It was with a happy heart that Mrs. Bennet bid farewell to the militia when they departed for Brighton. Colonel Forster's young wife invited Maria Lucas to join her as a companion—as Lydia was no longer available—but Mrs. Bennet expressed her disapproval to Lady Lucas in such a way that Charlotte was sent to accompany her sister.

The Lucases were extremely grateful to Mrs. Bennet for her superior insight when an express came from Charlotte. Miss Lucas wrote to inform her parents that Wickham had deserted the militia and attempted to take Maria with him! It was only Charlotte's presence that had prevented the elopement and led to Wickham's forfeiture of life for desertion during wartime.

Additionally, Charlotte had met a retired naval man by the name of Captain Benwick, who was attracted to her calm demeanor and pleasant company. Not only had Maria escaped ruin, but Charlotte returned home engaged to a sailor who had earned quite a bit of prize money during his time on the sea.

Maria's experience served as a good warning to Lydia and Kitty, who had also calmed considerably under the tutelage of Mrs. Hayter. They were each able to come out to society and comport themselves with propriety. They would never be sensible, and Lydia would always have her lively spirits, but they knew how to temper themselves in accordance with etiquette.

Each girl made a good match; Kitty with Mr. Goulding, and Lydia with Mr. Lucas. Both girls settled in Meryton, meaning that Mrs. Bennet was surrounded by almost all of her daughters. She missed Elizabeth in the north, but the two wrote often, and Mr. and Mrs. Bennet visited frequently—at least once a year for a month complete.

Fortunately for the Darcys, Georgiana married a man whose estate was not twenty miles from Pemberley, so they had at least one sibling living near them. They also stayed at Netherfield regularly when they visited Rosings or Longbourn.

Mrs. Bennet's meditations on her daughters and their lives were interrupted by a knock at the door. The maid opened it to admit a large crowd of the very people of whom Mrs. Bennet had been considering. She smiled as the large group entered the home, chattering gaily.

Yes, she thought to herself, *I will always be grateful for overhearing something that gave my life purpose.*

For I Am a Married Woman

William Collins discovered as a youth that with some polish and grooming, he could charm ladies as easily as the handsomest gentleman could. When he arrives at Longbourn to choose a wife from his cousins, Lydia is taken in by his compliments and declares that she should be the one to be put forth as Mrs. Collins. Meanwhile, Mr. Collins finds a friend in George Wickham. How will the friendship between these two rakes change the story?

Chapter 1

"What do you think he is like, Papa?" Elizabeth asked Mr. Bennet as he finished reading Mr. Collins's letter. "Do you think he could be a sensible man?"

"I'm afraid not, my dear," Mr. Bennet replied with a sigh as he took off his reading glasses. "The old Mr. Collins was an illiterate and miserly man; as Mrs. Collins died in childbirth, I'm afraid young William Collins was raised entirely by a father who most definitely did not behave as a gentleman should in any way. No, based on this letter, I expect the apple did not fall far from the tree."

The younger Mr. Collins arrived at Longbourn at the precise minute he was expected. Elizabeth casually wondered if he had made the cart and horse wait around the bend until the right moment. She had hoped—rather than believed—that the young man would prove to be better than his letter.

He was not.

Mr. Collins was a tall young man with a large form. He could also be considered handsome in the same way that Charlotte Lucas was. He was mannerly and well groomed, and Elizabeth's expectations began to rise as he descended from the buggy and made his bows to her father.

Then he opened his mouth, and the flowery words that fell from his lips almost made her laugh out loud.

"My dear cousins! It is such an honor to meet you. I had heard many reports of your beauty; indeed, your reputation has reached all the way to Kent. But I never expected to ever witness such loveliness as what is before me!"

As he spoke, he went down the line and kissed each girl on the hand. Jane, Elizabeth, and Mary did their best not to grimace, but Kitty and Lydia went into fits of giggles when it was their turn.

"And this must be the beautiful woman who has given birth to these angels," Mr. Collins said to Mrs. Bennet. "I almost mistook you for one of the daughters, madam, and it was only the lace cap on your head that prevented me from thinking my cousin had six daughters rather than five."

Mrs. Bennet blushed at this overt praise and batted her eyelashes. Her titters sounded exactly like those of her two youngest daughters, and Elizabeth bit her tongue to keep her amusement at bay.

"Yes, well, I do believe I am able to remember the number of children I have," Mr. Bennet said dryly. "Now that you have all become acquainted, we would do best to move indoors."

Mr. Collins immediately extended his arm to Mrs. Bennet, whose flush deepened as she took it. He then extended the other arm to Jane. The eldest Bennet daughter blinked at him in surprise before tentatively accepting his escort into the house.

As they moved inside, Mr. Collins continued to wax eloquent on the beauty of the women at his side. Elizabeth and Mary rolled their eyes towards each other behind his back while Lydia and Kitty took up the rear.

Once Mr. Collins had been shown to his room so he could refresh himself, the ladies retired to the drawing room to wait for dinner.

"Have you ever seen such a handsome and charming young man?" Mrs. Bennet asked enthusiastically. "So respectful and flattering. I daresay any of you girls would be lucky to have such a man as a husband. After all, not only is he everything a gentleman ought to be, but he has a good living and will one day be master of Longbourn."

She paused and looked around the room, then frowned at Jane. "But Jane is for Mr. Bingley," she declared firmly.

Jane's shoulders relaxed at this reprieve. It was clear to Elizabeth that Mr. Collins's offer of escort had discomposed her gentle sister.

364

"I quite agree, Mama," Elizabeth said, to everyone's surprise. "Mr. Bingley was here first, after all, and has paid some attentions to Jane. With his income, it would be cruel to allow a rival for her affections to drive such a suitor away."

"Then you shall have Mr. Collins," Mrs. Bennet said with satisfaction, to Elizabeth's horror.

Elizabeth opened her mouth to protest, but she was beaten to it by a very unlikely source.

"No, Mama! I want him!"

Elizabeth turned to stare at Lydia, who had stamped her foot to emphasize her point. She continued. "I want to be the first married of all my sisters! Then everyone, even Jane, will have to be below me because I will be a married woman."

It was all Elizabeth could do to prevent herself from gaping at her youngest, most foolish sister.

"Why, of *course* you shall have him!" exclaimed Mrs. Bennet. "What a wonderful idea! I had thought you might take a liking to one of the officers when they came, but marrying an heir to an estate is a much better plan for you, my dear girl."

Elizabeth felt the need to speak up. "Lydia, are you quite certain? Marriage is no game, and you don't know anything of his character."

"Oh, la, you're just jealous because I've stolen your beau," cried Lydia. "Don't worry, Lizzy. Once I am married, I will be more than happy to chaperon you to balls and dances."

"Heaven forbid," Elizabeth whispered to Mary, who nodded in agreement with wide eyes.

"Might I remind you that Mr. Collins has not paid particular attentions to anyone?" she continued in a louder voice for the entire room to hear. "We have only met him today. He may not be interested in you at all, Lydia."

Lydia and Mrs. Bennet looked at one another, then burst into raucous laughter.

"Who would not wish to marry my dearest girl?" cried their

mother, wiping tears from her eyes. "Lizzy, I think Lydia is correct! You are jealous of her winning Mr. Collins over you."

Elizabeth threw up her arms in surrender. "Very well, then. I wish you luck and joy in your endeavors."

With that, she stalked out of the room and went to her father's library. Knocking softly three times, as was her custom, she was bidden entrance.

"Papa, you will not believe the complete insanity that has taken over Mama and Lydia."

Mr. Bennet set his book to the side, and she quickly explained Lydia's sudden desire to marry Mr. Collins because he was somewhat charming, and being married would give her precedence over her sisters. He listened with amusement, then began to chuckle as she finished her recounting of the afternoon's events.

"Well, my dear, I will never be easy until Lydia is settled and out of my home. Mr. Collins may have her and take charge of her silliness, and I will finally have some peace, having gotten rid of my silliest daughter. I wish them all the best."

"But, Papa!" she protested. "Do you not think Lydia would be making a very imprudent match? Can you imagine her as a clergyman's wife, helping those in her parish? She knows nothing about his character nor the importance of such a decision that will affect her entire life!"

"She will not marry any more imprudently than her mother did, and is Mrs. Bennet unhappy? Lydia will have a comfortable home, and I believe that a man as sycophantic as Mr. Collins appears to be will make her happy if she can steer him right."

"Papa, we met him *today*. What if under all his charm and compliments he hides a vicious nature and will be cruel to her?"

"Lizzy, my dear, they would not be the first couple to marry foolishly nor the last. If he decides to ask me for her hand in marriage, I will not deny him. Think, too, of the comfort it will bring your family to know that you will not end up in the hedgerows upon my death."

He flicked his book open again and began to read. She tried to object once more, but he silenced her with a curt, "Leave it be, Lizzy. It is her life to ruin. Lord knows she could have done it in much worse ways and with more inconvenience to myself."

Sighing in resignation, Elizabeth returned to the drawing room, knowing that she would be fetched by a maid if she retreated to her bedroom until dinnertime.

When she entered, Mr. Collins was sitting next to Jane on a settee, with Lydia perched on a chair at his side. Elizabeth watched with a combination of amusement and dismay as the poor man attempted to compliment Jane but would be pulled away by Lydia's comments.

The same occurred throughout dinner, much to Mr. Bennet's amusement. Mr. Collins waxed on about his cottage, his patroness and her daughter, and the benefits of being Mrs. Collins. He directed this towards Jane, but Lydia took each comment for herself.

"You may imagine I am always available to pay little, delicate compliments to Lady Catherine and her daughter," he said. "I flatter myself that I have become quite accomplished at paying every attention to worthy ladies."

At this, he gave a significant look at Jane, who blushed and shifted uncomfortably in her seat.

"What an excellent coincidence!" cried Mrs. Bennet. "My Lydia absolutely adores attention and compliments, do you not, my dear?"

"Oh, yes, more than anything," Lydia agreed enthusiastically, batting her eyelashes furtively at Mr. Collins, who gave her a winning smile in return.

Once the sexes had separated and then rejoined one another, Mrs. Bennet took a moment to sit near Mr. Collins. Elizabeth saw them whispering and looking towards Jane and Lydia. At first, Mr. Collins looked perturbed, but when Lydia sat up straighter in her seat, causing her bosom to thrust forward, a glint came into his eye.

Nodding eagerly, he crossed the room and sat next to Lydia, all but ignoring Jane.

Elizabeth groaned to herself, but there was nothing she could do. Lydia would become Mrs. Collins.

Chapter 2

Mr. Collins whistled to himself as he walked down the stairs of Longbourn, running his hand along the stately polished handrail. After years of dealing with poverty and scorn from his father, his life was now looking to be complete.

While not blessed with the most handsome of countenances, Mr. Collins prided himself on the fact that he had a rather smooth tongue with the ladies. He had found comfort in the arms of many of the looser women in the village where he began to change into a man, and in return, he charmed them with pretty words to boost their low spirits when the proper ladies looked down on them.

During his years at school to eventually take orders, he was able to use that same flattery to work his way into the beds of ladies of the night without having to pay full price for their services. And now, as a vicar, he could give comfort in more than one way to a lonely wife whose husband did not fully appreciate her charms.

When he arrived at Longbourn, Mr. Collins could hardly believe his good fortune. All the Bennet daughters were quite lovely, especially the eldest. He paid his attentions to her, but it was clear by the end of the evening that she was too mild for his tastes. The second eldest could have been an option, but he saw her watching him warily and knew she was more intelligent than he would like.

The youngest, Miss Lydia, however… Now there was a girl who was ripe for the plucking if he had ever seen one. He was a bit surprised that she seemed so eager to command his attentions—he knew he wasn't the most handsome of men—but who was he to look a gift horse in the mouth?

With Mrs. Bennet in full agreement, it seemed he would be marrying the youngest of his cousins. Certainly she had some taming that needed to be done—especially to please Lady Catherine—but once she was in his control in his home and his bed, he had full confidence that he could shape her into the type of life partner he desired.

His thoughts were interrupted when he reached the breakfast room to find the majority of the Bennet family present.

"Oh, Mr. Collins!" cried Lydia. "We are so glad you are here. Would you like to walk to Meryton with us? We wish to pay a call on the regiment."

He frowned at her exuberance. "While I do enjoy a good walk—as it's good exercise—I am a bit hesitant to be introduced to members of the militia. Most officers who purchase a local commission do so because they cannot afford a higher rank. Many are not even gentlemen."

Lydia's face crumbled, and he could see the indecision in her eyes. Would she choose him, or would she choose her fancy for the redcoats? He almost grinned, as he could see the wheels turn slowly in her head. In fact, Mr. Collins had nothing against officers, but he wanted to see what choice she would make.

"Well, I suppose if you would rather not, we could walk somewhere else," she said, biting her lip uncertainly and looking towards her mother, who nodded her approval.

"Then again," he said, wanting to reward her for making the correct decision, "as a parson, I should not judge others before meeting them. *By their fruits ye shall know them,* says the Good Book. How can I lead people towards righteousness if I don't take the trouble to become acquainted with them?"

Lydia nodded furiously in agreement and clapped her hands with glee. "I can assure you, Mr. Collins, that the officers with whom we are acquainted have always been gentlemen."

"Then I would be delighted to accompany my dearest cousin

Lydia," he said with a broad smile and sly wink towards her. "After all, I would loathe to be parted from your fair company." He paused and looked around. "Will any of my other cousins like to accompany us?"

Everyone except Mary agreed that a walk into Meryton would be a good idea, and a plan was set in place. Once they had all finished their breakfast and changed their clothing, they put on their boots and began the well-worn path down to the small town.

Mr. Collins listened absentmindedly as Lydia chattered on about the ribbons she wished to purchase for a bonnet she had recently acquired. "It is hideously ugly, but I thought I might as well get it as not. I can always rip it apart and make something better, I daresay..."

He amused himself by envisioning how he would handle this sort of prattling when they were married. Of course, he didn't wish to crush her spirit *too* much. Otherwise he might as well marry her dull eldest sister. But with a few nudges in the right direction, he was confident he could direct her passions towards... other pursuits.

As they walked, Mr. Collins admired her form and pert bosom, which bounced against his arm that she held tightly against her. Yes, he would enjoy being married to her. It was worth putting up with her featherbrained wit in the daytime to have her warm his bed at night. Besides, he was sure he could find plenty to occupy her during the day that would keep them apart.

The group at last reached Meryton and almost immediately encountered several officers standing together on the side of the road. "Denny!" shouted Kitty, waving her hand to gain their attention.

Lydia looked as if to follow her sister, but one glance at Mr. Collins's purposefully raised eyebrow had her grip his arm even more tightly against her. "Does your sister always act so... indecorously?"

"That is why Mama often has me direct her," Lydia said boastfully.

Mr. Collins didn't miss the snicker that escaped from Elizabeth's mouth, but he chose to ignore it. "That is very good of you, Cousin Lydia," he said, patting her arm in approval. "I am quite pleased to have attached myself to the most ladylike and mature of women."

She preened at this compliment and sedately crossed the road at his side. Kitty had already rushed to join the officers. Elizabeth and Jane hurried after the girl, most likely to keep her in check.

Once all had joined the soldiers, Lydia proudly introduced everyone. "Mr. Collins, allow me to present these gentlemen to you. Here are Misters Pratt, Denny, and Chamberlayne. They are lieutenants who have recently arrived. Oh, and I don't know you," she said to yet another gentleman.

The officer called Denny stepped forward and bowed in response to Lydia's inquiry. "Please let me introduce you to my friend, Mr. Wickham. He just signed up to enlist in the regiment this morning and is still awaiting his uniform."

Greetings were exchanged all around, and Kitty eagerly invited all of them to a card party that evening at Mrs. Phillips. Lydia urged them to accept as well, but Elizabeth stepped in. "I don't believe, girls, that we have the right to extend the invitation on our aunt's behalf."

Lydia opened her mouth to protest, but Mr. Collins pressed gently on her hand. "Quite proper of you, Cousin Elizabeth."

Elizabeth looked at him with a mix of surprise and suspicion in her eyes, but he returned the look with one that he had perfected as a child: a mixture of innocence and blundering foolishness.

The newly arrived Wickham added his agreement and finished by saying, "However, if Mrs. Phillips makes the invitation herself, we would be more than glad to accept."

As if by design, an upstairs window of a nearby home was opened, and the lady herself called down to greet the party. Lydia began to shout an answer back, but Mr. Collins once again pressed her hand firmly. Instead, Kitty was left to display a lack of decorum in the streets, causing her elder two sisters to blush furiously.

Wickham gracefully accepted the invitation to the card party after Kitty urged her aunt to make the offer. When Mr. Collins met Wickham's eyes, what he saw made him want to laugh. *This man is no more an honorable gentleman than I am! It seems we might have more in common than I thought.*

Shortly after the debacle ended, two gentlemen on horses approached them. Mr. Collins was introduced by Jane to Misters Bingley and Darcy. *Ah, the suitor and his friend... Perhaps he is related to Lady Catherine? He certainly looks arrogant enough to be the nephew she claims is engaged to her daughter.*

Mr. Collins watched as Darcy turned red and Wickham turned white upon seeing one another. Eventually, Wickham tipped his hat, but Darcy whipped his horse around and rode quickly in the opposite direction. Poor Bingley, who had been speaking ardently with Jane, looked after his friend in confusion before making his farewells and mounting his horse once again.

Eyeing Wickham, who was doing his best to not appear discomposed at the encounter, Mr. Collins thought, *Yes, I think it would be a good thing to make friends with this man.*

Chapter 3

Elizabeth entered the drawing room of her aunt Phillips for the card party and looked around. She was unsurprised to see the officers already there, with Kitty sitting in the midst of them. What *did* surprise her was that Lydia stayed with Mr. Collins rather than joining her sister with the handsome redcoats.

Perhaps this marriage may be a better match than I originally thought.

There was still something about the way Mr. Collins looked at Lydia, however, that made Elizabeth uncomfortable. He was as obsequious and fawning as she had imagined him to be after reading his letter, but at times, there was a look in his eye that made her wonder if he was more intelligent than he seemed. It was as if his ingratiating, bumbling nature was merely a facade.

No, she wasn't quite yet ready to trust him completely.

She took a seat near the fire and amused herself by sketching the characters of her new acquaintances. After several minutes, the handsome Lieutenant Wickham approached and seated himself beside her. He began the conversation by asking about the county, eventually leading the conversation to the current residents of Netherfield.

"Do you know Mr. Darcy well?" he inquired.

"As much as I wish to," she said hotly. "I spent a few days in the same house as him when Jane took ill, and in spite of being of large property in Derbyshire, I find him to be quite disagreeable."

"Ah, yes, Pemberley. I know it very well. I grew up there, you see, and have been connected with Darcy as a friend since our infancy."

Elizabeth's eyes widened in surprise, and she listened as Wickham spoke of the living he had been denied and how he had been cast out of the only home he had known.

"That is quite terrible!" she cried out, not noticing she had ignited the attentions of Mr. Collins. "Why did you not take it up with the authorities?"

"I'm afraid it was written in such a way that it was able to be interpreted as merely a desire rather than a bequest. Besides, I cannot bring myself to make it known. Until I can forget his father, I could never disparage the son."

"What is this?"

The pair looked up to see that Mr. Collins had joined their conversation. Elizabeth was silent, still agitated by the injustices poor Wickham had suffered. She expected him to politely change the conversation to a new topic to keep the story private, but to her surprise, he repeated the entire thing to Mr. Collins.

"That does sound quite terrible," Mr. Collins said when Wickham's tale was finished. "You would have no doubt made a perfect man of the cloth."

"As you are, I'm sure," Wickham responded. "I truly regret being denied the opportunity to... help and comfort the men and *women* of a flock. There are so many ways to show them love in a way they may not have."

"That is precisely how I see it," Mr. Collins said. "I only wish my patroness, Lady Catherine de Bourgh, would allow me more freedoms in helping her daughter."

"Not Darcy's aunt?" exclaimed Wickham in surprise. "And his cousin, little Anne?"

"The very one," replied Mr. Collins. "*Miss* de Bourgh is the sole heir to Rosings Park, and I visit the household on a regular basis to provide spiritual counsel to both ladies. Based on your story, it appears Mr. Darcy is just like his aunt in preferring to arrange things according to his will and pleasure."

"I can only imagine Miss de Bourgh feels quite confined with such a life."

Mr. Collins sighed. "Indeed, and I wish I could do more to help comfort her."

The two men spoke to one another as if there was double meaning to everything they were saying. This was typical for Elizabeth and her father, as very few people were capable of understanding their wit, but this was on a different level. She couldn't help feeling as if she were missing an important piece of a puzzle.

She shifted uncomfortably in her seat, anxious to find a way to excuse herself and join a card game, but all the tables were full. As much as she loathed them, there was too much double entendre in the conversation for her to want to participate any longer. Her estimation of both men had sunk quite low, although she could not exactly say why.

"Perhaps one day I can be of service to her," Wickham suggested. "I met her several times when we were younger. Lady Catherine and Sir Lewis came to visit Pemberley several times. I found her to be quite timid and reserved, one who would take correction easily. Is she still that way?"

"I believe she is," Mr. Collins sighed. Then he brightened. "I say, Mr. Wickham, I have just thought of an idea. The curate who is covering for me while I am away is actually on loan from another town. What would you think of being my curate? I'm sure between the two of us, there is much we could do for Rosings and Hunsford."

"I'm afraid I was never ordained," Wickham replied, "but I did finish university."

"Well, then an ordination should be easy enough," Mr. Collins replied. "Lady Catherine has urged me to not only take a wife, but to find a good young man who could serve as curate for me. As it is her desire, I cannot think of why she would not help you attain the necessary requirements."

Elizabeth could stand it no longer. She muttered an excuse about her mother summoning her, then left the gentlemen to speak amongst themselves. Almost instantly, Lydia took her sister's seat and began prattling away about the fish she had won and lost. While the two gentlemen appeared attentive to her words, Elizabeth could see their silent communication over her younger sister's head.

There will be no good to come of that friendship, she thought. *There is something about both men that makes me uneasy. I wonder, could perhaps Mr. Wickham have been telling a falsehood about Mr. Darcy? After all, Mr. Wickham did say that he would not speak poorly of the man, but he had no qualms sharing it with my foolish cousin.*

That night after they returned home, Elizabeth tossed and turned in her bed, unable to fall asleep despite the late hour. She couldn't help but think that both men were more than they appeared to be, and that the two were plotting something.

There was nothing Elizabeth could do about the situation, however, though she vowed to keep an eye on both men as much as possible.

The next fortnight passed quickly, until soon it was the twenty-sixth of November, and she had just arrived with her family at Netherfield for the ball.

Elizabeth looked around the ballroom in awe. She had to admit, Miss Bingley certainly had talent with regard to decorating and being a hostess. She began to say as much when she reached her hostess in the receiving line, but Miss Bingley spoke first.

"Why, Miss Eliza," she said with a sneer, "how very... quaint you look in your dress."

Elizabeth gave her thanks with gritted teeth, unwilling to mar Jane's chances with Bingley that evening. The gentleman had already requested the first two dances, and Elizabeth hoped he would make a formal request of her father for a courtship at some point throughout the evening.

The music soon began, and Elizabeth watched Lydia stand up with her newly betrothed. Mr. Collins had officially asked for Lydia's hand in marriage that morning, a gesture that was filled with beautiful flowers and flattering words. Lydia and her mother were ecstatic about the situation, and the day had been filled with discussions of wedding plans in between what gowns would be worn that night.

The only shadow over the conversation had been Mr. Collins's insistence that the banns be called that Sunday, with the wedding to follow immediately after the required three weeks. Lydia pouted over this, especially when Mrs. Bennet began to wail about her inability to plan a proper wedding, but Mr. Collins remained firm.

"I must return to Rosings in a few weeks. It would be quite tragic if something were to befall me along the way, leaving us unable to marry at all. Longbourn would revert to the Crown and be lost forever."

Elizabeth was still in astonishment at how easily Mr. Collins had manipulated her mother. It was one more arrow in her quiver of evidence that her father's cousin was more intelligent than he claimed to be. This only increased her suspicions with regard to both him and Wickham.

She wished to watch them during the ball but was informed that Wickham had declined to attend due to the presence of Darcy. While she still felt he was one of the most arrogant men she had the unfortunate pleasure of knowing, she did not think him as evil as everyone else seemed to.

But their opinions are based on those of Mr. Wickham, and I do not trust him.

As the dance came to a close, she watched Bingley lead Jane to a quiet corner. Miss Bingley attempted to go after them, but she was distracted by the fact that Darcy was approaching Elizabeth, who watched the woman's dilemma with some amusement.

"May I have your next dance, Miss Elizabeth?"

Chapter 4

Elizabeth allowed Darcy to escort her to the ballroom floor for the supper dance. Her card had been filled by her cousin and a few of the officers, forcing Darcy to defer until later. She was a bit surprised he had agreed when she offered the supper dance, but she hoped it would give her time to discuss Wickham with him.

The dance began with some small talk; Darcy remained as taciturn as usual, in spite of her efforts to form some conversation. At last he said something that allowed her to bring up the subject she wished most.

"Yes, we do often walk to Meryton. When we saw you last, we had just formed a new acquaintance."

Darcy's lips tightened. "Mr. Wickham has the happy manners that allow him to make friends easily, but whether he can maintain them is uncertain."

"Really?" Elizabeth asked, intrigued. "I admit to having some concerns about the man, but I have nothing but my suspicions, which carry little weight without something tangible to base them on."

His eyes narrowed sharply, and he spoke in an intense, yet quiet, voice. "Has he done something to offend you?"

"No, nothing overt. There is just something about the way he and my cousin Mr. Collins speak. It is as if there is more to the conversation, but I cannot make it out."

"Mr. Collins?" Darcy's tone was one of surprise, and he darted his eyes to the man in question. "Forgive me, but your cousin does not seem the sort with whom Wickham would normally associate. He is a man of the cloth, is he not?"

"He is. He is also my father's heir, and his patroness is your aunt, Lady Catherine. Mr. Wickham related how he had wished to join the church but had been denied a valuable living your father had left to him. Mr. Collins has offered to retain Mr. Wickham as his curate, and the offer has been accepted. He will begin his new position upon my cousin's marriage to my sister Lydia."

Darcy's brow creased in confusion. "Mr. Wickham was granted a substantial sum to the tune of three thousand pounds in lieu of the living, and he declared he had no desire to take orders."

"I thought there was something about the story that seemed off. While you may be quite proud and callously above your company most times, I have never thought you to be wicked or cruel."

He seemed taken aback at her characterization of him. "Callous?"

"Forgive me," she said in a rush. "I should not have spoken so openly. In any case, I would have thought my cousin was being taken in, as he seems to be quite the buffoon—and he is choosing to marry Lydia, after all—but there is something about his manner at times that makes me uneasy. The way he and Mr. Wickham speak reminds me of how my father and I will discuss things above my mother's head."

Darcy had seemed to want to respond to her apology, but her further words changed what he was about to say. "Can you give me some examples?"

Elizabeth shared the conversation the two men had on the night of the card party about Lady Catherine and Miss de Bourgh. The more she related, the grimmer his face became. By the end of her narrative, his face was practically etched in stone. "I see why you have your suspicions. Were you a married woman, you would most likely be able to understand some of the subtext the two gentlemen discussed."

He hesitated, then added, "I cannot give you specific details, but please know you are very wise to not trust Wickham. He can be quite cunning, and even dangerous, when he thinks it would benefit him. If your cousin has befriended him—and I trust your judgment, given that you saw through Wickham's lies—you must be on your guard."

"I worry about Lydia," she admitted. "There is nothing I can do to prevent this wedding nor this friendship. It makes me very concerned for my future."

The dance came to an end, and Mr. Darcy escorted Elizabeth into dinner. After the guests had been seated and their food served, Mr. Bennet stood and tapped on his glass with his knife. "I am pleased to announce that not only will I be losing my youngest daughter to the married state, but my oldest daughter will soon follow. Lydia and Mr. Collins became engaged this morning, and Mr. Bingley just now asked me for Jane's hand in marriage."

Gasps and gossip flowed around the room. Elizabeth grinned broadly for Jane's happiness; her sister had never looked more radiant than at that moment. She turned to Darcy, who was looking at Jane and Bingley with a furrowed brow.

"Are you displeased with the news?" she asked him in a challenging tone.

He turned to her, surprise on his face. "No, I am not," he replied calmly. "I simply had not thought Bingley ready to make such a step, especially when he was uncertain of your sister's affection for him."

Elizabeth gasped. "How could there be any doubt? I have never seen my sister so affected by a gentleman before!"

"Your superior knowledge of your sister must, of course, give away to my own suppositions. She seemed to smile at him just as willingly as any other person. When asked my advice, I could only answer honestly: that I had never witnessed her display any symptom of particular regard."

"That's because she's shy! My sister keeps her feelings quite close, but that does not mean she does not feel deeply. I daresay she is very much in love with Mr. Bingley."

"Then I am very happy for them both," he said, giving her a small bow of the head.

She smiled at him, unable to help feeling impressed that the proud man was able to admit he was in the wrong and be happy for his friend.

"I hate to change the subject back to unpleasant things," he said, "but I'm afraid there is nothing I can do to help your sister or change the fact that Wickham will go to Rosings. I do own some of his debts, but circumstances prevent me from calling them in."

"Does he... is he blackmailing you?" she asked in a whisper.

He looked startled. "No, he would not dare do something that illegal, especially when my cousin Colonel Fitzwilliam—who is an officer in the regulars—would take offense at that. But Wickham *does* have information about someone for whom I care very much, and if I attempt to take direct action against him, I fear he will release that information and ruin their life. I cannot allow that to happen."

"I see," she said, sitting back in her chair in disappointment.

"For what it's worth," he said, "I do not think your sister will be mistreated. I will speak with my aunt and give her a warning about both men. While my aunt has firm opinions and the majority of her servants are sycophants, she does feel strongly about men who mistreat the women under their care. Your sister may not be happy, but she would not be in any danger."

A weight lifted itself from Elizabeth's shoulders. "Thank you," she whispered.

It was only the memory of Darcy's promise to keep Lydia safe that allowed Elizabeth to participate in the wedding preparations with any semblance of calm. The days were agonizingly long, but the weeks seemed too short. All too soon, Lydia was married and had driven away in the carriage with her new husband.

"One wedding down, one to go," Mr. Bennet said with a small

sigh of relief. "It is too bad Jane wasn't willing to combine weddings and do them at the same time." He gave his eldest daughter a small wink, who gave a shy smile in return.

"I wanted Lydia to have her special day," Jane said.

"It also allowed her to be the first married, which she will gloat about for the rest of our lives," Elizabeth said with a laugh.

The following weeks until Jane and Bingley's wedding were filled with preparations. Mrs. Bennet was distraught to not have a full six months to plan something that would meet her standards based on his income, but Bingley was eager to turn his wife into his betrothed.

It was with great happiness in January that Elizabeth stood up with her elder sister in the chapel at Longbourn. Darcy had gone to London shortly after the ball in order to celebrate Christmas with Miss Darcy, but the pair of them came to Meryton for the wedding.

Elizabeth was surprised that the tall, well-formed girl was painfully shy. It was difficult to pry more than a few words out of her until Elizabeth asked her about her favorite composers. Music, it appeared, was the key to getting Miss Darcy past her shyness.

Darcy, in his turn, was surprised that the Gardiners—who had come from London for both the weddings and Christmas—were such genteel people. Given that Mr. Gardiner was the brother of Mrs. Bennet, he had anticipated a rough man of trade from the docks. Had he not known their names, he would have mistaken them for people of fashion.

For her part, Miss Darcy was thrilled to meet the Bennet girls. "Imagine, Brother, a family with *five* sisters!" By the end of the wedding breakfast, she had secured promises to correspond from each of the girls.

Elizabeth's heart was weighed with sorrow as she watched Jane and Bingley drive towards Netherfield. It would be the first time since Elizabeth's birth that they would go to bed without speaking to one another, save the rare occasions when one traveled to visit the Gardiners. This was a permanent change that nearly brought Elizabeth to tears.

The Bingleys had decided to postpone a wedding trip until the warmer months, at which point they would travel to the north and visit Bingley's relatives. Elizabeth had been invited to accompany them, a proposal to which she agreed with alacrity.

Mr. Bennet was a bit hesitant in allowing the new Miss Bennet to travel so much that year. For some reason, Lydia had insisted Elizabeth be the first of her sisters to visit her at Rosings.

"Probably so she can show off her good fortune, as she still imagines me jealous that Mr. Collins preferred her," Elizabeth had said wryly to her father.

The wedding trip with the Bingleys would occur only a few weeks after her return to Longbourn, and only a few weeks after that, she had been invited to travel with her aunt and uncle Gardiner to the Peak district over the summer.

"What would I do without you, Lizzy? I will be left with only my wife and two silly daughters," Mr. Bennet complained to Elizabeth one day.

"You could teach Kitty and Mary how to play chess," she responded. "I daresay one of them will become good enough to best you."

"I will take that challenge," he said, "and if neither of them is able to learn well, you will have to return to Longbourn for at least a year after all your travels."

"Only if you promise to actually make the attempt!" she cried. "And if you *are* bested, you will owe me a new hat."

The two laughed as they shook hands in agreement. It was decided; Elizabeth would go to Hunsford in the spring.

Chapter 5

Elizabeth strolled along the path from the Hunsford Parsonage and made her way towards the grove of trees just on the other side of the perfectly manicured lawn at Rosings Park.

It was early March, and she had been visiting Mr. and Mrs. Collins for a se'ennight now. Thus far, it had been an interesting visit. Elizabeth was amazed at the love and devotion Lydia seemed to show Mr. Collins. She had expected to find her sister in low spirits with constant tantrums and scandalous behavior, but instead she was a more proper wife and mistress of a home than their own mother!

Lydia had also shyly confided to her elder sister that she believed she was with child already, which made Elizabeth want to close her eyes against the images the information produced in her mind.

For his part, Mr. Collins still troubled Elizabeth. He was just as fawning and submissive as ever, giving the air of a bumbling fool who lived for nothing but to serve his patroness, the great Lady Catherine de Bourgh. There were instances, though, where she thought she spied another personality underneath it all.

Wickham was also frequently present, as he was staying in a room he'd rented from a nearby elderly widow who needed a young man about the house for chores. The situation was beneficial to them both, as a curate's income was usually quite paltry.

"I don't anticipate this always being my situation," he told her one evening on the many occasions he dined at Rosings. "There are a few changes that may occur soon that will mean an entirely different set of circumstances."

He gave Mr. Collins a broad grin as he said this, which was returned with a sly wink. Once again, Elizabeth knew there was something going on that she wasn't party to, but she had no idea what to do about the situation.

At the end of her first week, an invitation came from Rosings to the parsonage, requesting their presence for dinner the following evening. Lydia's excitement knew no bounds.

"Oh, Lizzy, I cannot wait for you to meet Lady Catherine! She is the most elegant person I have ever met. And the lace on Miss de Bourgh's dresses is ever so fine! Lady Catherine knows all about how to run a household as well. She is constantly giving me advice. I don't know how I would manage without her!"

Elizabeth followed her sister and brother-in-law to Rosings, expecting nothing but amusement and interesting character study for the evening. To her delight and dismay, she was introduced to one of the most condescending persons she had ever met. The delight was in the strange character, but the dismay stemmed from the fact that she was subjected to quite an impertinent line of inquiry about the personal details of her life.

"I find it quite odd that Mr. Collins chose your sister to be his bride instead of yourself. You are, after all, several years older than Mrs. Collins, are you not?"

Before Elizabeth was even given the chance to respond, another question was thrown at her, this time about her accomplishments and talents. Practically unable to take a bite of food, Elizabeth was still hungry when Lady Catherine announced that dinner was over and tea would be served in the drawing room.

As there was no host, Mr. Collins and Wickham joined the ladies instead of having the traditional separation of sexes. Elizabeth sat next to Miss de Bourgh in an attempt to get to know the girl better, but she proved to be just as quiet as her mother was vociferous.

After only a few minutes, Elizabeth was called away to play the piano, Lady Catherine having been informed by Mr. Collins that she was quite talented at it. At the same time, Miss de Bourgh coughed several times and was promptly excused to her rooms to rest.

It was only when she had finished three songs that Elizabeth realized Wickham was no longer in the room. Upon asking his whereabouts, Mr. Collins gave her a look of such anger that she faltered in words. The man then turned to Lady Catherine and said,

"I'm afraid my curate was feeling a bit unwell and wished to retire early. He did not wish to interrupt your enjoyment of my cousin's performance, your ladyship, so he begged me to offer his excuses."

Lady Catherine gave a gracious nod and began to rhapsodize about the thoughtfulness of both Wickham and Mr. Collins. "I daresay, no other patroness in England has had as much skill at appointing livings as I do."

Finally, the tedious evening came to an end. As the three remaining guests gathered their things, Lady Catherine said, "It may be some time before I invite you to Rosings again. My nephews are coming to visit at the end of the week, and I expect Darcy and Fitzwilliam will be quite occupied with my Anne."

At this news, relief flooded Elizabeth. The tension she hadn't even known she'd be feeling flowed out of her body. She would no longer be the only person who was suspicious of Wickham and Mr. Collins. It had seemed evident to her that Lady Catherine had not taken Darcy's warning about Wickham's untrustworthiness seriously.

The days passed slowly as Elizabeth waited impatiently for not only Darcy's arrival but also for the ability to speak with him once he was here. She had told Georgiana about her plans to travel to Hunsford, but she didn't know if the letter had reached her friend or if the information had been passed on.

Finally, Saturday came, and Elizabeth sat at the window and pretended to read a book, although her eyes were fixed on the lane between the parsonage and Rosings, hoping to see a glimpse of a carriage with the Darcy crest.

The morning was uneventful, other than Miss de Bourgh riding out in her phaeton as she usually did. Elizabeth hardly paid any attention to the sickly, cross girl who rebuffed every effort Elizabeth had made to befriend her.

As the afternoon changed into evening, Elizabeth saw the carriage arrive. It went past the Parsonage and up to Rosings, and she finally felt as if she could breathe. Retiring to bed, she looked forward to church the next day, where she would hopefully see Darcy.

Several hours later, her sleep was interrupted by a pounding on the door. Jerking awake, she heard shouting coming from the outside. It sounded like Lady Catherine, so Elizabeth quickly put on her dressing gown and made her way downstairs.

Mr. Collins had just opened the door when she arrived, and Lady Catherine barreled into the room. "Traitor!" she roared, swinging her walking stick at Mr. Collins. It hit his temple with a sickening thud, and the man collapsed to the ground.

Lydia screamed and ran to her husband's prone body while Elizabeth gasped in shock. When the grand lady lifted her stick again, Elizabeth ran forward and seized it with both hands. "How dare you?" she cried out, pulling it away from the irate woman and backing away several steps out of reach.

Lady Catherine let out a scream of rage and started towards Elizabeth, when Darcy and another gentleman burst through the open front door.

"Aunt Catherine!" bellowed the stranger, leading Elizabeth to correctly assume this was the Colonel Richard Fitzwilliam of whom Georgiana and Lady Catherine had both spoken of.

Darcy rushed to Elizabeth's side. "Are you harmed?"

"No," she gasped out, "but Mr. Collins... she hit him on the head..."

Unable to say another word, she simply pointed to where the parson lay unconscious on the floor, Lydia weeping at his side.

Darcy cursed under his breath and turned to the door, where a manservant was standing. "Roberts, fetch the doctor immediately."

The man raced away, and Darcy turned his attention towards Lady Catherine, who was fighting against Colonel Fitzwilliam's hold.

"Take her into the parlor," Darcy said brusquely. "I'll tend to things here."

The colonel frog-marched his aunt out of the hallway and into the room, closing the door against her ranting and raving. Elizabeth winced as she heard a crash that sounded like a porcelain vase being thrown to the ground.

"What on earth is going on?" she asked him.

"My cousin Anne has eloped with Wickham," he said grimly. "My aunt blames your cousin for bringing the man here."

"But—but I saw her just this morning when she went past the parsonage!" Elizabeth cried, unable to comprehend what he was saying.

"Apparently she took her phaeton to a nearby town, where Wickham had rented a carriage. They have a full day ahead of us, as no one knew Anne had even left the house. She'd told her companion she was indisposed with a megrim and wished to be left alone. We only found out tonight because Aunt Catherine insisted she come down to greet us."

"How do you know she eloped? And with Wickham?"

"She left a note to her mother. Apparently, your cousin has been helping the two of them meet secretly."

"I *knew* they were up to something," Elizabeth said angrily. "I never thought it would be something this awful though."

The doctor arrived at that moment, and Darcy led him over to examine Mr. Collins. Once he had declared that it was safe to move the injured man, he and Darcy lifted him up and took him to his room. Elizabeth escorted a weeping Lydia to the mistress's chambers, where she cried herself to sleep.

After assuring herself that her sister was indeed out, Elizabeth went and knocked on the door to Mr. Collins's room. Darcy opened it, and he beckoned her inside, leaving the door open.

"How is he?" she asked, looking at her cousin's prone form on the bed.

The doctor made a grim face and shook his head. "The blow was quite intense and struck him on the softest part of the scalp. There's no way to know for sure, but I would be surprised if he ever awakens."

Elizabeth gasped and put a hand to her mouth. "Lady Catherine has killed him!"

"I'm afraid that may be the case," Darcy said somberly. "I must help Fitzwilliam take her back to Rosings. Doctor, do you have laudanum we can use to calm her until the magistrate arrives?"

The doctor nodded and pulled a small vial from his bag. Darcy took it, then hesitated. "I believe I will keep her sedated until my uncle can arrive. He is the only one who can control her, and this will not be easy. I will send an express immediately."

"What about Miss de Bourgh?" Elizabeth asked. "What will happen to her?"

Darcy shrugged. "She is technically the mistress of Rosings, but it is tied up in such a way that no husband of hers can have access to any of it. I don't think Wickham knows that. When the *happy couple* returns, my uncle can deal with them then. There is no possible way for me to catch them, even if my aunt hadn't completely lost her senses and required me to stay here."

"I wish I had been able to write to you, to bring you to Rosings sooner," she whispered. "This is all my fault. I knew there was something wrong."

He turned to look at her with wide eyes. "No, dearest Elizabeth, this is the fault of only the men who chose to make these decisions."

She gasped softly at his use of her Christian name, and he turned a bit pink. "My apologies, Miss Bennet. I did not mean to speak to you so informally."

Elizabeth shook her head. "No, you cannot take it back now. I did not think… that is, I never dared hope…"

Darcy reached forward and took her hands in his. "I have loved you since the moment I saw you come to Netherfield to care for your sister. I wanted nothing more than to be loved by you in the same way that you loved her."

Her eyes filled with tears. "I love you too," she whispered. "I did not always, you know, but I've come to see over the last several months that you are the only man in the world whom I could love so ardently."

"Marry me, Elizabeth."

"I will."

Epilogue

The memory of Darcy's proposal was the only thing that helped sustain Elizabeth through the following days.

True to his word, Darcy sent an express that night to his uncle, keeping Lady Catherine dosed with laudanum until the earl could arrive. Thankfully, the man did so before his duplicitous niece and her new husband returned from Gretna Green.

Whether or not Mr. and Mrs. Wickham lived happily ever after is up to the reader to decide. Anne's male relatives did their best to keep Rosings solvent over the years, but it was a frustrating process for all involved.

Mr. Bennet also came to Hunsford, having received Elizabeth's note by express. Although he was normally an indolent correspondent—he had been known to leave letters unopened on his desk for weeks at a time—the hasty nature and expense alarmed him enough to read it immediately.

Tragically, Mr. Collins only lived for three days before passing on in his sleep. He never knew that his wife was with child, as Lydia did not feel the quickening until the day after his death. It was only with great fortune and much prayer that the sixteen-year-old widow's grief did not cause an early delivery, but she was directed by the doctor to remain in her bed as much as possible until her confinement.

It was decided that Lydia should remain in the Hunsford parsonage until after the baby was born; the travel to Meryton was too risky. Instead, Mrs. Bennet came to join her daughter to help her through the process. Elizabeth worried her mother's nerves would make the situation even more delicate, but to her amazement, Mrs. Bennet proved to be sensible and useful during the time of Lydia's grief.

To everyone's great relief, Lydia gave birth to a baby boy, and the entail on Longbourn was broken. Shortly after Mr. Collins's death, his many infidelities and rakish behaviors came to light. Lydia refused to believe any of the rumors, but she allowed herself to be convinced that the master of Longbourn should carry the name of Bennet. Thus the child was christened William Collins Bennet.

The parson's murder was the catalyst that finally convinced the earl to remove his sister from Rosings entirely. He did not wish to send her to Bedlam, nor did he want the scandal of a trial and hanging. Instead, the magistrate gave him permission to secure Lady Catherine in a remote estate in Scotland, where she would spend the remainder of her life in seclusion, watched over by a doctor, several nurses, and her loyal lady's maid.

Elizabeth did not accompany Jane on her wedding trip. Instead, she married Darcy quietly in April, and they hosted the Bingleys at Pemberley.

Kitty remained at Longbourn, and Lydia's improved conduct once again influenced her elder sister, this time for the good. Mary joined Georgiana at Pemberley, and the two bonded over their shared love of music.

Eventually all three maidens found respectable matches and good marriages with husbands that respected and loved them.

For her part, Lydia never remarried. She remained dedicated to the memory of her husband—in spite of the atrocious claims of jealous women in Hunsford—and raised her son to be a kind, thoughtful man who would take care of Longbourn.

Elizabeth would always be grateful for Lydia's insistence that she be the first married woman of her sisters, as it helped Elizabeth see Darcy through clear eyes.

About the Author

Tiffany Thomas is a chocoholic former math teacher with Crohn's Disease and homeschooling mom of four kids. She and her husband Phillip (who is an engineer) work together on the blog Saving Talents. They enjoy spending time with their family, geeking out over sci-fi together, and saving money.

Tiffany discovered *Pride & Prejudice* as a teenager, and even made poor Phillip watch the six-hour version with her on their honeymoon when they got snowed in. After reading fan fiction for over a decade, she finally broke out into writing some herself, with the support of her husband (who still hasn't read any of her books).

A Gift for Readers

Thank you for reading *Pride, Prejudice & Permutations* by Tiffany Thomas.

If you enjoyed it, please leave a review on Amazon or Goodreads! A five-star rating means you think others will enjoy it as well.

Want to read another one for free? Just sign up for Tiffany's newsletter—no spam ever! Just a short weekly email with updates and freebies.

www.authortiffanythomas.com

You may also enjoy Tiffany's other works:

A Look Behind the Mask
What if Elizabeth Bennet had an experience as a young girl that taught her that a handsome face does not mean a man is trustworthy?

The Sins of Their Fathers
How would *Pride & Prejudice* be different if William Collins came to live with the Bennets at Longbourn as a young child? Will Elizabeth Bennet and Mr. Darcy still find their happily ever after?

When Summer Never Came
In this *Pride & Prejudice* variation, a worldwide disaster of epic proportions causes Fitzwilliam Darcy and Elizabeth Bennet to meet under extraordinary circumstances. In this retelling of Jane Austen's famous work, will Mr. Darcy and Elizabeth find their happily ever after?

Read on to learn more about each story.

A Look Behind the Mask

As a twelve-year-old girl, Elizabeth Bennet witnesses a traumatic experience that shapes how she views men. She learns the hard way that a handsome face can mask cruelty and depravity.

This experience forever alters her relationships with her sisters, her parents, and her friends.

How will a changed Elizabeth Bennet react to Fitzwilliam Darcy's insults at the Meryton assembly?

Can Elizabeth and Mr. Darcy overcome their altered pride and prejudices to find happily ever after?

A Look Behind the Mask is a full-length, clean *Pride & Prejudice* variation of 112,000 words and is a variation of Jane Austen's *Pride & Prejudice*.

The Sins of Their Fathers

Young William Collins spent his childhood under the oppression of an abusive father and an ill mother. When he becomes an orphan after a scarring tragedy, Collins is sent to live with his estranged cousins, the Bennet family, at Longbourn.

At the same time, Fitzwilliam Darcy passes through his own crisis. The unique relationship between the Darcy and Wickham families is revealed late one night when Fitzwilliam discovers his father's unsettling secret—one that affects George Wickham to the core.

Elizabeth grows up loving Collins as a brother, but when he befriends Darcy and Wickham, Elizabeth wonders about her cousin's choice of friends, and Darcy's overbearing pride. What she doesn't know are the heartaches of Darcy's past that shape his intentions now.

As the beloved characters of *Pride & Prejudice* grapple with their disturbing childhoods, how will the choices of their parents be carried on to the next generation? Can they find happiness, or are they doomed to a lifetime of misery because of the sins of their fathers?

The Sins of Their Fathers is a full-length, sweet regency romance novel of 85,000 words and is a variation of Jane Austen's *Pride & Prejudice*.

When Summer Never Came

In April 1815, the volcano Mount Tambora erupted in Indonesia, affecting the climate so that in 1816, there was cold and snow throughout the summer all across the world.

How would *Pride & Prejudice* be different if Mount Tambora had erupted ten years earlier, drastically altering the climate across the world? Would Elizabeth Bennet and Mr. Darcy still find one another in a year when summer never came?

Elizabeth Bennet has just experienced one of the most difficult years of her entire life. The loss of a beloved sister, a failed harvest, and the threat of freezing to death from a bitterly cold winter cause the inhabitants of Longbourn to do the unthinkable.

Meanwhile, Fitzwilliam Darcy is desperate to keep his family and his tenants alive. The scarcity of food due to a freezing summer has him taking extreme measures. His radical idea takes him, along with his friend Charles Bingley, to Netherfield, where his drastic experiment has the potential to save them all—or ruin his life forever.

Will the changed circumstances cause Elizabeth and Darcy to come together in unity? Or will his pride and her prejudice remain alive in spite of the terrible circumstances that are a result of the year without summer?

When Summer Never Came is a full-length, sweet regency romance novel of 130,000 words and is a variation of Jane Austen's *Pride & Prejudice*.